I0597085

The Shadow Contract

A Colin Pearce Adventure

by

Chris Broyhill

Copyright © 2017 by Christopher M. Broyhill.
All Rights Reserved. No part of this publication may be
reproduced or transmitted in any form or by any means,
electronic or mechanical, including photocopy, recording,
or any information storage retrieval system, without
permission in writing from the copyright owner

FIRST EDITION

Published by

Citadel Publishing LLC
Dover, Delaware, USA
2017

ISBN: 978-0-9988250-0-7

Paperback

Cover Design By: Robin E. Vuchnich

Acknowledgements

Writing these books is a lone creative process for me. As a result, I can get too close to the character of Colin Pearce and not see him objectively. To provide that objective perspective, I turn to two people I trust, my friend since high school, Matt Bille, and my wife, Denise Broyhill. Matt is a great writer in his own right and he is not afraid to provide blunt criticism where appropriate. He knows what makes stories work and he has a keen sense of technical feasibility. Denise is a voracious fiction reader so she has a solid sense of pacing, content and continuity. Between the two of them, I received input that made the story you are about to read much better than the orginal version, and I owe them both a huge debt of gratitude. Thanks for your perseverance and your persistence, Matt and Denise. This story wouldn't be what it is without you.

I had some technical assistance in the creation of this work as well. Mike Pacilio, the Chief Operating Officer of Exelon Generation, provided input on certain elements of the plot that deal with the nuclear power industry. Thanks, Mike. It's been a pleasure knowing you and working with you.

Neil Humphries and Brian Schuessler provided input on the feasibility of my helicopter scenes and helped to provide the additional color that my 12 hours of helicopter time could not. Thanks, guys.

Lieutenant General Bruno Clermont (Retired), formerly of the French Air Force and now an Air Force Advisor to the CEO of Dassault, provided expertise on the Dassault Rafale fighter. I had the pleasure of flying a Rafale simulator at Saint Dizier-Robinson Air Base in the fall of 2017 and Bruno was my gracious tour guide and host. Merci, mon ami.

Brent "Gunner" Reinhardt, a former F-35 test pilot provided input on my F-35 scenes. The F-35 possesses many capabilities and systems that are classified. While I had the pleasure of flying an unclassified F-35B simulator at Lockheed Martin's Global Training and Logistics center in Orlando, Florida, in the summer of 2016, my descriptions about the tactical display and capabilities of the jet are based purely on research and some educated guesswork. While Brent was able to provide some information to correct my descriptions, there was much he couldn't comment on, so any errors, exaggerations or understatements about the F-35's capabilies are mine and mine alone. Thanks, Gunner.

Finally, to you, my readers, goes the biggest thanks of all. Your enthusiasm for Colin Pearce is an inspiration and a bright spot in my life. I'm more grateful to you than you know.

To Those for Whom the Sky is Home

Prologue

Creating international incidents was getting to be a habit for me these days. After an aerial refueling over the North Atlantic, between Iceland and Norway, I was racing across the Baltic Sea to coast in over Estonia and cross the Russian Border just north of Lake Peipus.

I was in a borrowed F-35B that I had logged a whopping eight hours in – the time it had taken me to fly from Eglin Air Force Base to my current location. I would have preferred a Viper of course, but I needed a stealthy jet that would allow me to sneak across the Russian border and land vertically in a concealed location. I just hoped I didn't have to tangle with any Russian fighters on the way in or out. For all its technology, the F-35 was not a turning and burning machine and I didn't know how most of its systems worked. I was just hoping the jet's stealth would keep me hidden, because if it didn't, I was fucked.

I was on the trail of a killer named "The Shadow," and that trail would go cold soon. After killing nearly 60 people all over the world, the Shadow was about to disappear.

But I wasn't going to allow that to happen. The Shadow's latest victim was someone I cared about, and that's why I was here and not a CIA Ops team. The Shadow made the battle personal. And I was going to make it personal right back.

Tomorrow, the Shadow was to be made a Hero of the Russian Federation in a small ceremony in St. Petersburg. At the moment the medal was presented, I was going to put a .50 caliber bullet into the Shadow's boss and mentor.

Then, I was going to wait for the Shadow to come and find me.

If I lived that long.

CHAPTER ONE

Monday, October 18
1000 Hours Local Time
CIA Auxiliary Offices
McClean, Virginia, USA

You'd never know it was a CIA building from the outside. It looked like any other nondescript office building in a no-name office park in northern Virginia, with the usual brick and steel façade, dark glass windows and accompanying parking garage. Even the civilian security guard who gave me my parking card could have passed as normal, but his eyes were a little too sharp and his movements a little too precise. I was sure there was an automatic weapon nearby, and I was also sure that my face and license plate had been photographed and were being analyzed by a computer somewhere.

It wouldn't take them long to identify me. I was already in their database.

The garage was only about half occupied. I parked the Dodge Challenger in the first available slot on the second level and turned the engine off. After considering the environment of the building I was about to enter, I shrugged to myself and pulled the Colt .45 ACP Commander pistol and its holster from my right hip and locked it in the car's center console, along with the two spare magazines that I carried on my left hip. Then I got out of the car, donned my overcoat, and walked to the nearest stairwell, listening to the sounds of my shoes as they clicked on the cement floor.

I went down the stairs, onto the sidewalk at the bottom, and outside into bright and chilly October day. The sun was high in the blue Virginia sky, and the wind was brisk, sweeping down the tree-lined parkway and blowing the branches of the trees in a direction they were apparently used to bending, toward the end of the lane, pointing toward the building I was entering. I smiled at the irony of the subtle hint that nature was providing. *Here's where they are*, it seemed to be saying.

I strode up the concrete stairs, went through the glass doors and into the climate-controlled lobby. I silently commended the

CIA on their camouflage. The lobby looked the same as many similar spaces in buildings that weren't owned and operated by one of the world's most secretive organizations. The lobby's walls were shiny gray marble and featured the typical directory for the building's several floors. As I glanced at the directory, I wondered how many of the companies listed were ficticious. There was the usual security desk with the typical guy and gal in blue blazers with stock bored but pleasant expressions on their faces. There were banks of elevators beyond the desk and card-keyed gates to allow passage. I walked up to the desk and presented my driver's license.

"Welcome to Donovan Tower," the female guard said politely. She was in her mid-thirties and had black hair drawn into a severe ponytail. Underneath the loose-fitting security uniform, I was betting her body was tight and toned. She just had that look. "Can you tell us your name and who you're here to see?"

"Colin Pearce," I said, handing her my driver's license. "I'm here to see someone from the office of Brewster and Barnes."

"Legal trouble, Mr. Pearce?" the male guard asked after a moment. He was about my size and had wary and watchful brown eyes. He also looked athletic and fit. Neither of the two guards was anything like those I had encountered in similar posts in the past.

"No," I replied. "Just some real estate issues."

The male guard nodded. Apparently, our recitation of the required litany had been to his satisfaction. They knew who I appeared to be. They just needed to confirm it was me and that I was here at the right date and time as well as to confirm I wasn't under duress. The words I was given via my secure I-Phone had several variations to communicate different things.

The female guard had been looking down at a screen in front of her. She raised her eyes to me.

"You're not *equipped*," she said flatly. "We had been told to expect that you would be."

"I normally am," I said. "But given the nature of this facility, I left my *equipment* in my car."

She nodded. "Understandable," she said. "But given your credentials, unnecessary." She looked over at the male guard. "Clean," she said.

Apparently, I was scanned by something I had neither felt nor seen. Very thorough. As usual.

The male guard handed me a security badge. It had the word "VISITOR" in large letters at the top, my picture in the middle and "Contractor 09-017" at the bottom. My name did not appear on it.

"Wear this at all times," he said. "It will buzz you into the turnstiles to my right and into the waiting area on the 18th floor. They know you're coming." He motioned me around the desk to his right to the elevators behind him. "Have a good day."

I nodded and went through the turnstiles and found an elevator that serviced the 18th floor. After a quick ride upward, I stepped into an air-conditioned lobby area with a receptionist sitting behind a desk. She was a pert brunette with clothes that looked upscale and makeup that was slightly overdone. Letters that spelled "Brewster and Barnes" were emblazoned on the gleaming wooden wall above and behind her.

"Good morning, sir!" she said brightly. "You must be Mr. Pearce!"

"That's me," I said.

"Any trouble finding us?" she asked. "We're not the best-marked building in the office park."

"No trouble at all. The directions I received were perfect, and the signage was there if you knew where to look."

"Glad you didn't wind up in Alexandria," she said.

"Or in Reston for that matter," I replied.

She nodded at me. Another successful exchange completed. She typed a few words into her computer. "Mr. Brewster will be down to retrieve you in a moment."

I nodded. "Thanks very much."

I strode to the windows in the waiting area and looked out over the trees, roofs, and asphalt of the office park. In the distance, I could make out the obelisk of the Washington Monument and see an airliner flying down the Potomac river to make the visual approach into Runway 19 at Reagan National Airport.

"Nice view," I murmured to no one in particular.

"It ought to be," said a familiar voice behind me. "We pay enough for it."

I turned to find CIA Operations Officer Dave Smith standing there with a wry smile on his face. He was about my height, six feet two inches, had dark brown hair and moved like a cat. The jade green eyes in his lightly-lined face looked tired, but they sparkled with knowledge that he seemed eager to share.

"Nice digs," I said as we shook hands. "I thought you guys would be buried somewhere in the bowels of that huge building at Langley I've seen in the movies so many times."

He shook his head. "Langley is a hole," he said. "Difficult to get into, difficult to get out of, and the guards are so tight they think a fart is a threat to national security. Our whole section moved here a few years ago, and we like it a lot."

"Thanks for inviting me," I said. "I never thought I'd get to see the inner sanctum."

"Thanks for coming," Smith said, motioning me toward the doors next to the reception desk. "There's something the Director wants to talk to you about."

"Director?" I asked as Smith buzzed us through the doors with his badge. "Director of what?"

Smith grinned at me. "Relax," he said. "The big boss, Director Panetta, was tied up today. You'll be meeting our boss, the Director of the National Clandestine Service, Bryan Hansen."

"Wow," I said as the doors closed behind us. "To what do I owe this honor?"

"He's been wanting to meet you for a while," Smith said, guiding me through the maze of cubicles and workstations to an office at the edge of the building. "He's the one who authorized us to come after you in the first place, last year. Apart from us, he's probably your number one fan here."

"Always nice to be appreciated I guess," I said.

As Smith led me through the work area, an undercurrent of conversation was detectable, but as we approached the office Smith was taking me to, the conversation rose in volume. As I glanced to the side to see the focus of the conversation, I could see the workers motioning toward me and smiling. Those that made eye contact with me nodded my way, and I returned the nod, oblivious as to what we were nodding about. Then, as I approached the door of the office, a tall man with closely-cropped black hair and wire-rimmed glasses came out of the door and extended his hand.

"Bryan Hansen," he said. There was no presumption or attitude in his voice at all.

"Colin Pearce," I replied, liking him immediately.

The undercurrent of conversation behind me became a muffled round of applause which then erupted into a loud roar of applause complete with whistles and whoops.

"I'm impressed," I said to him over the noise. "Your folks must like you!"

Hansen shook his head in disbelief and looked sideways at Smith. "He doesn't get it, does he?"

Smith smiled at him and shook his head in return. "Nope. He never does."

Hansen looked at me, smiling. "This isn't for me," he said. "It's for you. These are the folks who have supported your last three ops for us. You've validated their hard work and made all of us look good. They're grateful." He put a hand on my shoulder and slowly turned me to face the still cheering office. There were men and women of all colors, shapes, sizes, and ages and they were looking at me with expressions of admiration, gratitude, and amazement. "Plus," he said, his voice barely audible above the roar, "I think many of them just wanted to see that you're a real person. There aren't many of our operatives who have made it through what you have." He raised his voice over the ruckus.

"Ladies and Gentlemen, if you didn't already guess it. This is Contractor 09-017. Colin Pearce!"

The applause and cheering erupted anew. I could feel my cheeks flush with embarrassment. I had never felt more awkward in my life.

As they clapped, I could see people talking to each other and hear snippets of conversation shouted over the roar.

"...shot down like eight jets...saved the presidents...been shot too many times to count...killed Ramon the Rock...."

"You're like a legend," Smith said in my left ear.

I looked over at him. "Please tell me you didn't bring me here for this," I said.

"Not at all," he said. "But I'm not surprised it's happening."

As I looked at the faces in the cheering audience, I could feel an air of expectation. These people wanted me to say something. They needed me to say something. When the noise level subsided, I raised my hands to shoulder level.

"I guess I should say thank you," I said as the voices died down. "But I'm not sure that would be adequate." Suddenly, there was a huge lump of emotion in my throat that I couldn't completely explain. "I don't know what I've done for you," I said, fighting to keep my voice from cracking, "but I know what you've done for me. You kept me alive. You kept me in the fight. I'm just glad I didn't embarrass you, and I'm glad I didn't embarrass our country. Thank you."

The cheers erupted again, and Hansen turned me back toward his office. I walked in quickly, anxious to leave the discomfort behind me and enter a place with some walls and fewer people. Hansen's office occupied about thirty feet on the side of the building. One wall was entirely glass, and it faced a few other buildings in the office park. Since it was on the opposite side of the building as the entry area, I could see jets departing from Dulles International Airport in the very distant background. There was a government-issue wooden desk and a rectangular conference table with a large-screen TV monitor on the wall at the far end of the table. The screen displayed the intro slide to a classified presentation with a warning appropriate to the clearance level of the material to be discussed - TOP SECRET / SPECIAL COMPARTMENTALIZED INFORMATION. As I looked around the office, I saw a few family pictures on the desk and a coffee cup with "World's Greatest Dad" inscribed on it in a childlike scrawl. Notably absent were the plaques and certificates of achievement found in the offices of most civil servants or corporate types who had climbed the ladder. Apparently, Hansen was secure enough in his accomplishments that he didn't need to remind anyone of what he had done.

I turned toward the table and saw the blond, surfer hair style of John Amrine. The blue eyes regarded me respectfully as he offered his hand. Amrine was slightly shorter than I was but wider, with a muscular physique barely contained in the dress trousers and shirt he wore.

"Great to see you again, John," I said, shaking his hand. "Thanks for having me down to the ranch."

"The least we could do, T.C.," he replied. "We've got something we need your help with."

I nodded. *So that's what this is about.*

There was a shorter, blonde woman standing next to him that seemed to be chafing somewhat at Amrine's choice of words, an observation that was evident due to the peeved expression on her tense features and the impatient gleam in her blue eyes. She was short, about five foot six, with dirty blonde hair pulled into a tight bun at the back of her head. She weighed about thirty pounds more than she should have, and the combination of her weight and her expression reminded me of an angry dwarf.

I couldn't resist shoving my hand at her. "I'm Colin Pearce," I said. "And you are?"

"Lucy Edmonds," she said, barely turning her head to me in acknowledgment. "Directorate of Support." She walked to the end of the room where a podium, with a laptop computer upon it, stood next to the large TV screen.

"Lucy's the one who has working the analysis on this project," Hansen said from behind me.

"Project?" I asked.

"Yes," Hansen replied. "Have a seat, Colin."

I sat down at the table as Edmonds looked at her laptop computer and seemed to prepare her remarks. I took the opportunity to gaze around the room some more. The conference table paralleled the window, and while there was room for twelve people, only five of us were seated there. Hansen sat at the end of the table nearest his desk, in the standard power seat. I sat on the side of the table to his right, facing the window with Smith and Amrine to my right. Across from me was a man who, up until now, had been silent. He was a thin, older man with wispy black hair, bright blue eyes and horn-rimmed glasses with thick lenses. He regarded a folder in front of him with an inquisitive expression on his face.

"And you are?" I asked.

The bright blue eyes looked up at me. "Henri Girard," he said with a trace of French accent, pronouncing his name ON-ree, in the French idiom.

"Mr. Girard is our shooter expert," Amrine said. "He's studied assassins all over the world. He analyzes methods, patterns, situations, and...styles. Like a..."

"Profiler," I said, interrupting him unconsciously.

"Exactement," Girard said.

I looked around the table and eyed each of them. "So, this is about the Shadow, isn't?"

Hansen smiled thinly. "So where did you hear that name?" He asked.

"In a hospital bed in San Antonio, several months ago," I said. "I was pretty drugged up, but the person who mentioned it sort of had all my attention."

Hansen looked at Smith and Amrine and raised his eyebrows questioningly.

Amrine nodded. "Yes, it was her."

Hansen nodded and looked at me. "She does that," he said.

"Director Hansen, can we proceed?" Edmonds asked, interrupting the interchange. It seemed her time was more valuable than ours.

"Please, Lucy," Hansen said. He picked up a remote control from the table next to him and hit a button. In a millisecond, the windows in the room changed from clear to opaque.

Edmonds began her presentation. For the next several minutes, I was provided a complete background on the assassin who the CIA had code-named, "The Shadow," a name that reflected the Agency's inability to get any significant intelligence on or sightings of the assassin since the killing began. Arising on the international scene out of nowhere about a year ago, the Shadow had been attributed fifty kills by the intelligence organizations tracking him, approximately four per month. The targets were seemingly unrelated, all minor governmental officials and business people, but they had taken place all over the world with no discernible pattern.

"Why haven't the cable news organizations gone crazy with this?" I asked, interrupting Edmonds. "This guy has killed 50 people! There has to be some reporter out there that has made the link."

Hansen nodded. "Some of them have, and they've been threatened to keep their mouths shut so that we can catch this guy before he causes a world panic."

"The other thing is that the Shadow rarely takes his victims in public," Amrine said. "Most of the time the victims are in their homes or hotel rooms. Sometimes they're getting on or off private aircraft or into and out of cars. The hits come when they're only in view or still for very few seconds."

I shook my head in reluctant amazement. "Damn," I said. "This guy must be good."

Across the table from me, Henri Girard nodded. "He is excellent," he said. "The shots are precise, take place at long ranges and in many instances, have mere seconds to be aimed and fired."

"Weapon?" I asked.

Hansen inclined his chin to Edmonds.

"Lucy?" He said.

Edmonds clicked forward a few slides and brought up a profile of a large rifle round on the screen. She didn't have to tell me what it was. I knew it on sight.

"The venerable .50 caliber Browning machine gun," I said. "Chambered in a sniper rifle. So, this guy wants to make a statement?"

Girard shook his head with a wry smile on his face.

"It is the ballistics of the bullet," he said. "Often, the Shadow, he does not have a clean shot at his target and needs to shoot through something to hit the target. There is not another round that can carry power through an obstacle and to the target like the .50 can."

Smith and Amrine were both nodding in agreement. Smith glanced over at me.

"Our snipers prefer the .338 Lapua. At the distances from which most of our shots are taken, the trajectory is a little flatter.

But if they must shoot through anything at all, or reach out and touch someone at extreme ranges, the .50 is the weapon of choice."

"Why?" I asked. "I know a little about the two rounds, but I've never compared them."

"It is the greater bullet weight and powder charge behind the .50," Girard said. "While the two bullets, the .50 and the .338, travel at the about the same speed, the .50 bullet is about 2.5 times the weight of the Lapua round and delivers much more energy on target. It also has about twice the maximum range of the 338."

"Wow," I said. "I had no idea. No wonder Ramon liked the .50. He wanted the power."

Hansen nodded. "He did. And the world is a better place without him and his brother in it."

I felt my left should tingle with Hansen's words. I was still recovering from the knife wound inflicted on me by Ramon "The Rock" Pétreo the younger brother of Miguel Hidalgo, the Mexican drug king, in my last outing with the CIA.

"Do you have a map of all the places and dates where these shots have occurred?" Something was pulling at my brain, and I wanted to change the subject anyway.

Edmonds exhaled, apparently somewhat miffed that she would not be able to complete her entire presentation in the order in which she had built it. But she pulled up a slide of the globe, depicted on a flat map, with red "pins" identifying the Shadow's victim locations and dates of the of shootings. It only took me a few seconds to satisfy my inquiry.

"He's got a private jet," I said, pointing at the screen. "He's engaging targets in places like Tokyo and Paris only a day or two apart. No way you do that on the airlines. The whole problem of transporting a big-ass rifle notwithstanding."

"Funny," Amrine said. "Almost like we've heard that before."

Edmonds was shaking her head insistently. "It can't be a private jet," she said, with a note of smugness in her voice. "There has been no pattern of aircraft with the same or similar tail numbers going to the same locations as the incidents."

I sat back in my chair and glanced around the table while I waited for someone else to speak up. No one did. I felt my jaw drop. "You're kidding, right? You need to compare the serial numbers, not the registration numbers."

Edmonds' eyes became wide. "What?" she asked.

I exhaled in disbelief. "The serial numbers. Every jet has a unique serial number, like the VIN on a car. The serial numbers are required for registration in the various countries. It's possible the folks operating the jet in question have multiple registration numbers for it and change them with magnetic plates or something. But they can't fake a serial number. The pattern is unmistakable, and the various governmental agencies in the different countries would catch it when the registration paperwork was processed."

I leaned back and thought for a moment. Then I brought my eyes back to the table. "If they had multiple registration numbers from different countries for the same serial numbered jet, the only place where it might be detected is at the International Registry. But that's voluntary, not compulsory." I nodded at them. "It could be done."

"But why have multiple registration numbers?" Smith asked. "Why not just make a registration number up?"

I shook my head. "Twenty years ago, that might have been possible. But now, when a flight plan is filed, especially in Europe, the registration number and owner is verified because that's how the controlling agencies, like Eurocontrol, bill the owner for services. A fake registration number would be a huge red flag."

Smith turned to Amrine and inclined his head toward me. "I knew there was a reason we brought him along."

"Oh my god," I said. "Your folks have to have thought of this."

"Not so much," Hansen said. "Once the DCS ran the registration number check they were convinced there was no correlation, so they went in a different direction."

"There's a little bit of political tension between the NCS and the DCS," Smith whispered, but not so quietly that Edmonds couldn't hear him. "Sometimes they forget who is operational and who is supporting."

I nodded. "We had the same problem in the Air Force."

Edmonds' face flushed. She killed the slide show and began busily typing into her computer. "Son of a bitch," she said under her breath a few moments later.

"Let me guess," I said. "A correlation."

She looked at me out of the tops of her eyes. "A few correlating events," she said, dismissively. "Nothing definitive yet. Our tech people will have to run more analysis."

"Run the correlation on both ends," I said.

"Why?" she asked, with acid in her voice.

"Because you could find relationships not only to locations of the events but also to airports where the aircraft returns. In fact, the correlation should be stronger there. Almost every private jet has a home base. And that might give you a clue to where your assassin lives."

The blank expression on her face made it clear she hadn't considered this.

"They're going to be busy for a few hours, Colin," Amrine said. "Do you have time for lunch?"

I made a production of checking my watch and my iPhone. "It seems I have the day free. I suppose I could squeeze some lunch in."

The target was number 51 on the list. His name was Adam Bruzek and he seemed to be another anonymous man, living in another anonymous apartment, in another big city.

But the Shadow knew better.

Bruzek had been approached and offered a very generous situation many months ago. He had refused.

And that was why the Shadow was here. In Prague. Looking through a 25-power telescopic sight into the picture window of the target's apartment, 842 meters away. The target lived well, on the top floor of a ten-story building, in an apartment that overlooked one of the many historic squares in the city.

The Shadow leaned into the weapon, a specially designed semi-automatic rifle, chambered in the .50 caliber Browning machine gun cartridge and built to break down into its component parts in less than 60 seconds. The magazine was loaded to capacity with 10 of the large cartidges but the Shadow doubted more than one would be needed. There wasn't much to shoot through today besides a pane of glass. The 29-inch barrel ensured the weapon's accuracy and the long, tubular suppressor helped to limit the amount of sound emitted by the powerful cartridge, especially the sound perceived downrange.

For the third time since arriving on post, the Shadow rechecked the distance to the target with a laser range finder. Then, the Shadow rechecked the windage and elevation settings on the scope and grunted in approval. The wind was dead calm today and the range of the shot was less than a kilometer, so Coriolis Effect would be minimal.

The Shadow regarded the time readout in the lower left side of the scope. 1730 hours local time. The Shadow lowered the scope to the front curb of the building and smiled. A nondescript sedan pulled up to the curb and stopped there.

Right on time.

In a moment, the driver was out of his seat and walked around to the rear, passenger-side door to open it for his rider. The target, a rugged-looking middle-aged man in a black suit and carrying a worn leather briefcase, shook the driver's hand and patted him on the back after climbing out of the backseat.

Seems to be a nice guy, the Shadow thought. That's too bad.

Then, the target walked into his building and the car moved down the street.

The Shadow shifted the telescopic sight's field of regard to the picture window and took a few deep breaths to relax. The weapon felt good against the shoulder and the hard plastic of the pistol grip felt good in the hand. The fingers of the right hand were curled firmly but not tightly around the grip and the right index finger lay outside the trigger guard until the appropriate time.

The door of the target's apartment opened as the target entered a few minutes later and he was greeted immediately by a dowdy-looking housekeeper and a little girl with bright blonde hair and a light blue dress. The little girl jumped into the target's arms, wrapped her arms around his neck and hugged him hard. The target nodded to the housekeeper, who seemed to say a few words. Then they exchanged smiles and she let herself out of the door.

After a few moments, the target slowly put the little girl down and the two of them made their way to the table in the dining area where the housekeeper had left their dinner out for them. The Shadow had watched her prepare the dinner after arriving on station two hours ago.

The table was oriented parallel to the front side of the building and the target seated the little girl in the chair to his right so that she was looking directly at the Shadow, over eight hundred meters away. The Shadow wasn't worried about being seen. The shooting position was far into a storage room in a building well down the street and the room was unlit and dark. The only possible sign of the Shadow's presence was the small window, which was open to the outside. The Shadow regarded the target through the scope's reticle and noted that with the target sitting at the head of the table, his profile was partially obscured by the drapes on the right side of the window.

Patience, the Shadow thought. It won't be long now.

Thirty-three minutes later the target and the little girl finished their meal and the target rose from the table, cleared their *plates and disappeared into the kitchen for a few moments. Then he returned with a small bowl of chocolate gelato for the little girl and presented it to her, bowing to her as if granting a wish. She clapped her hands in enthusiasm and began to eat the gelato as soon as the target placed it in front of her. The target stood over her, watching her, with a sad smile on his rugged features.*

The Shadow briefly considered taking the shot at that moment but decided against it. Assuming the routine stayed the same, the target would be alone soon enough. Collateral damage was to be strictly avoided and the Shadow interpreted that to mean collateral psychological damage as well. It would be one thing for the little girl to find out her father had died. It would be another for him to die in front of her. The Shadow had watched both parents die in considerable pain many years ago. Making others suffer the same fate was to be avoided at all costs. It was in the contract the Shadow provided to clients.

Of course, if a public message had to be sent, the Shadow was willing to make that happen. For a considerable increase in fee of course. Only a few messages had been needed in the course of the Shadow's brief but lucrative career. But today was not one of those days. Today was a simple elimination. The fact that the target died in the way he did would be message enough.

The target and the little girl left the table and watched television in the great room for about 90 minutes. At the normally scheduled time, the target went to the apartment's door and opened it to reveal a woman about the target's age. They exchanged a perfunctory kiss and he let her in. The little girl reluctantly rose from the sofa. The target helped her into her coat and then the two exchanged a long hug. There were tears in the target's eyes when they parted and in moments the little girl and the woman were gone.

The target cleaned up the dinner dishes and then turned off the television, perhaps letting the sound from the children's shows accompany him as he performed his tasks in the kitchen. Then, he seated himself at his desk in the study, facing out the study's window and looking longingly at the sky above him.

The Shadow regarded the rugged face through the scope for a few moments and felt a tinge of emotion for a lost father many years ago.

Don't humanize them, the Shadow thought once again. They're targets, not people.

It was time.

The Shadow didn't hurry. Hurriedness equaled sloppiness and the Shadow was a creature of precision.

With the right index finger, the Shadow pushed the record button on the rifle, located just above and in front of the trigger housing. The button activated power to a fiber optic lead inside the telescopic sight that captured high definition video of the view through the scope and saved it onto a flash drive inserted into a USB port on the side of the sight. All projects were recorded to provide irrefutable evidence of their successful completion.

The Shadow's index finger then found its way into the trigger guard and rested against the trigger, the first pad of the finger placed precisely on the wide, smooth strip of metal. The Shadow inhaled slowly as the crosshairs of the scope settled on the center of the target's chest. Then, the Shadow exhaled half a breath, and gradually took the slack out of the rifle's match- grade trigger.

The weapon fired a few milliseconds later and recoiled into the Shadow's shoulder with about the same force as a 12 gauge shotgun. The 750 grain .50 caliber bullet closed the distance to the target at 2,765 feet per second and impacted the target just over a second after leaving the weapon's muzzle. It hit him in the middle of his chest, tore through his body and spewed blood, tissue, and gore all over the bookshelves behind him. The target died instantly, the wistful expression on his face unchanged. His brain never had time to process his death. After a moment, he slumped forward onto his desk and lay still.

The Shadow had the rifle disassembled in seconds. The weapon's bullpup design and detachable barrel allowed it to break down without tools from its 45-inch length to twenty inches, not including the barrel. The stock, action, magazine, forend, and suppressor were placed into a specially designed denim backpack that seemed to be old and worn on the outside but was pristine on

*the inside, with pockets built to precisely hold each component.
The 29-inch barrel was placed into a white poster tube that was
quickly sealed with tape on both ends. In moments, the Shadow
was out of the door of the room and headed down the hallway. The
barrel and poster tube went down the first trash chute that Shadow
found along the way to the stairs.*

*"Fifty-one down, Anton," the Shadow said, opening the
door to the stairway. "Just a few more and we're done."*

CHAPTER TWO

Monday, October 18
1130 Hours Local Time
Legal Seafood Restaurant
McClean, Virginia, USA

"So, what the fuck happened to the efficient machine that brought down Miguel Hidalgo?" I asked later, as we sat around a table in the bar of a local restaurant.

"Well you might recall that we were under some pressure when we did that last operation," Smith said.

"But things have become worse since then," Amrine added. "We've had a new DCI, and several of the positions higher in the food chain have been filled by bureaucrats with no knowledge of the trade and who believe we live in a kinder, gentler world."

"Hansen seems pretty cool," I said. "Isn't he high enough to insulate you guys from some of the nonsense?"

"He's great," Smith said. "But the various directorates are in competition for resources. And Hansen can ask for anything he wants, but he's only going to get so much. Particularly when dollars are at stake or diplomatic niceties have to be dealt with."

"At the end of the day it's about resources," Amrine said. "And sometimes we get what we need, and other times we don't."

"And now would be one of those times we don't," Smith said.

I sat back in my chair in the predictably furnished place and sipped my Arnold Palmer, wishing it was a martini. The multiple TV screens in the bar were tuned to a news network and showed some man behind a podium, apparently speaking quite passionately about a certain topic. The closed captioning wasn't on, but the crawler said something about "Energy Secretary Pacilio speaks out against Russian Breeder Reactors." I found myself yawning. I turned my attention back to Smith and Amrine. "So, you've got this…person…flying all over the world and shooting about four people a month, and you can't get the resources to stop him?"

Amrine stared down unto his soda water and nodded slowly. "First of all, not surprisingly, it took several months for the police agencies of the world to communicate and for us to understand that there was probably one person performing all of these hits. That didn't happen until early summer, while we were working with you in Arizona. But even once we started putting the pieces together, we realized he hadn't killed anyone who is prominent," Amrine said. "And it hasn't been terribly public. So..."

"...there hasn't been any political pressure to stop him," I said, finishing the sentence.

"Exactly," Smith added. "And, as you might expect, with political pressure comes resources."

"Wow," I said, as much to myself as to them. "So, until the Shadow kills someone prominent, you can't get the support to pursue him."

"Or the analysis time," Smith said.

"Which brings us to one of the reasons you're here, T.C.," Amrine said. "You've achieved something of a status in the Agency. We were hoping to leverage that with the DCS to get them to look at the private jet angle again."

"The serial number correlation occurred to us as well," Smith said. "We just couldn't get them to devote the resources to pursue it."

"Now they have to," Amrine said.

"Because I have status," I said. "Jesus, guys. You should have brought me in earlier. I would have been happy to lend my 'status,' such as it is, to help you."

"It didn't matter so much before a week or so ago," Amrine said.

I cocked my head at him.

"Because until then, we couldn't find what we needed," he continued.

"And that would be?"

"A possible pattern," he said.

My eyebrows raised. "A pattern relating to what?"

"To something we would have never expected," Amrine said, inclining his chin towards the TV where Secretary Pacilio was

21

apparently still speaking about nuclear reactors. "Nukes. Nuclear reactors. It's just a hunch at this stage, but if we're right, it could be fucking huge."

##

We finished our meal about 45 minutes later, which for me had consisted of a Mahi fillet and a glass of sauvignon blanc. Apparently, Amrine and Smith had permission to splurge a little on the lunch bill because of my status.

"I wonder if my status can get me laid tonight," I muttered as Amrine had signed the check.

"Isn't General Petersen taking care of that?" Smith asked.

I shrugged. "She's hot and cold. She's so into her career that I don't hear from her much. We only see each other when she's on the road these days and when we do get together, she's more interested in sleep than sex."

Smith raised his eyebrows. "That's not what you said last summer."

I nodded sadly. Gail and I had spent two incredible weeks in the islands during the summer while I was recovering from a severe wound I had incurred during my last adventure. We spent most of our time on a clothing optional beach and Gail didn't wear a bathing suit the whole time we were there. We fucked each other like a pair of newlyweds.

I sighed. "Last summer was amazing. But since then she's been obsessed with getting her third star. I tried to visit her in San Antonio once and she made me stay in a hotel for 'appearances sake.' She wouldn't even spend the night. We'd talk and have a drink or two, then she'd fall asleep for a few hours, wake up and go home."

"Might have something to do with her husband," Smith said.

"What? She's divorced. Or at least she told me she was." I sat back and crossed my arms. "Wouldn't be the first married woman I've slept with and she probably won't the last."

"She is divorced," Smith said. "We checked into that."

"You checked into that? I asked, incredulously. "Who are you guys, the OSI?"

"No apologies," Smith said. "Married people having affairs can be a security risk. Depending on their career aspirations and how they feel about their partners, they can be blackmailed. And we knew she was aware of what you do for us. That's classified above the top-secret level. We needed to know what her status was so that we could judge whether she was a security risk. It turns out she is divorced…"

He left the sentence hanging.

"But?" I asked

"Her ex followed her to San Antonio from D.C. He's apparently trying to win her back."

"This would be the ex with no visible means of support, right? The one that doesn't work? I knew she was pissed about the alimony she'd have to pay, as well as the fact that he gets half of per pension, but I can't imagine that she'd take him back for purely financial reasons."

"You might be wrong about that," Amrine said. "He moved back into the house last week."

"Jesus," I said. "I never knew." I sighed. "You know, the thing is that she's amazingly smart. She's got like three masters degrees and an honorary doctorate. She's professional and she's aggressive. But smart and successful people can be stupid when it comes to relationships. Can't judge her for that."

"Nor do we," Smith said.

"She was in a low spot in her personal life and career back in the summer. I think she needed me to feel good about herself. Now her career is on the rebound, and her self-actualization squares are getting filled. I might no longer be useful."

Smith nodded. "We see that sort of thing all the time in government agencies and the corporate sector. It's often what makes people vulnerable to blackmail or bribes. She's a climber, T.C. Don't be surprised if she calls your relationship off."

"She's in town for a conference at the Pentagon. I'm supposed to see her tonight. Maybe I'll ask her."

##

We returned to Hansen's office soon after. He motioned us through the door with a phone to his ear.

"Fine, Lucy," he said into the handset. "Just send me what you have, and we'll work with it. I'll schedule a call with your director to get us more computer time."

He hung up and motioned us to the chairs around the table as he entered a few commands into the keyboard in front of him. Then he rose from his desk chair. "Give me a minute or two," he said. "Edmonds just sent me an email with what they've found so far. I'm sending it to the printer. I'll be right back."

I looked at Smith after Hansen walked out of the room. "No admin assistant or anything?"

Smith shook his head. "He's entitled to one, but he does without. Something about not wanting anyone to do his menial stuff."

"Wow," I said. "Tell me that he didn't always sit behind a desk."

Amrine smiled. "He was a field agent before he got married. Once he settled down, he put in for some of the leadership positions that were available and worked his way up to this one."

"But he never forgot his roots," Smith added.

"Kind of like colonels and generals in the USAF that never forget they were once fighter pilots," I said. "Pretty rare when the political correctness doesn't take over."

"Never has with him," Amrine said, grinning. "How do you think we got approval to recruit you?"

I laughed. "I guess I need to thank him for that. Maybe."

Hansen walked through the door a few moments later with a stack of paper in his hand. He sat down at the table with Smith, Amrine and me and handed each of us our own collated sheets.

"Our good friend Lucy Edmonds performed a quick correlation run on the locations of private jets, serial numbers, and locations where the Shadow has acted," Hansen said. "It's pretty basic. Just serial numbers that have arrived and departed from any of the airports during the timeframes we're interested in."

"She didn't look for a consistent pattern at all the airports?" Smith asked.

Hansen shook his head. "Apparently that was too much trouble."

"Unbelievable," Amrine said.

As they were talking, I was going through the list. It was ten pages of arrival and departure information sorted by date. Each line had the registration number, serial number and aircraft type listed along with the date and time of arrival or departure and the airport. There were well over a thousand of them.

I looked up at Hansen. "Did Edmonds leave copies of her slides so we can look at the chronology of the Shadow's hits again?"

Hansen nodded, rose and retrieved a file folder from his desk. Then he returned and placed it in front of me.

"What are you thinking, T.C?" Smith asked.

"I think that the CIA should spend more money on supercomputers for starters," I said. "But I'm also thinking that if I look at some of these city pairs and the travel time between them, I might be able to narrow down the type of aircraft we're trying to find."

I looked at the map and the dates. There was an accompanying table that gave more detail on each of the highlighted marks on the map. There were many large cities and accompanying airports that were identified, but that wasn't what I needed to see. I needed data about the airports themselves. I went through the first page of backup listings and didn't find the type of airport I wanted to see there.

"Damn," I said. "I was hoping he would have made this easier for us. Too bad he went after folks in all these big cities and not somewhere with a short runway."

Then, on the next page, two airports popped out of the list at me.

"Gotcha," I said.

"What do you have?" Hansen asked.

"Hang on just a minute. Let me make sure." I looked at the two airports and then at the dates again. "Holy shit," I said after a few moments. I pivoted the map, so it was oriented for Hansen to see.

"We have one hit on the 18th of September in London," I said. "And the next day, 19 September, this jet, C0622B, departs London City, Airport and flies to Bedford, Massachusetts. On the

21st of September, the next hit takes place in western Massachusetts. At Pittsfield."

I sat back in my chair and looked at them. "Gents, there's only one type of aircraft that can take off from London City and make it to the US without stopping for gas. It's the Falcon 7X. We can narrow our search to that aircraft type and run it against the other cities, dates and times."

"What makes you so certain this is our jet?" Amrine asked. "Besides the performance piece? Wouldn't it have landed at Pittsfield? There's an airport there."

"He would have had to clear customs at a US port of entry," I answered. "And a Falcon 7X is a flashy jet. He wouldn't have wanted to land at a small airport like Pittsfield. Too memorable."

I looked around at them and saw nods from each.

"Okay," I said. "I'll take the first three pages and look for 7Xs." I reached for the pen holder at the center of the table and retrieved a yellow highlighter. "You guys can divvy up the remaining ones."

Thirty minutes later, we had all the Falcon 7X arrivals and departures identified. That narrowed the field down to just under 200 entries.

"Okay," I said. "That's better. Now let's start looking for serial number alignment."

Ten minutes after that, a pattern became obvious.

"Houston, we have a winner," I said. "Serial number 077."

Amrine was shaking his head. "But this doesn't make sense, T.C. There aren't enough of them. There were 50 events, and we've got a lot less than twice that number of arrivals and departures."

"You're right John," I said. "That is an issue."

Hansen was standing and looking down at the sheets of paper. Then, he slowly began to nod to himself. "It's not his only jet. He has more than one."

"If we can access the national registration database for one of the countries Serial Number 77 is registered in, we may be able to a bead on the owner," I said. "You might find out how many other jets the owner has, assuming he duplicates registrations for all of his aircraft."

I looked at all the entries for 077 on the list. There were several different registration numbers from a few different countries, but it didn't take long to find one with a familiar pattern.

"And since we've identified N497PT as one of the registration numbers, I think our friends at the FAA might help us."

I looked at Hansen who was already moving to his desk.

"FAA dot gov," I said. "Click on aircraft and then aircraft registration."

We walked over behind him as he called up the web page.

"OK, click on search by N-number and then enter N497PT," I said.

Hansen did as he was told and in moments the registration information for the jet was displayed.

"There's the serial number, 077," I said.

"The owner is listed as Soehren Industries," Hansen said. "With an address in Las Vegas."

"Clever," Smith said. "Corporate registration records in that state can be the next thing to anonymous and difficult to search."

"Now go back out the search menu and select search by name," I instructed Hansen.

Hansen backed out the main menu, clicked on the name and entered 'Soehren Industries' in the search field. In moments, a list of aircraft was displayed.

"Jesus," Amrine said. "This guy must be pretty well funded. He's got three of them."

I was nodding. "You're right. Three 7Xs is a lot of expensive hardware. No wonder the correlation has been hard to see. Three jets with multiple registration numbers for each in multiple countries? It's like an international aviation shell game."

I walked back over to the table with the list of arrivals and departures. "But now we have the keys to solve it. What are the other two serial numbers?"

"063 and 071," Smith said.

I scanned the list again and highlighted the other serial numbers as I saw them. Hansen, Smith, and Amrine walked over to the table as I worked.   In a few moments, I was done, and I counted all the occurrences of the serial numbers in question.

"115 total," I said. "It fits if you consider there might have been reconnaissance visits to some of the locations before the hit there."

"Goddamn," Smith said. "We finally have a break."

I looked down the list. "The aircraft are registered in the United States, the Cayman Islands, Russia, France and Switzerland," I said. "As you search the various registration data, some of the owners will be fake companies, but you should be able to get a little closer to what you're looking for."

Smith was nodding enthusiastically. "You bet your ass we will. We'll farm this legwork out internally, so the DCS doesn't slow roll us again."

Amrine was eying me with a disturbing gleam in his eyes. "It seems that Uncle Sam paid to get someone in this room type-rated in the Falcon 7X. And having that someone on one of those jets to sniff around might not be a bad thing."

I grinned at him. "I wondered when that type rating was going to be put to government use. Obviously nothing in life is free."

"You know better than that T.C.," Smith said.

"What do you think boss?" Amrine asked.

Hansen shrugged. "Sounds like a good idea to me. So exactly how do we go about doing that?"

"Seems like we ask the contract business jet pilot here," Smith said. "What do you think, T.C.? Any ideas about how we make that happen?"

"I might have a few," I said.

CHAPTER THREE

Monday, 18 October
1845 Hours Local Time
Marriott Hotel Bar, Crystal City
Arlington, Virginia, USA

I looked at my watch as Gail entered the bar – almost two hours late. She had changed out of her USAF uniform and into a pair of tight jeans and silk shirt and looked beautiful, as usual. Her brownish-black hair flowed to her shoulders, and she had refreshed the usual makeup configuration that highlighted her deep brown eyes and wide, expressive mouth.

I rose to greet her and was awarded with a quick hug and kiss for my trouble.

"I am so sorry," she said as she took a seat across the table.

I nodded to the glass of wine in front of her. "I ordered you a glass of the cabernet. After a long day of meetings, I figured you could use it."

She raised the glass to her lips and took a long sip. "This is good!" she said. "Thank you!" She leaned back in her chair. "I couldn't get out of that damn meeting. General Santos just wouldn't shut up."

I smirked and took a sip of my martini.

"What?"

"This would be the Vice-Chief of Staff and the one you have some history with, right?"

She nodded. "I worked for him two assignments ago. We got along really well. He's the one who helped me get my first star."

And the one you're counting on to get your third, I thought. Gail had briefly told me about the two-days of meetings she was attending at the Pentagon. The subject matter seemed unrelated to her job as Commander of the Air Force Personnel Center, but now that I knew General Santos was hosting the meetings, the trip made sense. *Can't find time for us to get together,* I thought, *but you can sure find time for a trip to see the guy who might get you promoted.*

For about the millionth time since last summer, I wondered why I was still seeing her.

Gail's phone buzzed in her purse and she retrieved it in a show of lightning reflex that would have made a prize-fighter proud.

"Do you mind?" she asked. "I haven't been able to deal with email all day."

"Do what you have to do," I said.

I signaled the bartender and motioned for a second martini. The bartender was in her mid-thirties and had red hair that shimmered in the low light of the bar. I smiled at her and returned to my drink. The bartender reminded me of Sarah, the woman I had almost married six months ago. Sarah was a business jet pilot and a former centerfold model for Bachelor Magazine, with silky red hair and a body that men would kill for. We had connected, she and I, and through an amazing stroke of fortune, we had a baby daughter named Colleen. Colleen would be a year old in two months, and odds were high I wouldn't be there to celebrate the occasion. In fact, I probably wouldn't see either of them again, except perhaps to gaze from afar. After bringing down the most powerful drug lord in Mexico, the world had become very dangerous for people close to me. The CIA had taken both Sarah and Colleen into an international version of the witness protection program, and I had no idea where they were or what they were doing. I only knew they were safe – safe because they were away from me. Even now, with Miguel dead, the last words of his brother, Ramon, still haunted me.

"Others will come," he had said.

I believed him. And so, apparently, did the CIA and DEA, because continual chatter containing the words *vengar a Miguel*, avenge Miguel, was regularly intercepted. Both agencies believed that vengeance would begin with me or those close to me. I had warned Gail of the danger but she didn't seem concerned. I shrugged. *Not sure it matters*, I thought. *With as little time as we spend together, no one would suspect she meant anything to me anyway.*

The bartender brought my drink and set it on the table in front of me.

"Would you folks like any starters?" she asked us.

Gail didn't answer and continued to take care of email.

"I haven't looked at the menu, but do you have shrimp cocktail and a hummus platter on it?"

The bartender nodded.

"One of each please."

"I'll have those out right away," she said as she collected my old glass and made her way back to the bar.

I sat back and sipped my martini, relishing the taste of smooth gin as it washed across my tongue and down my throat. I glanced across the table at Gail, still engrossed in her email. I briefly considered broaching the subject of her ex-husband but quickly dismissed it. The discussion would generate tension between us and it wouldn't change anything. Besides, I wasn't sure I cared enough to make the effort.

Then my phone rang. For the first time since turning to her email, Gail raised her eyes and glanced at the screen of my phone as it sat on the table next to me. She glanced down at the number and the contact and looked up at me, her eyes widening slightly.

I took another sip of my drink and then raised the phone to my ear.

"The Shadow just did number 51," Smith said. "In Prague."

"Well shit," I said, sitting my glass on the table. "Any idea who or why?"

I left Gail at the table and walked into a hallway beside the bar where I wouldn't be overheard.

"The who we know," Smith answered. "And he was one of the top nuclear experts in the country."

I nodded unconsciously. "Sounds like your hunch was right."

"Maybe. But the cool thing is that we've located one of the jets. It's on the ground at Le Bourget, France getting fixed and it flew there from...Prague."

I nodded. "Le Bourget obviously has a Dassault service center there, but you knew that."

"Not sure we did," Smith said. "But we do now. Some members of our Paris office are working with Dassault and the

French Directorate General for External Security. Anyway, we're going to try to get you on the jet."

"How are you going do that?"

"The jet is having something called a fay-deck replaced?"

"It's an acronym," I said, interrupting him. "F-A-D-E-C. Full authority digital engine controller."

"Whatever," Smith said. "Apparently it generated some error code, so the crew flew from Prague to Le Bourget to have it fixed or replaced. Dassault will insist on a test flight and will require that you perform it. You probably didn't know this, but you've been a contract maintenance test pilot for Dassault for about the last two years."

I smiled thinly. "The things I learn about myself."

"You'll happen to be in Paris, just coming off another contract trip, and because of numerous sudden scheduling conflicts, you'll be the only person available to fly."

"I see," I said after a few moments. "When do you need me there?"

"Your flight is tomorrow," Smith said. "The test flight will be Wednesday afternoon, or whenever you get there, whatever is later."

"You guys have been busy. Holy shit."

"We have to pick up the pace a bit. If this nuke thing we're analyzing plays out, the Shadow may be onto a specific timeline and we need to get in front of it."

"Anything I need to know about?"

Smith paused for a moment. "Honestly, Colin, I don't think so. It shouldn't affect anything but the target choice. But…"

"But what, Dave?"

"If you hear anything about a trip to London, you need to get on it."

"Okay. If I hear something about it before the jet leaves Paris, we could have Dassault insist I fly on subsequent trips or something."

"Good idea. Keep your ears open when you get there."

"What time is the flight tomorrow?" I asked. "I'll have to go back to my townhouse and pack a bag."

"Go to a mall and buy what you need with the credit card we issued you. You have a flight from Reagan to JFK at noon. You'll pick up the flight to Paris from there. I'll email you the ticket info. Enjoy your evening with the General." Smith was laughing as he disconnected.

I walked back into the bar. Gail was sitting at our table and looking down at her glass of wine.

"What's up with your friends?" She asked as I approached.

"A trip to Paris. And a contract flight on a Falcon 7X."

"That doesn't sound so bad."

I looked at her for a moment and debated how much I would tell her. I opted for the truth. I wasn't sure if I was being honest or cruel. Maybe it was both. "It wouldn't be under normal circumstances. But that jet might be owned by one of the most dangerous contract killers in the world."

I sat back and sipped my martini and eyed her.

After a long moment, she spoke. "And what are you supposed to do?"

I shrugged. "Get in. Get to know the jet. Get to know the crew. Pass along what I see."

"And that's it?"

"For the moment," I said.

There was another long pause.

"But it won't stay that way. Will it?" She was looking directly at me now and with a look of concern in her eyes. I couldn't decide if I was touched or shocked.

"Probably not. The boys don't typically bring me in for the passive stuff."

She reached across the table and took both of my hands in hers. "After we finish the appetizers can we go upstairs and have dinner in the room?"

I nodded. "Sure. What did you have in mind?"

"I need to feel close to you," she said. "I want to snuggle up on the couch in our room and watch TV. I promise I'll put my phone down."

"Wow. Okay. Sure."

She laughed and squeezed my hands. "Don't act so surprised! You know I love spending time with you. When we're together I can forget about the Air Force and all the shit in my life."

I nodded, thinking of our time together last summer.

"I enjoy spending time with you too. It'd just be nice to maybe do it more often."

CHAPTER FOUR

Wednesday, October 20
2130 Hours Local Time
Lobby Bar, Hilton Hotel, Charles de Gaulle Airport
Paris, France

I was nursing a sip of the Highland Park 18 in yet another airport hotel when Smith called the next time. The vibration of the phone and the accompanying ringtone shook me from my reverie as I sat in comfortable corner bar chair, fighting sleep and trying my best to recover from the jet lag and the two-hour test flight I had flown that afternoon. After a fine French meal and some equally fine French wine, I was trying to stay awake just a little while longer so I could overcome the upcoming struggle for sleep. A long night of rest seemed heavenly, and I could almost hear the king-sized bed in my hotel room beckoning to me.

My iPhone continued to vibrate on the table next to me. The ringtone was AC/DC's "You Shook Me All Night Long," and I smiled as the strains of it reached my ears. Gail had changed the ringtone before I had left her yesterday morning as a reminder of our time together. I reached for the phone to prevent my thoughts from wandering any further.

"Hello Dave," I said.

"Hey Colin," Smith answered. "How's Paris?"

"Beautiful. But I haven't seen it yet on this trip. The airport Hilton is quite comfortable though."

"How'd the test flight go?"

"Routinely. We did just over two hours of droning up and down the coastline of France at altitude and watching the FADEC indications on the number 2 engine. No issues or anomalies, or so it would seem."

"Did you meet the crew?"

"Yes, and it's like a mini United Nations. The flight attendant is from Scotland, one captain is from France, and the other is an American."

"Is the American anyone you know?"

"His name is Mitch Grace. I don't know him well, but I've heard good things about him through my contacts in business aviation."

"Did you have a chance to interact with them at all?"

"Not really. Crews represent the owners of their aircraft and don't typically interact with representatives of service centers. I've been hanging out in the lobby here hoping one or all of them would show up and I could have a drink with him or them. I'm not sure how much longer I can last though. It's been a long day-night-day."

"How'd you leave the test flight today?"

"We said that we still needed to analyze the FADEC data, but the first indications looked good."

"Dassault isn't planning on returning the aircraft to service?"

I shook my head even though I knew Smith couldn't see me. "I told them not to, even though the FADEC's indications were normal."

"What's your plan then?"

I shrugged. "No idea. Just stall things until I either learn something or get posted as a crewmember."

Smith exhaled. I couldn't tell my plan wasn't as definitive as he would have liked it but the options were limited.

"Dave, I'm not the experienced field operative here. You are. If you have any advice or suggestions, I'd be happy to hear them."

"I don't have any. And that's the problem. Just do the best you can and..."

"Dave," I said, interrupting him, "one of the other crew members is here. It's the American. I gotta go."

"Colin!" Smith's voice took on a severe tone.

"Yes, Dave?"

"On the base of your phone, next to the power cord socket is a small compartment with an arrow on it. Inside that compartment are three small pills. If you have a chance, put the white one in the guy's drink."

I felt my guts tighten up a little. "I kind of like this guy, Dave. I don't want to kill him."

Smith laughed. "You watch too many spy movies. Killing people at the wrong time generates too much visibility and too many questions. The white pill won't kill him. It will just make him sick for about 12 hours."

I exhaled in relief. "We'll that's good. I'll see what I can do."

Smith laughed again. "Do that."

I clicked off the call, gathered my drink and made my way over to the table where the American crew member, Mitch Grace, was sitting. Mitch was slightly shorter than I was, about six feet or so, and unlike many in the business aviation industry, he was solidly built, with wide shoulders, a flat stomach, and muscular arms. His balding hairline was shaved close to his head, and his face was cherub-like with friendly blue eyes.

"Mr. Grace," I said, playing the part of the customer-oriented Dassault pilot. "Would you mind if I join you? Dassault might be buying."

"I don't know," Grace said, eyeing me with a wry expression on his face. "My standards are pretty high. If someone offers to buy me a drink, I feel forced to take them up on it."

"Sounds like we have that in common," I said, sitting down in the chair across the table from him. "Shall we order or wait for the rest of your crew?"

Grace shook his head. "They're not coming," he said. After a moment, a smile worked its way onto his features. "But then again, maybe they are. Just not here."

I raised my eyebrows and smiled back at him. "Oh really?"

He nodded. "I've only been on this contract for about two weeks or so, but the two of them seem to disappear a lot together."

"That happens."

He nodded again. "And it usually fucks things up when it does. But so far, I've not had to deal with it while we've been flying and that's all that matters to me."

"Makes sense."

The cocktail waitress, a svelte brunette with long wavy hair and bright red lipstick, arrived at our table to take drink orders. I held up my glass and indicated I was fine for the moment and motioned for her to take Grace's order. She leaned over to him, and her short black dress inched up the back of her upper thighs, exposing a goodly amount of stockinged flesh as she did so. Grace ordered his drink, a Jameson's with no ice, and smiled at me as she wrote the order down. Then, she straightened and made her way back the bar.

"You're welcome," Grace said.

"Nicely done," I replied. "Great view from my perspective."

"You can repay the favor when you order another one of whatever it is you're drinking. I'll enjoy the view as well but it will just make me think of my wife more, and I'm not sure that's the best thing for me with two more weeks on this contract."

"Where's home?"

"North Carolina. We own some land north of Greensboro and just built a house there. I miss it."

"North Carolina is beautiful. I can understand why."

"It's not just the land," Grace said, quickly looking away. "I have a great wife and small kids and miss all of them. I've spent a lot of time on the road in the last few months. It's getting old."

Suddenly an idea popped into my head. "Excuse me for just a second," I said.

I opened my phone and texted Smith.

I CAN PROBABLY BUY THIS GUY OFF. IS THE GOVERNMENT WILLING TO PAY TWO WEEKS OF HIS SALARY TO GET ME ON THE JET?

The reply came in seconds.

YES.

"Hey Mitch," I said. "Before we continue the evening, I have a business proposition for you."

His eyes sparkled. "I'm listening."

THE SHADOW - INTERLUDE

The Shadow removed the new barrel from the shipping container and began the process of cleaning it. Slowly, deliberately, reverently, the Shadow screwed the cleaning rod together and coated the bristles of the brass brush with the viscous liquid that was a combination cleaner, protectant, and lubricant. Then, the Shadow inserted the brush into the barrel's breech and pushed it through until the brush came out of the muzzle. After pausing a moment, the Shadow pulled the brush back through the barrel until it reappeared in the breech again. The motion of the rod and the brush was firm but careful, even tender. The rifle's 29-inch barrel was new, and the Shadow didn't want to take any chances on scratching or nicking the lands and grooves on the inside. The slightest damage to the metal ridges that would give the .50 caliber bullet its spin could compromise both the projectile's range and accuracy. These barrels were made just for the Shadow's use – by one of the most skilled gunsmiths in the world. They were works of art, and they deserved respect. Technically, this barrel, like the many that had preceded it and now were lying in trash chutes, dumpsters and rivers all over the world, didn't need to be cleaned. The gunsmith had cleaned it thoroughly after it had been finished. But the Shadow was a creature of habit and the pre-event cleaning was a ritual the Shadow never missed. It was always performed the before an event, in precisely the same manner. Consistency was what had made the Shadow successful. And consistency was based on doing the same thing, the same way, every time.

The brush went through the barrel and back a total of ten times. Then the brush came off the cleaning rod and was replaced by an attachment of approximately the same size and length but had an oval-shaped opening in the middle of it. The Shadow inserted a square cloth patch through the hole, reinserted the rod in the breech, and repeated what had been done with the brush. After the tenth trip through the barrel, the old patch was replaced with a new one, and the process was repeated.

The barrel cleaning complete, the Shadow screwed the barrel into the rifle's receiver and attached the forend, ensuring *that gas vents and piston lined up precisely. Then, the Shadow lightly coated a patch with some of the CLP liquid and gently swabbed the inside of the barrel's chamber, the inside of the receiver and the bolt, making sure that a thin layer of CLP remained on all the metal parts. The Shadow inserted the bolt into the action and finished assembling the weapon. A cartridge case containing a boresight laser was inserted into the breech, and the bolt closed behind it. The Shadow deployed the bipod legs from the rifle's forend and lowered the weapon to the ornate wooden desk that had been serving as a cleaning platform. The Shadow positioned the rifle such that the tiny red laser dot appeared on the far wall of the large hotel room and then peered through the telescopic sight on the weapon. The dot rested just below the crosshairs in the scope, and the Shadow smiled in satisfaction. The weapon still held its zero for 100 meters. Through the expenditure of several thousand rounds of specially loaded match ammunition, the Shadow had created a robust database for the performance of the .50 caliber BMG cartridge at ranges from 100 to 3000 meters. All that was left was for the Shadow to measure the range to the target and assess the wind and humidity, then use the tablet application to provide adjusted windage and elevation settings for the telescopic sight. At that point, it would become a function of the Shadow's patience and proficiency. Holding the scope's crosshairs steady on the wall, the Shadow inhaled slowly and then gradually applied pressure to the rifle's match-grade trigger. The snap of the hammer striking the firing pin came at exactly the expected time.*

The Shadow rose from the weapon and quickly disassembled it into four pieces plus the barrel and placed them into the backpack and a poster tube respectively. Then, the Shadow packed the poster tube into a long garment bag hanging in the closet and zipped the bag closed.

There was a sudden knock at the bedroom door that did not distract the Shadow from the work at hand.

"Ready for dinner soon?" The voice on the other side of the door asked.

"In about ten minutes," the Shadow answered.

The Shadow disassembled the cleaning rod and placed it and the other cleaning elements into a zippered pouch. The zippers were fastened together with a zip tie, and the pouch was ready for disposal. It would end up in an anonymous rubbish bin as the Shadow exited the hotel in the morning.

Chores done, the Shadow went into the lavish bathroom to ensure all clothes and accouterments were in place for dinner.

The London job was on for tomorrow, the Shadow thought. The shot from the Four-Seasons hotel to the Marble Arch wouldn't be one of the longest, but given the complexity of the environment, it also wouldn't be one of the easiest. But in the end, the results would be the same. The Right Honorable Robert Essex, a distinguished member of Her Majesty's government, and the opposition Labour Party's counterpart to the Conservative Party's Chancellor of Energy, would be dead. And the Shadow would be another million U.S. dollars richer. It would be the first of two very public events that were meant to send a message to the government of the United Kingdom.

The Shadow smiled.

Most snipers liked working in the darkness, plying their trade in secret, sneaking in, taking the shot and sneaking out. The Shadow had done that for most of the events assigned, but every once in a while, a public message was necessary. That meant there would be an audience to witness the event.

And the Shadow loved an audience.

CHAPTER FIVE

Thursday, October 21
1400 Hours Local Time
Descending through 20,000 Feet Over the English Channel
On the Jacko 1D Arrival into London City Airport (EGLC)

The flights from Le Bourget to Prague and from Prague to London, our current destination, had been busy, as most flights were in European airspace, with multiple frequency changes and radio calls in the dense airspace of the small and crowded continent. And now, about an hour after taking off from Prague's Havel International Airport (LKPR), we were on the descent into one of the most challenging airports in the world.

I was in the left seat of the Falcon 7X I had test-flown yesterday, N497PT. Between the agreement with Mitch and the pill I had given him, along with the work the CIA had accomplished in the background, I was pilot-in-command of the jet on its flight into London City Airport. The contracting agency had made it clear that I would be a crewmember for the flights today only, due to my lack of a complete background check.

Damn, all this effort is expensive, I thought as I sat in the cockpit and gazed at the clear blue sky in front of the jet and the typical European undercast below us. *And for what? Maybe a snippet of something that might help? Jesus.*

I had met the passengers that morning, and they seemed pleasant enough. The principal passenger was a Russian businessman named Vladimir Strelkov who specialized in commodity trading. He was in his late thirties to early forties with jet-black hair and dark eyes. He had a distinctive square chin and reminded me of a young Hugh Grant although with a more aristocratic appearance and demeanor. His companion, Alina, was one of the most beautiful women I had ever seen. Somewhere in that ageless middle-aged region in which well-preserved women reside, she had thick blonde hair that flowed to just below her shoulders and blue eyes with small flecks of gray in them. She had high cheekbones and wore just enough makeup to highlight her model-like features but not so much that she looked artificial. Her body was a study in female anatomical perfection with breasts that strained under the tight fabric of the silk top she wore, a thin waist and hips that accented an ass that was truly world class. But as physically attractive as she was, it was her manner and personality that made her truly beautiful. She was bubbly, funny, self-deprecating and incredibly friendly. After the appropriate greeting and hugs for the pilot and flight attendant who regularly crewed the aircraft, she wanted to know everything about me in the few short minutes after they boarded and before we started engines. I gave her a brief, edited version of my bio and she thanked me profusely for my service to the "cause of freedom." Then she gave me a hug and released me to my cockpit duties.

"Wow," was all I could say as I finished strapping into my seat and donned my headset.

"Zat is ze normal reaction," said the other pilot, a Frenchman named Jean Renaud. Jean was thin with dark hair and dark eyes, an easy smile, and none of the arrogance that sometimes characterizes the French. He was also a talented aviator and could probably land the fickle 7X better than I could.

"And you're not the first to have it, love," said the flight attendant, chiming in. Her name was Abigail Stewart, and she spoke with just a hint of a Scottish lilt to her voice. True to her heritage, Abby was red-haired and freckled and seemed almost plain-looking until she smiled. Then her face and her eyes lit up, and the effect was dazzling.

"We just love her, don't we?" Abby had continued. "She travels more than Vladimir does, and she's always been very friendly to us. Unlike some of the people we've flown before."

"I know what you mean," I had said. "I've had my fair share of high-maintenance passengers. It's nice to run into somebody who isn't."

"Nice of you to let me fly this leg Jean," I said as we continued the descent to 10,000 feet per the instructions London Control had issued a few moments ago. "I've done a lot of contract work, and when I'm not on maintenance flights, most of the lead pilots on the jets I've flown would have made me sit over on the right side."

"Well, you have had ze training, and you are good with the jet, n'est pas? Besides, we who have flown fighters must assist each other, eh?"

I nodded. "Yes, we do. And speaking of that, why don't I give you a quick approach briefing for the ILS to Runway 09 since you've been nice enough to set it up for me?"

"Bon!" He replied.

I relinquished control of the aircraft to him and displayed the approach chart on the lower center display unit. Then I briefly talked through the elements of the instrument approach, most of which were routine but a few of which were not.

"This is going to be a 5.5-degree glide slope instead of the normal 3.0," I said. "We'll fly the approach with the first notch of speed brakes deployed, and I'll start the round-out at about 100 feet as opposed to 50. I'm not going to try to make it pretty. I'm going to plan on a firm touchdown to kill some of our energy and then stop the jet as quickly as I can."

"Zat is a good plan," Jean said. "But you do not have to worry about not making it pretty. Your landings yesterday, zay were not pretty." He winked at me.

I smiled back at him. Fighter pilots gave each other shit. That was just how it worked.

Abby stuck her head into the cockpit and touched my shoulder. "Alina would like to sit in the jump seat and watch the approach. Do you mind?"

"No," I said, shaking my head. "Jean?"

He shook his head as well. "She makes the boss happy so we, we will make her happy."

"Great!" Abby said. "I'll get her up here and strapped in."

A few moments later, the lovely Alina was sitting on the jump seat behind Jean with seat belt, shoulder harness, and headset in place.

"Thank you very much for letting me sit up here with you gentlemen," she said. "I've ridden in the back for many of these landings but I always wanted to see what they looked like from the front."

I marveled at how devoid of accent her English was. She could have easily passed for an American.

"It is our pleasure, mademoiselle," Jean said. "But Vladimir, he will not miss you?"

"He's asleep," she said, laughing. "Too much exercise this morning and too much vodka on the way here."

Lucky him, I thought.

She leaned forward and looked out through the cockpit windscreens. I could see her face out of my peripheral vision. Her expression of was one of rapt attention and excitement.

"The view is so much better up here," she said. "I can see why you guys like this so much."

"Every day you can get air under your …rear end is a good day," I said, barely catching myself in time.

"Under your ass, you mean," she said, smiling at me. "I get that. So, our lives are in your hands Mr. American fighter pilot?"

"That's the way it appears ma'am," I replied. "I'll do my best not to scare you."

"Sometimes a little scare can be exciting," she said.

"Maybe in an F-16 or a Rafale," I said, nodding at Jean. "But not in a jet like this."

"It is our job to make the most exciting thing boring to you Mademoiselle," he said.

"Well you're no fun," she said, giving him a gentle push on the shoulder.

"Falcon November 497 Papa Tango," the VHF radio interrupted our banter. "This is London Control, descend and maintain 3,000 feet, altimeter 29.90. Turn right heading 270. Downwind. Perform landing checks."

"Damn this happens fast," I muttered under my breath.

"Always it does," Jean replied after acknowledging the radio call. "And always it is a little different."

"Could you ask him if he needs a speed here?" I asked. "I'd like to get slowed down a little early if possible."

Jean nodded and I heard him key the mic. "London, November 497 Papa Tango, what speed do you wish us to maintain?"

"November 497 Papa Tango, maintain two-five-zero knots until advised."

"Of course," I said. "Why would they let us slow down and get ahead of the aircraft."

"N'est pas!" Jean replied.

"What's the big deal about the speed?" Alina asked. Her voice was barely a whisper.

"It's always good to get ahead of the jet as soon as you can,"" I replied, watching the altitude click down in the head up display or HUD in front of me, and eyeing the small runway that was London City Airport as we banked up to make the turn to 270 degrees. "Obviously we want to be smooth as we slow and deploy flaps and the landing gear but sometimes we can't be." I turned around and looked at her. "And that pisses us off."

She smiled at me. It was an amazing smile.

"ALTITUDE!" Announced the Falcon 7X's alerting system.

"Four thousand for three thousand," I said automatically.

"One thousand to level," Jean responded.

The 7X leveled at 3,000 feet as the urban sprawl that was the east side of London spread out below us, interrupting the green of the fields and gray-blue of the Thames with a blanket of brown and black spots.

London City Airport passed down the right side of the aircraft. The airport was about 5,000 feet of runway and minimal supporting structures and occupied an island that had been reclaimed from the Thames in the same area that the eastern docks used to be.

"November 497 Papa Tango, London, contact Thames Director on 132.7."

"132.7 for November 497 Papa Tango," Jean said into the mic.

Jean checked us into the required frequency a few seconds later as the London City runway receded down the right side of the aircraft.

"November 497 Papa Tango, base turn in two miles, slow to final approach speed."

I shook my head in disbelief at how quickly we'd have to lose over 50 knots to configure the aircraft. I reached back on the center pedestal and pulled the air brake handle to the first detent.

Instantly, the center portion of the three air brakes on the top of each wing deployed and the aircraft began to slow, with the usual vibration generated by the spoilage of lift across the top of the wing.

"You warned me about this," I said to Jean. "You said it'd come fast. By the way, AB1 is selected and I'm just going to leave it there since we'll need it for the approach."

"Roger," he answered, nodding. "Zis approach, it always happens fast. Ze controllers, zay try to get too many airplanes in here."

"November 497 Papa Tango, Thames Director, turn right, heading 360, base leg."

I turned the heading knob on the guidance system control panel to the right and the big 7X banked up and began its turn to the north as Jean keyed the mic.

"November 497 Papa Tango, right to tree-seex-zero," Jean replied.

I continued to shake my head. I could see the square corner developing already. I glanced out Jean's side of the aircraft as we made the turn to the north. We were very close to the centerline of the runway. The chances of doing everything smoothly, on autopilot, were lost.

The airspeed tape in the HUD decreased through 200 knots.

"SF one," I said.

Jean was looking down at the pilot's display unit to check my speed. He nodded.

"Speed checks," he said. "Selecting SF 1."

Jean moved the Slats/Flaps handle from the CLEAN to the SF1 position. Instantly, the slats on the front of the Falcon's huge wing deployed and then the flaps rolled down to the number one position – about 9 degrees. The air noise in the cockpit rose noticeably, as did the vibration of the aircraft. The airspeed slowed to 170 knots and the throttles advanced automatically to keep it there.

I glanced out of the left cockpit window and saw that we were paralleling the Thames River. The majestic brown Hall of Parliament and the square spire of Big Ben were very close as was the hustle and bustle of the City of Westminster just beyond.

"Amazing," I said to myself.

"November 497 Papa Tango, Thames Director, turn right heading 060, maintain 3000 until established, cleared ILS approach runway 09. Contact London City Tower, 118 decimal 07."

"Of course," I said to know one in particular. "Why make it easy."

"AUTOPILOT!" Announced the 7X's warning system as I kicked the autopilot off. The late instructions given to us by the controller had us overshooting the centerline of runway 09 as we turned. The mechanics of the 7X's advanced autopilot weren't going to be enough. I was going to need to do this by hand.

Jean acknowledged Thames' call and was switching radio frequencies. I engaged the 7X's APPROACH mode on the guidance panel and began to follow the steering cues presented in the HUD. Below us, the runway we were to land on seemed impossibly close and impossibly far below us. But that was the mental picture a normal pilot would have. As for me, I had flown hundreds of simulated engine out approaches in the F-16 back in the day and a real one in the not too distant past, so the picture looked disturbingly normal.

"Gear down, SF2," I commanded.

Jean nodded his head and pulled the landing gear handle into the down position and then deployed the flaps to the second position even as he checked us in with London City Tower.

"November 622 Papa Tango, London City Tower, cleared to land runway 09. Plan to execute a 180 turn on the runway after landing."

The 7X's throttles retarded automatically as I nosed the aircraft over to intercept the 5.5-degree glide path. I centered the flight path marker in the HUD over the ILS steering cue and pushed forward on the sidestick very slightly to hold it there.

"SF3. Before landing checks," I said.

Jean nodded and toggled up the before-landing checklist on the lower right corner of the bottom multi-function display. Then he moved the flap lever to the last position.

"Landing gear?" he asked.

I glanced at the landing gear position indicator in my display unit. "Down. Three green."

"Slats and flaps?"

My eyes moved to the slats and flaps indicator in the display. The green slat was illuminated and the position indicator was abeam the 3. "SF3 indicating."

"Ze checklist is complete," he said.

I nodded. "And AB1 is set, per the approach requirements."

"I am showing you on ze course and ze glide path," he said.

"Me too. Now we just need to hold it there."

"It's really noisy," Alina said.

"It's always noisier in the front than in the back," I said. "We get the wind noise up here that you don't get in the back. All that air hitting the windscreen at anywhere from 120 to 350 knots generates quite a bit of kinetic energy."

I saw her nod in my peripheral vision. Below me and off the nose, the 4998 feet of the London City airport's runway was growing larger in the windscreen by the second. I glanced at the vertical velocity indicator in the HUD.

"1300 feet per minute," I said to myself. "That makes sense."

Alina was straining to see over the glare shield and down to the runway below. With the aircraft in such a steep descent and the higher angle of attack typical of an approach to landing, the runway was obscured from her perspective.

"And we're really shaking a lot," she asked. "Is that normal?"

I nodded. "We have the airbrakes extended to keep us from accelerating in the descent."

"ONE THOUSAND!" The 7X's ground proximity warning system or GPWS announced. We were 1,000 feet above the ground.

"Time to do some of that pilot shit," I muttered.

"The jet, she will want to nose up," Jean said. "You must not allow zis."

"She does and I won't," I said. "Feels a little bit like a bombing pass back in the day."

"FIVE HUNDRED! APPROACHING MINIMUMS!" The GPWS informed us that we were 500 feet from the ground and

100 feet above the approach minimums that Jean had programmed into the avionics.

"MINIMUMS! MINIMUMS!" Came a few seconds later.

"Runway in sight, landing," I said.

Jean nodded next to me. He was leaning forward in his seat, obviously anxious about the landing.

"THREE HUNDRED!"

I hit the autothrottle release button and took manual control of the throttles.

"AUTOTHOTTLES!" The 7X announced.

The runway below was growing larger rapidly and the temptation to raise the nose of the aircraft was strong. But like any precision maneuver, the round out from a steep approach had to be done by the numbers. I held the 7X's nose down and kept the steering cue centered.

"TWO HUNDRED!"

Now Alina could see the runway in front of us and she could also see how rapidly we were descending in relationship to it. In my peripheral vision, I could see her body stiffening with tension.

"ONE HUNDRED!"

I applied backpressure to the sidestick as I retarded the throttles to idle. The trick was to be smooth but not abrupt and also to allow the aircraft to touch down with a slight descent rate so that the landing contact with the runway would absorb some of the jet's energy and help to slow the jet down more quickly.

"FIFTY!"

I increased the back pressure just a bit to slow the descent rate a little more.

"FORTY!"

I checked the throttles in idle and held the stick where it was.

"THIRTY!"

The black asphalt of the runway seemed to reach up for us.

"TWENTY!"

The runway numbers went underneath us at over 100 knots.

"TEN!"

A little more backpressure now.

"FIVE!"

The touchdown came just a moment earlier than I expected. The main gear contacted the runway firmly but comfortably and I pushed forward on the stick to get the nosewheel on the ground as quickly as possible. At the same time, I applied firm pressure to the brakes as I deployed the thrust reverser located on the center engine. Jean, Alina and I were pushed forward into our shoulder harnesses somewhat but while the sensation was noticeable, it wasn't uncomfortable.

The 7X slowed to taxi speed a few seconds later with 1,500 feet remaining on the 4,998 foot runway.

"Tres bien!" Jean said. "Now let us get turned around before zay yell at us."

I nodded. I was already moving the jet to one side of the runway so that I could make the 180 degree turn to head back to the approach end. Even as I completed the turn, the landing lights of another jet a few miles out on final approach were visible.

"They do pack them in here," I said.

We shut the aircraft down a few minutes later and Jean unloaded the luggage while I walked Vladimir and Alina into the immigration office of the small executive terminal. I stopped at the glass doors of the entrance. "It's been nice flying you both," I said. "I hope I get to do it again sometime. You've got a great jet and Abby and Jean are two of the most professional flight crew members I've ever flown with."

"Dos vidaniya," Vladimir said in business-like fashion. He shook my hand firmly and went through the doors, leaving Alina and me alone outside.

"A pleasure to watch you work," Alina said, looking back at the jet. "You are very precise in what you do."

I nodded. "Precision is about discipline and discipline is everything."

She nodded in response. "Yes, it is," she said. Then she turned to me and looked me in the eyes. It seemed that time froze for a few moments. I got the distinct impression she was appraising me somehow. Just before it became uncomfortable, she smiled and raised her arms for a farewell hug.

As our bodies touched, she whispered in my ear.

"Discipline, steady hands, grace under pressure. You're a very intriguing man, Mr. Pearce." Then she gave me quick kiss on the left cheek and she was gone.

I don't get complimented that often, especially by people who don't work for tips. Her words seem to hang in the air, making the atmosphere seem heavy. I found myself pondering them and wondering if there was some deeper context there that I didn't understand.

"Huh," I said, as I watched her go through the automatic doors. "I wonder what the fuck that means."

The rooftop was just as the Shadow remembered it from her scouting visit. It was deserted and covered with numerous vents and fans behind which the Shadow could hide. In mere moments, the Shadow had found the pre-surveyed perch, removed the pieces of the rifle from the backpack and poster tube and assembled the weapon. The Shadow extended the bipod legs and placed the rifle on the chosen ledge and ensured it was in the shadows of the fan on the right side. The wind and humidity sensors were deployed next, and the tablet computer was activated. The Shadow raised the binoculars equipped with the laser rangefinder next and peered down London's Park Lane to the Marble Arch. The Shadow settled the rangefinder on the Arch itself and pressed the button to initiate the laser. In less than a second, 958 meters appeared in the display. The Shadow lowered the binoculars and entered the range into the application on the tablet computer. Nearly instantaneously the tablet returned windage and elevation adjustments for the rifle's telescopic sight. The Shadow removed the screw covers for the windage and elevation knobs and clicked the adjustments into both knobs before replacing the covers. Satisfied, the Shadow took up station with the rifle shouldered and dominant eye to the scope. The tablet computer, wind and humidity sensors remained deployed. If either of those conditions changed such that an additional adjustment was necessary, a low-pitched alarm would sound and alert the Shadow to make the corrections.

As the Shadow looked through the scope at the target area and took in the frenetic activity that was downtown London, a smile etched itself onto the full lips. A black government car pulled to the curb by the arch, and before it had even fully stopped, the Right Honorable Robert Essex jumped from it and headed to the area of the arch where the liberal speakers were popular. The Shadow didn't know what Mr. Essex was going to speak about, but the gist of it would be anti-Russian and anti-nuclear, and that was all that mattered.

As Essex stepped up onto the ceremonial soapbox where he would address the gathering crowd, the Shadow increased the magnification of the scope and zoomed in on Essex's face. Even from nearly 1,000 meters away, the Shadow would feel the arrogance emanating from the smug expression on the man's pale, wrinkled face. Apart from a few London Police officers, which was typical at a gathering like this, there no security the Shadow could detect. Not that additional security would have helped Essex, but it would have at least made this particular job more interesting. As it was, it was almost too easy.

The Shadow activated the video recorder, settled the crosshairs of the scope on the bridge of Essex's nose and exhaled slowly into the rifle. Then, after a brief pause, the Shadow inhaled deeply and stopped breathing. Unconsciously, delicately, the Shadow increased pressure on the trigger and held the crosshairs on the target. It was a matter of seconds now.

But then the unpredictable happened.

Just as the trigger went past the sear point and the hammer struck the firing pin, Essex suddenly bent forward, as if he had sneezed. The 750-grain bullet left the barrel and closed the gap between the Shadow and the target in just over a second, but it just missed the left side of Essex's head and hit a London City policewoman who was standing about ten meters behind him. The policewoman was wearing standard issue body armor, but it was no match for the velocity and energy of the .50. The projectile penetrated the front layer of bullet resistant fabric easily and entered her chest, rapidly slowing down as it expanded inside her flesh and transmitted its energy to her body, pulverizing her heart and killing her instantly. The projectile then attempted to exit her body through her back but the rear layer of bullet resistant fabric deflected it back into her body, and it tore down through her stomach and intestines, eventually embedding itself in her pelvic bone. The policewoman took a step backward as the bullet entered her body. Then, she slowly crumpled to the ground as if she had fainted.

As the Shadow watched the crowd react, it appeared that the policewoman's collapse was viewed with curiosity but not alarm. The Shadow wasn't worried about the sound of the gunshot. The suppressor was one of the most carefully designed in the world, and it drastically reduced the amount of sound traveling downrange. The sound that remained was quickly overshadowed *by the cacophony of noise that characterized a metropolitan area. Essex himself didn't even notice. He now stood straight up and was vigorously speaking to the assembled crowd. The Shadow placed the crosshairs on the bridge of the politician's bulbous nose again, repeated the breathing ritual and squeezed the trigger. This time, the bullet flew directly to its target, and as he spoke, Essex's head snapped back as the projectile entered it just above his nose and then a cascade of flesh and gore spattered out of the back of his head and on to many of the crowd gathered in back of him. The bullet ricocheted off the pavement behind and disappeared into the London Sky.*

The Shadow nodded in satisfaction. Another target down. Another million in the bank. In moments the rifle was disassembled and stowed along with the tablet computer and sensors. Task complete, the Shadow exited the rooftop via the same door used to gain access. Total time on the rooftop was a little under five minutes. The barrel was placed in a dumpster a few moments later, and the Shadow quickly vanished into the masses of London.

CHAPTER SIX

Thurday, October 21
2000 Hours Local Time
The Bar at the Dukes Hotel
London, United Kingdom.

I've probably been in several hundred bars all over the world during my travels, but the bar in the Dukes hotel ranked in my top five. The bar consisted of three rooms, all furnished with formal sitting chairs and ornate wooden tables, the centerpiece of which was the bar itself, contained in the middle of the three-room complex, a compact but rich testimony to the art of mixology. But as sumptuous as the furnishings were, it was the lore of the place that made it fascinating. During World War II, the Dukes Hotel lay on the route that James Bond author Ian Fleming took from work to his home, and it is where Fleming would stop for his evening drink. It is there that the James Bond martini was invented and the phrase *shaken, not stirred*, was originated.

I had arrived at about 1900 local time and after exchanging greetings with Alessandro, the master bartender, I was escorted to a two person table in the back of the main room about twenty minutes later. The Dukes Bar doesn't take reservations and is usually quite crowded in the evenings, so I considered myself lucky to be seated so quickly. A bar waiter appeared within minutes, and I ordered the classic gin martini right off the menu as well as a plate of hors d'oeuvres. In short order, the legendary Dukes martini trolley came to my table, and Alessandro himself mixed my martini. I'm usually quite specific about the way I order martinis, but to do so at Dukes would be the equivalent of telling a professional musician how to play his instrument. All the items for the martini were on the cart, Plymouth Gin, Dukes sacred vermouth and a martini glass, as well as a fresh lemon. The two bottles of liquor and the glass were all frosty, evidence that they had just left the freezer. In a deft series of motions, similar to the movements of an orchestra conductor, Alessandro poured a small amount of the vermouth into a martini glass with a flourish and then followed that with a long pour of gin with a greater flourish. Then, he cut a fresh twist of lemon and dropped it into the glass before presenting it to me to drink.

I accepted the glass and took the first sip immediately. The cold mixture danced across my tongue and seeped down my throat. It was heavenly. "Excellent, sir," I said, nodding at Alessandro, "as usual."

He nodded back and took the trolley away to serve other customers.

I took another sip and relished the taste again, allowing it to linger in my mouth a bit before I swallowed. Vermouth is under-appreciated as a martini ingredient. If you order a dry martini, most bartenders won't even put vermouth into it. But that does the martini a disservice. The slight essence of vermouth compliments the taste of the gin and makes the martini a much more enjoyable drink. This martini was a tribute to the art. It was smooth, delicate and delicious.

I sat back in my chair, and for the first time since I had arrived, I took in the people in the room. Every other table was occupied by parties of two or more, and in a notable contrast from most bars in the United States, there were no jeans, sneakers or flip-flops in the place. Everyone was dressed professionally in suits, jackets, or dresses and looked like they had either dressed for work or dressed for the occasion. I allowed my eyes to discreetly roam the room and took in the faces and expressions. There was an older British man and woman, silently enjoying their cocktails without saying a word to each other. At the next table, five men discussed the British stock and commodities markets, arguing their points vociferously and slapping each other on the back when they agreed with each other. Two tables down sat a young couple, probably American, sipping their martinis as they ogled the bar and talked to each other in near whispers. *Tourists*, I thought. *Maybe their first time in London.* On the other side of the room, there were two tables pulled together to accommodate a group of four middle-aged people, two men, and two women, obviously on their way to a late dinner. The men were dressed in expensive suits and the ladies in equally expensive dresses. After several hundred trips flying the rich and famous all over the world, I knew nice clothes when I saw them. They all looked affluent and happy. I envied them.

The final table in the room had two people, a man and a woman. The woman sat with her back to me and the man facing me. The man looked like a classic British gentleman. He had aristocratic features and was dressed in a suit that had to have come from Saville Row. The woman was blonde and seemed to be much younger than he was. She wore her hair up and above the chair I could see the upper part of what appeared to be an expensive black cocktail dress with a line of fine white pearls around her neck. Both she and the man seemed to be talking in hushed tones, and the expression on the man's face was one of angst and concern. As I watched, he reached inside his suit jacket and removed a business letter sized envelope. He pushed it across the table at her as he continued to speak. The envelope wasn't quite flat though, I noticed. It had something small but thick inside. It was very apparent that the man wasn't pleased with something. The woman shifted her posture and cocked her head as she replied, and I was struck with a sudden sensation of familiarity.

Who are you? I asked myself.

For reasons I didn't understand, I removed my iPhone from my jacket pocket, unlocked it and ensured the camera didn't have the flash enabled. Then I made a show of checking my email while I tried to get the phone into a place where I could unobtrusively get some pictures of the two at the table. After some maneuvering, I got a few shots of the man's face and the woman's back. I slowly sipped the rest of my drink with the phone in my lap as I waited for an opportunity to get a picture of the woman. But then she turned to address the waiter, and I saw her face in profile and found myself stunned.

Alina? What the hell are you doing here? And without Vladimir?

A thousand things ran through my mind at that moment, but probably the most concerning thought was the prohibition of crew members and passengers occupying the same space at the same time when outside of the aircraft. If you were a professional, it was probably the one of the most important rules you didn't break. You *never, ever,* socialized with passengers. Even accidentally.

Instinct took over at that moment. I finished the last sips of my martini and waved the waiter over to ask for the check. My entrancement with the Dukes Bar was over. I needed to get out of there.

The waiter was quick and efficient. In mere moments I was presented with the check, and I provided a credit card with which to pay. The waiter took it gracefully and ran it in minimal time. I added a healthy, although unnecessary, gratuity and signed the receipt. Then I slowly rose from my seat and hoped I could make it to the doorway of the room without being noticed by either Alina or her companion. I kept my head down and turned away from the two of them as I approached them and attempted to sidle by them on my way to the exit from the room.

But no such luck.

"Colin?" I heard Alina's voice ask as I walked past them. "I didn't know you were here! What brings you to this place?"

I stopped, painted a surprised expression on my face, and reluctantly turned to the two of them. The man seemed irritated that their conversation had been interrupted by Alina's question. Alina's face was more interesting. It bore a combination of bemusement and curiosity.

"This is one of my favorite places in London," I said. "I come here whenever I'm in town."

She nodded. "So you're a martini drinker?"

I nodded in return. "The evening isn't complete without a good one."

She smiled at me. "Isn't that the truth. Especially after working hard during the day."

I smiled back. "I don't think I worked that hard, but a good martini is a good martini." I motioned to our surroundings. "Especially here. This place is like Mecca for martini drinkers."

Her smile broadened. Then, she suddenly seemed to remember the gentleman sitting at the table with her. She motioned toward him.

"This is Mr. David Ackerman. He's a business partner of Vladimir's. Vlad was supposed to join us by now but he must have gotten delayed."

I extended my hand toward Mr. Ackerman. "Colin Pearce," I said. "Nice to meet you, sir."

Ackerman begrudgingly extended his hand and shook mine like a wet noodle. Handshakes were always a tell for me. You show me a guy with a limp handshake, and I'll show someone who is either unengaged or gay. The latter didn't bother me at all, but the former certainly did.

"How do you do?" he said in a thick, posh, British accent.

"Would you care to join us, Colin? Vlad will be here soon."

"I'm sorry Miss Alina," I said slowly. " I have to get to my hotel because I have an early flight tomorrow on British Airways."

She nodded with a knowing expression on her face. "Whatever you say, Mr. Pearce. Have a safe flight back to the US."

She rose to give me a farewell hug, and it might have been my imagination, but this one seemed a little closer and a little tighter than the one earlier today. For a moment, I could feel her firm breasts against my chest.

Damn! I thought.

"Take care of yourself, Mr. Pearce," she said, the warmth of her breath hanging on my ear.

When the hug ended, I saw a look in her eyes that I didn't expect. It was a mixture of knowledge and sadness. Like she knew something I didn't.

I smiled at her and said something I probably shouldn't have as I look back on it now.

"Don't worry, Alina," I said. "I've been trained to do just that."

CHAPTER SEVEN

Monday, October 25
1000 Hours Local Time
Sports Stadium, Anne Arundel Community College
Arnold, Maryland, USA

The track felt good under my feet, and the cool autumn air soothed my lungs as I pushed myself around the quarter-mile of pavement. After several days of sitting in airliners or 7X cockpits, it was great to be outside again. The months of running and doing aerobic interval training were paying off, and my legs were growing stronger. With each stride, they felt more and more comfortable propelling my body at a greater speed. I no longer struggled for breath, but I diligently monitored my pace so that my heart rate stayed within the appropriate bounds. Being a middle-aged guy had its limitations.

I would have rather been in the weight room of course. But thanks to the damage caused by a huge knife in my left shoulder a few months ago, the use of my upper body was somewhat limited, at least for a while. So I had turned to core training and interval training as a way to keep myself in shape while I waited for my return to the iron. I was a little thinner than I would have liked. I was down to 210 pounds, but I could tell my aerobic capacity was increasing significantly, so that was a bonus.

I rounded the track's final turn and headed down the straightaway. After this lap, I'd take a few minutes of active rest and allow my heart rate to settle. That was the regimen. Run or jog two laps, walk up and down and back and forth across the stadium's steps, then another two laps and repeat. I typically punished myself for about 45-60 minutes when I did this, and today I planned to lean toward the lower number because I was seeing Gail tonight.

I found it interesting that she had managed to find another conference at the Pentagon so soon after the last one. I briefly wondered if it had to do with seeing me or working her next promotion. But I knew the answer to that question.

I retrieved my towel from the fence in front of the concrete bleachers and wiped my brow as I trudged up the first flight of steps. The steps weren't particularly high or even especially steep, but they provided me just the right amount of activity to ensure my heart rate didn't completely return to normal. I reached the top, walked along the upper row of seats and descended the next flight of stairs, wiping another stream of moisture from my head. The temperature was a mild 70 degrees, but I was sweating profusely. It wasn't a function of my weight or age. I had always perspired heavily once my metabolism shifted into high gear. I heated up quickly and cooled down slowly. Great attribute for losing weight and staying in shape but not so good if you were trying to get a shower and get out of the door in the morning.

I looked around the empty stadium as I reached the bottom of the second flight of stairs and made my way to the next flight. I seemed to have the place all to myself. It wasn't a stadium really; it was just an athletic field with a set of concrete bleachers built into the hill on one side. I had come across the place by accident, trying to find a shortcut between Richie Highway and US 50 a few years ago, and since I was always trying to find random venues for exercise these days, this stadium seemed to fill the bill. Especially since it was on the way to Washington D.C.

Two couples appeared on the track, walking in from the parking lot through the gate on the south side. They seemed innocuous. There was an older man walking with a younger man and an older woman walking with a younger woman. It was the age spacing that lured me in. It looked like a set of parents walking the track with their child and spouse. Four happy people out getting some exercise in the temperate autumn air. There were neighborhoods all around here. It made sense. It fit. Which is why my brain processed what my eyes perceived and then categorized it and dismissed it.

No threat.

I continued up and down the stairs, and they continued along the track. The two women walking in front of the two men, all four engaged in animated conversation. I reached the end of the bleachers and accomplished the steps again, back in the other direction. When I replaced my towel on the fence and made my way back out onto the track, I noticed that the two women were now a good twenty-five yards or so in front of the men. The older man seemed to have some difficulty walking, and the younger man was staying by his side. I passed the men first as I started around the track and then the women a few moments later. Neither group looked at me as I passed. The younger man was speaking intensely to the older man and the younger woman was doing the same with the older woman. It didn't seem like the older folks were saying much at all.

I rounded the far curve of the track and proceeded down the straightaway near the bleachers. I kept my eyes on the track in front of me, but my peripheral vision regarded the two groups of people opposite me automatically, without my willing it. I had always been very observant of my surroundings, and it had become more of a reflex than a deliberate effort. The two conversations continued with the younger people gesticulating to make their points more emphatically. The older people didn't seem interested and looked my way more often than not.

I felt my stomach tighten for a moment and then quickly dismissed it.

Jesus, Pearce. Lighten up.

I rounded the near curve of the track and retrieved my iPhone from my left pocket, regarded my playlist for a moment or two and then put the device on pause. I jogged up the far straightaway and caught up with the two men. I looked over at them as I passed, smiling and nodding at them.

"Good morning!" I said between breaths.

The two of them nodded back at me, the younger man smiling in return as his Asian features rendered a friendly gaze. The older man didn't even look at me as he nodded. He kept his gazed fixed on the way in front of him.

I returned my eyes to the track in front of me.

A few seconds later, I passed the two women and greeted them in the same fashion. Again, the younger person returned my greeting and the older did not. And again, the younger was Asian, and the older was not. If they were parents and children how could both kids be Asian and both parents not be?

The import of that question hit me about the same time as the two .22 slugs did, precisely placed right in the middle of my back. The twin impacts felt like two hard fingers through the bulletproof under-armor I was wearing. The soft "popping" sound of the weapon barely reached my ears.

A flurry of options ran through my head but few of them viable. Even if I had been faster on my feet, the odds were I couldn't outrun a gun. There was only one thing to do. I made a show of falling forward to the track in front of me, just as I heard two more rounds sizzle through the air above my head and two more popping sounds behind me. As soon as my body hit the pavement, I rolled onto my back and lifted the .45 caliber AMT backup pistol I carried. The little gun only held six shots and wasn't good outside of about 7 yards, but it was all I had. I lined the gun's sights up on the Asian woman behind me and was dismayed to see that the older woman she had been walking with was lying on the track next to her, a pool of blood surrounding the gray hair.

I squeezed off two shots, pulling the long, double-action trigger as quickly and smoothly as I could. The little gun bucked in my hands, and one of the rounds smacked into the Asian woman's right shoulder and spun her around like ballerina doing a pirouette. Her weapon flew from her hands and clattered to the track next to her.

Behind her, the Asian man was raising a pistol of his own that looked larger and uglier than his partner's. I aimed the small .45 at his forehead, hoping the tiny gun's short barrel could get the rounds to his midsection. I pressed the AMT's long trigger carefully but quickly, and the little gun fired just about the moment I felt a line of fire open up along the left side of my neck.

The .45 round from my weapon crossed the gap between us and tore a gaping red hole in the Asian man's right cheek, snapping his head back like the top of a Pez dispenser and driving him backward and down to the track. I was on my feet in seconds and running toward him as he fell, holding the AMT in front of me and mindless of the blood running down the left side of my neck.

The Asian woman was trying to regain her feet as I got to her, and I shot her in the left eye as I ran by. I reached the man a few moments later and kicked his gun away as he struggled to raise himself. I put my knee on his chest and shoved the hot muzzle of the weapon against his forehead.

"Who hired you?" I shouted at him, my ears still ringing from the little .45's blasts.

His face was a grotesque mask of pain and gore, and his teeth were visible through the gaping hole in his cheek. He smiled at me through the mess and before I could stop him, he grabbed my gun hand with his, slid his thumb inside of the trigger guard, and forced me to pull the trigger. The little AMT fired a final time and as the echo died away, tranquility regained possession of the mild Maryland morning.

"Jesus," I said reflexively.

I pulled his dead fingers from my weapon and slowly stood, trying to process the events of the last few moments. I saw the elderly man lying face down on the track next to me and shook my head as I pondered the pointlessness of it all. The elderly couple were obviously intended as camouflage for the younger assassins, so I wouldn't either contextualize them before they opened fire. Nevertheless, they were probably someone's parents and possibly someone's grandparents.

The logistics of the situation occurred to me as the sirens in the distance woke me from my reverie. I pulled the iPhone from my pocket, found the contact I needed and punched the number.

"Smith," the familiar voice answered.

"Any chance you can get a sanitation crew down to the Anne Arundel Community College. Quickly maybe?"

"What?"

Smith was normally pretty quick on the uptake, but it was clear that he was having trouble processing my request.

"I need a sanitation crew, Dave. I just killed two assassins on the track here."

I was looking down at the track as I spoke and I saw that there was a small pool of blood next to my left foot.

"Oh yeah," I said. "Have the crew bring a medic with them. I'm pretty sure I've been shot. Again."

"Damn, Colin!" Smith said, his mind obviously now in full gear. "Sit tight. We'll send a clean-up crew ASAP."

"You might want to talk to the county police and state troopers too," I said. "I hear sirens coming my way, and this will be tough to explain."

"Copied. What happened?"

I looked at the carnage around me as I thought about the answer to his question.

"No idea. But I hope it's not Miguel and Ramon reaching out from the grave."

CHAPTER EIGHT

Monday, October 25
1700 Hours Local Time
Crystal City Marriott Hotel
Arlington, Virginia, USA

I slid into the restaurant's booth across from Gail and put my iPhone on the table next to me.

"I take it your boys got back to you?" Gail asked, looking up from her salad. Her flowing dark hair fell to her shoulders and the black knit top she was wearing clung to her superb torso like a second skin, emphasizing her perfectly formed breasts. She watched me look back at her, and a wry smile etched its way onto her face. "Well?" she asked at last.

"What did you say?" I asked her. "My mind kind of went blank there for a minute."

"Hold that thought," she said, her smile widening. "You were talking to your boys."

"I was," I said. "The car in the parking lot matching the keys in the Asian man's pocket was a rental, picked up at Philadelphia International Airport two days ago."

"So, they were following you," Gail said.

"I don't know," I said. "I'd like to think I would have noticed. Although I don't have a CIA watch team looking after me these days, so I guess it's possible."

"Any word on who they are?"

"The Agency is still checking," I said. "Nothing yet." I replaced my napkin in my lap and picked up my fork. "Salad ok?"

Gail nodded at me. "It's a good Caesar. And it's got a decent bite to it. Not so damn creamy like most of them are."

"Awesome," I said. "Tell me about this conference you're going to. I can't believe you were able to get another conference here so quickly after last week."

"It's a follow-up. Last week was about the colonels; this week is about the state of personnel affairs in general. I'm sure glad I didn't spend my whole career doing this personnel shit. It's important, no doubt, but it distracts you from the mission."

"I'm sure," I said. "But if my own limited experience in leadership taught me one thing, it taught me that taking care of your people is what makes the mission possible."

"Point taken," Gail said, nodding. "But you're evading me and changing the subject." She waved her fork chidingly at me. "If those people weren't following you, then what?"

I shrugged. "No idea right now. They found me at a place that I told no one about and had time to recruit two people to act as a distraction before they tried to take me. That would bespeak of a degree of notice and preparation. Smith and Amrine are trying to understand what that means."

"And no idea who they were working for?"

I shook my head. "Nope. Someone with ties to Miguel would be the obvious answer, but it may not be that simple. Especially when he's been dead for six months."

She nodded, and there was silence for a few moments as we both worked on our salads. We were at a chain steak house, the one with two first names, that was less than a mile from the hotel. We had walked there earlier, eager to get out into the autumn air. Walking along with her, together, hand-in-hand, seemed like the most natural thing in the world. Unfortunately, with my morbid sense of destiny, I couldn't stop thinking about how I, or the events that surrounded me, would eventually fuck it up. Assuming Gail didn't ditch me for the sake of her career in the meantime.

"What now?" Gail asked as she pushed her salad aside.

I shook my head helplessly. "Wait and see what happens, I guess?"

We didn't have to wait long.

An hour and ten minutes later, after a great steak, dessert, and a fine single malt, the Oban 14 actually, we made our way back to the hotel along the sidewalks of Crystal City. We could have gone underground. The maze of office buildings, residential complexes, and businesses that constituted this suburb of Arlington were connected by a series of passageways. But Gail and I both wanted to feel the autumn air again.

We had rounded the corner of a large office building and turned down the street that led to our hotel when I heard the tire squeal. It was faintly audible above the jets that were flying above us into Reagan airport and the noises of the city. But my ears perked up at the sound, and my body went into high alert mode.

There are times in your life when seconds matter and you wish there were more of them. Gail was walking to my right, inside of me on the sidewalk, and closest to the building nearby. I heard the car engine roar behind us and barely had time to disengage my arm from Gail's and pivot to face the oncoming threat. I pushed her behind me and tried to cover her body with mine while I reached underneath my jacket to retrieve the Colt Commander holstered on my right hip.

I heard the first bullets hit the sidewalk and concrete around us as my right hand found the Colt's rubber grip. The car was a dark, nondescript four-door sedan with both windows on the passenger side open and the muzzles of two suppressed automatic weapons visible through the frames of the doors. The power of the brain to observe details while under stress never failed to amaze me. I could see the two shooters, clad in black, with black masks on their faces, but with eyes that were clearly visible. The eyes of the shooter in the front seat were dark and angry and surrounded by olive skin. The eyes of the shooter in the back were different. The skin around the eyes was lighter, but the eyes themselves were dispassionate and dissimilar. The right one was blue, and the left was gray. It struck me as odd that someone in a profession where anonymity was a requirement would have a physical trait so distinctive. Of course, he or she probably didn't care in this instance because they didn't think their targets would live long enough to remember.

But they hadn't counted on the Kevlar vest I wore, and they hadn't counted on the hours I had spent on the firing range. Even as the car slowed directly alongside us, and the bullets began to careen into the sides of the building next to us, the Colt had cleared my holster, and my right hand was bringing it to firing level. I pressed the trigger as the front sight aligned with the front seat shooter. The gun bucked in my hand and geyser of red gore replaced the gunman's right eye. I reacquired the sights and fired into the side of the driver's head as I felt the sting of shards of concrete and brick hitting my face. The car turned wildly to the left, and I found myself eye to eye with the rear-seat gunman who was now trying to regain his balance and bring his weapon to bear once again. I fixed the Colt's sights on his face and sent 200 grains of .45 ACP projectile his way, hoping to end the fight. But the gunman was fast and managed to move his head even as the Colt recoiled in my hand. He let loose with a few rounds of his own, and I felt three solid impacts on my chest, which pressed me into Gail and pushed us both against the building behind us.

But his firing stopped as the car accelerated away and to the left. It veered across the narrow street and smashed into a parked SUV as it increased speed. There was a loud crunch of metal, followed by the sound of glass sprinkling onto the pavement.

I quickly turned to Gail and looked her over. Her eyes were wide, and she was breathing heavily, but she seemed to be none the worse for wear.

"Are you okay?" I asked her as I felt her arms and opened her jacket to look for blood or holes in the cloth.

She nodded at me rapidly.

I gave her my phone.

"The code is zero nine one seven. Go around the corner, find a place to hide and call Dave Smith in my contact list. Tell him you need a cleaning crew and describe what happened. He knows who you are."

She nodded again and then grabbed the lapels of my jacket.

"What are you going to do?" she asked.

"Finish this," I said. "But I want you safe."

She kissed me and then ran down the street away from me, as fast as her high heels would allow her to move.

I turned to the crashed sedan and walked toward it, replacing the magazine in the Colt as I moved. The entire front end of the car had collapsed, and the hood had been forced open and up. There was crushed glass from the side windows on the black asphalt around the car, and it reflected the street lights in an odd pattern of orange, yellow and white sparkles. The windshield was pushed out of its frame and lay at an angle to the hood, the Plexiglas still intact but cracked in several places.

As I approached the car, I bent down and made my way around to the left side. The rear passenger door was open and there a very faint trail of dark drops of liquid leading from it. Apparently, I had hit the assassin in the back seat after all. I moved to the right side of the car as quietly as I could and lifted myself up just enough to peer into the rear seat with my gun at the ready. The seat was empty. But a suppressed weapon, an H & K MP-5, was left behind.

"Too big to carry on the street," I said to myself.

A quick glance in the front of the car confirmed that the passenger and the driver were both dead. I reached inside the front passenger window, past the driver's body and turned the car's ignition off as I looked up and down the street. There were far too many places for someone on foot to hide, and I had other considerations. I engaged the Colt's thumb safety and replaced it in the holster. Then I walked down the street to rejoin Gail.

"This doesn't make any sense," I said to myself as I walked. "No sense at all."

##

"Any idea what the fuck is going on, Dave?"

We were gathered in Gail's suite at the Marriott, me, Gail, Dave Smith and a CIA medic who was looking the two of us over. Gail was lying on the bed while the medic examined her, and Smith and I were standing in the adjoining living area.

Dave Smith shrugged his shoulders. "We have no idea. No activity other than some chatter since you put Ramon and Miguel down last summer and now two events in less than 12 hours. I've been pinging our networks since this afternoon, and they've heard nothing. Is there anything you can give us that might help?"

I started to shake my head and then stopped. "There might be. The shooter who got away had mismatched eyes. The right one was blue, and the left one was gray. I've never seen anything like that before."

Smith nodded thoughtfully. "We'll run that through the system. It doesn't ring a bell right now though."

"General Peterson," the medic said from the other room. "It looks like you're okay. No strikes, no collateral injuries."

"Except for nearly spraining my ankle running in those damn FMPs," Gail said sardonically. "Damn street was downhill, and I couldn't stop."

"Colonel Pearce?" The medic called. "You're next. Jacket, shirt and vest off please."

I raised my eyebrows at Smith and began removing my jacket as I walked in the bedroom area of the suite. I put the jacket on the bed and noticed that there were a few holes in the sides of it. Apparently, a few of the assassin's bullets had grazed the sides of me as well as hit me in the chest. I had never even felt them.

"Guess I need a new jacket," I said. "Brooks Brothers suits aren't cheap, Dave. Can I bill the government for this?"

"Sure," he said. "Just don't hold your breath waiting for the expense to be approved. We have a new budget director named Reedy who has more budget sense than common sense."

I unbuttoned my light blue dress shirt and pulled my arms out of it. The three holes were visible in the cotton fabric.

"Have to add a shirt to the bill," I said as I tossed the shirt onto the bed. Then I undid the Velcro strips on the sides of the thin Kevlar vest and found another surprise. There was a mess of coagulated blood on my left side, just above my hip bone, where the two sides of the vest left a gap along the side of my body.

I sighed. "I seem to be making a habit of getting myself shot these days."

The medic was already walking over to me with his bag in hand. He was a younger man of medium build with a dark mustache and a serious demeanor. He was wearing a softball jersey, jeans, and sneakers.

"Sorry to take you away from your game," I said. "I had no intention of engaging anyone this evening. Especially after I saw one of your colleagues earlier today."

"It wasn't my game," he said as he dropped his eyes to my wound. "It was my daughter's. First thing I've been able to attend after 36 hours on shift."

"Then I'm doubly sorry."

"No problem," he said. "That's why the government pays me the big bucks to moonlight as a medic when I'm not doing trauma surgery."

He sat down on the end of the bed and probed the wound with his fingers, and I winced.

"Tender?" he asked, looking up at me.

I nodded.

"There's something still in there," he said. "You probably caught a ricochet off the building or something."

"I guess I'm not so lucky after all," I said.

"Yeah you are," he said as he retrieved a syringe and a vial from his bag. "This looks like it's just a flesh wound or light penetration. It caught you in the gap in your body armor. If the projectile had been larger, had more energy or caught you at a different angle, it could have penetrated further and might have killed you."

"And it's obvious they were using subsonic rounds and a submachine gun," Smith added. "If they used an assault rifle, the vest wouldn't have done you much good."

"Good points, I guess," I said.

The doctor wiped the wound down with alcohol and injected me several times around the wound site.

"Novocain," he said without looking at me. "I'm probably going to have to dig a little to find that thing."

"Be careful with that stuff," Gail said as she walked around the bed to watch. "Don't get it too close to the more vital regions. I might have plans for him later."

I shook my head and smiled at her. "You realize I've been shot twice today?"

She nodded at me. "You're not going to have to move much. I can do all the work."

I was well familiar with the intensity of emotion and desire that was often generated after life threatening events. It seemed that Gail's dormant libido was being rekindled by her brush with death earlier this evening. Gunshot wound notwithstanding, I was just enough of a male pig to take advantage of that.

"I might be able to help a bit," I said.

I felt pressure below and looked down. The doctor had an instrument that looked suspiciously like tweezers inside the wound and had a gloved hand on the outside of my body, his fingers following the tweezers as he moved them.

"Ah," he said after a few moments. "Here it is."

He carefully pulled the tweezers out of the wound, and I saw a substantial chunk of twisted metal between the jaws.

"Damn," I said involuntarily.

He looked up at me. "A nine millimeter, judging by the size of it." He looked over at Smith. "I presume you want this for analysis?"

Smith nodded.

"You've got the gun," I said. "What do you hope to learn?"

"We'll do a metallurgical and spectral analysis on it," he said. "You'd be surprised at the minor variations in metallurgy that different manufacturers use. We have a database with all sorts of samples in it. We might be able to tell you what part of the world the round was manufactured. With a little luck, we'll be able to tell you the company and maybe even the plant."

"Damn," I said. "That's some high-tech shit."

Smith laughed. "Well, we are the CIA."

The doctor cleaned the wound and stuffed a small roll of gauze into the hole. Then he put a flesh-colored bandage over it. He retrieved a biohazard disposal bag from his case and put the instruments, the bloody gauze he used to clean the wound, and his gloves, into the bag. Then he pulled several bandages out of his medical valise and handed them to me along with a small bottle of pills.

"Clean that wound and replace the bandages twice a day," he said. "You won't have to stuff anything in after one or two more times. And the pills are antibiotics. Take one now and take one per day until they're gone."

I nodded at him. "Wilco."

The doctor stood and collected his bag.

I offered my hand. "Thanks, Doc. Don't take this the wrong way, but I hope I don't see you again."

He smiled at me tiredly. "No offense taken. Have a good night."

Smith followed him to the door, and I heard them exchanging a few words before the door clicked shut. Then Smith returned to the room.

"Before I leave you two, we're going to have to do something to get you both out of circulation for a bit while we try to figure out what the hell is going on." He inclined his head toward Gail. "General, I think we're going to find some conference for you in a faraway place where we can keep an eye on you."

Gail shook her head. "I can't. I have meetings next week. I can't miss them."

"Gail please," I said. "This is different. If these guys are associated with Miguel, there are no rules in the game. And if they're not, we don't even know who we're dealing with or what they're capable of."

She nodded after a few moments. "Well if you're going to send me away, what are you going to do with Colin? He needs protection worse than I do."

Smith grinned slyly. "I have an idea about that," he said, looking between the two of us. "We're going to send him to a school where he'll be surrounded by people with guns. Big guns."

"He ought to be right at home then," she said.

THE SHADOW – INTERLUDE

The Shadow picked up the secure cell phone on the second ring.

"Yes?"

"Based on your observations, we went after Mr. Pearce," the old man said.

The Shadow was saddened but not surprised. "And?" the Shadow asked, with a sudden touch of apprehension.

"We missed," he said.

The Shadow felt a sudden surge of unexplainable happiness. "What happened?"

The old man's voice breathed exasperation. "We tried it subtly with contractors, and we tried it via brute force with our team and missed both times. Four dead and Vassily is injured."

The Shadow felt an increase in heartbeat and thought for a long moment.

"Are you still there?" the voice asked.

"Yes," the Shadow answered. "So there's something about Mr. Pearce that we missed."

"Apparently," the man said. "The contractors were top notch, an Asian team we have used before. I sent our team as a backup and ended up tasking them when the Asians were taken down. Our team was part of my protection detail. All former Spetnaz, as you know. A retired Air Force pilot should not have been able to take them all down. He's been trained. We'll tear his life apart and get some answers."

The Shadow's mind wandered as the old man spoke. Colin Pearce was a killer. And he could be a kindred spirit. Maybe they could meet again? The old man's gruff voice awoke the Shadow from the daydream.

"Are you ready for the next job?"

The Shadow nodded even though she knew he was far away. "Yes."

"It will be a very long range shot, dushka. Your longest ever."

"I am ready, uncle," the Shadow said, now realizing the conversation had shifted from English to Russian.

"I believe you," the old man answered. "No one can shoot like you do. Your stepfather taught you well."

The Shadow felt a pull at the heart for the father figure lost long ago but pushed it aside to focus on present matters. "Perhaps we could bring this man closer to us before the final engagement."

"How?"

"Don't we have another project, in Switzerland, before the final one? Why not use the same crew agency as last time and ask for him? I could get close to him and get some information. Depending on what I find out, I could take direct action myself."

There was a long pause.

"We both know you're not trained for that, dushka. But having your enemies close is a well-proven strategy. After the upcoming London project, we may set it up. In the meantime, we'll dig into him." The old man paused. "We are almost there, dushka. You realize that, yes?"

"Yes, uncle."

"Soon you will be wealthy beyond your dreams and able to live anywhere you like. And you will have done your country a service beyond measure."

The Shadow swallowed hard. The money was appealing, but it was serving her country, the country of her birth, that made her especially proud. "I live to serve the Motherland."

"I know you do, dushka," her uncle said. "It's one of the many reasons I love you. Now get some more study time in for your next target."

"Yes, uncle."

The call ended without further words. The Shadow put the cell phone down and walked to the penthouse window and gazed out over the bustling activity in the metropolis below. She thought about the strange attraction she felt for this man she had just met, and the words were uttered involuntarily before the Shadow even thought of them.

"Who are you, Colin Pearce?"

CHAPTER NINE

Friday, October 29
0845 Hours Local Time
Firing Range, GLX Sniper School
Scottsdale, Arizona, USA

"You have to feel it," the voice in my ear said. "It's more than ballistics and environmental conditions. Anyone can shoot a rifle; that's technical skill. But not everyone can make the shot. That's artistic skill."

My right index finger was slowly squeezing the trigger on the highly-modified AR-10 rifle. The round, black bulls-eye of the paper target, 1,000 yards down range, was centered in the cross-hairs of the 12 power Leopold telescopic sight. The shoulder piece of the rifle's plastic, collapsible stock rested snugly against my shoulder, and the bipod supported the weight of the heavy barrel, a round, silver cylinder that was 30 inches long. My right hand held the weapon's grip, and my left rested over my right as if I was firing a pistol. I had held my breath as I continued to squeeze the weapon's match-grade trigger while I tried to keep the cross-hairs centered.

The AR-10's report made a loud, popping sound through my electronic ear muffs and the 7.62 x 51mm round went downrange at about 3,000 feet per second. A ragged hole appeared in the paper target, in the black bulls-eye, but about a half-inch right of the center.

"That will do," said the instructor as he looked through the spotting scope. "But there's still room for improvement."

He was an ex-marine scout sniper named George Phillips. A short, hard man about my age, he looked as tough as a piece of tanned leather and showed the scars of several years on active duty all over the world. He was a retired Gunnery Sergeant, and we were permitted to call him Gunny Phillips or just Gunny, but that was as familiar as we were allowed.

I grunted in acknowledgment as Phillips rose from his place next to me and moved to the next student. Then I settled back into my position, re-centered the crosshairs on the middle of the bullseye, exhaled slowly and took up the slack in the trigger once again. The rifle's discharge was a slight surprise, as any good shot should be, and the second round hit the target at almost the same place as the first, widening the existing hole only slightly.

"Mister Pearce!" Phillips called, looking up from the spotting scope at the next student's position. I didn't realize he was still watching me. "Why the fuck would you put two bullets in the same hole when the hole isn't dead center?"

I looked over at him. "Wanted to make sure my error was consistent I guess."

"So you like to fuck up consistently?"

I cocked my head at him and slowly shook it. *Typical Marine,* I thought. But he was right.

"Did the first shot feel good? Did you like it?"

It did feel good, I thought to myself. I nodded.

"Then fucking correct!" he said. "Look at your range card and click the error out!"

I smiled to myself and looked down at the range card I had developed for over the last week. While I had corrected my scope for range accurately, I had not accounted for the wind well enough. I clicked the rifle's safety on and set the butt of the rifle down on the mat I was laying on. Then I unscrewed the cap over the windage screw for the scope, turned it one click in the direction to compensate for the minuscule angle change at 1000 yards and replaced the cap. I settled back into position, shouldered the rifle once again and looked downrange at my target through the scope. I inhaled slowly and then exhaled even more slowly. My finger unconsciously applied pressure to the AR-10's trigger and once again, the rifle went off against my shoulder without my willing it.

A new hole opened up in the paper target. At the exact center of the bullseye. I lifted my eye from the scope and glanced over at Phillips.

He looked back at me and nodded. "Well don't break your arm patting yourself on the back, Pearce," he said. "You've got about fifty more rounds to fire today. Switch to the 1200-yard targets."

I shook my head as I regarded the range card I had assembled over the last few days. It listed distances and elevation corrections for the telescopic sight I was using. I needed to apply some additional clicks to the elevation screw on the scope to compensate for the greater bullet drop at 1200 yards versus 1000. I knew an additional windage adjustment would be necessary as well. The wind would have a slightly greater effect due to the longer projectile time of flight, but I was undecided as to how much. I did a little quick math and elected to apply another click of windage correction. Corrections complete, I pivoted the AR-10 to the first 1200-yard target on the left and set my eye to the scope.

"Did we correct for everything Mr. Pearce?" Gunny Phillips called to me from five feet away.

"I think so," I said. "I increased elevation per the range card and even clicked in a little more windage."

Phillips nodded. "That's good, but it's not everything. What else must we consider at longer ranges?"

"Coriolis," I answered.

"Exactly," he said. "Did you apply those corrections as well?"

"Yes Gunny, I did. Those are built in the adjustments on my range card."

The instructor nodded again, a degree of satisfaction on his rugged features. "Put your first one dead center, Colonel, and I'm buying tonight. If not, you are."

I nodded back at him. "Pressure's on I guess."

I returned my eye to the scope and settled into the weapon once again. The crosshairs were centered on the bullseye of the 1200-yard target, and even with the magnification of the sight, the bullseye appeared as a small black circle. As I inhaled and held my breath and began the trigger squeeze, I felt the wind pick up slightly from left to right. Without consciously thinking about it, I shifted my point of aim one mil dot to the left and continued the squeeze. The AR-10 fired, and the bullet began its flight downrange.

"Well hot damn," Gunny Phillips said. "I'm not sure I believe this. Especially from an Air Force guy."

I looked through my spotting scope and saw a single hole in the dead center of the bullseye on my target. I blinked my eyes and looked again. The hole was still there.

"So what happened when you aimed?" Phillips asked.

"I felt the wind increase little, so I aimed a mil into the wind," I said. "Seemed to be the thing to do."

"Didn't you have calculations you could have consulted?"

I shook my head. "Not at the moment." Phillips allowed a grin to etch itself into his weathered face. "That would be the art of the shot," Phillips said. "There are some great shooting technicians out there who are outstanding shots. But someone who is an artist will put them to shame every time."

I was reminded of a discussion I had with my Air Force Academy roommate Burt Magnusson, several years ago, in which we had used the same terminology to refer to pilots. Technicians were the folks who could repeat what they had been taught, sometimes to perfection; and artists were those who could make a leap of understanding and execution without having had all the training. Technicians could only understand what they had learned; artists naturally extrapolated beyond what they had learned. It seemed the same concepts applied to snipers.

"Keep shooting Mr. Pearce. Graduation isn't until the end of the day, and there are no shortcuts here."

"Yes, Gunny."

About 50 rounds and several targets later, the shooting phase of the training was over, and I was cleaning my weapon, along with my three fellow students, all of whom were civilian contractors working for various federal agencies. There wasn't much talk about who did what for whom. Through our limited interaction this week, I had learned that I was a late addition to this course and that this special one-week sniper orientation school was limited to only those with certain pedigrees, like protection specialists working at a very high level. It seemed the CIA had applied enough pressure to get me through the door.

After the weapons were cleaned and graduation certificates handed out, Gunny Phillips motioned for me to stay behind. He led me into his cozy office and offered me one of the two seats next to a small table against the far wall. Then he opened a waist-high wood cabinet and produced a bottle of the AnCnoc 12-year-old single-malt scotch and two tumblers. Without formality, Phillips poured a healthy amount of the light amber liquid into each glass and slid one across the table to me.

"One shot," he said, raising his glass.

"One kill," I answered, clinking my glass off his.

I nosed the glass and absorbed the whiskey's light aromatic aroma with a little lemon and honey at the front. Then I sipped the luscious stuff and held it in my mouth for a second or two before I swallowed. The palate was smooth, spicy and fruity and the finish was long and soothing as the whiskey went down.

I nodded at Phillips. "Good choice. I haven't had the AnCnoc in a while. This is like catching up with an old friend."

Phillips smiled back and reached over to his desk, retrieved a file, and tossed it over to me. "Here's my analysis of your sniper."

My face must have registered some surprise.

"I consult for the Agency from time to time. Your boys Smith and Amrine had me do it while you were here. I'm surprised they didn't ask me earlier. Apparently, they've been chasing this guy for some time."

I nodded. "Nice."

"My full summary is in that folder. I don't connect to the Internet when I do this type of work. Too many ways electronic copies of things can wind up in the wrong hands. Read it and send it to your boys when you're done. Or you can give it to them if you'll see them anytime soon."

"Will do. So what are your thoughts about our shooter?"

Phillips shook his head. "I'm not impressed. This guy is a technician, not an artist. He's about brute force, not finesse." He looked across his glass at me. "I don't like to brag, but sometimes the background is useful for credibility. I've got 137 confirmed kills in places all over the world, most of which I can't talk about. And I've been an instructor for over 30 years. I'd wager you have more inherent talent than our sniper does. There is no artistry to the shots. It's all about brute force. Which is why…" Phillips took a slow sip of his scotch and relished the taste of the amber elixir for a few seconds. "He uses the .50 BMG for all his shots. Trained snipers use the tool best suited for the job. For me, if I'm inside 700 meters, I'll use the good ole 7.62 NATO or .308. Great cartridge for those ranges. Shoots flat, travels fast and isn't too hard on the shooter. Between about 700 meters and 1200 meters, I'll use the .300 Winchester Magnum. The bullet is about the same weight, but muzzle velocity and trajectory are better. Above 1200 meters, it's either the .338 Lapua or the .50 BMG depending on whether I have to shoot through something or not. Both guns are punishing on the shooter, but the .50 is larger and heavier than the .338 and a bitch to carry if you need to change stations quickly or egress in a hurry. For most situations, the .50 is too much gun and most of the shots this guy has taken, the .50 was way too much gun. Why would he risk the difficulties of repeatedly smuggling a big-ass rifle to multiple locations all over the world when most of the shots could have been taken by a smaller one? There are only two reasons I can think of. Either he's trying to make a statement, or he's never been trained to appreciate the value of different cartridges for different tasks."

"Smith and Amrine think it's all about the power of the .50 versus the other calibers. They have an advisor named Girard who seems to agree.."

Phillips shook his head slowly. "I'm not buying it. I don't think the shooter knows any better. "You know, there were pieces in the incidents that didn't fit. Things that didn't make sense. But I was looking at them in the context of professional snipers. I don't think this guy is a sniper at all. He's a rifle shooter, no doubt, but he's never been trained as a sniper. Tell your boys they need to look for target shooting champions, Olympic rifle shooters, that sort of thing."

He took another sip of his whiskeys and sat back in his chair with a look of disbelief on his weathered face. "And this guy isn't just in it for the money," Phillips said after a few moments. "He's trying to set some bizarre fucking record."

CHAPTER TEN

Friday, October 29
2030 Hours Local Time
Hilton Resort Hotel
Scottsdale, Arizona, USA

Gail and I were in our suite at the Hilton, in our usual posture, me sitting on the sofa with my legs propped up on the nearby coffee table and her lying down with her head in my lap. I had stopped at a liquor store on my way back to the hotel and bought a bottle of the AnCnoc. The amber nectar was caressing our throats as we relaxed.

Dinner had been underwhelming and the conversation had been strained, in spite of my attempts to engage her with what I had learned about the Shadow from Phillips. Gail wasn't happy about being here. In spite of her protestations, the CIA had managed to convince Gail's boss that she needed to go to Luke Air Force Base directly from the Pentagon. Her boss had come up with the idea of her hosting a late-notice seminar on pilot retention. She had arrived in Phoenix on Wednesday and had stayed on base at Luke for the last two nights, claiming that she was tired to make the drive to Scottsdale. Today, after her last event, she drove to east side of the valley and joined me at the Hilton. At dinner, her impatience with the situation reminded me of a pot of water that was boiling and might soon overflow. Being here, with me, took her out of the political arenas for her job, either back at Randolph AFB in San Antonio or at the Pentagon. Cooling her heals in Phoenix, even if it might be for a worthwhile cause, put her out of the game. And she hated that.

But the scotch seemed to be relaxing her. Her head rested on my lap and her eyes were closed. She had a semi-smile on her features and she was turned slightly toward me, almost like she wanted to get close to me. Her dark hair cascaded over my lap and framed her striking facial features and with her dark red lipstick, she looked like a grown-up version of Sleeping Beauty. But even as I appreciated her beauty, the reality of our situation made me shake my head. In many ways, we were good together, but her career would always come first and her loyalty to her ex-husband, for reasons I couldn't understand, would always influence her actions. She was stuck in a prison of her own construction and refused to use the key in her hands.

Besides, I thought, *my heart will always belong to Sarah. Even if I can never be with her.*

Gail's eyes opened and she looked up a me for a moment before leaning up with her arm outstretched. I retrieved her scotch glass from the side table and handed it to her. She took a long, slow, sip and then handed the glass back to me. Then she lay down and put her hands behind her head.

"This sniper of yours," she began.

I raised my eyebrows, surprised she even remembered the conversation. "We can't call him that anymore. Phillips said he's not a sniper. He's a target shooter."

Gail smacked my legs playfully.

"What the fuck ever," she said. "I get your whole artist versus technician thing you and Phillips talked about, but you know what? I think this guy might be somewhere in between. He reminds me of those guys who copy paintings because they have some talent but no originality. They can copy the motions and the techniques, but they can't generate anything new. This guy never does anything new. He likes to shoot people at long range, and that's all he does. Every scene is a repeat of the last but at different ranges and with some different angles. But they're all essentially the same thing."

I nodded respectfully at her. "That's a great observation. But I'd think consistency would be first among the considerations. You're a golfer. Why do you use the more reliable clubs in your bag and not necessarily the longest? If you know you can get to the green in two with a three wood and five iron, I bet you'll hit those clubs. You won't hit a driver unless you have to."

"Or unless I'm really comfortable with it."

"Well, there is that that."

I leaned my head against the back of the sofa and stared at the ceiling. Between Phillips' words earlier and Gail's words now, I could feel something tugging at me. I just didn't know what it was.

"By the way," Gail said, "I should tell you. I don't think we're talking about a guy here. I think the Shadow is a woman."

I snapped my head up from the back of the sofa. "Why?"

"More a feeling than anything else. The incidents are obviously very well planned, but they're also very neat and antiseptic. Like the shooter is fussy and doesn't like to get blood on her hands. Also, as much as the shooter strives to make a statement, she also doesn't want to defy convention too much, like she's dressing up or decorating a room or something."

She looked at me to see if I was buying it. I guess my face was blank.

"You know the odds are against that. According to the boys, the data indicate that most paid killers, whether they do it for fun or money, tend to be male."

"That would explain why she isn't a military-trained sniper," Gail said. "How many women are?"

"Not many."

"No. But there are a lot of Olympic class rifle shooters who are female. And those girls can knock the eyes off a fly at the indoor ranges they shoot at."

I nodded. "Another good point," I conceded.

"Just something to consider," Gail said.

She raised herself off my lap and reseated herself so that she was straddling me. I gave her glass to her and she sipped it slowly while looking me in the eyes. "You know, I've been thinking about something this week," she said.

"And what would that be?"

"How easy it is to be with you," she said.

I nodded. "It is easy. That's a good thing."

"You relax me. And it's hard for me to relax. I want you to know I appreciate it."

"I'm glad. You relax me as well."

"There might be something else we can do to relax."

"And what might that be?"

Gail took my whiskey glass and put both hers and mine on the side table before sliding her arms around my neck and bringing her mouth to mine.

"I'll show you," she said.

The Shadow completed the cleaning ritual and packed the pieces of the rifle into the backpack and poster tube. Then, she walked into the expansive bathroom and disrobed. The bath had been drawn earlier with precisely heated water and exactly the right combination of bath salts to smooth her body and allow her mind to wander. Next to the tub, a snifter of Courvoisier XO lay waiting, the aroma of the cognac wafting through the bathroom enticingly. The Shadow sank into the tub slowly and let the steamy water slowly rise onto her extremities and torso while allowing her eyes to close and her mind to enjoy the moment.

Tomorrow would be a record.

The shot would be taken from just outside of 3000 meters. The time of flight of the projectile would be just over 4 seconds and assuming the target didn't know it was coming, the effect on impact would be devastating. The Shadow lifted the glass of cognac to her nose and slowly relished the bouquet.

It was interesting that the finer, more complex things in life required more time to prepare, whether it was a fine cognac or the world's longest rifle shot. The Shadow had been practicing and obtaining the equipment for this event for months. The barrel for the shot was a masterpiece of the gunsmith's art. It was 32 inches long and specially tooled to increase the spin rate of the projectile before it left the muzzle. It had taken the gunsmith many attempts over several weeks to get it right. The telescopic sight was a newly developed model of Russian design with gyro-stabilization, a built-in rangefinder and automatic corrections for wind and elevation based on the ballistic data programmed into it. One of the first models of its kind off the assembly line, the Shadow had been waiting for the sight for better part of the last year. The cartridges themselves had been hand-loaded by the Shadow's armorer and were guaranteed to leave the muzzle at exactly 2,850 feet per second – every time. The Shadow had a magazine of ten of the cartridges in the backpack, and those were the result of days of trial and error to get the powder charge and bullet seating height as close to identical as possible.

Then there was the practice. Hours and hours on the open air firing range. Trying to get the shot groups even tighter and more consistent. Hundreds of rounds fired. The Shadow's shoulder was sore from the continual pounding it had taken from the rifle's butt stock.

But tomorrow the fruits of the all the labor would be realized.

The Shadow raised the glass of cognac to her lips and took a slow, deliberate sip. She smiled as the liquid oozed across her tongue and down her throat. The delicate taste toyed with her taste buds and left a slightly warm sensation in her throat.

There was yet one complication in her life that needed to be dealt with before the big job – the one that would set her up for life - a complication by the name of Colin Pearce.

Where had he come from? She smiled as remembered his cool swagger and his confident but self-deprecating manner. He was older than she was, and she adored older men. He was tall and muscular and good looking, in a bad-boy sort of way. He had dark brown hair that he combled straight back and warm hazel eyes. But what had attracted her to him had been the look in those eyes.

He was like she was.

It had been a very long time since the Shadow had wanted a man. Now it seemed the very man she wanted might be after her.

And the thought of that made her wet on the inside.

##

Nine hours later, the Shadow was in position. In London again. Looking through the telescopic sight and down into the middle of Trafalgar Square – 3005 meters away. The nest was an empty office in a tall building well away from the square and from which the Shadow could make a quick exit.

A circle of glass had been cut from the window through which the Shadow would take the shot. The rifle's suppressor was about half a meter inside the glass, close enough to allow the Shadow some maneuvering room but back far enough it wouldn't be easily seen by observers in the many police helicopters patrolling the skies. The legs of the rifle's bipod rested on a pillow, which in turn rested on a desk. The Shadow sat behind the desk, in a padded office chair, probably the most comfortable seating she had ever experienced since beginning this new career.

Three years ago. That was when the Shadow first started killing people for a living with a rifle – something she had never been trained to do, in spite of ten years in the military. The Shadow had been a competitive rifle shooter since her childhood when she had learned to shoot so she could spend more time with her stepfather, hunting and controlling varmints on the farm where they lived. She had killed her first rabbit when she was five and the act of killing had not inspired any emotion in her. It had seemed a natural part of life. Over the years of her childhood, she had killed over a hundred small and large animals and the lack of emotion she felt was constant. But what did inspire passion in her was the desire to make the perfect shot. As she graduated from .22 rimfire rifles to heavier, centerfire weapons, she learned to shoot at further distances and relished the challenge of putting a single round into an animal's head at the increased ranges. She and her father often went to the local firing range and soon she was outshooting him with every weapon he owned. The range master noticed her skill and encouraged her to shoot competitively. By the time she was fourteen, she was dominating every contest she entered at the range and the range master, a former competitive shooter, spent time with her every day after school, showing her the finer points of professional marksmanship and increasing her skills at ranges of 1,000 meters and beyond. When the time came to decide on a college, she found herself highly sought after by several schools for their collegiate rifle teams, but it was the school from one of the mountain areas of her country that got her attention. They wanted her for their biathlon team, even though she had never skied in her life.

She smiled as she sat at the desk, looking through the telescopic sight and remembered the first time she had donned the Nordic skis, a moment that was quickly followed by her first fall. But she had mastered cross-country skiing quickly, with the same persistence and concentration that she had used to master shooting. Soon she was dominating biathlon events at the collegiate level and was invited to join her country's winter Olympic team. She competed in the 1998 Winter Olympics in Nagano, Japan. But while she didn't miss a single shot on the 10-kilometer course the multiple times she skied it, her skiing just wasn't in the same league as the women on the European teams, and she didn't receive a medal.

After graduating from college, she joined the military, hoping to put her shooting skills to work for her country in a different way. But her hopes were short lived. Women were not allowed in combat, and she found herself in the intelligence field, gathering information on events and persons that her service found interesting. She lost herself in the art of information gathering and became adept at researching the backgrounds of people her service had designated as enemies or potential enemies. She rose through the ranks quickly and was sure she'd be staying in the military for an entire career.

But then her mother and stepfather had died. Slowly. Horribly. And she felt like she had lost the only constants in her life. After burying them and selling the farm where she had grown up, she felt directionless and hopeless. She resigned from the military and traveled the world on the savings she had accumulated while she served.

And she discovered an uncle she had never known. In Russia. He invited her to live with him and his wife, and he found her a job in the government. After a year or so, she began to feel like herself again.

And that was when the mob found her. She was in her mid-thirties, beautiful and voluptuous and a perfect candidate to be a kept woman for one of the many government officials the mob wanted to control. She was abducted from a nightclub and had resisted her kidnappers ferociously, nearly killing one of them and injuring another. When she was taken before the mob boss, in an abandoned warehouse on the outskirts of the city she lived in, he asked her why he shouldn't kill her.

"Because I have a skill you can use," she had said.

The men around her had laughed. "All women have that skill."

She had shaken her head. "If you have a rifle, I can show you."

And that was three years ago.

She spent the next two years traveling to various parts of the country and abroad, eliminating targets she was assigned. She did all her own observation and research and planned each project thoroughly, leaving nothing to chance. When it was time to perform, she used all the expertise she had accumulated over the years and took the shot from as far away as she could, to increase her proficiency. Her first kill had been a banker that the mob said was skimming money. She shot him from 300 meters away with a 7.62mm rifle and a four-power telescopic sight from a room at the end of the street where his bank was located. As the banker collapsed to the street, she had felt the same satisfaction in the perfect shot she remembered from longs ago. And she experienced the same lack of emotion over the death involved.

Over the next two years, she became one of the mob's most used assassins, and her bank account grew substantially.

Then had come the fateful meeting with her uncle.

He summoned her to his office and asked the same question that she had hoped the military would have several years ago.

"My friends tell me you are very skilled," he had said, "Would you like to use those skills in the service of your country?"

The events of the last 24 months fell into context then and she should have been angry. But instead, she was grateful once her uncle explained what she would need to do. She had a chance to avenge her mother and stepfather's deaths. And she had a chance to serve the country of her birth.

That was about a year ago.

And now she was about to make a kill that would not only break all the record books but also send a clear message to those who would interfere with her country's goals. Of course, the fact that she would also put a substantial amount of money into her bank account was an added benefit.

It was time.

The target's limousine entered the square and slowed to a halt. The target's security detail deployed from the limousine and joined their colleagues already in position. As she watched them through the telescopic sight, the security personnel gazed around the crowd and the surrounding buildings in their typical, precise, tight, visual search patterns. She smiled grimly. It would do them

*no good. She was shooting from a distance far outside their ability
to see or detect.*

*The target exited the limousine and walked purposefully to
the small stage and dais that had been erected in the square. The
assembled crowd cheered at his approach, and he waved to them
enthusiastically as he walked up the stairs and strode to the dais.
His stride was confident and the expression on his face cheerful as
he removed the notes from his jacket pocket and prepared to speak.*

*He was a handsome middle-aged man with wavy black hair
and bright, green eyes.*

But he would not be allowed to utter a word.

*Because he too had been offered a deal he had refused to
accept. And his words today could turn the tide of the country
against the will of the Motherland.*

*The Shadow centered the crosshairs of the telescopic sight
on the chest of the handsome prime minister of the United
Kingdom. She started the video recording, and squeezed the
trigger.*

CHAPTER ELEVEN

Saturday, October 30
0930 Hours Local Time
Hilton Resort Hotel
Scottsdale, Arizona, USA

I was in the hallway of some kind of office building. It was night and the floor, walls and ceiling of the hall were bathed in a dim red glow generated by the exit signs over the doors at each end. There were individual office rooms on the two sides of the hall, each with its door open so that I could inspect them as I passed. The outside walls of the building were glass and as I slowly worked my way down the hall, I could see the lights of a city far below when I looked inside each room. The building seemed impossibly thin. I was reminded of a visit I once paid to the 99th floor of the Willis Tower, in Chicago, where I could look out both sides of the building at once and see nearly 1000 feet straight down. But that hallway had been short and this one seemed very long. And the more progress I made, the longer the hallway seemed to be.

You're looking for someone.

The realization occurred as I found the pace of my search increasing and I began to run down the hall, quickly looking inside each room. The spacing between the rooms on the left and right sides of the hallway was offset so that no two doorways were across from each other. I could only run a few steps before I had to stop, look into a room and then run to the next one.

Someone is going to die unless you find him.

My pace quickened and I could feel my heart beating rapidly in my chest. I was panting now, like I was running a race, and I felt a sensation of helpless panic taking hold of me.

I continued down the hall. Running. Stopping. Looking. Running. Stopping. Looking.

You're never going to find him.

But then, as I ran, stopped and looked into yet another non-descript room on my right, there he was, seated at a desk, in the middle of the room with a large rifle on a bipod in front of him. He was staring into the rifle's telescopic sight, focused on the target in front of him. A hood obscured his features but also kept him from immediately seeing me.

The room had no glass in its window and I was abruptly conscious of the noise of wind and car horns honking in the distance. I became aware of how heavily I was breathing and how much noise I was making. I held my breath and slowly moved into the room, hoping to take the shooter by surprise.

But even as I stepped toward him, the room seemed to suddenly compress and I was right behind the shooter, just over his right shoulder. He lifted his face from the sight and slowly turned toward me, his features still obscured by the hood. I reached back for the gun that should have been on my right hip, cursing myself for not having it in my hand already.

The shooter was now rising as he turned and I felt arms going around my neck. Small arms. Delicate arms. And then, finally, the features of his face became visible and I found myself looking down at a beautiful female face with blue-gray eyes and blonde hair.

Holy Shit!

I bolted upright in bed, breathing rapidly and with the blood roaring in my ears. My phone rang and vibrated on the nightstand. I felt Gail stirring alongside me. She mumbled something and then her breathing sank back into a regular pattern. I fumbled for the phone and placed it against my ear. Smith's voice pierced the calm darkness of the hotel room.

"The mother fucker just struck again," he said. "The prime minister of the United Kingdom is dead."

"Jesus," I said, still panting. "That's going to leave a mark."

"Catch you a busy time?" Smith asked. I could hear a degree of impatience in his voice.

"No. I was sleeping. I was having a weird dream." I tried to blink the sleep from my eyes as I stared at the line of light on the carpet to the right of the bed. The Phoenix sun was streaming through a gap in the curtains and individually illuminating the strands of fiber in the multicolored carpet.

"Do you have your passport?" Smith asked.

"Never leave home without it."

"I'm sending a jet to the Scottsdale Airport to get you. John and I are on our way to U.K. We'll meet you there. I'll text you the details. It will take a few hours for the jet to get there."

"Got it. I'll be standing by."

I hung up and tossed the phone on the nightstand. Then I rolled onto my back, and Gail snuggled up next to me and put her head on my chest.

"The U.K.?" she asked, sleepily. "Why do they want you there?"

I shook my head. "I don't know. The Shadow is long gone by now. I don't know what they hope to gain by me being there."

"Maybe they need your mind?"

I snorted and kissed the top of her head. "Fat chance," I said. "They've got a lot of minds that are better than mine."

"But those minds are used to thinking inside the box," she said. "And you don't do that."

"Maybe not," I said.

"When are you leaving?"

"In a few hours. They're sending a jet to get me."

She nodded. I could feel her hair moving against my chest. "Can we just stay here, like this, a little longer? I have a flight to catch too, but I don't want to get up for a while."

"Sure," I said.

Gail drifted off to sleep a few minutes later and I felt her even breathing against my chest and under the arm I had around her. Sleep was the furthest thing from my mind.

The British Prime Minister, I thought. *Holy shit. That raises the bar to a new level.*

While I was in France and the U.K., stopping the Shadow had seemed almost like an academic exercise. It was important but not critical. Then the Shadow had killed the Labour Party's Energy Chancellor and now the Prime Minister. Stopping the assassin had become critical. And apart from maybe getting on one of the assasin's jets, I had no idea how I could help.

But the anxiety from the dream and my gut told me how it would all end. I would come face to face with the Shadow and it would be the Shadow or me. I couldn't decide whether I feared that or welcomed it. Maybe it was both.

CHAPTER TWELVE

Sunday, October 31
0900 Hours Local Time
Trafalgar Square
London, United Kingdom

It was a typical humid English day. The air in London was heavy with fog and low clouds. The square was cordoned off, and hundreds of people looked on from beyond the police barriers. There were many officers from the U.K.'s various law enforcement and investigative agencies combing the square for evidence, and there were several vehicles parked in random order throughout the expanse of asphalt and concrete.

But it was eerily quiet. And gloomy.

As Smith and I exited the car we had been provided, the sound of the doors shutting seemed to echo across the square, and many of the faces of the officials present looked in our direction. The long façade of the National Gallery was devoid of activity, and the wide steps to its magnificent doors were vacant. The statue of Admiral Lord Nelson seemed to brood down upon the square from atop its tall column and lent an air of gravity to the scene that was unfolding below it.

It took a moment or two for me to understand.

"They're in shock," I whispered to Smith, gesturing tactfully to those around us.

Smith nodded. "This is the first time a sitting Prime Minister of the U.K. has been assassinated. We've had several presidents assassinated and many more attempts. Sadly, the whole thing is a bit more," he paused to think of the right word, but I could have chosen it for him, "routine in the U.S. than it is here."

"Good for us," I said, shaking my head.

"Yeah, really. That damn energy minister is shot less than a mile away from here a little over a week ago and now this. The Shadow is ramping up his game."

"How do you know it was the Shadow?" I asked. "Seems a little out of his his normal league."

Smith nodded. "True. But the wound was a big hole, like a .50 caliber, and it impacted well before anyone heard anything that sounded like a rifle shot."

"So not from close by in other words."

"Nope," he said. "And it would be tricky. There are several large buildings but finding a sightline to the square would be difficult. The Scotland Yard and MI-5 folks will be working the reverse azimuth problem shortly."

We continued walking over to the area of the square directly in front of the tall column with the statue of Nelson on top of it. The platform and dais from which the prime minister was to speak were still in place, and forensic analysts were on their knees on the carpet behind the podium, with latex gloves on their hands and knee pads over their coveralls. As we approached, a man with a bushy head of surfer-blond hair turned toward us.

"Hi John," I said, extending my hand. "Thanks for the free trip to London."

"You're welcome, T.C.," John Amrine said, with a grim expression on his face. "I wish it was under better circumstances."

I nodded. "Me too. While I'm grateful to be here, I'm not sure what expertise I can provide." I gestured to the square around us. "You've got to have some of the best investigators in the world here. Plus the two of you and the Agency have been following the Shadow for a long while. You've got to know more about him than I do."

"Maybe not," Amrine said, with the same grim expression on his face. "You know the 7X you flew into London not too long ago?"

I nodded and began to feel a tightening in my guts.

"One of its sister ships is here. With Canadian registry."

"Of course," I said. And then Gail's words and the events of the last week or two ran together in my mind.

"Jesus!" I said. "I saw her in the bar at the Duke's Hotel that night!"

"Who?" Smith asked.

"Alina! The principal's companion!" I fumbled for my phone. "I forgot all about this!" I turned on the phone, selected the photo app and found the pic I was looking for. "I didn't get a good picture of her, but I got one of the guy she was sitting with."

I showed them the picture, and they both shook their heads in unison.

"Goddamn," Amrine said. "You're going to need to make a statement to the guys from Scotland Yard and MI5."

"Who is that guy?" I asked. "She told me his name but I forgot it."

"David Ackerman," Smith answered. "He's the Conservative Party's Chancellor of Energy."

"And probably the next Prime Minister," Amrine added. He eyed me. "Did you hear or see anything?"

"No," I said. "But I saw him push something across the table to Alina. It looked like a letter-sized envelope, but it wasn't flat. There was something irregularly shaped inside of it."

"Bank token?" Smith asked his partner.

Amrine nodded. "Could be," he said. Amrine looked at me again. "Anything else?"

"This guy, Ackerman, wasn't happy with Alina. I gathered that something had gone wrong."

Amrine nodded again. "It fits. The Shadow missed Essex with the first shot. Apparently, he sneezed at exactly the right moment, and the bullet missed his head by inches. It hit a young policewoman standing behind him and killed her instantly. She happened to be pregnant. The papers had a field day with that. Even though they had no information on who the shooter was."

"But the Shadow killed Essex though, right? What's the big deal?" I asked.

"The Shadow bills himself as a one-shot, one kill assassin," Smith said. "Two shots for one kill hurts his reputation."

"Maybe Ackerman didn't like paying the standard price for a less than perfect job," Amrine said.

The wind in the square became a little cooler just then, and I realized that once again I was in the middle of something that I did not understand. I shook my head unconsciously. "So why am I here?" I asked. "You could have gotten any of this information over the phone."

"Because you're the only person in this entire crew," he gestured to the officers around us, "that may have been in the company of the Shadow," he said. "Maybe you'll see something here that they won't know enough to look for."

I shrugged. "Maybe. Not sure I know where to begin."

Amrine motioned to the platform and dais next to us. "Jump up and see if anything strikes you."

The forensics personnel had moved on. I stepped up onto the raised, rectangular, platform, and looked around. The rows of wooden chairs on either side of the dais were scattered about, and some had been turned on their side as their occupants had made a hasty exit. It looked a little like a game of musical chairs gone bad. The dais itself stood pristinely untouched, a few papers from the speech the prime mister had planned to deliver still lay distributed about the surface.

"How far into the speech was he when the shot came?" I asked.

"He never got started," Amrine answered. "The Shadow took him out before he ever uttered the first word."

"Damn," I said. "Any idea on the topic of the speech?"

Amrine nodded and smiled grimly. "Britain's energy future. And why it was important to use facilities that were of British design and manufacture."

"And not someone else's," I said.

It was Smith's turn to nod. "Like the Russians."

I turned to them. "What are you guys not telling me?"

Amrine raised his hand. "We'll discuss later. But for now, just look around, please. Let's respect what has happened here and try to help these people."

I nodded. I looked at the area behind and around the dais for the telltale signs of blood or tissue spatter. I frowned as I studied the carpet on the platform and the asphalt behind it.

"Doesn't look like the bullet exited," I said.

"It didn't," Smith said.

"Isn't that unusual for a high-velocity rifle round?" I asked. "Even with soft-nosed bullets?"

I saw Amrine nod in my peripheral vision. "Unusual sure, but not unheard of. Sometimes the round strikes a bone or enters the target a weird angle. And sometimes…"

"It doesn't have much energy when it reaches the target," I finished the sentence for him. Suddenly Gunnery Sergeant Phillips' words echoed in my ears. "Damn," I said. "It's about the record."

"What?" Amrine asked.

"Have they found the shooting site yet?" I asked.

"No," Smith answered. "They're still looking. Everywhere within about 1,000 meters."

"They need to push the search out further. This shot was about the record."

"The record?" Smith asked.

I turned to look at both of them. "Don't you remember what Phillips said?" I asked. "I told Dave all about it."

I raised my head and did a slow 360-degree view of the skyline around us.

"Phillips said the Shadow wasn't a sniper. She was a target shooter and wanted to set some bizarre record."

"She?" Amrine asked.

"That's Gail's input. I shared some of the reports you sent me with her."

I could see the grim expressions on both their faces.

"Relax," I said. "She knows the drill. What's more important is that she knows how to keep her mouth shut. Gail thinks the Shadow is a woman. After having been aboard the aircraft in question, the odds are 50% that's true and that business with Alina at the bar makes a stronger case for it." I continued to survey the skyline around Trafalgar Square. "So they haven't started their analysis of the shot direction yet?"

"No," Amrine answered. "That team hasn't arrived. Should be soon though."

I pointed to a tall glass building on the skyline that was barely visible with the low clouds and fog.

"Tell them not to bother," I said. "They'll find the shooting position there."

"You mean the sniper's nest?" Smith asked.

I looked down at him. "The Shadow isn't a sniper. She's a target shooter. And that building is the furthest one from here that I can see. That's where you'll find the position. I'm positive of it."

Amrine motioned to some of the officers next to him. "Can you find Inspector Dawson and ask him to come over here please?"

As he spoke, I looked into the foggy distance and regarded the glass and steel of the skyscraper beyond. When I had been stationed in the UK, twenty years previously, shiny skyscrapers were an oddity on the London skyline. Today they seemed to be everywhere.

I shook my head as I regarded the structure. She had fired from there. I was sure of it. It was like I could feel it somehow. Suddenly the memory of yesterday's dream flashed into my consciousness and I felt a chill across the back of my neck.

"It was you, Alina," I said to myself. "You were there. Why do I know that?"

THE SHADOW – INTERLUDE

The Shadow stood among the people surrounding Trafalgar Square and watched the many teams of officials scrambling to analyze her work. She was attired in a long Burberry coat and matching hat. She wore large sunglasses that covered the upper portion of her face and even though the weather didn't require them, they fit her style perfectly, completing her guise as a typical affluent Londoner.

As she regarded the square, an Audi sedan rolled slowly by her, official lights flashing, accompanied by a few blurts of the siren as it made its way through the crowds. She glanced inside and saw a familiar profile.

Could it be him?

The police around the cordon allowed the sedan through the barriers, and it stopped near the raised platform at the base of the pillar with Nelson's statue atop it. As the occupants exited, she found herself holding her breath.

It was Colin Pearce!

The tall, muscular, man exited the vehicle and strode toward the platform with purpose. This was the first time the Shadow had been able to watch him from afar. He walked confidently, like there was no one he needed to impress. Like there was no one he feared. She remembered the conversation with her uncle. This was a man who killed four would-be assassins and wounded a fifth in one day. She could almost feel a quiet, deadly power emanating from him.

She wanted him.

The thought occurred to her with a sudden intensity that took her by surprise. A smile crept onto her face. At last, someone who might be her equal.

Colin was accompanied by another man who was as tall as he was, but thinner, with light brown hair and a grim expression on his face. The two walked over to a third man who was shorter, but stockier and had a mop of surfer-blond hair on his head. After a few minutes of conversation, Colin jumped up on the platform and looked around. Then, without warning, he turned in her direction and surveyed the London skyline behind her. He pointed to something above her head and in the distance.

He had identified the building she fired from. He knew her. He understood her.

The Shadow's smile grew wider, and she felt more drawn to him. The game was on. It had become personal for them. She knew that once they were together, he would want her. Every man she had ever met wanted her. But she had resisted them all. She wanted someone who was worthy of her.

Maybe Colin Pearce was that man.

It was time to bring him close and find out what he knew. And find out who he was. She reached inside the Gucci purse and retrieved her smartphone, her hands trembling slightly as the butterflies awakened in her stomach.

PEARCE IS HERE, she texted. WORKING WITH THE AUTHORITIES AND TRYING TO TRACK ME. LET'S USE HIM AS CREW ON THE SWISS TRIP. WE NEED TO FIND OUT WHAT HE KNOWS.

She waited for her uncle's reply while she continued to watch the scene in front of her. Colin dismounted the platform and rejoined the two men who were with him. Then a few members of the Scotland Yard team were motioned over by the blond man. In moments, cars were dispatched from the square. The barricades were opened, and the cars headed up the street next to her.

She knew where they were going.

They'd find the place where she had fired from, along with the shell casing she'd left them. And they'd know that she had set another record for the conditions and the round.

HE SHOWED THEM WHERE THE NEST IS, she texted her uncle. WE NEED TO KNOW WHAT HE KNOWS. I CAN GET THAT INFORMATION.

The pause was momentary.

OK, came the reply. WILL GET HIM AS CREW. BUT I WILL QUESTION HIM ALSO. YOU KNOW WHERE.

Her heart leaped inside her chest, and she raised her eyes to look at Colin once again. She smiled at him, and waved, just so he alone could see it.

And then she vanished into the crowd.

CHAPTER THIRTEEN

Sunday, October 31
0923 Hours Local Time
Trafalgar Square
London, United Kingdom

"No way," I said to myself as I saw the woman in the Burberry and sunglasses looking at me. "No fucking way!"

She was about five feet ten but could have been wearing heels, and between the coat, the hat, and the sunglasses, there was no way to distinguish any identifiable features. But it was like I could feel her. There. Watching us. Watching me.

As the Scotland Yard cars sped off to investigate the building I had identified, she waved at me.

"Holy fucking shit!" I screamed and bolted toward the area where she was standing.

"What?" Smith and Amrine yelled, almost in unison.

"She's here!" I yelled back them, over my shoulder. "She's watching us!"

I reached the barrier and slipped between two barricades and shot up the street, looking for any sign of the coat, the hat or the sunglasses. After about ten yards or so, the crowd thinned out, and I looked around me.

She was gone. No trace of her at all.

"Damn!" I said as I stopped and Smith and Amrine caught up to me. "She was here. She looked right at me and waved at me."

"That's pretty gutsy," Smith said.

"She must be pretty sure of herself," Amrine said. "There are more surveillance cameras in London than in just about any major metropolitan city in the world. There will be footage of her. I'll get some folks from the Yard on it." He pulled a smart phone out and dialed a number.

"Probably not her first attempt at doing this sort of thing," Smith said.

"Jesus," I said as I continued to look around us. The gray brick and stone structures around us seemed to mock us as we stood there. *We absorbed her*; they seemed to say. *And you'll never find her.* I shook off the feeling as several thoughts careened through my head like bumper cars at an amusement park. *What was she looking for? What was she waiting for? Did she know I was going to be here?*

A car pulled alongside us a few moments later, and Amrine motioned for all of us to get inside. As soon as the doors had shut, Amrine barked two words at the driver. "Scotland Yard," he said.

Forty-five minutes later we stood in a darkened audio-visual room with a bank of TV monitors against the far wall. The technician at the console was an older, balding man with a set of wire-rimmed glasses worn very low on his nose. But his knowing hands worked the control screen in front of him with the proficiency of a concert pianist, and soon he had the footage we needed called up on three separate monitors in front of us. He pointed at the three screens as he spoke.

"These three are synced," he said. "The screen on the far left is the camera at the side of the National Gallery, at the corner of Charing Cross Road and Duncannon Street. The one in the middle is across the way and down about half a block, right about where William the Fourth Street intersects with Charing Cross. The one on the far right is where St. Martin's Lane intersects William the Fourth Street. It's the only way she could have fled on foot and not be noticed."

He typed a few more commands into his keyboard. "The time is 0900 on all cameras. Here we go." He clicked once more.

Immediately the three screens came alive with motion as cars began to roll, albeit slowly, and people began to move. The action was less than I would have expected but then again it was Sunday and the day after the Prime Minister had been shot.

I focused my eyes on the group of people nearest the square and looked for the coat and the hat. At first, it was difficult, but then, the car that Smith and I had taken into the square became visible, and as it made its way to the barricades, a person at the front of the crowd turned and looked at the car, and stared for just a moment too long.

"There," I said, pointing at her image on the screen. "That has to be her."

She had chosen her apparel well. The dark coat, hat, and sunglasses made her look affluent but anonymous, and she blended well with the horde of Londoners around her. As we watched, she turned her attention back to the center of the square and observed Smith, Amrine and I as we went about our initial analysis of the events in the square. Then, as I turned to point at the buildings behind her, her body posture changed a little. She crossed her arms and nodded slightly, almost in satisfaction it seemed.

"Well that's it, T.C.," Smith murmured. "She's on to you."

"Jesus," I said.

Then she raised her hand into a bride wave and turned back into the crowd. And she disappeared into the crowd as we watched.

"What the fuck?" Amrine exclaimed. "Where'd she go?"

"'Ang on," said the video operator, with a bit of cockney accent in his voice. He backed the footage up about 15 seconds and accessed a pull-down menu on his screen. "This should slow it down a touch," he said.

The footage replayed from the moment of the wave at a very slow speed. As she turned and walked into the crowd, she seemed to squat down for a moment or two, and there was some motion that was hidden by the crowd and the camera angles. Moments later, a new head reappeared in the crowd with a different hat and glasses and even with a different coat. Before the color scheme had been dark but now everything was light gray. The perfect urban camouflage color. The face wasn't visible of course, but it was her.

"Holy shit," Smith said. "That was fucking slick. Fifteen years of covert ops and I've rarely seen something that smooth."

"What happened?" I asked.

"She changed clothes," said Amrine in a peeved tone. "Something any trained operative under surveillance is taught to do if they think they're being followed." He shook his head. "And I'll second Dave's observation. That was fucking slick."

"So did she have another outfit stowed somewhere or something?" I asked.

"Possibly," Smith said. "More likely the coat and hat where reversible and she just ducked out of sight and took them off and and put them back on again."

As we watched her continue up Charing Cross street, she turned on to William the Fourth Street and maintained a normal, leisurely pace. Then, suddenly, she turned left down a side street and disappeared from view.

"Let me guess," Amrine said. "No surveillance on that street."

The video operator cursed under his breath and entered some commands on the keyboard and pulled several more cameras up on the screens in front of us. Each new camera showed a new view of the street at about the same time frame, and every one of them showed her disappearing from view.

"She's a planner," I said, stating the obvious.

"That she is," Smith echoed.

"Good," I said. "That might make this easier."

Amrine and Smith turned to me with bemused expressions on their faces. I wish I had taken a picture of them, side by side, the blond and the brunette.

"How do you figure?" Amrine said at last.

"The way to fuck up a planner is to get inside their decision loop and fuck with their plan," I said. "And that's something I'm good at."

Smith nodded, a thin smile etching itself into his features.

Amrine retrieved his phone from his pocket and glanced down at it. "You might have the opportunity to do that sooner rather later," he said. "Your crewing agency is asking for your services again. To fly the 7X in question."

"Wonderful," I said. "Just when I thought this trip couldn't get any better."

CHAPTER FOURTEEN

Sunday, October 31
1830 Hours Local Time
Grafton's Restaurant
London, United Kingdom.

The day's activities complete, Smith, Amrine and I were enjoying drinks and dinner at a local restaurant they were familiar with. We were sharing a superb bottle of 2005 Chateau Greysac Bordeaux while we waited for the waiter to bring our food. I had ordered the Beef Wellington on Amrine's recommendation, and after a long day without much time for a meal, I could hardly wait for its arrival.

"So let me ask the obvious," I said. "When I meet the jet for my *trip,* day after tomorrow, why don't you just grab everyone on board and do the interrogation thing?"

"Because we need to know who's been paying for the hits," Amrine said patiently as he sipped his wine. "The Shadow is just the mechanism. We need to know who is pushing the buttons."

"Okay," I said. "So since I seem to be in this for the long haul, maybe you could talk to me about the Russians and what you've discovered."

"It seems to be about energy," Smith answered after a moment.

"More specifically, nuclear energy," Amrine added.

I must have had a baffled look on my face

"I know," Amrine said with a rare expression of embarrassment. "That's why it took us so long to see it."

"Nuclear energy? They've killed 52 people over nuclear energy? You're going to need to explain that one."

Smith and Amrine looked at each other and Amrine tilted his head toward me. Apparently, this was something they'd had to explain several times.

"Ok, I guess I'm elected," Smith said. He looked at me. "So how much do you know about nuclear power?"

I shrugged. "Not much. I know it powers a lot of naval ships, and some reactors provide power to cities. I know the tree-huggers don't like it, but the reactors seem to produce power just fine for folks who need it."

Smith nodded at me. "You know about as much as we did. Here's the executive summary. Nuclear energy provides about 11% of the world's electrical power. There are places in Europe and the Far East where that's the only source available. France gets three-quarters of its power from nuclear reactors, several other European countries and many in Asia get anywhere from 20 to 50% of their power from nukes. In the US, about 20% of the electrical power we use is generated by nuclear power plants."

"And the tree huggers hate it because it generates no carbon signature at all, so it's actually green," Amrine said. "But because it's nuclear, they think it's evil. It drives them fucking nuts."

"Bottom line," Smith said, "is that it's big money and has big impact, but it occurs in the background because no one talks about it much."

"Ok," I said. "So why are people being killed?"

Smith held his hand up to silence me. "We'll get to that." He took a sip of his wine before continuing. "There are two main issues confronting the nuclear industry today. First, many of the plants are old and need to be replaced, but no one is in a hurry to build new reactors because the capital investment is huge."

"And the regulations governing construction are extensive and tedious," Amrine interjected. "Not to mention the pushback from all the environmental groups."

"It makes companies not want to invest in new plants," Smith continued. "The biggest nuclear generator in the US is a company called Enteron, and the CEO has gone on record as saying that without reduced regulation and government subsidies to put them on a level playing field with other subsidized non-carbon energy sources, his company will be out of the nuclear business in 10 to 15 years. And there is no replacement for that generation capability on the horizon."

"What about renewables, hydroelectric power, wind, solar, and all that?" I asked.

Amrine shook his head. "Sounds good when the politicians say it, but it's not realistic. Not enough capacity. Especially with a growing population. And besides, while your average environmental activist might love to make signs and protest nuclear energy, they don't like windmills or solar panels in their neighborhoods. Brings the property values down you see."

"Not to mention that a large part of the world's energy is generated by burning coal and that's being forced off the grid by environmental groups as well," Smith added. "Even the clean coal with a much smaller carbon footprint. If you believe in the whole climate change thing."

"Okay," I said. "I'm getting that there is something of an energy crisis brewing. So, let me guess, new nuke plants are the answer, right?"

Smith made a pistol with his right thumb and index finger and pointed it at me while he took another sip of wine with his left hand. "Bingo," he said, after he swallowed. "But they take anywhere from 8 to 10 years to build, depending on the area of the world. Add all the prerequisite environmental studies and public hearings required, especially in the US and Europe, and you've got another 2 to 3 years on top of that."

I was starting to see the square corner. "So time is running out to get ahead of this impending crisis," I said.

They both nodded but said nothing. Instead, they sat back and looked at me to see if I would put the pieces together.

I sat back as well and took a sip of my wine and let the luscious liquid rest on my tongue while I thought. The answer swam to the surface of my consciousness a few moments later.

"The Russians have a solution," I said. I thought back to the TV news crawlers I had seen the last few days. "Breeder reactors."

Smith and Amrine looked at each other, then back at me.

"Not too bad for a fighter jock," Smith said.

"Let me guess," I continued. "They're less expensive, safer and take less time to construct than typical reactors. They're also probably more environmentally acceptable."

Amrine nodded. "At least the Russian prototypes are," he said. "Theoretically at least. They also produce more fuel in the process of generating, so they're self-perpetuating in a way. The Russians are pushing the technology hard, especially in Europe and the Far East, although they're trying to sell to America as well. They've sponsored multiple tours of their three prototype facilities with free private jet transportation, lavish parties, the works."

"So what's the problem then? We're supposed to be open to globalization and international cooperation and all that."

"It seems that the technology the Russians are selling doesn't work," Smith said, looking down at his glass. "The physics aren't there. We've reached out to some folks at the Nuclear Regulatory Commission, and while a few believe what the Russians are advertising, most don't. Apparently, there is physics shit that can't be changed when it comes to safely sustaining and containing low-level chain reactions, in spite of what the Russians might say."

"Some nuclear experts throughout the world have spoken out about the Russian reactors," Amrine said. "They've examined the tech data the Russians have provided and said the prototypes and the plans don't match. They've also gone as far as to accuse the Russians of marketing a product they know will fail so that when the plants do fail, the buyers will be dependent on Russia for electrical energy."

"Wow," I said, sitting back in my chair. "That seems a little extreme. You guys are in the threat business. What do your experts say?"

Amrine shrugged, and Smith gestured with his hands.

"It's the Russians," Amrine said. "They can be utterly un-fucking-predictable."

"And their economy has been in the shitter since oil prices fell," Smith added. "They could be open to anything that will bring additional hard currency into their country."

"But if that was the real intention wouldn't it take a long time?"

Amrine smiled at my naïveté. "Don't forget. The Russians don't think like Americans or any other western country for that matter. They take the long view of everything. The ruling class can afford to. It's not like they'll get voted out of office."

"Wow, so it could all be real," I said.

"Could be," Smith said, nodding. "We're still checking it out, but it could be."

"So you said there were two problems," I said.

Smith nodded again. "People are the other issue," he said. "With the the future of the nuclear energy industry in question, fewer and fewer people are getting into it as a career. The regulatory requirements for the necessary expertise to operate and manage nuclear plants are detailed and extensive. As a person ascends the nuclear ladder, he or she accumulates very specialized knowledge and experience that makes them somewhat irreplaceable if something should happen to them."

I smiled grimly. "Like maybe getting themselves shot," I said.

"Exactly," Amrine said. "We've been going back through the records of all the Shadow's hits, and it seems that the majority of them had spoken or were speaking out against the Russian reactors."

"And by the way," Smith added. "Guess what country is generating more nuclear experts than it needs?"

"Russia," I answered. "Holy shit. So if they take experts in other countries down, they have the supply to replace them. And get their people into place." I shook my head in unwilling admiration. "It's fucking brilliant," I said. "Diabolical. But still fucking brilliant."

"And that would be the Russians in a nutshell," Amrine said. "From their politics to their economics, even to their organized crime activity, the Russians are utterly ruthless in the pursuit of their goals."

"But isn't the use of an assassin who fires a big-ass rifle unsubtle, even for the Russians?" I asked.

"That's a good question," Smith said. "And we've wondered about it as well. Russian mobsters typically like to send a message when they whack someone, but if you were trying to subtly execute a plan to take over the nuclear energy industry, it doesn't seem that blowing people away would be the best answer."

"Especially after yesterday," I said.

They both nodded.

"Can't get much more visible than that," Amrine said. "Still can't believe they whacked the prime minister of the U.K. It defies the pattern and that, along with Essex, brings the whole deal out of the darkness and into the light. If the cat wasn't out of the bag before, it will be now."

"The press is going have a fucking field day with this," Smith said. "Because now, all the other hits will be all over the news and the police and counter-intelligence agencies of the world are going to look like idiots."

"Maybe that's part of the game," I said.

"Might be," Amrine said. "With the Russians anything is possible."

"So what else do you know about the people the Shadow is taking out?"

"Until recently, the targets were highly placed members of the nuclear industry in several countries like the UK, France, Germany, Japan, and Brazil," he answered. "Even a few in the U.S."

"All of whom are irreplaceable, at least in the near term," Smith said. "It's too bad we didn't put the pieces together until recently, we might have been able to warn some of them. But it doesn't seem to matter, because now the Shadow is going after members of governments that are part of the decision process on energy alternatives for their countries. The Energy Minister of the Czech Republic was killed about two weeks ago, then David Essex, the Ministry of Energy here in the UK."

"Damn," I said. "But why not the Energy Ministers of other countries and why the Prime Minister here?"

"Maybe because the only European country that hasn't signed an agreement with the Russians is the UK?" Smith offered.

"And let me guess, the guy sitting with Alina that night in the bar, David Ackerman, supports the Russian initiative in the U.K." I said.

"And he will probably be the next P.M," Amrine added.

"The stakes must be pretty fucking high," I said. "Jesus. Is he getting a kickback from somewhere?"

"MI-6 and Scotland Yard are working on that. So far, nothing." Amrine said. "But the Russians are experts at paying people off with no electronic or paper trail."

The waiter arrived table side and the food was presented to us. We lapsed into silence as we ate. British cooking is probably the most underrated on the planet. While the typical pub food might lack some originality, at the upper end of the culinary scale, British cuisine stood its ground against both the French and Italians. The pastry on my Beef Wellington was soft and flaky, and the meat inside was utterly succulent. I tried to restrain myself and relish the dish but my hunger got the better of me, and I consumed the entrée in minutes, not even pausing to take a drink of wine between bites.

"Damn, T.C.," Smith said as I came up for air. "I guess you hated that."

"Yeah it sucked so much I might have to have another to make sure," I said.

"If you can wait that long," Amrine added.

"And that would be the issue," I said.

I buttered a piece of bread for myself and ate it in between bites of my side dishes, the ever present new potatoes and peas that seem to be on the short list of sides in the U.K. After a few moments, I felt my hunger beginning to ebb and decided not to order another helping of the Wellington. As Smith and Amrine continued to eat their food, I poured some more wine for the three of us and pushed myself back from the table a bit.

"You may be one of the faster eaters I've ever seen, T.C.," Smith said between bites.

"I probably am, and it's not a good thing," I said. "My whole family ate fast and the 20-minute meals we had at the Air Force Academy sealed the deal. I've been a fast eater ever since. Comes in handy when you're eating in a cockpit or an FBO, not so much when you're out for fine dining."

Amrine and Smith's phones both buzzed at that exact moment and sudden vibration of both of them, loudly, at once, against the wooden table almost made me jump out of my seat.

"Jesus!" I said reflexively.

"A little tense are we, T.C.?" Amrine snickered as he reached for his phone. His smile vanished as he unlocked the device and read the message that was displayed. His mouth opened, but it was Dave Smith, who was looking at the same message on his phone, who supplied the words.

"Well I'll be damned," he said.

They looked at each other for a moment and then back at me. The air was heavy with their silence.

"What?" I asked

Amrine was the first to speak.

"The analysts have been doing some digging. The 'Vladimir' on your jet, isn't Vladimir Strelkov like the manifests indicated. His real name is Vladimir Novak, and he's the COO of the PDR Corporation. That's the company that makes the breeder reactors we've been talking about."

My mouth dropped open, but I didn't speak.

"It gets better," he continued. "He's the son of Anton Novak, who just happens to be the Russian Energy Minister."

"Pretty fucking convenient," I muttered. "Seems the Russians aren't encumbered by ethics regulations for members of the government."

"Apparently not," Amrine said, shaking his head. "One of the things you learn in this job is never to be surprised by weird shit, but sometimes it still makes you shake your head."

"Well get ready to do that again," said Smith, still reading the message on his phone. He scrolled to the bottom of the message and then scrolled up and down again, as if re-reading, just to make sure what he read was real. "So it seems Vladimir has a cousin and Anton has a niece," he said. "And her name is Alina."

Amrine nodded like the information didn't surprise him at all. He raised his eyes to me. "And she seems to have a thing for you, T.C., given the wave and all."

I remembered the body contact and her voice in my ear and nodded. "Which means she's fucked up, like all women attracted to me are. But I guess we already knew that."

A long moment followed, and Smith and Amrine looked at me across the table as a smirk found its way onto both of their mouths.

"And you want me to get close to her and find out what she knows," I said. I hung my head in disbelief. "Jesus," I said at last. "You guys must have an awful lot of confidence in my prowess with the opposite sex."

"The past speaks for itself, T.C.," Smith said. "You've got a knack for getting women to talk while they're on their back." He smiled to himself at the rhyme.

"If she doesn't kill me first," I said sardonically,

Smith shook his head. "Doesn't gain her anything," he said. "And it could cost her a lot, especially now that she knows you're working for the good guys. She's got to figure we'll be tracking you and the moment we don't hear from you we'll come after her."

"That would spoil her schedule," Amrine added. "And there's always a schedule."

CHAPTER FIFTEEN

Monday, November 1
1930 Hours Local Time
The Bar at the Dukes Hotel
London, United Kingdom.

The first leg of my trip was supposed to depart from the London City Airport tomorrow and go to Gstaad Airport in Switzerland. In theory, I had traveled from the US to London last night, arrived this morning and was scheduled to meet the crew at the airport tomorrow morning after 24 hours of rest at a local hotel, the Hilton at Green Park. A series of airline reservations, tickets and hotel reservations had been created to provide the backup documentation if anyone checked.

I probably should have stayed at the bar in the Hilton. It was a great hotel and had a better than average selection of single-malt. But I was restless and often when I felt restless, I made my way to a place that provided familiarity and comfort. Which was why I was back in the bar at the Dukes Hotel, sipping another superb martini and watching some of London's upper crust pass their evening.

My fellow patrons were mostly business people tonight, nearly all of them were younger than I was, dressed in fashionable suits and animatedly discussing the details of the day. I sat back in my comfortable chair and stared into my martini glass as the glow of the alcohol slowly came over me. My task over the coming days would not be an easy one and the flying duties would be the least of it.

There was an unspoken code that existed in business aviation and it was probably as old as the industry itself; the crew didn't mix with passengers. While the relationship between crewmembers and the passengers they carried could be an intimate one, it was understood by both that the crew was 'the help' and the passengers were those who paid. Crossing the invisble line between crew and passengers, even when done innocently, came at great professional peril for the crewmember involved. On one of my contract trips in the Gulfstream IV, I had seen a first officer reprimanded for being friendly and talking to the principal's girl friend too much. He was dismissed after the next flight we flew together. In another instance, I had heard of an entire crew that was fired because the aircraft owner's wife thought they were getting 'too close.' And there were many other similar anecdotes out there.

I took a long slow sip from my glass and thought about my options. They weren't attractive. Alina's words in my ear notwithstanding, I was going to have to cross the line and attempt to get close enough to her that she would talk to me about who she was and what her plans might be. That would require me to get very close indeed. If Alina was receptive, I might have a chance to learn something. If she wasn't, then I'd probably be fired and sent home with no information at all. Assuming she didn't kill me, of course.

Then there was the act of trying to get close to a woman who might be a serial killer. The whole contract assassin element aside, she still had killed over 50 people, perhaps more. I had known some dangerous women in my time, but none of them had either the bodycount or the cold determination that Alina had shown, assuming she was actually the Shadow.

I reflected back on the last time I was in London and the brief interactions Alina and I had shared. She was ravishingly attractive, and ordinarily, that would be enough for the typical visually-oriented male. I had slept with my fair share of attractive women that I knew little about. But what lay inside people had always mattered to me and if I learned something about a woman that seemed ugly to me, I never looked at her the same way again. Alina was a killer and the brutal core of what lurked inside of her would taint her attractiveness to me, or at least, I hoped it would.

She's a killer. But you are too. The thought appeared in my mind immediately, like it had been hovering there, waiting to jump into my consciousness.

"Yeah, I know," I sighed to myself. "That's what I'm afraid of."

"Is this seat taken?"

Speak of the devil, I thought.

I snapped out of my reverie to see Alina standing before me in a tight black sheath dress that displayed her amazing figure superbly.

"Uh, no," I said.

She smiled at me and delicately slid into the chair immediately to my right. A Dukes bartender appeared out of nowhere and took her drink order.

"Whatever he's having," she said, gesturing to me.

In mere moments, the Dukes Martini Trolley appeared and the bartender produced a classic gin martini with decidedly more flourishes than he had generated when he had made mine several minutes earlier.

"Cheers," Alina said and offered her glass.

I clinked mine lightly against hers.

"Cheers," I replied.

"To another safe trip in your capable hands," Alina said, smiling over the top of her glass. She leaned back in her chair, and angled her body so that she was facing me. "I knew you'd be here." Then she took a sip of her martini and watched my face as her words filled the space between us.

I kept my face impassive as I regarded her and raised my glass to my lips, proud of myself that I could keep my hands steady in the process. While her words could be interpreted one way on the surface, there was a depth of meaning there that was not lost on me.

"Well," I said, "after an overnight flight from the US and an early arrival today, a martini at my favorite bar in London was most welcome this evening. It will help me sleep better tonight. I remember you and I were here the same night a little while ago. I'm flattered you recalled that I liked this place."

I made a slight show of looking around the room. "Are Vladimir, Jean or Abby going to join us?" I asked. "Or perhaps your friend from the other evening?"

She smirked at me. "No," she said. "They didn't know you'd be here. *I* knew you'd be here." She took a slow sip of her martini without taking her eyes off me. "And I think you've been in London for longer than since this morning."

"I can't discuss the business or the accompanying travel arrangements for other clients," I said after a long moment. "I sign confidentiality agreements with them. Just as I signed with the agency that supports your aircraft."

She nodded slowly. "Confidentially is important. But so is trust."

"I agree with both of those statements."

"So what if the objectives of one of your clients conflict with the objectives of another? What do you do then?"

I allowed a slight smile to form on my lips. "I favor the objectives of the client who pays me more. What else?"

She laughed at that. "We're going to get along fine," she said, with twinkles in her eyes. "Just fine indeed."

"So," I said, trying to find exactly the right words, "how does a lowly pilot type like me rate the company of someone like you?" I tilted my head toward her appreciatively. "You could be with anyone you wanted."

"I've taken an interest in you. I've got this feeling there's a lot more to you than meets the eye."

"Not sure how to take that," I said, smiling at her. "Either you don't see much on the surface that's appealing or you find me very mysterious."

She kicked me playfully and giggled at me.

"So you'll pardon my asking," I said. "But is Vladimir busy tonight or something? As a crew member I hardly ever socialize with the passengers of jets I fly and especially not when they are as beautiful as you are. I don't want to get in trouble with him."

She smiled at the compliment but then I saw a few emotions cross her face, just under the surface of her striking features. There was something she wanted to say but knew she could not. After a few moments, she shrugged. "He has business. I am able to do as I wish."

"I see."

"And that frees me up for the entire evening."

Alina crossed her magnificent legs. It took every ounce of discipline I could summon not to look up her dress. "And do not assume that Vladimir makes all the decisions about where the jet goes," she said. "And who is aboard it."

I nodded at her. "You would not be the first significant other to have responsibility for a business jet. I've seen that scenario before."

"So women in charge of things don't bother you or threaten you?"

I shook my head.

"Good," she said. "Then perhaps after these drinks, you'd allow me to take you to dinner?"

##

Dinner was one floor below the bar in the hotel's restaurant and it didn't disappoint. We started with smoked salmon that was sliced so thinly it was diaphanous. The salmon melted in the mouth and there was exactly enough toast to offset it. After sorbet to clear the palate, Alina and I shared a Chateaubriand that was cooked to perfection and came with the appropriate assortment of vegetables and starches accompanying it. Alina ordered a splendid Bordeaux after announcing she was paying for the meal. The wine danced across my tongue between bites of the fork-tender beef. We talked as we ate. She asked me about my history and I gave her an edited version of my childhood, USAF career and work in business aviation since retirement from the service, obviously omitting my labors for the CIA over the last 18 months or so. She, in turn, told me about growing up in the Ukraine and attending the University of Colorado in the US, at which point I complimented her on her accent-less English but I must have had a puzzled look on my face.

"What?" She asked.

"How do we go from growing up in the Ukraine to going to college at UC?"

"Chernobyl," she said.

I sat back in my chair. "Okay, I'm lost now."

"We were very poor in the Ukraine. My father left or died when I was very young. I didn't even know who he was."

"I'm sorry about that."

"Thank you. But it was a good thing because my mother was single when she met my stepfather. He was part of the containment team brought in from the U.S. to deal with the reactor incident after it happened. The Russians didn't have the expertise to assess the damage and seal the site, so they brought in outside help. My step-father was part of the team. My mother was one of the locals hired to cook for them and feed them. She was grateful for the work."

I looked her and smiled, wondering if perhaps I had found the first nugget of information that might reveal who she was. I didn't know how much of what she was saying was a cover story and how much of it was real.

"How did they talk to one another?" I asked. "She spoke Ukrainian or was it Russian and he spoke English, right?"

"Ukrainian and Russian are both East Slavic languages, so they're very similar although there are a few differences. But he spoke Russian because his family was of Russian ancestry and he took Russian as a language in college. It was one of the reasons he got the job."

"I see," I said, making numerous mental notes to relay to Smith and Amrine later. "So when did you move to the U.S.?"

"About 1988. It would have been sooner but it was difficult for him and my mother to get married because they were of different nationalities. He ended up having to sponsor both of us for immigration and then he married her when she got her green card."

"Where did you live?" I asked.

"On a farm outside of Rockford, Illinois. It was my stepfather's family's property but he wasn't into farming. He worked at a nuclear power plant there and my mother tended the farm, not that there was much tending to do. The land was contracted out to commercial farming. We had a few dairy cows and hens. I grew up with fresh milk and eggs every day."

"That's awesome!" I said. "Nothing like fresh from the source. So how much land did you have?"

"About a 1,000 acres or so. Plenty of room for a young girl to run and play. I was quite the tomboy, and that delighted my stepfather. He and I spent hours walking the land together and hunting. He taught me to shoot."

I took another sip of the Bordeaux to give me some time to process what I had just heard and to decide where to direct the conversation from here. The shooting thing was a revelation but it was also possible that she was baiting me.

"So how are your parents doing?" I said, changing the subject. "Do ever get back to Rockford to see them?"

Her eyes quickly dropped to her drink and a sheen of moisture suddenly appeared on them. "They both died a few years ago from cancer caused by the radiation. It devastated me."

Instinctively, I reached across the table and placed my hand on hers. "I'm so sorry. I lost both of my parents to cancer many years ago. It still hurts and it still sucks."

Alina nodded and raised her eyes to mine. "Thank you. You're probably one of the few people I've told who understands." She searched my eyes for a second and then looked directly into them as she spoke. "Did their deaths make you angry?"

I shrugged. "If I was angry, I guess I was angry at them. They both smoked like chimneys and they both got a strain of cancer that only occurs in smokers. My mom lost all of her hair in the chemotherapy and radiation treatment, felt sorry for herself because men weren't flocking all around her and drank herself to death. My dad wasn't around much when I was growing up but we were starting to form a bond when he died." I squeezed her hand. "I'm a little jealous of the relationship you had with your stepdad. I never had anything like that."

She smiled sadly but in her eyes, I saw a bitter anger that startled me.

"I take it you were angry?"

She nodded once, a single, harsh move of her lovely chin. "They were taken from me," she said. "They should have lived many more years."

There was a distinct pause after her last words like there should have been more to follow. Like there was another sentence or thought that was left unfinished.

And I will have my revenge.

The thought materialized in my mind like it had grown there. For a moment, I couldn't decide whether she had said it or I had thought it. But regardless, I knew those were the next words. I was certain of it.

Jesus. This has all got to be tied in somewhere. My stack of mental notes for Smith and Amrine continued to grow. I just hope I remembered them all.

It was time to lighten the conversation.

"So how did an Illinois girl wind up going to college in Colorado?"

Her eyes turned from darkness to sparkles in an instant and she smiled modestly. "I was a recruited athlete."

"Wow! What sport? Downhill?"

"No," she said, eyeing me carefully as she continued to hold my hand. "Biathlon. I was a rifle champion. All I needed to learn to do was cross-country ski."

Holy shit, I thought. I felt a cold chill creep up my back as I nodded respectfully to her.

"Very cool," I said, proud that my voice was rock steady. "So how did you do?"

"Pretty well, I guess," Alina said, still scrutinizing me intensely. "I was part of the U.S. Olympic team in 1998."

George Phillips' words echoed in my ears. *"...rifle shooter, no doubt, but he's never been trained as a sniper. You need to tell your boys they need to look for target shooting champions, Olympic rifle shooters, that sort of thing."*

I felt a chill on the back of my neck. I was looking at the Shadow. There was absolutely no doubt in my mind.

"That's remarkable," I said, probably just a fraction of a second too late. "Did you get a medal?"

She looked at me for a moment before answering. I had the distinct impression she had gleaned something from my behavior that was telling.

Alina released my hand and swirled her wine before taking a long sip. "I didn't medal," she said, at last, eyeing me over the top of her glass. "My shooting was perfect but my skiing wasn't quite on par with the Europeans. I had only been skiing for a few years. They had been doing it their entire lives. I missed the bronze by three-tenths of a second. Gold was only a second above that."

"I feel honored to be in your company," I said, bowing my head to her. "That's pretty darn respectable. The closest I've come cross country skiing is a Nordic track machine. I shot expert with the M-16 in the Air Force but the course wasn't very demanding. Not sure I could hit a damn thing with a rifle these days and the only kind of skiing I'm interested in is the kind where gravity does the work for me."

Alina smiled at me and her eyes sparkled once again. "Thank you," she said, watching me with the smile still in place. "Maybe we could shoot against one another some time."

"Not sure how well I'd do there," I said, looking right back at her. "But I'd try to give you a run for your money."

"It could be fun."

"Yes, it could be."

The waiter arrived to clear the dinner dishes and the moment dissolved. Dessert followed dinner and whiskey followed dessert. Alina steered the conversation to my background and that's where it stayed for the rest of the evening in spite of multiple attempts on my part to turn it to hers. She was curious, asking multiple questions about my career in the Air Force and my journey in business aviation. She seemed particularly interested in the life of a contract pilot and the different aircraft and people I had seen. She was flattering and laughed in all the right places when I related anecdotes from those situations. Occasionally, as we spoke, her hands would brush mine on top of the table or one of her legs would rub against mine under it. Sometimes the contact would linger, other times it would be momentary, but intense. It was a classic seduction technique, a shortcut to breaking through the barrier of the intimacy of touch.

And I was completely falling for it. The electrical charge that passed between us when she touched me was powerful and intoxicating and terrifying. I felt drawn to her in a way that I never experienced.

She rose to go to the restroom and I respectly rose with her. As she walked away, I watched her hips move under the tight fabric of the dress and took a deep breath. Then I swigged the dregs of the Bordeaux that remained in my wine glass.

"So much for you being turned off by what she is," I muttered to myself.

When she returned to the table, I walked her upstairs so that she could to catch a taxi to her hotel. I tried to keep my distance from her, but as we walked, our hands brushed, and she enfolded her fingers with mine. I felt my heartbeat increase and the typical schoolboy butterflies in my stomach.

We walked out to the curb in front of the hotel and waited silently for a few moments as the taxi the doorman had called made its way to the hotel. Alina released my hand and drew herself up alongside me, apparently snuggling for warmth. I put my arm around her waist and she pushed herself against me even further. I didn't feel the coolness of the London evening at all. My cheeks were flushed and the blood was racing in my veins.

Her taxi pulled up to the curb and I disengaged myself to open the door for her. She reached up to me, put a hand around the back of my neck and pulled my mouth to hers. Her lips were soft and full and while the kiss was brief in duration, it was intense with promise.

Then she was into the cab and gone.

I stood on the sidewalk and watched the taxi's taillights recede. I should have felt a sense of accomplishment. I had successfully taken the first steps to get close to Alina and get the information the CIA needed. Yet as my head cleared, I realized it wasn't that simple. The odds were high that I might be playing right into her hands, but that didn't scare me. I had been there before and triumphed in the end. The problem was that I couldn't believe the intensity of the attraction I had for her. It was deeper than mere physical attraction; deeper and darker, and I had a sickening sensation about the source of it.

"Damn it, Pearce," I uttered into the noisy London night, "what the fuck have you gotten yourself into?"

CHAPTER SIXTEEN

Tuesday, November 2
1000 Hours Local Time
London City Airport (EGLC)
London, United Kingdom.

The London sky had cleared and presented a beautiful azure blue as I did the exterior inspection on the Falcon 7X. I looked at the nose wheel and wheel well with the flashlight I had taken from the cockpit. Once I was satisfied there, I proceeded to look at the nose of the aircraft and ensure there were no blockages in the four "smart probes" mounted on both sides of the jet's sleek nose.

After making my way along the fuselage, around the right wing, and inspecting the right main landing gear, I climbed into the service compartment to check the hydraulic reservoirs and the "S" duct. The 7X is a tri-engine aircraft and the number 2 or "center" engine, has its inlet above the fuselage at the rear of the jet, but the engine itself is mounted in the fuselage, so the air duct that routes air to the engine is shaped somewhat like an "S." Unlike the number 1 and number 3 engines, which are pylon-mounted on the left and right sides of the aircraft respectively, the fan blades of number 2 engine are not visible from the outside of the aircraft. I opened the access door to the "S" duct and inspected the number 2 engine carefully. Every time I opened that door and stuck my head up into the inlet I had fleeting memories of the scene from *The Omen* movie where David Warner's character had his head sliced off by an errant sheet of glass.

But my head remained stubbornly attached to my body, and I retreated into the service compartment again and secured the door. Then I completed the rest of my inspection of the aircraft and climbed the airstair to the cabin.

"You're cleared to start the APU, Jean," I said as I reached the top of the stairs. "Apparently it's still an airplane."

"Mais bien sur!" he said and began to run the checklist.

I turned to the galley and spoke to Abby. "Can I help you load the catering or ice or anything?"

She shook her head, and the red hair swirled around her. "No, but thanks very much for asking. Got it all under control. It's only Alina today, and she just wanted a light salad for the trip to Gstaad."

"Vladimir isn't flying today?"

Abby shook her head again. "He's going to catch up with her later. In Scotland, I think."

"I guess I should have looked at the itinerary that was emailed to me yesterday," I said sheepishly.

She smiled at me. "No worries," she said. "That's what Jean and I are here for."

I made my way to the cockpit as the Jean started the auxiliary power unit or APU, essentially a small jet engine mounted inside the aft fuselage of the jet that provided power for the avionics and cabin as well as air for starting the engines. Jean was in the right seat, which was a bit puzzling since he was the lead pilot on the aircraft.

"Hi, Jean!" I said. "Ca va?"

"Ca va bien!"

"So why aren't I sitting on the right side pushing buttons and raising the gear."

He looked over his shoulder and smiled at me. "Mademoiselle Alina, she says you are to fly ze jet. Apparently she wants to see your skills again."

I laughed. "Such as they are. She must be easily impressed!"

"Perhaps not," Jean said, with an admiring expression on his face. "She is Russian after all, n'est pas?"

"I guess," I said as I slid into the pilot's seat, "but I think that makes her more a of a glutton for punishment than demanding. Especially with my landings."

I seated myself and began strapping in.

The APU reached 100% RPM, and its generator kicked on. Jean slowly and deliberately activated the various power allocation switches on the overhead panel and turned on the interior lights. He then used his cursor control device and selected the system synoptic page on the lower center display unit and called up the test page.

"So we're going to Gstaad airport today? Isn't that the one with a tiny little runway in between two big mountains?"

Jean nodded as he ran the various system tests. "And zen we get to fly to Samedan, the highest airport in Europe."

"Hopefully the runway is longer."

"About 2100 feet longer or so. You will have to read a short briefing and take a quiz online while we're on the ground in Gstaad to be legal to land at Samedan."

I looked over at him. "Wait a minute. Gstaad has the shorter runway, but I don't need to take a test to land there?"

Jean shook his head as he clicked on another test key. "C'est fou; it is crazy. But zat is Switzerland."

I finished clicking the seat belts in place in the rotary buckle and reached behind my head for the shoulder straps.

"What the hell is she going there for?" I asked. "What the hell is she going to either place for?"

Jean shrugged. He called up the weather radar display in his pilot display unit so he could run the weather radar test and then looked over at me after he activated it.

"Who knows?" he asked. "Perhaps lunch with a girlfriend or somezing. It is too early for ski season."

I nodded. "So it would seem."

Jean finished the self-tests a few minutes later. He rose from his seat to exit the cockpit. "She should be here anytime, so I will go in and wait for her. You must download the flight plan and program the aircraft for departure. We will not get our clearance until just before engine start, but you can use ze departure procedure to get an idea of ze settings."

I nodded at him.

He reached the cockpit entryway and turned back to me. "You are ze captain, but I would recommend you set climb mode with V-two plus 10 in manual speed," he said. "We must maintain v-two plus 10 to 3,000 feet."

"Oh yes," I said, nodding my head. "And we climb out with reduced power as well, right?"

"Qui. About 15% less than maximum. I will set zat for you at 400 feet AGL."

"Got it," I said. "I had the London City course when I got typed in the jet, but of course I forgot all that departure stuff until now."

"Too much whiskey, n'est pas?"

I looked back at him. "That and martinis!"

Jean put on his jacket and walked down the airstair. I turned to my tasks in the cockpit. I downloaded the flight plan using the aircraft datalink and loaded it into the flight management system or FMS. Then I verified the waypoints along the route with the printed version of the plan that Jean had left in the cockpit. Once that was done, I made the necessary entries in the FMS system for the enroute portion of the flight plan as well as for the departure from London City.

I finished programming the jet and looked up just in time to see Alina exiting the doors of the executive terminal with Jean at her side, pulling a roller bag behind him and carrying a small hangup bag. Alina looked radiant in a tight white leather jacket with matching calf-high boots and white designer jeans that hugged her body. She had a worn denim backpack over her shoulder and carried something that looked like a poster tube. She looked up at the cockpit as she approached the plane and smiled at me. Then, Jean headed to the back of the aircraft to stow her bags, and she came up the airstair. A few moments later, she entered the vestibule behind me, and I heard her and Abby exchange greetings.

"Another one of your landscape paintings?" Abby asked.

"Apparently people seem to like them," Alina answered in a self-deprecating tone. "I can't understand why."

"Well from the one I've seen you've got real talent," Abby said. "I'm not surprised at all."

"You're very kind," Alina said.

I heard her come forward to the cockpit. As I turned my head to greet her, her lips found mine and her right hand caressed the side of my face. Unexpectedly, I felt my heart begin pounding in my chest, and I felt myself stirring below the waist. Our lips parted, and she eyed me at close range for a few seconds.

"If you get us to Gstaad and St. Moritz safely, I'll buy you dinner tonight," she whispered. "And who knows what may happen after that."

She winked at me and smiled. Then she left the cockpit. As I watched her superb ass retreat toward the cabin, I felt the oddest combination of emotions I had ever experienced. There was keen anticipation about what could occur to be sure. But there was also a distinct feeling of deep, dark, foreboding dread – like I'd be walking into a place from which I could never completely escape.

"Damn," I muttered to myself.

Jean climbed the airstair and entered the jet a few moments later. "We are ready for departure?" he asked.

"Mais bien sur!" I answered, over my shoulder.

"Bon!" he said, pushing the DOOR LIFT button just inside the cockpit on the upper left panel. The main entry door's hydraulic motored whined as it powered the heavy door up into rthe etracted position and I heard the characteristic thump as Jean engaged the door's locking handle.

"The door, she is shut," Jean said.

"The light, he is out," I replied.

Jean chuckled as he made his way into the cockpit and seated himself. "You are quite ze American smart ass today," he said with a smirk on his face.

"Everyone has to be good at something."

Jean strapped in and donned his headset. After a quick check of the intercom to make sure we could hear each other, I briefed him on the current airport information and walked him through the departure settings I had programmed into the jet's avionics. He nodded when I had finished the briefing.

"We are ready for engine start, n'est pas?"

I nodded in response.

Jean keyed the mic button next to his cursor control device on the center console.

"London City Ground, Charlie 0622 Bravo, ready for engine start with information echo."

"Charlie 0622 Bravo, City Ground, cleared via the Dover 5 Uniform departure, maintain 3,000 feet, squawk 1454."

Jean read back the clearance, and we ran the BEFORE STARTING ENGINES checklist. I started the engines in the usual 2, 3, 1 order and Jean and I performed our portions of the after engine start flows. We then accomplished the digital flight control checks and finished by running the AFTER START checklist to make sure we weren't missing anything. Everything was appropriately set.

"Ready to taxi?" Jean asked.

"You bet," I said.

"City Ground, Charlie 0622 Bravo, taxi."

"Charlie 0622 Bravo, City Ground, can you take off within the next 5 minutes?" the controller asked.

Jean looked over at me, and I nodded at him.

"Affirmative, Charlie 0622 Bravo," Jean answered.

"Charlie 0622 Bravo, taxi up to and hold short of holding point Alpha and monitor the tower on 118.075," the controller said. "Be prepared for an immediate takeoff after the next arrival."

"Up to and hold short of point Alpha, Charlie 0622 Bravo," Jean repeated.

"This won't take long," I said as I advanced the 7X's three power levers.

"It never does," Jean said as he called up the TAXI checklist on the ECL, "I wish all airports ran as well as zis one."

Jean ran the checklist which consisted of only three items and then tabbed down to the LINE-UP checklist.

"Care to check your brakes?" I asked him.

He nodded and extended his feet to make contact with the brake/rudder pedals.

"My brakes," he said.

He pushed forward on the pedals slightly, and we felt the aircraft slow just a bit.

"My brakes, zay are good," he said. "Your brakes."

"My brakes," I replied. "Here comes the TR."

I pulled the thrust reverser handle on the center engine back as I kept my eyes on the ramp/taxiway in front of us.

"Transit," Jean said, looking down at the center engine display on his PDU. "Deploy." The words were displayed successively on the N1 gauge in the display.

I pushed the TR handle back into the stowed position.

"Transit," Jean said. He waited a few seconds and then announced, "Stowed."

"Jean, per our briefing, I'll do a static takeoff and we'll use normal procedures and call-outs until we get to 400 feet and then you retard the power 15% to about 83 percent N1 RPM per engine. We'll leave the flaps deployed and climb out at V2 plus 10 until we level at 3000 feet. At that point, I'll ask for FMS speeds, and when we reach VFR, I'll ask you to clean the wing. After that, we'll be flying normally. Any questions so far?"

He shook his head.

"That's if everything goes normally. If bad things happen, before 80 knots, we'll abort the takeoff for anything that either of us doesn't like. Just call 'abort, abort, abort, ' and I'll get on the brakes and TRs. Please back me up on the airbrakes. Between 80 knots and V1, we'll abort for an engine fire, failure, loss of directional control, TR deployment, runway incursion or any red CAS message. A loss of directional control is defined as one of the main gear crossing the centerline of the runway headed in the opposite direction. After V1, we'll take the emergency into the air, climb to 3,000 feet and level off before running any checklists. I'll fly and talk on the radio, and you can run the checklist. If we have to land immediately, my vote is not to come back here but go to Stansted, which is very close and has a longer runway and normal approaches. Questions or comments?"

"Non," Jean answered. "Good briefing."

I slowed the aircraft to a stop as we approached holding point Alpha. "I'm ready for takeoff when you are," I said.

Jean hit the SWAP button on the control panel just under the glare shield in front of him and switched between the ground and tower frequencies. Then he dialed the departure control frequency into the ready position below the tower frequency, all the while listening to the tower frequency to ensure he didn't step on anyone else's transmissions when he spoke.

"City Tower, Charlie 0622 November ready to go, runway 09," he announced after a few moments.

"Charlie 0622 November, City Tower, hold short, arriving traffic."

"Charlie 0622 November holding short."

As if on cue, a Boeing 737 roared into our field of vision from our left, water vapor streaming from the wings as the pilot arrested the 1,400 feet per minute descent rate generated by the steep 5.5-degree glide path and forced the wings to generate several tons of induced lift in the process. The low pressure across the tops of the wings condensed the humid air into trails of water vapor, and the trails went by us, a few hundred feet away, as the big jet settled to a landing on the airport's short 4998-foot runway. I had a quick mental flashback of seeing those same trails of vapor coming from the wings of an F-16 I was fighting a little over a year ago at an island base far, far away. Twin puffs of smoke were emitted as the 737's main gear made contact with the runway and the thrust reversers deployed from the jet's two engines immediately.

"Charlie 0622 Bravo, City Tower, line up and wait, be ready for immediate departure."

Jean acknowledged the clearance and began the actions necessary to prepare the jet for takeoff as I advanced the 7X's three throttles to take the runway.

"Line-up checklist," I said.

"Slats and flaps," Jean said.

"SF1," I answered, verifying the slats were deployed and the flaps were in the number one position.

"Trims," he said.

I glanced down at the trim indicators for the elevator, ailerons, and rudder. All were in the neutral position.

"Checked," I replied.

"Landing lights," Jean said.

I glanced up at the landing light switches. Both were in the PULSE position where the two lights, located on opposite sides of the fuselage, blinked in an alternating pattern. I also glanced at the anti-collision light switch and noted the switch was dark, indicating the strobe lights were flashing as well.

"Pulse for now," I answered.

"Transponder," Jean said.

I glanced down at my PDU and saw TA/RA displayed just below the stack of radio displays. The transponder was ready to provide air traffic control position and altitude data for our aircraft and ready to provide traffic collision avoidance systems, both on our jet and other aircraft near us, the information needed to avoid collisions.

"TA, RA," I said as I turned the Falcon 90 degrees to the right tightly, to line up along the runway and utilize as much of the scarce surface before us as I could.

On the runway in front of us, the 737 had made a 180-degree turn and was taxiing towards the runway exit at the far end of the commercial ramp, about 1,500 feet down the runway.

"Damn," I said. "That's a lot of airplane to take into a small airport like this one."

I saw Jean nod in my peripheral vision. "Qui," he said. "I am very glad we are in zis aircraft and not zat one."

Just as the 737 began to turn off the runway and onto the commercial ramp, the radio crackled once again.

"Charlie 0622 Bravo, cleared for takeoff."

"Cleared for takeoff, Charlie 0622 Bravo," Jean answered as he toggled the landing light switches to the STEADY position.

"Ready?" I asked Jean.

"Mais qui," he said. "Push it up."

I advanced the throttles smoothly and steadily up to the maximum position and waited for the engines to stabilize. The three Pratt and Whitney 307 engines spooled up in typical fashion, somewhat sluggishly initially and then more rapidly as the N1 or fan RPM approached the top of the scale. In a few seconds, they were stabilized at about 98% RPM each.

"Power's up," I said.

"Three good engines," Jean replied.

I smoothly released the brakes, and the 7X leaped forward, eager for flight.

"One, two, three airspeeds," Jean said, his eyes scanning the airspeed tapes in my pilot display unit or PDU, the standby PDU and his PDU, all of which were fed by separate air data systems.

The airspeed tape in the HUD in front of my face accelerated rapidly.

"Eighty knots," Jean said after only a moment or two.

The black pavement of the small runway was flashing underneath us, and the dotted centerline was a blur as it passed below the nose. I could see the end of the runway rushing towards us.

"V1," Jean said.

I took my right hand off the throttles and placed it on my cursor control device, just behind and to the left of them. Once V1 was attained, we weren't aborting the takeoff no matter what happened, so the hand off the throttles was a safety measure to ensure that if an engine failed or something else occurred, the pilot wouldn't pull the power back inadvertently or subconsciously.

"Rotate," Jean said a few seconds later. "And do not be gentle about it."

I applied back pressure to the 7X's sidestick controller, and the nose rapidly pitched up towards the dull London sky. The heavy jet seemed to jump from the ground and as I felt the wings take to load of the aircraft, I continued to rotate the nose upward to pull the flight path marker in the HUD to the steering cue that rested at about 12 degrees nose high.

"Positive rate of climb," Jean said.

"Gear up," I commanded.

He pushed the landing gear handle up with his left hand and watched the gear display in his PDU to ensure the main gear and nose gear retracted normally.

"400 feet," he said a moment later. "My throttles."

"Your throttles," I said.

He reached for the throttles and slowly retarded them until all three were stabilized at about 83% RPM.

"Power is set," he said. "Your throttles."

"My throttles," I said.

The 7X settled into the reduced power climb and seemed to claw at the sky as it ascended. The lateral navigation system began to command a turn to the south, and I banked the jet up to the right to follow the steering cue. The big jet seemed somewhat frozen in space with a hefty nose up attitude due to the continued flap deployment and low airspeed alongside the lower power setting. The wispy clouds of the English overcast started to fly by us and envelop portions of the wings and jet itself. The gray expanse of the Thames river began to recede, and the urban sprawl that was southeastern London became less and less visible as the jet flew into the dark clouds. In moments, we were surrounded by gray mist. I concentrated on keeping the flight path marker in the steering cue as we continued the turn towards Dover and maintained the climb. I glanced at the altitude tape in the HUD.

"ALTITUDE!" the 7X's warning system announced.

"Two thousand for three thousand," I said.

Jean nodded. "One thousand to level," he said.

Even as the gray mist went by us, I could feel my eyes beginning to squint, and I noticed the darkness of the mist was waning and the clouds were becoming more white than gray.

"Thin layer," I said subconsciously.

"Mais oui," Jean said.

The jet's steering began to command a level off as we approached 3,000 feet and I gently applied forward pressure on the sidestick to push the nose down.

"I'll take FMS speeds, Jean," I said.

He reached over to the speed selector on the guidance panel in front of us and toggled the speed selector from manual to FMS. The speed window changed from the 132 knots, which had been our V2 plus 10 speed, to a series of dashes, indicating the flight management system now controlled our speed. As the jet leveled, it began to accelerate.

"Auto-throttles," I said.

Jean punched the A/T button in front of me, and the jet's performance computer took control of the jet's throttles and pushed them forward to push the aircraft faster.

"Above VR," Jean said a few moments later.

"Clean the wing," I responded.

Jean hit the lever that retracted the 7X's flaps and slats, and the slat/flap indicator in my PDU read CLEAN after a few seconds. The jet seemed to settle into normal flight, and the auto-throttles continued to accelerate it to 250 knots, the standard speed below 10,000 feet.

"Autopilot," I commanded.

Jean hit the autopilot button on the guidance panel, and my PDU registered its actuation with AP indicated in the top center of the display.

"Whew," I said, turning to him. "That happened quickly!"

He nodded with a look of satisfaction on his face. "Tres bon!" He said. "You did well!"

"Must have been the great set up," I replied.

Eventually, we were handed off to London Control and climbed to high altitude for the flight across the English Channel and France. The flight across that portion of Europe was busy and quick, as flights there typically were. But the weather cleared as we crossed into France and the deep green of the European countryside spread out below us. Soon, we could see the snow-capped peaks of the Alps in the distance, and shortly after that, we were descending over southeastern France, toward Lake Geneva and southwestern Switzerland.

Even though the flight was short, I had expected Alina to make an appearance in the cockpit as was her typical fashion but apparently, that wasn't going to happen on this flight. As we were defending through 30,000 feet, Abby came forward to ask if we wanted a bottle of water or anything before landing. After Jean and I had both politely refused, Jean asked her the typical question business jet pilots ask a flight attendant.

"Everything okay in ze back?" he asked.

Abby nodded. "She's studying a folder or something," she said. "She's very engrossed. You know how she gets."

Jean nodded. "Can't imagine what keeps her attention," he said.

I felt a slight pull in the back of my gut. I had an idea what it might be.

"Zo," Jean said a few moments later. "We have talked about the landing in Gstaad but let us go over it one more time."

I nodded at him.

"You will need to kick ze autopilot off as we come through about 10,000 feet. The airport is at about 3,300 feet MSL, but we will have to fly up ze mountain valley manually while we descend to get zere. We need to try to find ze runway as soon as possible so that Swiss radar will clear us for ze visual approach. If we delay reporting ze field in sight, zay may keep us up higher for a longer time and zat will make the approach much more difficult."

I nodded again. I was familiar with the need to get the runway in sight early to fly a more stabilized approach to a mountain airport. I had flown several charter flights into Colorado's Aspen airport and if you couldn't pick up the field by about 4,000 feet above it and 15 miles away, the approach could become very challenging indeed.

"Since ze winds are favoring runway 08, Swiss radar will probably descend us over Lake Geneva and vector us east. Eventually, we will descend into the valley where ze village of Chateau d'Oex is. Ze airport lies over a small ridge at the end of the valley. You will have to make a slight right turn and zen a greater left turn to align with ze runway as you descend on to your final approach to ze field. You will have to get very close to ze ridge on ze final phase of the approach, so if ze ground prox gives you a momentary warning, you can disregard it if you have a clear view of ze end of the runway. Once we land, don't worry about ze brakes. Get ze nosewheel down, brake hard and let ze anti-skid stop ze jet."

"Sounds good," I said. "We'll see if I can make all that happen." I looked over at him. "3,500 feet of runway, right?"

Jean moved his head from side to side, communicating a degree of ambiguity. "About 4,600 feet of pavement," he said. "But only about 3,500 usable for landing due to ze displaced threshold."

"Roger that," I said.

French air traffic control handed us off to Swiss radar as we approached Lake Geneva. As we approached it from the northwest, the lake appeared as a crescent of bright blue water nestled into the large valley with white fields and surrounded by snow-capped Alps. As I looked to the right, I could the gray shapes of Geneva's buildings and the main runway of its international airport at the lake's southwestern-most point. I had flown several approaches into that airport, and the procedures tended to be somewhat challenging for they required steep descent gradients and decreases in airspeed concurrently, an aerodynamic combination that was not possible without drag devices like air brakes or flaps deployed.

"Charlie 0622 Bravo, Swiss Radar, Descend and maintain flight level 100. Turn left heading 070."

"Charlie 0622 Bravo copies," Jean said into his mic. "Out of flight level 200 for 100. Left to 070."

"Here we go," I said as I turned the heading knob to 070.

The big jet gracefully banked up and began the left turn.

Jean nodded and adjusted the altitude selector. "Flight level 100 set."

I glanced down to my PDU to confirm that the flight director has taken the input. 10000 was displayed in the altitude selector box on the upper right portion of the display. "I see one zero zero," I replied.

Jean pointed toward the eastern shore of Lake Geneva. "I would hurry ze descent," he said. "It would be good if we were at flight level one hundred by the end of ze lake."

I nodded in response as I rolled the manual descent knob on the guidance panel to command 2,500 feet per minute in the descent. I glanced down to the waypoint list in the upper middle display unit. "About 12 miles from the edge of the lake to the airport?"

"Oui," Jean said. "And we must lose about 7500 feet in zose 12 miles while not running into any of ze mountains surrounding the airport or on ze way in."

"We'll get dirty as soon as we get down," I said. "So what's the terrain differential between the airport and the mountains around it?"

Jean moved his left hand from side to side in a gesture of approximation. "Ze Alps are not zat tall in this part of Switzerland," he said. "Not like zay are further south where ze Matterhorn is. Le Rubli overlooks ze airport, and he is only about 7,500 feet. But the airport is at 3,300 feet, so the differential is just over 4,000 feet."

"That's respectable," I said.

I was watching the airspeed increase in the HUD in front of me. As it approached three hundred knots, I reached down to the air brake handle and pulled it back to the first notch. The 7X began to vibrate as the panels extended on each wing and the aircraft's acceleration was abated.

The blue waters of Lake Geneva spread out before us as the 7X pitched over further to maintain the descent rate I had commanded with the increased drag from the air brakes. We were about halfway across the lake, and the snow-capped Alps in front of us presented a horizon of craggy peaks, draped in white and ringing the azure sea below.

"Wow!" Alina's voice said from behind us. "What a view!"

"I'll say," I whispered, looking at the scene in front of me.

"Do you guys mind if I sit up here again?" Alina asked. "We've been in here a few times before, but Vlad has always wanted me to sit in back with him."

I looked across the cockpit at Jean.

"Mais certainment!" Jean said. "Abby, can you get Alina strapped in please?"

"Of course," Abby said.

"ALTITUDE!" the 7X alerted us that there were one thousand feet remaining to our selected altitude.

"One-one-zero for one-zero-zero," I said.

"One thousand to level," Jean replied.

The 7X leveled off gracefully, and I left the speed brakes extended to slow us down. I dialed 190 knots in the speed command window on the guidance panel. Behind me, I could sense that Alina was settled into her seat and watching the terrain in front of us.

The mountains were much closer now, and I could see the entrance to valley that led to Gstaad-Saanen airport in the distance. As I glanced down at my PDU, I saw much the same depiction in the synthetic vision system in the display. Synthetic vision was part of the upgraded EASy II avionics system. It used data from the terrain avoidance database to construct a visual representation of the terrain and was amazingly accurate. In the distance, where the airport was, a cyan-colored runway was presented on the depiction, with a long line of cyan dots or "breadcrumbs" leading to it.

"Jean," I said. "We're idiots."

"You are just now discovering zis?" he said, smiling at me.

I pointed down to my PDU. "We don't need Swiss radar to find the field. You've already programmed waypoints to get us there, and we can use the synthetic vision to get us to the runway. Let's just cancel and go VFR. I think two fighter pilots can find their way up a valley to an airport with this kind of technology."

"Tres bon!" he said. "Main bien sur! Why did I not think of zis?"

"Is this the only one of your 7X's that has the EASy II upgrade?" I asked.

He nodded.

"You probably haven't had this when you've come in here before," I said.

He nodded again. "C'est vrai." Then he keyed the mic button on his cursor control device. "Swiss Radar, Charlie 0622 Bravo would like to cancel IFR and proceed VFR to Gstaad."

The controller didn't pause a moment. "Charlie 0622 Bravo, cancellation received, squawk VFR. Saanen altimeter is 1022 hectopascals. Good day."

"Wow," I said. "Seems like he couldn't get rid of us soon enough."

"Zis is a very busy corner of the country with ze traffic into Geneva," Jean said. "We are also under some of ze arrivals into Milan. He has plenty to do."

"Can you give me direct to Chateau d-Oex?" I asked. And plug in an altitude of about 5,500 feet there so I can get on some kind of vertical profile."

Jean nodded and set work with his cursor control device. In a few moments, there was a cyan line on the navigation display between our position and Chateau d-Oex.

"L nav is available," Jean said.

I hit the LNAV button the guidance panel, and the 7X corrected its course a few degrees to follow the command. As the airspeed decreased through 200 knots, I retracted the speed brakes.

"I'll take SF1 Jean, and you can set 5,500 feet in the altitude window."

"Roger," he said.

Jean rolled the altitude selector to 5500 and moved the flap handle to the SF1 position.

I pushed the AUTO DIS button on my sidestick.

AUTOPILOT! the 7X warning system announced.

The jet was in my hands now.

"Jean, please path me down to intercept 5,500 feet over Chateau d'Oex so I can have some idea of how I'm doing on the descent."

Jean rolled the vertical command knob downward. On the vertical profile below the navigational display, a magenta line appeared. He continued to roll the knob down until the magenta line intersected the altitude label over the Chateau d-Oex waypoint. In my HUD, a steering cue appeared that gave me both lateral and vertical guidance to the waypoint. If I kept the flight path marker over the top of the steering cue, I'd fly right to the waypoint and get there at the right altitude. But I'd probably hit a mountain on the way down, so I kept my course to left of the steering for now.

"Jean I'm going to slowly descend just to the left of these two peaks in front of us then turn toward Chateau d'Oex and steepen up the rate of descent. We'll stay at SF1 for now, but I have a feeling we're going to have to configure in a hurry when the time comes."

I saw him nod in my peripheral vision. He was entranced by the snow-covered wonderland in front of us, just as I was. We were descending into one of the most stunning areas in Europe and the beauty surrounding us made it difficult to find words to describe it. I kept the flight path marker in the HUD clear of any terrain and maintained the commanded descent rate of about 1,000 feet per minute.

Jean pointed out in front of the aircraft. "Do you see zis ridge in front us that comes north out of ze easternmost of ze two peaks?"

"I do," I answered.

"Just beyond it is the village of Rosiniere," he said. "As soon as you see ze lake by ze town, start to increase ze descent."

"Wilco," I answered.

We crossed over the eastern shore of the lake, and I edged by the first of two peaks.

"Zat first peak is Rochers de Naye," Jean said. "Ze second is Dent de Corjon."

The mountains were still lower than we were but the terrain was rising toward us as we proceeded east. I could see a building of some sort and a few squat cylindrical shapes nearby near the top of the first peak.

"Interesting buildings over there," I said.

"Somezing with ze Swiss self-defense force I am sure," Jean said. "Zay have stuff all over ze Alps."

The first peak was lower than the second, and because it was early in the winter, patches of green showed through the snow near the crest and became more prominent as the elevation decreased into the valley before us.

"Zis is a good rate of descent," Jean said, looking over at me briefly. "Keep it coming down just like zis."

I nodded, noting that my altitude was decreasing through about 9,000 feet.

There was no activity or sign of life at all on the top of Dent de Corjon as we passed by it a few moments later. This peak was slightly higher than its predecessor and had a much deeper blanket of snow on top of it and the surrounding ridges.

"Zhere is ze lake next to Rosiniere," Jean said.

I was already turning the aircraft to pull the flight path marker down the valley to the right of us and toward Chateau d'Oex. I pushed forward on the sidestick slightly to increase the rate of descent and reached back to deploy the air brake to the first position to ensure we didn't accelerate past flap limiting airspeed. Per my usual technique, I kept my right hand on the air brake handle, in the event I needed to close them or open them further and also to preclude my forgetting they were deployed. As I rested my hand there, I felt another hand reach up and gently enfold my fingers, give them a slow, gentle squeeze and release them. I glanced back over my right shoulder quickly, to catch a radiant smile from Alina. Her eyes were warm with adoration and admiration, and I felt the connection between us grow in intensity.

The altitude in the HUD was decreasing through 7,000 feet. We were about 2 miles from Chateau d'Oex. Not quite on a normal glide path but not too far off either.

"You want to give them a call, Jean?" I asked.

The Frenchman nodded and entered the frequency for the tower at Gstaad-Saanen airport. "Saanen Tower, Charlie 0622 Bravo, five miles west for landing."

"Charlie 0622 Bravo, Saanen Tower, continue. Number two after a Challenger on two-mile file final. Winds 090 at 4, altimeter 1022 hectopascals."

"Charlie 0622 Bravo copies. We will continue."

"FMS speeds, Jean," I said.

He clicked the speed selector over to FMS speeds and the jet instantly selected 170 knots as the speed for SF1, and the jet slowed another 20 knots.

"Gear down, SF2 Jean."

Jean glanced at his PFD to verify the speed, then he lowered the gear handle and reached back to actuate the flap handle. Instantly, the air noise and vibration of the landing gear deployment reached the cockpit, and the mild roar of the wind became audible. We flew over the town of Chateau d'Oex at 6,000 feet, still descending. The village looked like a scene from a postcard, with a downtown area in the heart of the valley and chalets on the hills going up either side. There were gray puffs of smoke coming from several chimneys, and the streets were active with vehicles and pedestrians.

I looked down at the waypoint display and confirmed it was cycling as we passed the waypoint for the town. I was probably going to lose sight of the runway for a few moments as we reached the far end of the valley and flew over the ridge, so the mileage display had to be accurate.

"About four miles to go," Jean said. "And you are at 5,500 now. Zis is good."

I nodded to acknowledge him, keeping my eyes on the valley ahead as I retracted the air brakes to the closed position.

"Remember to fly it as we briefed it," Jean said. "Follow the valley and make ze turns. It will give you less time to align with ze runway, but you will be better able to keep your speed under control. On zis tiny runway, being on speed is everything."

"Copy that," I said. "Let's go SF3, before landing checks."

Jean actuated the flap switch once again and the flaps deployed to the landing position. The jet slowed to the programmed approach speed of 118 knots. It was in this regime that the 7X earned a good portion of its reputation. For being a large jet with almost 6000 miles of range, it could fly slower than many jets with less range and passenger capacity during the final approach phase.

I glanced up the valley and over the ridge just to the right of the nose in time to see the gray asphalt of the runway. It looked pristine, a strip of pavement surrounded by a field of white snow. And then, as we descended below 5,000 feet, the runway sank slightly below the ridge, the eastern end of it barely visible. We were now about three miles from the airport and about 1700 feet above it. There was still a lot of work to do.

"Landing gear?" Jean asked.

I glanced down at my PDU. "Down, three green," I answered.

"Slat and Flats?" he asked.

"SF1," I replied.

"Before landing checklist is complete," Jean said. He looked out of the windscreen at mountains around us and the runway beyond.

"Zis is looking good. In about another mile, you will start the turn. Keep it coming down."

"Will do," I said.

As we flew down the valley, the ridge between us and the airport decreased in elevation, so I was able to maintain contact with the airport area and the eastern end of the runway. We were still too high above the field and too close to it to be on a normal glide path.

"Just about time for ze turn," Jean said. "You see ze runway?"

"Yes," I answered, but I can only see the far end, not the near end."

"You are not missing that much, zere is a displaced threshold. When you line up, you will still have time to get down."

The ridge down the right side of the valley and in front of us seemed to slope quickly downward as we approached it. Suddenly, I could see the entire length of the runway. I instinctively banked to the right to fly toward the centerline of the runway.

TERRAIN! TERRAIN! the ground proximity warning system announced

I looked into the HUD to make sure the flight path marker was clear of any immediate obstacles.

"We're clear," I said. "At least for now."

Jean nodded. "As we briefed, zat happens every time we come in here."

As he spoke, I was already turning to the left to line up with the centerline of the runway. Even with the painted numbers of the displaced threshold, about one-third of the way down the pavement, I still needed to descend to get on a three-degree glide path. I pushed slightly forward on the side stick and increased the descent rate a little more as I rolled out on the runway centerline.

"Now remember, do not be kind on ze touchdown or on ze brakes," Jean said.

I nodded as I continued to fly. The terrain was reaching up on both sides of the jet as I descended to the runway, like the valley was opening its arms to us. There were no visual approach slope indicator lights on the runway, but I was finally able to put the flight path marker on the threshold of the runway at just about a three-degree angle as indicated by the pitch ladders in the HUD. I disconnected the auto-throttles as we crossed the last tree line short of the runway so.

AUTO-THROTTLES! the 7X warning system announced.

As the pavement of the runway approached the nose of the jet, I slowly began to retard the power to bring the speed back from approach to reference speed, a difference of 5 knots. The pavement went under the nose, and the painted lines of the displaced threshold awaited us about 1,000 feet down the surface. The GPWS then began its usual countdown.

ONE HUNDRED! it said.

I ensured my aim point on the pavement was correct and slowly worked the power back.

FIFTY!

The painted threshold line was just in front of us now as we continued to descend.

FORTY!

The threshold went under the nose, and I checked the power in idle.

THIRTY!

I kept the jet's attitude constant. Ordinarily, I would have begun the flare at this point but today wasn't about a smooth landing. It was about getting stopped.

TWENTY!

I fought myself not to raise the nose. Still too early.

TEN!

Now it was time. I slowly began to lift the nose to kill the jet's descent rate.

FIVE!

The nose was coming up, but I wasn't going to kill all the descent before touchdown. I checked the VVI in the HUD. About 200 feet per minute.

And then we were on the ground with just a light thud as the main gear touched down. I pushed the nose forward and applied the wheel brakes, pushing the toe portion of the pedals nearly to the floor. At the same time, I pulled the thrust reverser lever on the #2 engine aft. The brakes kicked in first, slowing us quickly and immediately. But then the TR deployed and wound up to full thrust, and we decelerated rapidly, stopping well before the end of the painted runway surface with another 1,000 feet to go beyond that for the turnoff to the small ramp area.

"Tres bon!" Jean said, slapping me on the back. "Zat was as good as I have ever seen anyone do zis approach."

I exhaled gratefully. I was astounded by the performance of the 7X once again.

"Amazing jet!" I whispered, more to myself than anyone else.

"Amazing pilot!" Alina said from behind me.

I felt myself begin to flush with embarrassment.

"I guess we just taxi forward to the ramp area down and on the right?" I said to break the moment.

"Oui," Jean said. "I will get us cleaned up and get ze after landing checklist."

A few moments later, we were parked in the small ramp area and had the engines shut down. Even as Jean and I cleaned up the post-shutdown checklist, Alina was unstrapping herself and making her way to the rear of the jet. A few moments later, we had the door of the aircraft open, and Jean and Abby went down the ladder to greet the ground crew. I climbed out of the cockpit to stretch my legs and wait for Alina to deplane.

She collected her backpack and the poster tube and came down the aisle. She blew me a kiss before she reached the door.

"Enjoy your day," I said, my brain struggling for words. "Hope you and your friend have fun."

"I will," she replied, winking at me. "He's just dying to see me."

And then she was gone.

I grabbed a bottle of water from the ice drawer in the galley and retreated to the cabin, anxious to sit and clear my head.

After a long moment, I retrieved my phone from my pocket and texted Smith and Amrine.

WE'RE IN GSTAAD. SHE'S HEADED DOWNTOWN TO SEE A FRIEND WHO IS "DYING" TO MEET HER. I THINK SHE'S GOING AFTER SOMEONE.

SO DO WE, came the response a few minutes later. BUT WE DON'T HAVE ENOUGH EVIDENCE TO SATISFY THE SWISS AND WE DON'T HAVE ANYONE ON THE GROUND THERE. SIT TIGHT. CATCH UP WITH YOU IN ST MORITZ.

ROGER, I replied.

And then I put my head against the seat's leather headrest and gazed out the window at the beautiful Swiss countryside.

And wondered what the hell was going happen next.

For the first time in her career as an assassin, the Shadow was having difficulty concentrating. Her face felt warm and flushed, and her body felt a source of inner heat that she had never experienced. Even though she was shooting from an outside location for this event, she wore only a thin leather jacket and jeans but felt no chill from the cold mountain air around her. She regarded her target area, a balcony on the Gstaad Palace Hotel in the valley below her and it was everything she could do to focus through the eyepiece and project into the shot she was about to make.

The target for today was Gerhard Frober, and he was a departure from the typical targets she had taken in the past. He wasn't an engineer or a governmental official; Frober was a writer, well respected in the arena of international affairs. His family was quite wealthy, and he often used the Gstaad Palace as a writing retreat, and it was from here that some of his most controversial work had been created.

Work that could not be allowed to continue.

Frober was a creature of habit, and he lived by a schedule. If the routine served today, he would step onto his balcony between 1230 and 1245 to smoke his afternoon cigar before returning to his work.

The Shadow glanced at the time display in the reticle of telescopic sight.

1229. Any moment now.

The Shadow again verified the wind, humidity and range readings and re-ran the calculations in the application on her tablet computer. The shot was just over 1,000 meters today, so the tolerances weren't as tight as they had been in London, but precision was still important.

The Shadow felt her loins tingle unexpectedly as she lay on the insulated shooting mat and peered down into the valley. She had not been with a man in a very long time. Not since she was in the American Army, years ago. She had dated a fellow officer for several months, but nothing had come of the relationship. There had only been the shared experience of Army life and sex - no real link or connection.

But she felt something distinctly different with Pearce. There was a connection with him on a primitive and physical level. Like they were the only two creatures of their own, unique species. He was just like her. He could understand her. And she could understand him. They could be happy together.

Without willing it, her thoughts drifted off into fantasy. She had visions of she and Pearce walking a beach together, hand-in-hand, the warm sea caressing their legs as their toes trod the wet sand. Then she saw them in a large bed, surrounded by linen curtains that were waving in the ocean breeze. Their bodies were entangled and their mouths were exploring each other. He was looking down at her, tenderly, lovingly and his hands were gently touching her face and pushing her hair behind her ears. She sighed and closed her eyes.

Sometime later. Moments later. Gerhard Frober bent over to extinguish his cigar out in the ashtray on his balcony.

The Shadow opened her eyes to see the squat, bald man straighten and begin to turn his body to go back indoors. She scrambled to regain a correct shooting posture and center her crosshairs on the target's body. She activated the video feed and hurried to squeeze the trigger.

The weapon fired and 750 grains of .50 caliber projectile went down range.

And missed the target cleanly.

The heavy projectile shattered a pane of glass on the balcony's ornate French doors and disappeared into the darkness beyond.

But the sound stopped Frober's retreat, and he turned to look back across the valley and directly into the Shadow's sight.

The Shadow centered the scope's crosshairs on the center of the flabby chest, inhaled slowly and exhaled half a breath, and then she slowly squeezed the trigger.

The weapon fired again, and this time, the huge bullet found its mark. Flesh, blood, and gore spewed onto the now shattered glass on the ground behind Frober.

Sometimes, depending on the placement of the shot and the physiological shape he/she was in, the target stayed alive for a few seconds after bullet impact. The Shadow had taken to watching those last few moments of expression in the lives of her victims. Sometimes there was disbelief in the dying features, sometimes surprise, and still other times there was sadness as well.

This time, however, as the Shadow watched her target sink to his knees and regarded his face, she saw something there she did not expect.

There was an expression of comprehension and even acceptance. Frober knew why he'd been killed. He even looked like he had been expecting it. But there was something else there that was more troubling on the chubby Swiss face.

Frober was smiling as he died.

CHAPTER SEVENTEEN

Tuesday, November 2
1330 Hours Local Time
Gstaad-Saanen Airport (LSGK)
Saanen, Switzerland

The two hours and fifteen minutes on the ground at the Gstaad-Saanen airport had passed quickly. We had put some fuel on the aircraft to minimize the handling charges levied by the airport authority and had a quick bite of lunch brought to us by our handler. After we had eaten, I pulled out my laptop, connected to the internet through the 7X's satellite communications system and studied the pilot briefing material for our next destination, the Engadin Airport, or Samedan as it was more commonly known. Once I had reviewed the material a few times, I took the online quiz, downloaded the certificate of completion onto my computer and emailed it to Jean. He needed it to complete our landing authorization with the Samedan airport authority.

While billed as Europe's highest airport at 5,600 MSL in elevation, Samedan was going to be quite a bit less challenging to get into than Gstaad-Saanen had been. The airport lay in the middle of a long valley, and the approach and departure paths to the single runway seemed to be relatively clear of terrain. The runway itself was 5,900 feet long, which made the margin of error much greater than where we had just landed. But even with that, flying in the mountains was never routine, and I had no illusions about the amount of work Jean, and I would need to do to get us out of Gstaad and into Samedan. With London City as a starting point on today's itinerary, we were mounting quite the trifecta of challenging European airports.

"Colin?" Jean's voice called to me from the cockpit.

"Yes," I answered.

"Alina just texted me. We need to be ready to leave in 30 minutes."

"Roger that," I said. I hurriedly shut down my laptop and stowed it in my computer bag. Then I came forward to the cockpit, taking a moment to stow my bag in the forward lavatory/closet on the way.

I slid into the left seat while Jean programmed our flight plan into the FMS. The distance to destination was only about 109 nautical miles and would last about 15-20 minutes depending on how much we were vectored by Swiss radar. We'd blast off out of here, immediately climb to FL180 to clear the terrain and get into radar coverage, and then immediately descend to land at Samedan. It was going to be a very quick, action-packed flight. And as was typical with all flights in Europe, we wouldn't get our final ATC clearance until just before starting engines and would have to ensure everything was set up before takeoff during a taxi run that would probably last 2-3 minutes.

"We will make ze initial altitude FL150," Jean said. "But we will set ze takeoff safety altitude at 8,000, so we can clean up ze airplane at a lower altitude."

I nodded. "Makes sense to me."

I opened up the flight management window in the lower center display unit and programmed the pre-takeoff and takeoff settings into it, including setting TOSA at 8,000 feet. Once I had computed the speeds for takeoff and sent them to our PDUs as well as to the HUD, I activated the takeoff mode of the aircraft and ensured everything else was set.

Jean looked over at me. "What are your thoughts for ze takeoff briefing?"

I thought for a moment. "Well, static takeoff obviously and we'll use all the pavement, but up to V1, nothing changes. If we get airborne with an issue, I say we get above the mountains and find a long runway. Like Geneva maybe."

Jean nodded. "Zis works for me."

I glanced out of the cockpit and saw Alina walking onto the ramp through the door of the small executive terminal. In milliseconds, the butterflies had reemerged in my stomach.

Get control of yourself. She's a fucking serial killer and she probably just killed someone. Stay on mission.

"Zat is odd," Jean said. "She did not bring her backpack with her. I hope she will not remember it when we are halfway to Samedan."

I barely heard him. It was like he was talking from the bottom of a barrel. Ignorant of my internal battle, Jean slipped out of the cockpit to greet Alina on the ramp – the duty of every business aviation captain. I remained, struggling to focus on what I needed to do and dreading what the evening might bring. But with the dread came an acute sense of longing that reached deep inside of me.

Jesus, I thought. *What the fuck is the matter with me?*

I shook my head in frustration and reached for my phone to send Smith and Amrine a quick text and see if they had learned anything about Alina's activities today. I needed something to help my concentration.

Almost as the phone hit my hand, a pair of lips kissed me on the right ear, and I almost dropped my phone.

"Well hello, sexy!" Alina's voice whispered. "Who are you texting when you should be obsessed with me?"

"Just a friend."

I turned to face her as she seated herself on the jumpseat. She looked radiant, as usual. The blonde hair was tousled in a stylish, but sexy fashion and her blue-gray eyes sparkled mischievously. Her cheeks were flushed with either exertion or desire and her lips, glistening with dark red lipstick, were barely parted. She stared at me with an expression of pure, unadulterated desire.

"Did you have a good time?" I asked after a long moment.

She nodded. "But I might have been a little distracted," she said, with a sexy smile.

I smiled back at her and swallowed hard. "I know the feeling."

I became aware of Jean and Abby standing in the vestibule beyond the jumpseat, apparently ignoring us and making small talk, so they didn't interrupt Alina. I didn't blame them. Had situations been reversed I would have done the same thing.

"Did your friend like the painting?" I asked.

If I hadn't been looking directly into her eyes, I would have missed it. There was the briefest glimmer of confusion there, for a fraction of a second, and then she found herself.

"Very much so," she said, glancing away. "She's wanted one of my mountainscapes for a long time."

"Great," I said. "So, a successful visit."

Her eyes snapped back to mine for a moment, her expression one of intense curiosity. I realized then that my question could be taken differently. I kept my expression innocent and open. After a moment, the smile was back on her face, and she nodded at me.

"Well let's get you on to St. Moritz," I said. "So, you can have another good visit there."

She smiled and kissed me. "Can't wait for later," she whispered before she left the cockpit.

A few moments later, Jean slid into his seat and began strapping in as I turned my body forward and tried to compose myself. Once he had his headset on and we could not be overheard, Jean spoke very softly through the intercom. "Alina, she *likes* you, n'est pas?"

I nodded slowly.

"It is unusual for her," Jean said. "I have been flying her for a year, and I have never seen zis before."

I rubbed my eyes and exhaled. "I don't know what's going on." Then I looked over at him. "And I know it's not good to have any involvement between crewmembers and the passengers."

Jean nodded with a grim smile on his face. "We have to know our place," he said, softly.

"Amen to that," I replied. "And trust me, I'll never forget mine. So, what do you say? Let's start this thing and get the heck out of here."

"Tres Bon."

"Before start checklist, please."

"Parking brake?" Jean asked.

"Set," I replied, touching the handle to make sure the brake was in the first detent.

"Anti-collision lights?"

I reached up to hit the button and looked out through the windscreen as I did so. Two white BMW sedans with bright orange stripes and light bars drove onto the small ramp at high speed and stopped, one in front of our jet and the other in front of a

Beechcraft King-Air, that was parked next to us. As soon as the vehicles halted, two men exited each of them, clad in gray uniform pants and royal blue parkas. Each man had a sidearm strapped to his thigh and an assault rifle strapped to his chest. When their boots hit the tarmac, they shouldered their weapons and held them at the low ready position.

"Jean?" I asked. "Any idea what's going on?"

Jean looked up from the checklist and gazed outside. "Ze Swiss Politzei. I will see what zey want."

As Jean exited the cockpit, I put my hand on his arm. "Don't make any sudden moves with these guys and keep your hands in plain sight," I said. "It would also be wise to leave your jacket off so they can see you don't have a weapon under it. I have a feeling they're looking for someone."

Jean's eyes narrowed slightly. "Why do you think zat?" he asked.

"Intuition."

Jean nodded and stepped into the vestibule.

"Ze Swiss Politzei are outside," he announced to Alina and Abby. "Zay have blocked us from taxiing. I will see what zay want."

Jean pulled the handle for the main entry door upward, and the heavy door slowly lowered itself. As soon as it stabilized, Jean went down the stairs. From my perch in the cockpit, I turned off the anti-collison light and watched him approach the two policemen. The one on my left was tall and thin and sported a thin black mustache. As Jean approached, the policeman held his left hand up, in a halting motion. Then, he appeared to ask Jean for his passport. Like all good international pilots, Jean kept his passport on his person – as did I. As he reached for his passport, black moustache spat a word at him which I could only guess was something like "slowly" because Jean's right hand stopped and then reached into his right pants pocket very cautiously and deliberately. While Jean retrieved his passport, the second Swiss policeman, a shorter fellow, took a step back and watched Jean and his partner very closely.

The first policeman reviewed Jean's passport very thoroughly, taking his time going through all the pages, one by one.

I could hear him questioning Jean about all the destinations in the passport, and I smiled to myself. International jet captains often had so many stamps and visas they had to get extra pages for their passports. Finally, black mustache gave Jean's passport back to him and motioned for him to go back up the stairs into the aircraft.

The two men followed Jean around the nose of the aircraft as he came back to the airstair. It seemed they wanted to board the aircraft. As I looked to my right, at the Beechcraft King Air parked next to us, I could see the crew and passengers of that aircraft were getting a similar treatment from another pair of policemen.

"You don't know exactly who you're looking for or exactly where they might be," I said to myself. "But why would you check an aircraft for them?"

The answer occurred to me almost as soon as I uttered the words. Because the CIA had tipped them off. *Damn*, I thought. *She did whack somebody today.*

A few moments later, Jean came through the main entry door with a perplexed look on his face, shrugged his shoulders at me and headed rearward into the aircraft cabin. The mustached Swiss policeman followed him up the stairs while the other policeman waited at the base of the airstair. By the time black mustache entered, I had unbuckled myself and pivoted in my seat. I had both of my hands in plain sight and held my passport for his examination. As soon as the policeman looked into the cockpit, I slowly extended my hand with the passport toward him. He nodded and took it with his left hand. I noticed that he had taken his hands off his rifle and the weapon hung across his chest, muzzle down. I had no doubt that he had his right hand in very close proximity to the sidearm holstered on his right thigh.

"American?" The policeman asked, in a distinct French accent.

"Oui," I said. "Contract pilot."

He nodded and returned my passport after a quick perusal of the pages.

Interesting, I thought. *You guys know the person you're looking for isn't American.*

Black mustache proceeded aft into the cabin and examined Abby and Alina's passports. He finished with Abby's fairly quickly but spend considerable time looking through Alina's and questioning her, in French, about her various destinations. My French was spotty, but I kept hearing a French word that sounded like "citizen" and the words "Etas Unis" and "Russie" repeatedly.

She's got dual citizenship in the US and Russia, I thought. *That's got to be fucking rare.*

Alina remained pleasant and charming throughout the conversation, based on what I could see of her and the tone of voice I could hear. She smiled a lot and shrugged repeatedly as if she couldn't understand the policeman's concern about her citizenship. Finally, the policeman handed her passport back to her and issued Jean a command that I understood.

"Nous devrons chercher les bagages," he said.

Great. They're going to search the bags.

Jean turned to me. "The Polizei, they want to search our baggage."

I nodded. "On the jet or inside?" I asked.

Jean exchanged a few words with Black Mustache.

"On ze jet will be fine it seems," he said.

Over the next 30 minutes, we each took our turn with the policeman in the aft of the jet. This particular 7X had three passenger areas. The area closest to the cockpit and galley had four seats all covered in beige leather, two facing each other on each side of the aisle in a club configuration. In the center area, there was a conference table with four seats that occupied one side of the cabin and a small credenza against the other side of the jet. In the rearmost area, there were two leather chairs facing each other on left side of the cabin and a color-coordinated cloth-covered divan, or sofa, on the right side. It was on the divan that we each were instructed to bring our bags and open them for the policeman. Black Mustache was very clear about wanting to see the crew's bags first, and he went through them very quickly, first me, then Jean and then Abby. Not surprisingly, given his long conversation with her, he spent the most time going through Alina's things and even though she only had a purse, a roller board bag, and small hang-up bag, he went through every compartment of each one of them and felt every item of clothing, including some very lacy and frilly underthings.

Alina seemed entirely unbothered throughout the process and stayed good-natured and conversational as the search continued. She smiled often, seemed to make a joke every once in a while, and was completely cooperative. After about fifteen minutes, another policeman entered the cabin, and he and Black Moustache had a quick conversation. Then Black Mustache issued a command to Jean.

"I must go outside with ze other Poletzei and assist them to search ze other compartments of ze aircraft," he said. "You will stay in here with Abby and Alina?"

"Of course," I said.

I probably should have been concerned about the proceedings. After all, I was flying aboard the transportation platform for an international contract killer, and there were probably weapons and other incriminating evidence somewhere on the aircraft. But I found I was more curious than I was apprehensive - curious as to if and what the Swiss might find and even more curious as to what they might do if they did.

Given the possible circumstances, Alina's demeanor had been a study in composure. I couldn't understand every exchange between her and Black Mustache, but I never heard her raise her voice, never saw her tense her body, never detected a tightening of her facial expression. She either felt she had nothing to fear or was the best actress I had ever seen.

But the best explanation was the obvious one. She was a professional. This was what she did. In addition to all the non-professional shit between us, I felt more respect for her growing inside of me.

But then I remembered Jean's observation in the cockpit as Alina made her appearance on the ramp. She didn't have the backpack with her. He had expected her to leave the poster tube behind; the "painting" had been in that. But she didn't return with the backpack.

I looked over at her as the Swiss policeman finished his inspection and she closed her bags. I couldn't help smiling and shaking my head in admiration.

They're not going to find anything because there's nothing to find, is there Alina?

As if she had heard my thoughts, Alina turned, flashed a brilliant smile and winked at me. We were airborne on our way to Samedan 15 minutes later.

CHAPTER EIGHTEEN

Tuesday, November 2
1600 Hours Local Time
Engadin/Samedan Airport (LSZS)
Samedan, Switzerland

Alina's limousine whisked her away to her hotel moments after we had shut down the engines, leaving Jean and I to go about the tasks of putting the 7X to bed as Abby tidied up the inside of the aircraft. Jean monitored the fueling process while I reinstalled the various pins and covers on the exterior of the jet. Out of habit, I disconnected the nose gear torque link and pinned the assembly into the proper position for a tow bar to be attached to it. As I recovered from my crouch under the nose of the aircraft, Jean was standing there with a smile on his swarthy features.

"That is always a good idea, n'est pas? Unpinning ze torque link."

I nodded. "Never hurts. And it might save you some damage if the towing crew doesn't quite know what they're doing."

"Well," Jean said, motioning to the aircraft around us, "At least zay have plenty of other aircraft to damage first!"

While the ramp area here was larger than the one at Gstaad-Saanen airport, it wasn't nearly as large as many ramps at mountain airports in the U.S., but it was still packed with Gulfstreams, Global Expresses and Falcon 2000s, 900s and even a few other 7Xs. This was truly a European playground.

"Zay have finished ze fueling," Jean said. "I brought ze level up to 15,000 pounds for ze hop to Edinburgh on Thursday."

I nodded. That was the fuel level he and I had agreed upon when we arrived. Unlike many captains who used contractors, Jean had consulted me for many of the logistical decisions to be made with the jet, both earlier when we were at Gstaad, and since we had landed here. Even though many of the decisions were minor, it was nice to be included like a real crewmember.

"I guess we're good to go," I said. "Assuming Abby is done in the back."

The flight from Gstaad had been short and picturesque. It wasn't every day a pilot had the privilege to fly above one of the most beautiful mountain ranges in the world at just a few thousand feet above the peaks. The visibility had been crystal clear from horizon to horizon, so there were snow-capped peaks as far as the eye could see in either direction. Fortunately, in spite of the great visibility, the winds had been light so there was no mountain wave turbulence to contend with and the ride was smooth. As predicted, we spent only a few minutes at altitude before we began the descent into Samedan. Unlike the approach into Gstaad, there were no hard turns required to align with the active runway, Runway 03, and we simply descended as we flew down the valley and landed. The approach was less challenging than either Aspen or Vail back in the United States.

We unloaded our baggage from the aircraft, locked the doors to the cabin, baggage area and aft service compartment, and disconnected the aircraft batteries. As we completed our tasks, a black Mercedes passenger van arrived planeside to take us to our hotel. After bringing the vehicle to a stop, the driver leaped out to introduce herself. She was a lithe female in a tight but professional chauffer's uniform with skin the color of cappuccino. I recognized her immediately, and it was everything I could do to stay in character.

She had said her real name was Isabelle the last time we saw each other but I had known her as Sharona Brown on two previous adventures. She was one of the deadliest people I had ever met.

I guess the CIA thought I might need backup. About time.

Ever the polite Frenchman, Jean extended his hand. "Good evening Mademoiselle!"

She shook it firmly. "Schmidt," she answered. "Janine Schmidt."

"Enchante!" Jean replied. "I am Jean Renaud, ze captain of zis aircraft." He motioned to Abby. "Zis is Abby Stewart, our flight attendant."

Abby stepped forward and the two women shook hands. "Nice to meet you," Abby said.

"You also," Janine/Sharona/Isabelle replied.

"And zis gentleman is Colin Pearce, my contract pilot," Jean said, gesturing to me.

I stepped forward and offered my hand. "I guess you say guten abend in this part of Switzerland. A pleasure to meet you."

"You as well Mr. Pearce," Janine said.

Then she turned to all of us. "May I load your things so we can get you to your hotel?"

"Sounds good to me," I said. I turned to Jean. "Where are we staying by the way? I probably should have asked that before."

"Ze Kulm hotel downtown," Jean said. "We always stay in ze same hotel as our passengers," Jean said. "So zey have access to us if zey need it. And we wind up staying in some very nice places! All expenses, zay are covered!"

I kept my face impassive as my mind processed this revelation. Another one of the business aviation "thou shalt nots" was the crew staying in the same hotel as the passengers. It kept relationships professional and avoided any undue familiarity. This was only the second time in my career when I had been booked into the same hotel as my passengers, and I couldn't help thinking about how the previous time, in Cabo San Lucas, Mexico, didn't end well.

"Wow," I said after a moment. "That's quite generous."

"The Kulm is gorgeous," Abby said. "And they have an amazing spa! I get a massage and a facial every time we stay there. You'll love it!"

As we were talking, Janine had opened the van's rear hatch and was loading our luggage. She finished quickly and motioned for us to board the van. "Mr. Pearce, may I presume this is your first time in St. Moritz?" Janine asked.

"It is," I said.

"Perhaps you'd like to ride up front with me so I can point out some sights on the way in?"

I turned to Jean and Abby. "Will you two be offended if I ride up front with our lovely driver?"

"Absolutely not!" Jean said. "Enjoy ze sights!"

"I will apologize," Janine said as Jean and Abby entered the van, "the partition between the front seat and the passenger compartment is stuck in the raised position. I hope this won't be too inconvenient for you."

Jean shook his head. "Pas problem," he said. "It is a short ride anyway."

Janine bowed her head slightly in appreciation. "Merci, Monsieur," she said.

Janine ensured Jean and Abby were in and seated and then she motioned to me to enter the passenger side of the van as she entered the driver's side. As soon as we were strapped in, she put the vehicle in gear, and we were off. We drove across the small ramp and through a perfunctory security gate, and then Janine made a right turn, and we were on the airport access road, headed toward another complex of buildings.

The sun was beginning to set, and the orange glow of the fading sunlight bathed the entire valley before us in a palette of soft light. Snow covered the highest part of the peaks around us, but fields in the valley were still lush and green, as were the evergreen trees in the valley and on the mountainside. Janine made a right turn as we entered the industrial complex and followed a perimeter road.

"The quickest way to town requires us to go out of our way just a bit," she said cheerily. "Let me put some music on so you can all relax."

She hit a switch on the dashboard, and the sound of some electronic pop music emanated from the passenger compartment. She pointed toward a scenic peak in the distance and spoke as we drove.

"The music will keep them from hearing us," she said. "That mountain is Piz Ot, it overlooks the town, in case your friends ask."

I glanced over my shoulder and noticed the partition between us and the passenger compartment was a pattern of translucent and opaque plastic. If Jean and Abby were even watching us, it would be damn difficult for them to see anything.

"To what do I owe this honor," I said. "I thought I was going to be all alone on this little trek."

Janine ignored the question. "Your girlfriend took out a prominent journalist in Gstaad," she said. "We alerted the Swiss police as soon as it occurred but they obviously didn't succeed in detaining your aircraft."

I smiled. "She's not my girlfriend. But I think I figured out how she transports her weapons. She left the jet wearing a backpack and carrying a poster tube. She claimed the poster tube contained a painting for a friend of hers. When she returned to the jet, she didn't have the poster tube or the backpack. When the Swiss police searched the jet, they found no weapons."

Janine looked over at me and smiled, then pointed down the road toward the sunset as we entered a traffic circle. "And your thoughts are?" she asked.

"I'm not a weapons expert, but a .50 caliber bullet would probably require a fair amount of metal to fire it. I'm betting the rifle breaks down, and she carries the smaller pieces in the backpack and maybe the barrel in the poster tube."

Janine nodded as she turned onto a two-lane road that headed south. We were pointed in a different direction now, and I could see the lights of a village in front of us sitting in the shadows of the valley.

"The Brits found one of the barrels in the trash at the Intercontinental Hotel in London after she whacked Essex," Janine said. "Apparently she leaves the barrels behind after she shoots."

"Did they do any metallurgical analysis on it?"

She nodded. "Ironically, the barrel blank was manufactured in the U.S., but the steel came from China. The gunsmithing work was first-rate, but anonymous. No links to anything there."

I frowned. "Still isn't smart. She's leaving clues behind."

"Maybe. But it would make a ballistic match damn challenging if she was ever caught. And if she ditched the rest of the weapon, there would be no way to tie it to her."

"So how did she know to ditch it today?" I asked. "Jean noticed she didn't have it and he made it sound like she forgot it or something."

"You need to watch him and the FA," Janine said. "Neither one of them is completely kosher. Jean did some mercenary work after he left the French Air Force and Abby's family has ties to crime syndicate in Scotland."

"Of course, she does," I said, looking out of my window as we entered another traffic circle and turned southwest. "I wondered why the two of them kept appearing on the flights. It could have been a coincidence, but in a flight department with three aircraft, you wouldn't typically see the same crew two trips in a row."

I looked over at Janine. "You didn't answer my question."

She shook her head tightly. "We don't know how Alina knew. She may have a contact in the Swiss police force."

Janine pointed down the road in front of us. "This road takes us right into St. Moritz. Your hotel is on the lake there. It will only take us a few minutes to get there. I put a small package into your bag when I loaded it. Some things you may find useful."

"Understood."

Janine looked over at me and tilted her head toward me with a grim smile on her face. "You need to get Alina tell you everything she knows about what they're planning."

"I know," I replied. "And it might be easier than I thought because apparently she likes me a lot. Can't help but think there might be more to it though. I'd love to think I'm irresistible but I know better than that."

"Oh, I don't know," Janine said. The smile on her face went from grim to coquettish in a fraction of a second. "You can be irresistible when you want to be. I saw evidence of that in Cabo."

"Now you're humoring me," I said. "You're a hot young thing in incredible shape, and I'm just an old guy with delusions of grandeur."

Janine laughed and pointed out of the left side of the van. "You can't see it from your side, but there's a cool restaurant at the top of the hill here called Lej da Staz. Food is slightly above average, but the view is incredible."

"Maybe my *girlfriend* and I will go there."

Janine smirked at me. "Any idea how long you'll be in town?"

I nodded. "Until the day after tomorrow. We're flying to Edinburgh on Thursday."

"Morning or afternoon?"

"Jean didn't say. I'll get that information to you."

"In the meantime, we'll try to find out what/who she might be after in Edinburgh."

Some buildings and lights went by on the right side.

"That's St. Moritz north," Janine said. "There are a few hotels, restaurants and other attractions there, but your hotel is in St. Moritz proper. Just ahead."

"Are you sticking around to babysit me?"

Janine shook her head. "I don't think so," she said. "I was pulled off another operation to get you the package and talk to you. But I have to get back to what I was doing."

I nodded. "Ever busy."

"That's me," she answered. She looked across the cab at me again. "Speaking of busy. It looks like you recovered from your injuries well."

I shrugged. "I can't push the iron as much as I'd like for a while but everything seems to be working well enough. I've been doing a lot of aerobics and core work until my shoulder heals."

Traffic started to envelop us we entered St. Moritz. While a town of only 5,000-ish in full-time population, St. Moritz gave off a different vibe than some of the American resort towns I had been to. With its distinctly European ambiance, it was quaint and charming and sophisticated and worldly all at once - a hybrid of Alpen village and center city with a ski flavor thrown in. It reminded me of Aspen or Vail but with a lot more class.

As we drove through the busy streets, I saw some of the standard designer names go by on the formal storefronts – Versace, Prada, Gucci – and the usual assortment of beautiful people going in and out of the ornate boutiques. We negotiated another few traffic circles and then turned on the street where three rectangular buildings dominated the lake side of the street, all of which were connected and merged into a grand entry hall with four columns on the street side.

"Holy shit," I said. "This place kicks Cabo's ass. It's not meant for lowlifes like me. They're going to have to fumigate my room when I leave."

Janine laughed. "You'll fit in just fine." She reached across the seat and squeezed my right hand for a moment. "Be careful, Colin. There's still a lot about all of this we don't know, and this Alina chick might play praying mantis with your ass and kill you after she fucks you."

I sighed. "For once in my life, I'm actually hoping it doesn't go that far. But if it does, that thought occurred to me as well. I presume there's a weapon in the package."

"Kimber .45 combat commander with an extended threaded barrel. Custom suppressor, three magazines and fifty rounds of ammo, Glaser safety slugs."

"Sounds like you've thought of everything."

"One of the reasons we pushed the Swiss police to search the jet was so that Alina and the crewmembers would see that you were unarmed. They won't expect you to have a gun. You can use that to your advantage."

"If I do, who do I call?"

"There's a card in the package with a number. We always keep a cleaning crew around you when you go into the field, Colin," Janine flashed me a dazzling, knowing smile. "We know how you are."

She stopped the car in front of the columned entryway and resumed her chauffeur identity. "Here we are!" she said merrily.

Janine stepped out of the van and opened the side door, so Abby and Jean could exit. Then she opened the van's rear compartment and began unloading bags. I made my way back there as quickly as I could and took my roller board bag, extended the handle and placed my computer bag on top.

Formally attired bellmen in blue uniforms, replete with caps and greatcoats, descended upon us just as Jean and Abby reached the rear of the van. The two of them made absolutely no effort to participate in the loading process as the bellmen lifted their bags onto a trolley. They seemed to be accustomed to this drill.

"Help with your bags sir?" one of the bellmen offered in completely unaccented English.

"No, thank you," I said. "I carry other peoples' bags for a living. It wouldn't feel right for someone to carry mine."

The bellmen nodded respectfully and pulled the trolley away.

"I hope you enjoy your stay!" Janine said.

She shook Jean's and Abby's hands and produced a business card that she presented to Jean.

"If you need further transportation services while you are here, please feel free to call us."

Jean nodded. "Merci, mademoiselle. Your service has been excellent."

Janine bowed in gratitude. "Merci, monsieur." She turned to me. "I hope you enjoyed your little tour, Mr. Pearce."

I extended my hand. "It was great. Thanks for taking the time."

She shook my hand. "It was my pleasure."

Janine returned to the van and sped off into the St. Moritz evening.

Moments later we walked through a pair of beautiful wooden French doors and into the most magnificent hotel lobby I had ever seen. Persian carpets covered rich hardwood floors, plush formal furniture was precisely arranged into conversation groups, and the window treatments were made of perfectly color-coordinated fabric with textures and sheens that shouted of a no-expense-spared mentality.

Jean introduced himself to the receptionist behind the main desk, and after effusive greetings were exchanged, we were presented key cards in elaborate folders complete with maps of the hotel, vouchers for spa treatments and chocolates for our palates.

"Abby and I have plans zis evening," Jean said. "So we will bid you adieu. Perhaps we will join up tomorrow at some time."

I nodded. *I bet you two have plans,* I thought. "That's more than fine," I said. "I feel a martini or two at the bar coming on. I hope you enjoy your evening."

Jean and Abby headed off to their rooms, which were in one of the northern buildings of the hotel and I turned to head to the southern wing. Negotiating my way did not take much time. In spite of the hotel's size, there were only 172 rooms in the place. Before long I was walking through the door of my deluxe room. It was on the large side for a European hotel room and quite sumptuous. The room featured rich fabrics, ornate wood and a spectacular view of Lake St. Moritz, which was now lit by the lights of the village. I was sure there would be an amazing view of the mountains in the morning.

I took off my suit jacket, threw it on the bed, and began to unpack my bag. As promised, a thick manila envelope lay between a few layers of clothing. I smiled to myself as I pulled the envelope out of the bag and began to open it. Janine/Sharona had only been in the back of the van for a few seconds. The fact that she had managed to get the envelope into my bag so carefully, in so short a period, spoke volumes about her tradecraft.

In the envelope were the items she had described, a Kimber 1911-style Commander automatic in .45 ACP, three magazines, a suppressor, a plastic zip-lock bag of cartridges and a few pairs of nitrile gloves. The CIA had thought of everything. Never load a weapon you might have to use and dispose of without a pair of gloves. Technology had reached the point where fingerprints could be pulled from spent shell cases.

Once I had finished testing the weapon and attaching the suppressor, I loaded it and looked for a place to stow it. It needed to be hidden in a place where it would avoid a cursory search but where I could get to it quickly if required. After a considering the room for a few minutes, I found a spot that met my requirements and stored the weapon. Then I removed the gloves and unpacked the remainder of my few things.

As I opened the wooden doors of my room's wardrobe, I found a garment bag hanging there with a plastic bag wrapped around the hangar. The garment bag contained a black Armani tuxedo with a formal white shirt, black tie, and matching cummerbund. The plastic bag contained a pair of Gucci shoes, socks, t-shirts, underwear, cufflinks and shirt studs. There was even a watch-sized box with the Rolex logo on the outside.

Tacked to the suit bag was an envelope with a note inside.

Drinks at the Altitude Bar at 7. Dinner in the K restaurant at 8. Hope everything fits! Can't wait to see you in it! A.

CHAPTER NINETEEN

Tuesday, November 2
1900 Hours Local Time
Kulm Hotel
St. Moritz, Switzerland

After a quick shower, I dressed and headed down to the bar. As I waited for the elevator to arrive, I regarded my reflection in one of the ornately framed mirrors in the elevator vestibule on my floor.

I hardly recognized myself.

I had no idea how she had managed it, but the tuxedo looked like it had been tailor-made for me. Between the cut and sheen of its rich fabric, the stylish Gucci shoes and the understated but elegant Rolex, I felt like I was dressed to play a role. What a difference a few thousand dollars of style made.

I stepped off the elevator and walked down to the lobby a few moments later. If I had any fears that I'd be overdressed, they were allayed as soon as I entered the main lobby and headed toward the Altitude Bar. While there were the ever-present jeans on some of the lobby patrons, most the people in the area were clad in formal or semi-formal evening wear - suits, cocktail dresses, and the occasional evening gown. The bar at the Duke's Hotel had been dressy. The lobby and bar here were a step up from that.

The Altitude bar was busy but not packed when I walked in and made my way to the bar itself, an elaborate wooden affair with a large mirror behind it and several rows of glass shelves which displayed the bar's substantial selection of spirits. I couldn't help smiling as I walked through the area and assumed a seat at the bar. After airplane cockpits, bars were my favorite places in the world. While they might vary in character and décor, they seemed to all have the same effect on me. They calmed me and brought me to myself.

As soon as I was seated, the smartly dressed bartender immediately came over to me and introduced himself as Hans. He was about to ask me what I wanted to drink but then his gaze went over my shoulder, and I heard the mild rumble of conversation in the bar go instantly quiet.

I didn't have to turn around to know what was happening, but I did anyway. Once again, I attempted to steel myself with the knowledge of what she was, of who she was, and what she had done. But as I turned, the sight of her took my breath away and all of that was forgotten.

Alina was walking toward me in a long black gown with a gemstone inlay that reflected the light in a pattern that made the gown look iridescent. Her shoulders were exposed except for thin spaghetti straps that seemed to be barely sturdy enough to hold the gown on her. The top of the gown plunged to a wide V-neck that just contained her breasts and bottom of the gown featured a thigh-high slit up her left leg. Her blonde hair fell around her shoulders evenly, and her neck was adorned with a diamond necklace that sparkled even more than the gown did.

She floated across the room to me, and I rose from my seat to greet her. Her arms went around my neck, and our lips met for a quick but intimate kiss.

"Good evening darling," she said, as she seated herself next to me. "You look fantastic! I'm glad everything fit!"

"You're the one who looks fantastic. Every man in the room wishes he were me right now."

"I haven't worn anything like this in years and didn't have evening clothes in my suitcase. As soon as I left the airplane today, I went downtown and did some quick shopping for both of us."

"It must have been pretty quick," I said, pulling on the lapel of my jacket for emphasis. "This fits amazingly well. I can't imagine tailors working overtime in Saint Moritz."

She smiled. "I cheated a little," she said. "Your tux came from an Armani store that specializes in rentals for the many formal events here. When Jean reloaded the bags after the search today, I had him look at your clothes to get your sizes." She put her hand over her mouth in a gesture of modesty. "I hope that wasn't too intrusive."

He also had a chance to finish the search the Swiss police started, I thought.

173

"If it resulted in me looking like this, you can be as intrusive as you want," I said. "So, do I turn into a pumpkin at midnight or something? Or do I need to turn this in somewhere tomorrow?"

She smiled at me. A radiant, intimate smile. "Everything is yours to keep." She lowered her voice to a whisper. "But I may make you earn it."

I smiled back at her and raised my eyebrows. "I hope I'm worth it."

"You will be," she said, taking my hand.

For a few moments we just looked at each other and I could feel understanding and comprehension passing between us even though no words were spoken. For reasons either emotional or pragmatic, perhaps both, Alina wanted me. I could feel the pull of her desire. And for all my awareness of her nature, desire for her was growing inside me as well. There was energy between us that was a perceptible force and slowly gaining intensity - a connection fueled by the darkness that lurked inside our souls.

Years ago, I had read a book about the mannerisms and behaviors of adult children of alcoholics and how two people who had never met before, but shared the same parental dysfunction, could find each other and without really knowing each other, feel a strong bond due to their shared childhood experience. It was the same sort of bond I could feel growing between Alina and me, only ours was far stronger, and far darker.

If you fall for her, you'll lose a piece of yourself that you'll never get back. The thought seeped into my head even as I gazed at her and lost myself in her beauty.

Hans reappeared and asked for our drink orders, breaking the moment. Thank God.

I deferred to Alina, but she conceded back to me and said she'd have what I was having.

"Hans, I've heard the hotel has a substantial gin list."

"We do," he said, with a mild German accent. "Probably the best in the city."

"You know, in some of the cities I've traveled to, that wouldn't be much of a claim. But I guess in Saint Moritz that's a different story."

He nodded modestly.

"So, do you keep any of your gin in the freezer?"

He looked at me like I had asked him something very strange and shook his head. I could see Alina smile in my peripheral vision. She knew exactly why I was asking the question.

"Hans, I'm going to be very specific, with no insult intended. Okay?"

"Of course, sir."

"Two Plymouth martinis. Very, very dry. That means vermouth swished around in the glass and then dumped out. With a full slice of lime in each. And please shake the gin as hard as you can shake it. We should be able to ski on them when you're done."

Hans grinned at me. "Very good, sir. We may have to name a martini after you." He pulled two chilled martini glasses from a cooler under the bar and set to his work.

"That sounds yummy," Alina said. "How did you come up with it?"

"Trial and error mostly," I said. "I got the initial idea from a friend of mine and then just sort of refined it. I've never really been a vodka guy, so that option was out. And I don't like the taste of olives in a drink. I like the element of fruit in it, and the kiss of vermouth in the drink takes the edge off the gin. I'm not sure it will be as good as the martinis we had in the bar at the Dukes Hotel, but we'll see."

"I'm sure they'll be great."

"So, talking to Jean and Abby, I got the impression you guys come here somewhat often."

Alina shrugged. "A few times per year. My uncle has a residence here. You and I will stop by there for a little while tomorrow. I have to talk to him for a bit and pick up some things. Besides, he wants to meet you."

"So he's in town?"

She nodded. "He has offices in Moscow and Saint Petersburg. He likes to get away as often as he can. Especially during the late fall and winter. He says that if he has to be cold, he'd prefer to be luxuriously cold."

"Can't fault him there," I said.

Hans brought our martinis over and set them down before us. "I hope these will be to your liking, sir," he said.

I nodded to him. "I'm sure they will be, Hans."

Alina and I picked up our glasses.

"What shall we drink to?" she asked.

"New acquaintances who feel like old friends?"

Alina nodded and for a moment, I thought I saw her eyes glisten with moisture. We lightly clinked our glasses together and then sipped our martinis. The Plymouth gin was ice cold and perfectly set off by the small tinge of vermouth and the tartness of the lime.

I turned to Hans, who was discreetly eying us from a few feet away with an expectant look on his face. I raised my glass at him. "Well done, sir!"

He nodded in gratitude and attended to one of his other patrons.

"These are spectacular," Alina said, as she took another sip of her drink. "So, new acquaintance who feels like an old friend, here's to an evening getting to know each other better!"

We clinked glasses again and then Alina leaned back in her chair and shifted her position, drawing her right leg up under her and allowing the slit of her dress to reveal more of her lower body. I looked down involuntarily and saw a tiny flash of black lace for just a moment. As I raised my eyes, Alina caught my gaze and smiled at me.

The dinner that followed was one of the best in my life. The K restaurant featured French-Mediterrean cuisine and after spicy prawns and a light salad, Alina and I shared the largest lobster I had ever seen, cooked to perfection and stuffed with crabmeat. The lobster was complimented by a spectular Pouilly-Fuisse and the tastes of the shellfish and the wine blended perfectly.

Alina and I made small talk for most of the meal. We discussed our different college experiences in the state of Colorado and laughed over the typical antics of children passing into adulthood while they're away from home for the first time. All the while, I could feel the connection between us slowly strenghthening. The walls were coming down and where last night had been about cutting through the initial barriers to physical intimacy, tonight was about a deeper intimacy. Alina was anxious to understand me and in spite of my reservations, I found that I was anxious to understand her. During breaks in our conversation, I mentally tried to convince myself that my interest in her was about the mission, about getting information, but I knew that wasn't it. In the back of my mind was a growing sense of desperation at the realization that she and I were alike. We were both killers for hire. The orders might come from different places, but at the end of the day, we both killed and got paid for it. Although we could be on opposite sides of arbitrary lines between right and wrong and good and bad, that didn't change the reality of what we were.

After dessert, Alina and I had whiskey at our table instead of retreating into the bar. The Kulm's array of single-malts was impressive. I chose the Tomatin 18 with the Oloroso Sherry finish. As with all of Tomatin's offerings, the 18 was delicate and intricate. The nose featured grapes and raisins with a touch of cinnamon. The palate was sweet and full with notes of sugar, honeycomb, and cocoa along with a slight taste of oak. The finish was long and powerful with the flavor of oak and just a hint of pepper.

Alina and I sat at a table in the corner of the intimate dining room, near a fireplace made of gray bricks. She eyed me as she sipped her whiskey and she shifted her weight as she crossed her legs under the table.

"Did I tell you I was in the American Army for a while?" she asked.

I shook my head. "No. I don't think you did. What did you do?"

"I was an intelligence officer at the division headquarters level. I specialized in signals and human intelligence. I loved the work but I would have rather done something that got me into combat."

"Like what?"

"Oh, I don't know," she mused, looking up at the ceiling for a moment, then back down at me. "Maybe something where I could shoot a rifle."

"Like an infantryman?"

She shook her head and held my eyes with hers. "No. Something that would have made better use of my rifle skills. Maybe more like a sniper."

And there it was. It was either intimate revelation or thoughtful bait. Maybe it was both. I was thankful for the amount of alcohol I had throughout the evening because it kept me from shaking. I took another sip of the Tomatin and let it settle on my tongue as I contemplated a response. I did my best to keep my expression neutral and thoughtful.

"Well, I'm sure you would have made a good one given your success in the Olympics," I said.

She nodded in appreciation. "Thank you. There are many people who think women aren't capable of such things."

"I know. Toward the end of my Air Force career, we began training women in the F-16. A lot of my fellow male pilots didn't think women could fly and fight as well as a man could. But they were wrong. The women ran the same gamut of talent as the men we trained. Some were good, some weren't, but it was always about ability and application, never about gender."

Alina nodded again but I sensed that her mind was wandering. I watched her face as she looked into her whiskey glass for a moment and her eyes appeared to lose focus. She seemed lost in thought and I wondered where her mind was. I didn't want to press the conversation into dangerous areas but I didn't feel like I had much choice.

"So how does a U.S. Army officer wind up in Russia?"

She seemed to not hear the question and continued to stare into her glass. I was about to repeat it when she shifted her eyes to mine and spoke.

"Have you ever killed anyone, Colin?"

The question smacked me in the center of the forehead like a battering ram. *So much for subtlety,* I thought. I nodded as I considered my reply. Odds were high she'd seen a full dossier on me. I had to play it truthfully but carefully.

"Of course," I said after a long moment. "I flew combat missions in the first Gulf War. I'm sure I killed a lot of people. I'm just not sure who they were."

She smiled at me and shook her head. We both knew that wasn't the answer she was looking for. The conversation was headed down a difficult path. We both wanted honest words from the other but we couldn't reveal how much we knew, or how we knew it.

"But that was easy," I continued. "Because it wasn't personal." I took another sip of my whiskey. "I was shot down during the first Gulf War and taken prisoner by an Iraqi infantry squad. They beat me up for a while but then they got sloppy. One of them got too close to me with a weapon and I took it from him and killed him, along with all the members of the squad."

Alina nodded and her smile broadened. "And what was the weapon?"

You know as well as I do, I thought. "A knife. A big knife. I still have it."

"So you cut their throats. How did it make you feel?"

I smiled at her, very aware that I didn't mention how I had used the knife. But suddenly, I knew what this conversation was about for her. It wasn't about her trying to gain information. It was about her trying to understand me and the connection we had. So I gave her the answer she wanted. It just happened to be the truth.

"Good," I said. "I liked it."

I saw moisture in her eyes for the second time in the evening. She reached across the table and took my free hand in hers.

"Did it bother you afterward?"

I shook my head. "No. Never."

She raised my hand to her mouth and kissed it. The gesture was impossibly tender and intimate. I could feel more of the walls coming down between us.

"Me neither," she said, softly. So softly I could barely hear it.

We sat in silence for several moments and then she gathered her purse and rose to leave. I rose to leave with her but she motioned for me to stay.

"Finish your whiskey," she said. "It's too good to waste. I need to get some rest. We have a busy day tomorrow."

"We do?"

She nodded and smiled at me. "Yes. I'm going to take you shopping! Then I was thinking of massages later in the day, before we go to meet my uncle."

"Sounds great to me? When and where do you want to meet?"

"Breakfast in the Grand Restaurant at 1000?"

I nodded to her. "I'll be there."

She held her arms out to me and I went into them and held her close. I could feel her sigh against me. "I wish we didn't have to leave so soon."

"You own the airplane. You control the itinerary. We can stay as long as you want."

She shook her head against me. "I'm on a schedule. I have to be in Edinburgh by mid-day on Thursday. I have an appointment I can't miss."

The word *schedule* made me tense involuntarily. I felt a knot form in my gut.

Alina must have sensed my tension. She put her head back and looked up at me.

"What?"

I shook my head. "Nothing. I guess I was just hoping for more time with you."

"Well, I will be traveling to the U.S. soon. Maybe you could meet me when I get there?"

I raised my eyebrows. "I could do that. Where will you be going?"

"Lake Tahoe. I hear it's beautiful. I've never been there."

"It's God's country," I said, nodding. "One of the most beautiful places on earth. I'd love to meet you there and show you around. Any idea when?"

She shook her head. "I have an errand to do there for Vladimir, but I'm not sure exactly when he needs me there to do it. I know it will be soon."

"That's great. It will be something to look forward to."

"Yes it will," she said.

Then she kissed me, another brief but intimate kiss. I could feel her holding herself in check, like she wanted to go further but was consciously restraining herself.

When our lips parted, she looked up at smiled. But it was a smile that seemed to convey both sadness and knowledge. I was reminded of the expression on her face when I had seen her at Dukes the first time and I felt something pull at the back of my brain.

I slowly sank back into my chair and I watched her walk away, the curves of her magnificent ass clearly visible beneath the long, black gown. She stopped at the door to the dining room and looked over her shoulder and blew me a kiss before disappearing into the lobby beyond. I had a keen sense that tomorrow would bring me deeper into danger with a woman who was impossibly beautiful and completely deadly.

The problem was that I didn't seem to care.

CHAPTER TWENTY

Wednesday, November 3
0945 Hours Local Time
Kulm Hotel
St. Moritz, Switzerland

Freshly showered and dressed for the day, I sat on the bed in my room, listening to the 80s music softly playing on TV and staring at my phone. It had been a rough night. I had tossed and turned and not slept. Even after martinis, wine and multiple whiskeys, my mind would not let go of its obsession with the dark bond that connected Alina and me and the similarities between the two of us. I was due to meet her for breakfast in 15 minutes and I couldn't decide whether I was excited about the day ahead or dreading it.

Before showering, I had texted Smith and Amrine a brief message about today's itinerary. ALINA TAKING ME TO MEETING WITH ANTON THIS AFTERNOON. SAYS SHE NEEDS TO "PICK UP SOME THINGS." PRESUME IT IS WEAPON BUT NOT SURE.

The reply from Smith came back so quickly it was obvious he had been waiting for me. IF SHE HAS WEAPON IN HER POSSESSION AND ANTON IS THERE, WE CAN TAKE THEM. WILL HAVE TEAM STANDING BY.

Wonderful. A team standing by. That meant they had expected trouble all along. I shook my head as I looked at Smith's words on my phone. As pleasurable as the day's other activities might be, I knew I would be stepping into the lion's den when I met Anton this evening. The ensuing conversation might start out as a cordial exchange, but it would end up as an interrogation and I had no doubt about the Russians' ability to extract information. While I had a high threshold for pain, I had never been tortured by someone who knew what they were doing and I had no desire to find out what my tolerances were in that regard.

I briefly considered making excuses and saying I was ill or even quietly packing my things and leaving. But I had never been one to turn my back on the mission. Besides, intertwined with all of this was the connection I had with Alina and the desire to see her again.

She's your other half. She's just like you.

I bowed my head and exhaled.

"Jesus," I said to myself. "I sure hope not."

At that moment, the words from one of the 80s songs playing on my TV reached my ears. The song was Tears for Fears' Mad World and the words resonated with me.

And I find it kind of funny,
I find it kind of sad,
The dreams in which I'm dying,
Are the best I've ever had.

I listened to the entire song until it faded away and I sat there, shaking my head at my predicament. *What a world. What a mad, fucking world.*

##

Alina was waiting for me when I arrived at the restaurant. She greeted me warmly and it might have been my imagination, but her lips seemed to linger on mine a second or two longer than they had last night. She was a vision of loveliness with her long blonde hair pulled into an elegant pony tail and wearing boots, a wool skirt and a silk top that hugged her upper body enticingly. She had ordered mimosas and we toasted the day before us.

"My uncle can't wait to meet you," she said. "I told him about you and he's fascinated by some of the things you've done."

I bet he is, I thought. "That's kind of him," I said. "It will be nice to meet him too."

"We won't stay long, I promise." She took my hand in both of hers. "I have a wonderful evening planned for us tonight."

I smiled back at her and tried to detect even the slightest trace that she wasn't being truthful. But her eyes were steady and unblinking and her grip on my hand was tender and sure.

"My suite has a balcony with a beautiful view of the lake. I'd like for you to see it."

I felt a warm surge of desire flow through me, like the temperature of my blood had suddenly increased by several degrees. "I'd like that very much," I said, and meant it.

God help me.

"I stayed up all night thinking about you," she said, squeezing my hand gently as she spoke.

I nodded. "Me too."

"I haven't been with many men. Partly because I've been…," she looked away for a moment, "so busy for the last few years but also because I've haven't really met anyone who could handle who I am." She swallowed hard and looked down at my hand in hers. "Or handle what I am."

It was my turn to swallow. I remember the look of disgust in Christine Billings' eyes after I beheaded one of the guards holding us captive in my last engagement with the CIA. We had spent an intimate weekend together but after she saw the violence I was capable of, she couldn't seem to get far enough away from me.

"I know what you mean," I said after a long moment.

"I know you do." She raised my hand to her mouth and kissed it, for the second time in twelve hours. "That's why we'll be good together." She released my hand and retrieved the menu from the table in front of us. "Let's eat! We've got a big day ahead of us!"

I ordered the Eggs Benedict and Alina ordered Eggs Florentine, along with another round of mimosas. The eggs seemed to be cooked perfectly and the hollandaise sause was whipped to perfection, but I barely tasted anything. Alina talked throughout the meal about our day, the places where we would shop, the spa in the hotel where we could get our massages, as well as manicures and pedicures, and the meal that we would have tonight, served privately on the balcony of her suite. My head was swimming as she spoke. I didn't know if she was truthful, delusional or a consummate liar. I did know that one way or the other, the evening wasn't going to end the way she was describing. For reasons I couldn't identify, that deeply saddened me.

You want her as badly as she wants you, my conscience said to me. *You want her because she's like you are.*

I know, I responded. *Goddamn it.*

The shopping was all about me. Alina led me into several designer shops and bought an entire wardrobe for me. I was measured for suits and together, we selected fabrics for three of them. Then we choose shirts, ties, shoes, belts, and various accessories. All while the stores' staffs provided us glasses of champagne that never seemed to go empty. I tried to stop Alina from spending so much money, but she was enjoying herself and would have none of it. The tailor-made items were to be shipped to my home in Delaware when they were finished. Much of the rest of the merchandise was sent back to my hotel and the remainder I carried, in those bags with the designer trademarks on them that I had loaded into business jets for passengers so many times.

"I could get used to this," I said as we exited the final store.

"You'll have to bring some of these things to Lake Tahoe with you," Alina said. "So, I can see you in them."

"I can wear some tonight."

Her eyes grew distant for a moment, but then she nodded and smiled at me. "I'd like that," she said.

After returning to the hotel, I dropped the bags off in my room and then met Alina in the hotel's spa. We traded our clothes for robes and went to the nail salon for manicures and pedicures. While my schedule didn't allow for many of them, I believed having someone who knows what they're doing work on your hands and feet was one of life's true luxuries. The results of the two treatments were impressive, but I always enjoyed the process itself. It was fun to be fussed over for a brief period. I was fascinated by watching someone else display their ability to focus on the details of a repetitive, mundane task and perform it well. For some reason, it restored my faith in the human condition.

As we sat down in the pedicure chairs to begin soaking our feet, Alina gave very thorough instructions to the technician who would be administering her treatments. When my technician asked if I had any special requirements or instructions, I shook my head.

"Just do what you do for everyone else," I said. "I'm sure I'll be delighted."

Forty-five minutes later, with freshly done hands and feet, we were led to a treatment room for a couple's massage. I had a lingering glance at Alina's nude body as she casually doffed her robe and climbed under the sheets of her massage table, face down. Her body was even more spectacular out of clothes than it was in them. I shed my robe and hung it on the back of the room's door. Then I slid under the sheets on my table. I looked over at Alina before I put my face in the face cushion and she looked back at me and gave me a radiant smile of appreciation.

Two attractive Swiss masseuses worked us over for about 90 minutes and managed to make me forget about the tension of the coming evening. When they were finished, they slipped out of the room as we lay there on our backs on the massage tables. I kept my eyes closed and my breathing even as I came back to myself.

"Would you mind keeping your eyes closed while I get up and put my robe back on?" Alina asked after a few minutes.

"I'll do my best," I said. "But it will be an awful temptation."

"You're a disciplined man. You can handle the temptation."

I laughed as I closed my eyes. "I'm a lot more disciplined in some ways than in others."

I heard her get off the table and pad over to the stool where she had left her robe. Then I heard her walk over to the door.

"Safe to open my eyes?" I asked.

"Not yet," she said.

Then I felt her lips on mine. I smiled, expecting the usual brief but intimate kiss. But this time, she surprised me and kissed me hungrily, engaging my tongue with hers and breathing heavily against me. I responded in kind, pulling her to me and wrapping my arms around her. We remained entwined for several minutes, exploring each other's mouths and enjoying the sensation of our bodies pressing together. We were both naked and oily under the terrycloth robes and it would have taken mere seconds to be naked against each other, but there seemed to be a mutual agreement of restraint between us and we kept the robes on and were content to enjoy the kisses and the embrace.

A knock on the door interrupted the moment and Alina lifted herself from me. She looked down at me glowingly and stoked the side of my face.

"Meet me out front at 6-ish?" she asked.

I nodded. "I'll be there."

She kissed me again, in the usual quick but intimate fashion, and left the room.

I heard her slip out the door and say something to the masseuses, who were waiting in the hallway with the usual cup of water. She asked them to let me have a few minutes and I was grateful for the interval. A certain part of me was going to need some time to calm down before I could roam the halls in a robe.

##

We left the hotel at 6:05 pm for Anton's residence in a taxi. The sun was just setting as the Mercedes E320 made its way through the quaint streets of the city. The ride would only last a few minutes since her uncle's house was on the lake just down from the hotel. Although geographically close, the roads were such that walking between the two places wasn't feasible, especially in the spiked heels Alina was wearing. She paired a red cocktail dress with the shoes, and it clung to her magnificent figure perfectly. She also wore a Versace overcoat to keep her warm in the late fall air. I wore my typical navy-blue suit, with one of my new shirts and a new pocket hankerchief, but without a tie, at Alina's suggestion. She held my hand and put her head on my shoulder as we rode.

"This has been a wonderful day," she said softly. "I wish it didn't have to end."

"Me too," I said, turning to kiss the top of her head lightly.

"I have something you're going to need. Actually, something both of us are going to need."

Alina reached inside her jacket and retrieved a small flask. She unscrewed the top and took a long drink, then handed it to me.

"What is this?"

"Macallan 18," she said. "Anton can be pretty intense. It's good to get loosened up before you meet him."

Trust can be a dangerous thing sometimes. Particularly when it makes you sloppy. I took the flask and drank a healthy shot of the smooth whiskey without even thinking about it and handed the flask back to her.

We crossed over a short bridge on the lake's northern tip and drove by a small hotel. Then we entered a wooded area with houses on both sides of the road. It reminded me of some of the upscale housing developments I had seen in the United States. We reached a traffic circle, took the first turn and then drove down a road that paralleled the lake shore. A few moments later, we came to a house at the end of the road. It was a grand, two-story affair that looked like an Alpen cottage on steroids with walls that alternated stone and wood and wooden eaves that extended many feet beyond the front of the house. I was betting there was a spectacular view out of the back.

Alina paid the taxi driver, and we exited the vehicle. It took a little effort for me to find my balance. Alina steadied me and put her arm around me as we approached the house's front entrance. A man dressed in black pants with a black parka appeared from the shadows around the porch and examined us. I had trouble focusing my eyes on his face but as my vision settled, I saw that he had the hard look of a man who had spent a lot of time in the field. He carried a pouch over his right shoulder, and I was betting there was a submachine gun of some kind inside.

I blinked my eyes and smiled. "Like the mailman in *Three Days of the Condor*," I said to myself.

"Legkiy, Sergei," Alina said in Russian. "Eto prosto ya."

Sergei didn't seem to be satisfied. "Kto on?" he asked, inclining his head to me.

"Moy gost," Alina answered. "Moy dyadya znayet, chto on pridet."

Sergei spoke into a mic that was concealed into his collar and then nodded at Alina. She led me onto the wooden floor of the porch and knocked on the large wooden door of the house. I found that I had to concentrate on the mere act of walking.

"I forgot to mention that my uncle travels with a security detail," she said as we waited for someone to come to the door. "Former Spetsnaz. They're great at protecting him, but they don't have any manners at all."

I nodded as my head swam. I knew that there were questions I should ask and observations I should make, but at the moment, I couldn't summon the mental will to assemble them.

"Whoa," was all I could think of to say. "He mush be purty important."

"Or paranoid," Alina said, winking at me.

The door opened a moment later, and a clone of Sergei opened the door with the same look and wearing the same outfit, sans the parka and pouch. He had an H & K MP-5 hanging from his shoulder, and he looked both of us over suspiciously. I could barely keep my eyes open as I looked at him, but I was able to settle my gaze on his face after a moment or two. And I noticed something odd. His eyes were different colors. The right one was blue, and the left was gray.

I felt an intense memory in the back of my brain.

"I've sheen you…" I said as my knees gave out.

"Da," said a male Russian voice.

"Catch him, Vassily," I heard Alina say. "He's too big for me."

I fell forward and felt muscular arms go around my body and under my armpit.

"Anton will not like this," said the voice.

"Anton doesn't always get what he wants," Alina said.

Their dialogue transitioned into Russian and I lost track of it. The last thing I remembered was the thud of a heavy wooden door slamming shut and wondering it was the door to my tomb.

"You drugged him, dushka! You were not to do that!"

The Shadow ignored her uncle and stroked the side of Colin Pearce's face as he lay unconscious on the sofa in her uncle's great room.

"How will we learn anything now?" he demanded.

"How much more do you need to know?" she asked in reply. *"You know what the Chinese provided. He works for the American CIA and they're using him to get to me."*

"Then why should he live?"

"Because we've got him and there's nothing he can do now. Because he's special to me. Because he's like me."

The Shadow traced Colin's cheek with her fingers. Such a strong and troubled face. She wanted to make those troubles go away.

"All we have to do is take him out of action until we finish the jobs in Scotland and California," she said. *"I've paid for a two weeks of hotel for him. We'll drug him and keep him there and I'll come back and get him."*

"And if the CIA comes and gets him?"

"You have influence with the Swiss government. Make sure they don't."

Her uncle exhaled impatiently. *"That will take a lot of bribe money,"* he said.

The Shadow turned to him. *"I've done everything you've asked of me,"* she said.

"And you've been extremely well paid!"

"But so have you, uncle, from your investors and from the government. And I'm the one who has to disappear when all of this is over, not you. If I'm going to spend my life in hiding, I want to have someone to spend it with." She turned back to Colin and looked down at him. *"I want him."*

Silence hung in the air between them for several moments. The Shadow continued looking at Colin's face and stroking his hair.

"Very well, dushka," said her uncle at last. "I loved your mother very much. The least I can do is to grant my niece's request for happiness."

The Shadow rose from the sofa, walked across the expansive wooden floor and gave her uncle a warm hug. "Thank you, uncle."

Anton accepted the embrace but then pushed them apart and looked down at her. "But we will do this my way. You will need to trust me. I will have to work this with my contacts in the Swiss government and their state police."

"I will trust you, uncle."

"Sergei and Vassily will take Mr. Pearce back to his room and Jean and Abby will look after him until I can get staff in place tomorrow morning. And in the meantime, you and I can have dinner at your favorite restaurant. How does that sound?"

"Wonderful," the Shadow said.

"Vassily, get Sergei and get Mr. Pearce back to his room! Quietly and safely please."

The Shadow returned to the sofa and knelt on the carpet next to it. She brushed back Colin's hair and gently kissed his lips.

"It will be better like this, my angel," she said. "You will see."

CHAPTER TWENTY-ONE

Thursday, November 4
0700 Hours Local Time
Kulm Hotel
St. Moritz, Switzerland

When I crawled back to consciousness, sometime later, I was laying on the bed in my hotel room, hands zip-tied in front of me and feet duct taped together. Tears for Fears was still playing on my TV. The music seemed to be on a loop.

All around me are familiar faces,
Worn out places, worn out faces,
Bright and early for their daily races,
Going nowhere, going nowhere.

I stared at the ceiling of my room and listened to lyrics as they repeated. *Jesus,* I thought, as I lay there. *It is a mad, fucking world.*

My eyes focused and I suddenly noticed I wasn't alone in the hotel room.

Jean and Abby were seated on the sofa in the alcove of my room overlooking the lake. Both of them were watching me.

"So, mon ami," Jean said. "You wake just in time for us to put you to sleep again."

"What are you talking about?" I asked, trying to sound as groggy and out of sorts as possible. It didn't take much of an act.

"Alina said we were to drug you before we fly to Scotland today," he said, rising from the sofa. "Alina, she seems to be quite fond of you."

"Lucky me," I muttered.

"Not so much," Jean said. "You see Abby, she has a lethal dose of heroin for you." He paused for a moment to scratch his nose. When he did, I noticed he had a Glock pistol in his same hand he scratched with. The Glock didn't have a suppressor attached, and Jean's index finger rested carelessly inside the trigger guard.

You might be a professional pilot, I thought. *But you're a fucking amateur with a gun.*

"But unfortunately, Uncle Anton, he has other plans. You are a, how do you say it, a lose end. Tant pis pour vous, I think."

"So I guess he's the one paying the bills," I said. "I wondered about that."

Jean nodded. "He is ze one who hired Abby and me. I bought ze jets for him. Did all ze registration work. I had to bribe some people in ze various registration divisions of a few countries, but we made it work. We fooled everyone until you."

Jean walked over to the bed and sat down at the foot of it. "How did you do it?"

I shrugged. "It wasn't difficult. You thought all they would search was tail numbers. I had them search on serial numbers."

"Ah, mais bien sur," he said. "Of course."

"Which reminds me," I said. "They will probably come through that door just about any minute. If you two were smart, you'd get out of here before they do."

"Oh, we will," Jean said. "As soon as we get ze call to give you ze injection."

"Why the precise timing?"

"Anton wants to make sure he and ze security team get to ze airport and on ze jet first. I have my regular first officer warming up ze jet. When zay get zhere, zay will call me."

As if on cue, his phone rang, and he stood up to walk back over to the sofa to retrieve it. "Looks like your time may be up mon amie," he said over his shoulder.

Fucking amateur, I thought again. *If you're going to hold me at gunpoint, at least keep the gun on me.*

I raised my arms over my head and brought them down in front of me, breaking the zip tie instantly. Then I rolled off the bed on the floor nearest the closet and stuck my hand between the bed's mattress and box spring. The cold metal of the Kimber's grip greeted my hand. I had it out in a second and trained in front of me as Jean came around the corner of the bed, his gun carelessly held by his side. I centered the Kimber's sights on the center of his chest and fired twice, the two suppressed reports filling the air of the room. Two huge red spots appeared on his white shirt. The Glock fell from his hand, and he slumped down and collapsed to the floor.

Almost immediately, I heard something hit the bed above me, and I rolled away from it just in time to see Abby coming over the side of it, syringe in hand. Her Scottish features were twisted into a mask of hate and anger.

I swung the Kimber to her and shot her in center of her forehead and in the left eye.

"Sorry honey," I said as she rolled off the bed and onto the floor. "You shouldn't have brought a syringe to a gun fight."

There was a knock at the door just then.

"Housekeeping," a female voice said.

I put the gun aside and began ripping the duct tape from my feet.

"No thank you," I said as I sprung to my feet to get to the door. "No service today."

"Are you sure, Mr. Pearce?" the voice asked, this time in a familiar tone. "It sounds like you might have a mess to clean up in there."

Sharona?

I ripped the door open to find Janine/Sharona/Isabelle standing in the hallway next to a maid's cart, clad in the hotel's housekeeper uniform. Hers seemed to fit a little better than most of them though.

I cocked my head at her. "You know I've always had this fantasy about doing the maid."

She smiled at me and shook her head. "Well you seem to be just fine." She looked up and down the hall. "Be a fucking gentleman and hold the door open so I can pull this damn cart in."

"Yes, ma'am."

She wheeled the cart in. It might have been my imagination, but her cart seemed to be a little bulkier than most I had seen. As soon as the door shut behind her, she looked over my handiwork.

"Nicely done, Pearce," she said. "Now we need to get the cleaners in here."

"First, we need to call the boys. Alina, Anton and the security detail are at the airport. They're going to take off for Scotland within the hour. Alina has an 'errand' to do there, and she has to be there by mid-day."

Sharona nodded. "We know. We're going to let them fly there. The Brits will take them on UK soil. If her weapon is on board, they can be linked to deaths of both the PM and Essex. It actually works out well that you're not with them."

I shrugged. "Sounds like you guys have got it figured out."

"Sometimes we get lucky."

"How did you end up being here? I thought you were assigned to do something else."

"I was," she said. "I was here to observe Anton. When you showed up there, and Alina drugged you, it changed our game plan."

"I thought you guys were going to take them at his house."

She shook her head. "Damn Swiss wouldn't let us. Something about their neutrality status and a US team versus a Russia governmental official."

"Well, that sucks."

"Now you know why we're letting them fly to the UK unencumbered."

"Well they're going to have some trouble with that," I said, gesturing to the bodies on the floor. "They don't have a crew for the damn jet now."

"I'm sure they have a back-up somewhere," Sharona said. "Russians are planners. Even when they do bizarre shit like this."

There was another knock at the door, and Sharona opened it, allowing two men in nondescript coveralls to enter. She motioned to the bodies and to the cart, and the two men nodded. Then she looked at me and gestured to the alcove where the sofa was.

"Probably should get out of their way," she said.

I nodded, and we walked over to the sofa area together.

"What now?" I asked. "Alina said something about an 'errand' in the U.S. at Lake Tahoe sometime soon. I got the feeling that was the last one she had to do before the task was completed."

"Shouldn't matter. If we take them in the UK, we'll have them. The Brits might even let us rendition them to a place where we can do a little enhanced interrogating and find out what they're up to. In the meantime, you get to go home." She gestured to the rows of designer shopping bags. "With all your booty."

Sharona's phone rang, and she fished it out of one of the pockets of her maid's uniform. "What's up Bart?" she asked.

I smiled. Bart was John Amrine's handle because of the blonde hair and the faint resemblance to the Bart Simpson cartoon character. I knew he hated the nickname. Which made it even funnier.

"Well of course they did," she said. "Fuckers." She looked at me. "The 7X changed its flight plan. It's going to Saint Petersburg now."

"And they'll change tail numbers or get a new jet, and you guys will lose them," I said. "Alina has to get to Edinburgh."

Then a thought occurred to me. "You need to get the boys to check if any chartered aircraft came into the airport here and flew from here to Edinburgh. You need to do that right now."

Sharona eyed me strangely and then repeated what I had said to Amrine. I heard him acknowledge it and she ended the call. "What are you thinking?" she asked.

"What if the Swiss Police ratted you guys out again? They may have blocked your raid, but I bet someone told Anton and Alina you had asked for it. Assuming they did, Anton and Alina would have known the only place where you guys got the information about the meeting with Anton and the gun, is from me. That changed the landscape for them. They had to assume you guys knew they were going to Edinburgh and could have someone waiting for them. Especially after they made a run at me."

"Makes sense. But honestly, we all thought she was just taking you there for interrogation," Sharona said "And Swiss or no Swiss, we would have gone in and taken you if things had gotten hairy."

"Glad I didn't have to wait for that. I'm not sure how much they would have had to bust me up before you guys made the call."

Sharona punched my arm playfully. "Not too much. So before they can ask you any questions, she drugs you so they can't."

"I had no idea that even happened. The drug came on so suddenly that I didn't really have time to think about it or analyze it."

"She did it to save you," Sharona said quietly. "She did it so they couldn't interrogate you. Apparently she didn't trust her uncle to not damage you."

I remembered the last kiss we had shared in the massage room and the way she felt against me as we drove to Anton's house. "I guess I made an impression."

"I guess you did. But we also thought Anton might overrule her, which is why I was here this morning. We were waiting for the Frenchman to take the call and then I was going do a forced entry and save your ass."

"Sorry I didn't wait for you," I said. "You probably would have done this a little neater than I did."

I glanced over at the bed and saw, much to my surprise, that the two bodies were no longer visible. The two cleaning technicians were replacing the bedding.

"Just about done here," one of them said to Sharona.

She nodded to them and turned back to me. "So why do you think Alina is still going to Edinburgh? She could have lied to you about that."

I shook my head. "I don't think so. She wanted me to know what was going on. She needed for me to know she was pulling the trigger. She mentioned that she was on some kind of schedule and that Edinburgh was part of it. Besides, when Jean said who would be on the jet, he didn't mention Alina."

Sharona's phone rang. "Yes?" she answered.

"Well fuck us," she said. "We'll have to stand the Brits down. Goddamn it." She looked at me. "Charter flight this morning, early. Jet came in from Zurich, picked up one female passenger and flew her to Edinburgh. Landed about 30 minutes ago."

"Tell Amrine he needs to get me to Edinburgh ASAP," I said.

Sharona nodded. "Did you hear that Bart?" she asked into her phone. She nodded and looked at me. "He'll work on that."

"Did you guys ever look into who she might be targeting there?"

Sharona shook her head. "No. Once we decided to intercept them we stopped pushing on the research."

"You need to get rolling on that too," I said. "I can't do any good if I don't know who she's after."

She nodded. Then I heard Amrine's voice come over the phone into her ear as well as a few laughs.

"What's he laughing about?"

"He got you a ride to Edinburgh, from your friends at Dassault."

"Another Falcon? What kind?"

She shook her head and smiled. "Rafale fighter. Dassault has been demo-ing them to the Swiss Air Force. There's a two-seat version on the ramp at the airport here. They were going to do a high-altitude airport demo this morning. The Swiss have released it to us for a few hours."

"Guess they feel bad about facilitating another assassination."

Sharona shrugged. "Or maybe we just got lucky."

"I've always said I'd rather be lucky than good."

She nodded. "Me too. Any day."

CHAPTER TWENTY-TWO

Thursday, November 4
0930 Hours Local Time
45,000 feet and .99 Mach
Somewhere Over Northern France

Not too much later, I was seated in the rear cockpit of a Dassault Rafale B fighter, watching the clouds zip by below as the sleek jet cut through the blue European sky. I smiled under the French-made oxygen mask and shook my head in amazement. Of all the ways in which I had thought this saga with the Shadow/Alina would go, I never imagined myself to be back in a fighter as part of it.

I gazed around me, taking in the glass displays and the array of information presented. As much as I loved the Viper, the Rafale's clean cockpit made the Viper's look antiquated. There were many additional features as well. My favorite so far was the HUD repeater display that was mounted on top of the rear seat glareshield and provided the actual view through the front seater's HUD, with the horizon and clouds clearly visible in it. It was quite an improvement on the rear seat of the Viper, where I had spent many hours training young fighter pilots at Luke AFB, years ago. All we had then was a two-tone view of the front seater's HUD data, barely visible in one of the small multi-function displays in the panel. The data provided some situational awareness to the IP in the back seat, but it was largely useless.

There were three more display screens below the Rafale's HUD display. Two smaller screens were mounted in the panel above my knees and a larger display was mounted between them. This larger display was called a "heads down display" and it provided a graphical depiction of the all the information the jet's sensors were detecting and combined that information in a format that allowed the pilot to easily process it. The head's down display was close to my eyes because the Rafale, like the Viper, featured a side-stick controller on the right console, which allowed the pilot to sit much nearer to the panel. As I looked down into the center display, I could see the jet's position on a moving map as well as the programmed course of flight. It reminded me of the INAV display in the Falcon 7X, but with more detail. In addition to the position, navigation and terrain data, the heads down screen also displayed any airborne aircraft within the scan limits of the jet's onboard radar and infrared/optical systems. The amount of information seemed overwhelming. I wondered how the pilot prioritized targets in a multi-bogey environment.

Fortunately, I knew the pilot.

"So, B-Rock, tell me again how a career Viper foreign military sales guy ends up in the cockpit of a Rafale demonstrator?"

A low rumble of laughter came through the Rafale's intercom. "Just be lucky I guess," Brock Black said. "You should now all about that, T.C."

Brock "B-Rock" Black had been the second surprise awaiting me when I had arrived at the Samedan airport before takeoff. Brock had spent an entire career working foreign military sales in the F-16 and had flown the jet all over the world. He had also done a little moonlighting for the CIA from time to time. We had shared a previous adventure over the summer and I had wondered what became of him.

"You fly a pretty smooth airplane for someone who can't have too much time in the jet," I said.

"Wish I could say it was me," he replied. "The jet has a great autopilot and it even has auto-throttles. Did you notice that both engines are controlled by a single throttle mechanism?"

I looked down at the left console.

"Actually, I don't think I did. I'm not sure I even noticed how many engines the jet had with as quickly as I was suited up and stuffed into this thing."

There was indeed only one throttle. Unlike the throttles in the 7X, this one didn't move when the auto-throttle mode was engaged. Just in front of the throttle, on the console, were two switches, which I presumed were used to engage or disengage the engines from the throttle mechanism.

"Pretty sweet," I said. "A lot more ergonomic than those two monster throttles I had back in the A-10."

"This is a hell of a jet," Brock said. "Too bad someone is trying to sell the technology to the Chinese."

"The Chinese again? Didn't we just do this last summer?"

"Apparently after you shut down that F-35 pipeline between that Mexican drug lord and China, they had to try another source for technology. Their J-31 program is still not going so well."

"So they're trying to steal technology from this jet to fix it? That seems a little backward. I mean it seems like there's a lot of advanced shit on this airplane but it's not in the F-35's generation."

"You'd be surprised, T.C.," Brock said. "The Rafale is in generation of its own, between the Viper and the F-35. It's just about as nimble as the Viper and handles better in low-speed, high angle-of-attack conditions because of the canards. The avionics and sensor suites use a technology called data fusion which combines all that display shit on the head's down display on the center of the panel. It's got long-range optical and infrared sensors that work together with the electronically scanned radar to detect targets. The radar also has a terrain following feature that works with a terrain database and a navigational system that is accurate to inches. The jet can receive data from off-board sources and transmit what it sees to other aircraft or stations."

"Seems like a lot of stuff for the pilot to absorb."

"That's the beauty of it. The pilot doesn't have to assimilate all the data, the jet does it for him. That's the whole data fusion thing. And that's why the head's down display is graphical instead of actual. It lets the pilot see the big picture without having to do a lot of analysis. Did you notice that the head's down display is focused at infinity, like the HUD is? Lets you transition between the two without your eyes having to shift their focus. Pretty good thinking. Oh, and by the way, if you don't hang a lot of external shit on this airplane, it's damn hard to see on radar."

"Holy shit!" I laughed. "You should be a salesman for Dassault, B-Rock!"

He laughed in return. "Well that's essentially what I'm doing. I was placed on the test, development, and demonstration team for the Rafale a few months ago. After the whole F-35 business."

"How did that happen?"

"Once I was cleared by the USAF for the F-35 thing, Smith and Amrine said they had a job for me. They said it would get me out of the country for a while and let things cool down. Next thing I knew, I was at Dassault's headquarters in Paris, talking to this retired French Air Force general who is the assistant to the CEO of Dassault for French Air Force matters. Nice guy by the name of Bruno Valmont. He said he was worried about technology transfer from the Rafale program to the Chinese and wanted to put someone into the program who had no allegiances to anyone to find out what was happening. Now here I am."

"The fact that you were a fighter pilot and spoke fluent French probably didn't hurt."

"No, it didn't."

A radio call instructing Brock to switch frequencies interrupted our conversation. Brock complied with the controller's instructions and checked in with the new controlling agency, London Military Radar.

"London Mil, Tazer 11," Brock said. "Flight level 450. Direct Edinburgh."

"Tazer 11, London Mil. Radar contact. We have your special clearance. You can maintain your altitude and speed for as long as necessary."

"Special clearance?" I asked over the intercom.

"You bet," Brock said. "Your boys worked with Eurocontrol and got us clearance through all the airspace red tape. We can go direct as fast and as high as we want. When we get about 50 miles from the field, I'll put the boards out and we'll do a high-speed descent to a five-mile initial."

"Nice!"

"And it won't be long," he said. "We're crossing over the English Channel now. We'll be starting the descent in about twelve minutes or so. At nearly ten miles a minute, time goes by fast."

"So no breaking the Mach over the continent, eh?"

"Nope. Gotta stay just under and be a good neighbor. This is a French jet and I need to keep up appearances."

Brock called up the airport terminal information service broadcast for Edinburgh on the Rafale's auxiliary radio.

"Edinburgh International Airport Information Bravo," the recorded Scottish voice intoned. "Zero nine five five zulu weather. Wind 250 at 10 knots, visibility 5 miles in light mist. Ceiling 4,500 broken. Temperature 13 Celsius. Dewpoint minus 2 Celsius. Altimeter 10.01 hectopascals. Arriving and departing runway 24. Arriving aircraft expect vectors to the visual approach runway 24. Inform controller on initial contact that you have information Bravo."

I nodded to myself as the broadcast concluded and Brock rechanneled the aux radio. I had flown into the airport previously so I was familiar with the layout.

"I've been here a few times B-Rock," I said. "If you need any help getting around after you land, let me know."

"I may at that," he said. "Let's see where they send us after we're on the ground."

"Roger that."

"About time to start down, T.C.," Brock said. "Hold on to your shit. This is gonna happen quick." He clicked the mic button. "London Mil, Tazer 11 is ready for descent."

"Tazer 11, London Mil. Contact Scottish Mil for that on 131.52."

"Do you have a UHF for that?" Brock asked.

"Apologies, Tazer," the controller replied. "Scottish on 276.45."

"Tazer's gone 276.45," Brock said. Then he released the mic button. "I hate fucking VHF. I don't know how you civilian guys do it. It's so crackly."

I nodded. "I agree. Quality of UHF communication is much better."

"Scottish Mil, Tazer 11 checking in at flight level 450. Like to start down and get vectors to five mile initial to Runway 24 at Edinburgh."

"Tazer 11, Scottish Mil. Turn right to heading 360. Descend and maintain 4,000 feet. Need you level there in ten minutes. Edinburgh altimeter 10.01."

I smiled at the light brogue in the controller's voice. I loved the way Scottish people spoke.

"Tazer 11 right to 360 and out of 450 to 4,000," Brock replied. "We'll hurry down."

The jet smoothly rolled 180 degrees and I was suddenly looking directly down, through the top of the canopy, at the cloud-covered Scottish countryside. Then I felt the onset of about 2-3 g's as Brock pulled the nose below the horizon. I smiled to myself. He did exactly what I would have done in a high-performance aircraft when a rapid-descent maneuver was required.

"God, it's great to be back in a fighter," I said.

Brock chuckled. "You could do this shit all the time if you wanted to. I know lots of folks that would pay you to work for them doing this sort of thing."

"If only," I said.

The throttle on the left console came back to the idle position, indicating Brock had disengaged the auto-throttle mode. I felt the jet begin to rumble as the air brakes were deployed. I looked around and behind me to see if I could see where they were mounted. The back of the fuselage was smooth. I couldn't see anything in the airstream.

"Hey B-Rock," I asked. "Where are the boards? I don't see them."

"This jet doesn't have a dedicated air brake," he said. "Dassault left it off to save complexity and weight. But one of the cool things about a digital flight control system is that you can program the regular flight control surfaces to do more than one thing. When I hit the air brake switch on the throttle, the FCS uses the elevons and canards to provide the braking function. Pretty effective."

I nodded to myself. It was effective. We were about 20 degrees nose low, descending at about 5,000 feet per minute and the airspeed was staying under the Mach. The sleek jet seemed to be falling toward the billowy blanket of clouds below us.

"So what, 300 knots below 10,000 feet in this thing instead of 250?" I asked. "Like the Viper?"

"We have special clearance," Brock said. We'll get down to 300 knots at some point before we pitch out but I'm not going to rush to get us there. You're in demand, T.C. I have to get you to your destination ASAP."

"Nice to be wanted, I guess."

I sat back in my ejection seat and sighed. The truth was that I had absolutely no idea what good I would be when we landed. Apart from possibly identifying a shooting perch, assuming we even knew who Alina was after and where that person would be, I couldn't think of anything else to do.

"Damn," I said to myself. "Damn. Damn. Damn."

"What's on your mind, T.C.?" Brock asked.

"I don't know how much Bart and Bruiser told you but we're trying to stop a contract killer from whacking someone in Edinburgh today. And after insisting that they get me here as soon as possible, I don't have the slightest fucking clue what to tell the folks who will be meeting me."

The clouds suddenly enveloped us as we descended into them. I glanced at the HUD display on the console above the glare shield. We were going through 7,000 feet on our way to 4,000. As I gazed into the HUD, I felt a tinge of familiarity looking at the flight information displayed there. And then I realized that Rafale's HUD was nearly identical to the one in the 7X.

Wow, I thought. *HUD and digital FCS. I guess there is something about this military to civilian technology sharing that Dassault boasts about.*

"Tazer 11, Scottish Mil. Turn left heading 300 and descend and maintain 3,000 on the QNH of 10.01."

"Tazer 11 copies left to 300 and down to 3,000," Brock replied. "I'm going to maintain my speed until 5 mile initial."

"Tazer, Scottish Mil. Cleared as requested. Contact Edinburgh approach on 229 decimal 5."

"Tazer's gone to 229.5. Good day."

The whisps of cloud were passing around the canopy rapidly now. I watched in amazement as they went by. It had been a very long time since I had penetrated IMC, instrument meteorological conditions, in a fighter, with a full view of the world around me. It was a wondrous sight to see the pillows of white moisture surround us as we tunneled through them.

Brock turned to the left and continued the descent to 3,000. We were flying at about 480 knots and slowly decelerating. He reminded me of me. Speed is life. More speed, more life.

Suddenly, the clouds were gone and the deep green on the Scottish countryside came into view down the left-hand side of the jet. I remembered my geography from when I had flown all over England in the A-10, so long ago. We were just off the coast of North Berwick with the North Sea to our right. In front of us, the Scottish coast stretched to Aberdeen. To our northwest lay the Scottish highlands with its treasury of single-malt distilleries. I licked my lips reflexively under the oxygen mask.

"Edinburgh approach," Brock said, mimicking the local pronunciation of *edin-boro*, "Tazer 11, leveling at 3,000."

"Tazer 11, Edinburgh approach. Turn left heading 270. Field is at your 11 o'clock, ten miles."

"Tazer 11, roger. Looking." I heard the click as Brock released the mic button. "Well shit, T.C.," he said. "You've been here before. Where the fuck is the field? All this green British shit looks the same to me."

I looked out of the left side of the canopy.

"Okay, you see the bridge that crosses the river at the end of the bay?" I asked him.

There was a pause.

"Got it," Brock said.

"Look left. Do you see the urban sprawl of downtown Edinburgh?"

"Yep."

"Look exactly between the two and you should see the airport."

"Out-fucking-standing," Brock said. "Said just like a FAC. I see it." He clicked the mic. "Edinburgh approach, Tazer 11, field in sight."

"Tazer 11, Edinburgh approach, report a five-mile initial with Edinburgh tower on 235 decimal 7."

"Tazer 11's gone to tower."

Brock banked the fighter to the left and turned us over the bay to point us down the runway heading of 240. The descent continued. I made a quick calculation in my head.

"Pattern altitude should be about 1,700 feet," I said. "The field's at about 130 feet."

"Don't know what I'd do without you, T.C.," Brock laughed. He keyed the mic. "Edinburgh tower, Tazer 11, five mile initial."

"Tazer 11, Edinburgh tower. Make right traffic."

I could see Brock's head moving around in the front cockpit. He was looking for something.

"Damn, T.C.," he said at last. "You must rate. We're the only jet in the fucking pattern."

We leveled off at 1,700 feet and the airspeed crept back to 300 knots. We coasted in just north of downtown Edinburgh and flew toward the green expanse of southwest Scotland. Before I knew it, we had passed over the approach end of the runway and Brock was banking up into a right turn.

The military overhead pattern is the most efficient way to get multiple aircraft onto a runway, particularly when the aircraft are returning from a sortie as a formation, which is typical for combat missions. Today, we were single ship, but that didn't stop me from enjoying the experience. As we made the 180 degree turn to the downwind leg at 60 degrees of bank, I saw the green countryside pass beneath us and watched the deep blue water of the bay come to our nose again. And as we rolled out, I realized that the last time I had flown an overhead pattern, it had been on a lonely island in the middle of the south Pacific, over a year ago. I felt a lump form in my throat.

God, I love this shit, I thought. *God help me, I love it so.*

Brock deployed the landing gear and I heard the wind noise increase as the drag of the gear entered the airstream. I could see him looking over his right shoulder, checking his distance and orientation from the runway, deciding when to come off the "perch," and make the 180 turn to final.

"The Rafale be just like the Viper, T.C.," he said. "The flaps deploy when you lower the gear. No other action required."

We weren't quite to the coast when Brock banked up and began the descending turn to final. The final turn in the overhead pattern was a precision maneuver. The pilot had to lose 1,200 feet of altitude and turn 180 degrees to arrive on a one mile final at 300 feet above the field. It required judgment and finesse to execute properly. Especially when performing the maneuver at an airport the pilot had never seen before.

"Tower, Tazer 11, right base, full stop," Brock said.

"Tazer 11 cleared to land. Wind 250 at 10."

"Cleared to land, Tazer 11."

Brock flew the turn brilliantly. He worked the descent rate and turn rate to arrive on final at exactly 500 feet on the altimeter and precisely on airspeed.

"Dude," I said, "You're an artist!"

We touched down a few moments later and Brock held the nose up in the aerobrake for a few minutes to allow the sleek jet to slow down using aerodynamic forces before using the wheel brakes. Then he lowered the nose to the runway and stepped on the pedals. We turned off at the next taxiway and then he turned us east on the parallel taxiway.

"Tazer 11, contact ground on 252.75," the tower controller instructed us.

"Tazer 11's gone to ground on 252.75," Brock replied.

As he switched frequencies in the front cockpit, I heard Brock chuckle. "Damn T.C.," he said. "This is impressive. Look in front of us."

I canted my neck and looked around Brock to regard the view in front of the jet. There were at least 10 airliners in line for takeoff for the runway we had just landed on.

"They held them so we could land," Brock said, stating the obvious. "Haven't seen that for anyone but the president." He keyed the mic. "Edinburgh Ground, Tazer 11, clear of the active but no idea where we're going."

"Tazer 11, Edinburgh Ground. Continue straight on Taxiway Alpha, then right on Lima and right on Golf into the southeast apron. Park next to the helicopter. There's a marshaller waiting for you."

"Tazer 11, straight on Alpha, right on Lima, right on Golf," Brock replied. "We'll follow the marshaller." He released the mic button. "Helicopter eh? Quite the reception."

"I guess. I hope all of this hasn't been wasted."

We taxied by the main commercial airline apron and then made the right turn onto taxiway Lima as instructed and then onto taxiway Golf. The entire southeast apron was empty except for a blue and yellow helicopter that was parked in center of it, with its blades turning. Next to it were several men in uniforms, one of who had his hands up, marshalling us toward him.

"Hey T.C." Brock said. "Don't sweat this. Bart told me a little about your mission, and I get that you don't know what you'll do."

He applied the brakes to slow us down as we approached the marshaller and then brought the Rafale to a smooth stop.

"Hands up," he said.

"Hands are clear," I answered.

I assumed ground personnel were under the jet, pinning the landing gear or performing other functions to make the jet safe to shut down. It was always a procedure for crewmembers to keep their hands away from the controls when ground personnel were under the aircraft. If the controls were bumped, the hydraulically assisted surfaces could maim or kill someone who was struck by them.

"You have this way of making shit happen, T.C.," Brock continued. "It doesn't matter if you don't know what's going on or what you're doing, you always seem to get lucky and make shit happen. It's what you do."

He looked over his left shoulder so that I could see the left side of his brown face and he smiled at me. "And that makes you a fucking menace to the people you're up against. Now get out there and be a menace to this killer chick and stop the shit that she's trying to do. If anyone can do that, you can."

THE SHADOW – EVENT 54/55

The Shadow was ready. She had verified the range, sampled the atmospheric conditions, and fed the data into the tablet application. Now, with the telescopic sight adjusted for the shot, her rifle rested on its bipod, poised for action.

The Shadow peered through her binoculars and regarded the hotel where the target was staying. Unlike the two previous events, today's engagement wasn't about sending a message. It was about furthering her uncle's agenda and protecting the family.

The target was one Andrey Toth, the chairman of the Moscow board of governors for WANO, the World Association of Nuclear Operators. Toth had been one of the few Russian nuclear energy experts to resist Anton's push for the breeder reactor export program. While that could have presented difficulties, Toth resided in the wrong political circles, so his influence was limited. At least in the Russian Federation. As far as Anton was concerned, Toth wasn't an obstacle; he was annoyance. Like a pebble in one's shoe.

But even annoyances must be dealt with from time to time. Especially if they compromise the family.

Toth was here because he had been invited to speak at the University of Edinburgh's School of Physics. But that wasn't the only reason he was in the Scottish capital. He was also using the visit as an opportunity to spend time with his mistress, who was his executive assistant, and who had come with him from Moscow aboard a chartered jet.

The Shadow shook her head as she focused the binoculars. She despised cheaters. Her stepfather and mother had almost divorced when she was a child because one of them was cheating. She couldn't remember which one was the guilty party; she just remembered the arguments and the tears and the gut-wrenching uncertainty she had felt. Andrey Toth had three young children, and his wife was Anton's daughter, the Shadow's cousin. Anton had endured his daughter's tears long enough. So today, the annoyance that was Andrey Toth would cease to exist. And Anton would see the end of his daughter's pain. The Shadow was happy to help.

Toth's speech was at 1300 hours, local time. If the reports were accurate, he liked to sleep late with the mistress and enjoy morning "activities." As she scanned the windows of Toth's hotel room, waiting for a glimpse of her prey, the Shadow thought of Colin Pearce and smiled.

CHAPTER TWENTY-THREE

Thursday, November 4
1100 Hours Local Time
Edinburgh International Airport (EGPH)
Edinburgh Scotland, United Kingdom

The EC-135 Eurocopter lifted off the tarmac gracefully and ascended into the dull Scottish sky. I was still strapping into the observer's seat on the left side of the aircraft and getting my helmet into place as we climbed westward. I smiled to myself as I buckled the chin strap.

From one helmet to another, I thought.

Some crews wore headsets in helicopters, and some wore helmets. The helmets the pilot and I were wearing were blue and very similar to the plastic helmets with the integral visor assemblies that were prevalent in my early days in the USAF - before the advent of the lightweight helmets made of gray composite material. I reached up to the plastic visor housing above my forehead, unlocked the single visor and pulled it down and then pushed it back up again, just to make sure it moved freely. As I locked it back into the retracted position, the helo reached 500 feet on the altimeter, and the pilot made a slow turn back to the east, toward the city. In front of us, the dull gray buildings of Edinburgh lay in shadows from the overcast above.

I located my comm cord and pushed it into the jack mounted on the pedestal between the pilot and me.

"There you are," said the voice of the pilot as I got the cord into place.

"How do you hear me?" I asked.

"Loud and clear, mate," he answered over the intercom. "How do you hear me?" His voice was deep and had just a touch of Scottish brogue. He sounded like Sean Connery.

"Five by five," I said

"Sorry about the lack of help getting you strapped in, mate. We had to get out of there quickly. They were holding departures for us to get airborne." He glanced over at me. "You must be important Mr…"

"Pearce. Colin Pearce," I said. "And trust me, I'm nobody special."

"Special enough to get me scrambled on my day off," he said, not sounding disappointed at all.

"Well sorry about…"

"No worries," he said with a wave of his left hand. "I'd rather be flying than sitting on my arse watching the telly anyway." He looked over at me and smiled. "Bill James," he said. "Pleased to meet you. The gent in the back is Constable Fred Smithers."

I looked over my shoulder and saw another figure in a blue flight suit and helmet in the rear compartment. He waved at me.

"Hello," he said.

I nodded at him and returned my gaze to the front. The Eurocopter was configured for observation work. In addition to the cyclic control between his legs and the collective lever at his left side, Bill's side of the aircraft had a full instrument panel with electronic flight displays. On my side, I had duplicate flight controls and nothing else. But I also had a completely unimpeded view of the city through the clear Plexiglas canopy.

"The view is outstanding," I said.

Bill nodded. "Meant to be that way. We typically fly with a police observer in that seat. They can see a lot more without a panel in the way. There should be a hard plastic case to the left side of the center console there." He inclined his head to indicate the location he was speaking about. "There's a set of gyro-stabilized binoculars in there. It's too bad we only had the spare bird available today. The primary birds have optical and thermal imaging camera systems."

I opened the case and retrieved the binoculars. As I closed the lid on the case, a saw a flash of green to the left of the helo and turned my head in time to see a small golf course go by.

"That's Ravelston," Bill said. "Only a nine-hole course but great views of the landmarks while you're playing. My dad's a member there."

I turned the binoculars over in my hands until I saw a switch on the right-hand side.

"The first position is the light. The second is the gyro-stabilization system. Ever use gyro-stabilized binoculars before?"

I shook my head.

"Well we're in a vibrating helicopter obviously," Bill continued, "so they're a must for observation. They won't make the image completely still, but they'll stabilize it enough that you can tell what you're looking at."

"Sounds good," I said. I glanced over at him. Bill was wearing a blue flight suit with a nametag and a few patches on the shoulders. "Scottish Police?" I asked.

He shook his head. "No. Bond Air Services. We're the private air support for the Scottish Police. It's contracted over here in the U.K., not part of the department like it is the states."

"Interesting," I said. "Then it's got to be more efficient. Anytime you can get the government out of something it tends to work better."

He grinned at me. "That's the truth, isn't it?" he said. "Fred is police though. He's even armed if we get into trouble."

"Good to know," I said. "So where are we going?"

Bill shrugged. "I'm headed downtown but beyond that, you'll have to tell me. Our instructions were to pick you up and take you wherever you needed to go."

"Great," I said. "That makes two of us who don't know what to do." I retrieved my iPhone from the leg pocket of my flight suit and opened the message app. I was somewhat shocked to see there were no messages there.

"Well, shit," I muttered.

ANY LUCK ON A TARGET IN EDINBURGH? I texted Smith and Amrine.

I thought for a moment and decided to pursue the obvious. "Bill, do you have access to a list of official conventions, meetings or gatherings in the city today?"

"I don't, but I bet Fred does," he said. "Fred?"

"I can find out," Fred said. "But can you be more specific? Depending on the week or the day, there can be a hell of a lot of them."

"Something energy related," I said. "Particularly nuclear energy. Let's start there."

"Understood," Fred said.

Bill motioned toward the back seat with his collective hand. "He's got a data terminal back there as well as a printer," he said. "He should have a list for you in moments."

"If they've registered," Fred added. "That's the limitation. We only have a list of the gatherings that have been officially registered and have had permits issued."

"That should cover it," I said. "The shooter will be after someone attending a high profile event. That is assuming she's not targeting someone who lives here."

"Won't be able to nail that down anytime soon," Bill said.

I shook my head. "Probably not."

There was silence on the intercom as we drew nearer to the old section of Edinburgh. I could see distinct shape of Edinburgh Castle only a few miles away now. I could also make out the rectangular glass roof of the Scottish National Museum. There was white, round-domed building just to the south. It looked familiar to me from when I had toured the city years ago, but I couldn't remember what it was.

"What's that white domed building?" I asked Bill. "Just south of the National Museum."

"The University of Edinburgh is around there," Bill said. "I'm not sure of the name of that particular building."

"McEwan Hall," Fred said from the back. "It's the graduation hall there. I saw my brother graduate from the College of Physics there a few years ago. Big auditorium."

I nodded to myself. "Now, I remember," I said.

"I'm just going to set up an orbit around the downtown area until we figure out where we're going, okay?" Bill asked.

"Sure," I said.

"Nothing energy related," Fred said after another few minutes.

"Of course not," I said. "That would be too easy."

I gazed down through the Plexiglas at the streets below, bustling with business people and tourists. Even under the dull overcast sky, the streets teamed with flashes of color from the cars, the storefronts, and the people. I shook my head in frustration. Everyone I could see was having a normal day today and would probably be with family, friends or loved ones tonight. Everyone except for one poor soul who was going be on the receiving end of a .50 caliber bullet.

"Damn, Alina," I said into the intercom. "Where the hell are you?"

The Shadow heard the noise of the approaching helicopter but dismissed it because she was seeing movement in the hotel room she was monitoring. She put the binoculars aside and shouldered the rifle. She adjusted the focus on the sight as she settled into the weapon and waited for her target to appear. One of the room's windows was centered in the crosshairs of the sight. The white window frame looked like it had been freshly painted and it was shiny, even in the dull light. She could see diaphanous curtains behind the frame. The curtains were still, but there was motion on the bed that lay beyond. She could see two bodies, apparently locked in the throes of passion and moving rapidly. She couldn't determine which one was Andrey and she also couldn't quite distinguish enough detail to establish a point of aim.

The sound from the helicopter was getting louder. The Shadow looked up from her weapon to watch the blue and yellow aircraft fly overhead and in front of her. She wasn't worried about being spotted. She was inside a room on the top floor of an apartment building. Anton has ensured that the flat stayed available for her use as he had ensured that Andrey would be given a room facing the flat. As usual, the logistics were excellent and this time, even comfortable. The Shadow smiled as she remembered his words on the phone this morning after she had landed.

"Only one more after today, dushka. And then you will be rich, a hero of the Russian Federation and you will be free. You can rejoin your Mr. Pearce and spend the rest of your life with him what you wish."

Her body tingled as she remembered her time with Colin and she felt a lightness in her heart. Colin would understand why he had to be sidelined. She had to finish her mission. So they could be together.

Her eyes detected more movement in the hotel room. It seemed the couple was getting adventurous. They were getting up from the bed. The Shadow had the layout of the room and knew there was a sofa in front of the window.

A few moments later, the naked torso of a woman appeared in the window, and then her face, as she appeared to kneel on the sofa. A man's body appeared behind her, and as the woman's mouth opened in pleasure, the Shadow knew they were coupled.

This would be perfect, she thought. Both cheaters die with a single shot. While in the very act!

She leaned into her weapon and started the video.

CHAPTER TWENTY-FOUR

Thursday, November 4
1120 Hours Local Time
1,000 feet and 100 knots over City Centre
Edinburgh, Scotland, United Kingdom

"Do you have any helo time, Colin?" Bill asked.

We were maintaining our orbit around the downtown area of Edinburgh while Fred was continuing his search in the city databases to see if there were any other possible gatherings where the Shadow might make an appearance.

"About 12 hours," I said. "I had some extra money a few years back and was thinking about getting a helo rating. I started a private/commercial transition course at New Castle County Airport in Wilmington, Delaware. But I gave it up after a while. I didn't know what I'd do with it. I'm a contract business jet pilot. I didn't think I'd ever get enough helo hours for anyone to hire me to fly one for them. Just didn't seem to make any sense."

Bill nodded. "Tried to do a fixed wing transition a few years ago. Same for me, job opportunities didn't justify the cost."

"Well you had the easier time of it," I said. "Helicopters are much more difficult to fly than fixed wing aircraft are. Not sure why fixed wing pilots make so much more money." I laughed. "Must be the glamor."

"Well you do get to fly big-wigs and go exotic places," Bill said with a smirk on his face.

"And carry luggage and serve food and clean lavatories and deal with temper tantrums from people who never get told 'no.' Like I said, real glamorous."

"I've just flown soldiers and cops around," Bill said. "Guess I've been lucky."

"It's always great to fly people who appreciate the service you provide and the professionalism it takes to do it well."

I felt my phone vibrate in my hand. It was an incoming text message from Smith.

EVENT IN TAHOE IS A WANO MEETING. TWO
DAYS FROM NOW. ALL THE NUKE BIGWIGS WILL BE
THERE.

"WANO," I said. "What the hell is WANO?"

"How do you spell it?" Fred asked. "I'm online. Might as
well do something useful back here."

"W-A-N-O," I said.

It only took him a few seconds.

"World Association of Nuclear Operators," Fred said. "It's
an industry nuclear safety group, based in London but with
governing boards in Atlanta, Moscow, Paris, and Tokyo."

"Makes sense why she'd go after that," I said. "Just a
question of who she's targeting there."

"Wait a minute," Fred said. "I've seen that acronym today.
On one of my searches. It didn't pertain to a meeting or gathering
about energy, so I didn't mention it." There was a pause. "Where
was that? I know I saw it." A few more clicks. "Ah, there we are.
At my brother's college, that's why I ran into it. It's one of my
bookmarks. There's a speech about nuclear physics being given
today by an Andrey Toth. He's the Chairman of the Moscow Board
of Governors for WANO."

I looked at Bill and shrugged. "Not sure it's relevant, but
it's the best lead we've got. When's the speech, Fred?"

"1300 today. Not for about ninety minutes or so."

"She had to be here early," I said to no one in particular.
"Why did she have to be here early if he wasn't going to be in
public until one?"

I texted a message to Smith. ANDREY TOTH IS IN
EDINBURGH. CHAIRMAN OF MOSCOW BOARD FOR
WANO. RING A BELL?

I could see the little bubble on the screen of my iPhone as
Smith composed his reply. I looked over at Bill while I was
waiting.

"Sure is nice to stay in cell coverage while you're flying," I
said.

He nodded. "Comes in handy, doesn't it?" he said.

TOTH AGAINST ANTON'S PROJECT. POSSIBLE
TARGET.

My mind flashed through the portfolio of Alina's previous work. The majority of her victims had been taken in isolated locations or in their homes or hotel rooms through the window.

"Holy shit," I said. "She's going to take him in his room! Fred, can you find out where he's staying? We need the room number, floor, and exposure. As soon as possible."

"On it," Fred said.

Bill banked the helicopter up and headed it away from the castle, across the train station and toward a hotel with a tall clock tower extending from the top. He glanced over at me.

"Probably the Balmoral," he said. "Best place in town."

"Been in the whiskey bar there," I said. "Something like 400 single-malts. It was like paradise."

"Single-malt fan are you?" Bill asked, smiling.

"My favorite stuff on earth. I have over 50 bottles in my collection at home."

"Man after my own heart. There's a great pub in the north part of the city. Named after the writer Sir Arthur Conan Doyle. Well, maybe we can share a dram or two and swap war stories when we're done with our business today."

"I'd like that," I said.

"Got it," Fred said from the back. "He's in a deluxe room on the southeast corner of the hotel. Fourth floor."

"Smart thinking," I said. "She can take the shot from either side. Damn."

"She'd be hard to find anyway," Fred said. "Lone shooters always are."

"Let's do the easy thing then," Bill said.

"What's that?" I asked.

"Go hover outside the window of the room and scare the victims away! If they stay away from the windows, your shooter can't get them."

"Good call!" I said. "Fred, can you get with the local constabulary and have a team sent up to Toth's room to warn him? Just in case?"

"Will do," he said.

Bill was already bringing the helicopter down to an altitude level with the fourth floor and slowing it to less than 50 knots. The four tracks feeding into Edinburgh's Waverly station went underneath the helicopter as we crept toward the hotel. I wondered what Andrey Toth would think about finding a police helicopter outside his window. I had a brief flashback to Alina's invitation to dinner on her balcony in St. Moritz and the intensity of our time together. I found myself longing for her. Even as I attempted to stop her from killing another human being.

Jesus, I thought to myself. *This is so fucked up.*

"Well looks like we'll be interrupting something," Bill said, laughing.

"What are you talking about?" I asked.

"Look at the corner room we're interested in," he said. "Mr. Toth is having a little pre-speech tryst!"

"Get over there quick, Bill!" I said. "He's totally exposed."

Bill tilted the cyclic forward and we moved toward the building more rapidly, still laughing. "I'll say he is!"

The Shadow was just starting to press the trigger when the helicopter entered the telescopic sight's field of regard. She watched the faces of Toth and his whore as they registered surprise and shock and then both figures retreated from the window.

No! The surge of rage was sudden and intense and surprising.

The Shadow had never experienced emotion when she was on the job before. She was always dispassionate. Calculating. Distant. The targets were merely targets. Not people. She didn't care whether they lived or died. She only cared about the precision of the shot and the amount of money in her bank account.

But today was different. The people she was engaging deserved to die. And no one was going to stop her. These meddlers had foiled her plans to put two cheaters in the ground.

How dare they!

Without thinking, the Shadow pivoted her weapon to the right side of the cockpit, settled the crosshairs on the helmeted figure seated there and squeezed the trigger.

The .50 caliber round closed this distance to the target at 2,750 feet per second. As the weapon recovered, the Shadow saw pilot slumped over, and the helicopter immediately began spiraling to the left and down and away from the building.

The Shadow brought her sight back to the room's window. Hoping. Perhaps even praying.

Sure enough, Andrey Toth and his whore stood there. Now covered by sheets, watching the carnage about to take place as the helicopter headed downward.

She smiled and squeezed the trigger of her weapon twice more.

CHAPTER TWENTY-FIVE

Thursday, November 4
1137 Hours Local Time
100 feet and 0 knots ... and descending
Edinburgh, Scotland, United Kingdom

For the second time in several days, I found myself in a situation where life was all about reaction time. And again, I was lucky.

Even as Bill slowed the Eurocopter into a hover outside Toth's window and began the pedal turn to point the helo away from the building and toward Alina's avenue of fire, I felt a sudden knot form in my gut. We were going to be in the sights of a .50 caliber weapon, aimed by a woman who was deadly accurate with it. We had no armor, no countermeasures, no defenses.

Without even willing them, my hands began to move toward the helo's flight controls, the cyclic and collective, although I wasn't sure what I'd do if I had to fly the damn thing.

I never heard the bullet come through the windscreen. There was a dull thud and a scream from Fred through the intercom. Then Bill slumped into his shoulder harness and released the controls.

Immediately the helicopter began slowly turning to the left and descending. There wasn't time to think. There was only time to do.

I rushed my feet onto the pedals and applied pressure to the right one to stop the left rotation. At the same time, I pulled up on the collective to arrest the descent. I looked below us. We were over the flat roof of some sort of shopping complex that was next to the Balmoral, but was we continued to rotate, we drifted south, over the multiple metallic, pitched rooflines of the Waverly Station. They seemed to be slowly climbing, reaching for us. The sensation was similar to an aircraft settling to the ground during the landing phase. My peripheral vision saw the horizon rising around us, even as we continued to rotate. It was like sinking into a crater made of dull, gray, buildings.

I felt an odd isolation. There were no people or cars directly beneath us or around us, just the pitched, metallic roof of the train station. As we continued downward, I felt some assurance that at least we might not kill anyone else in the crash – unless someone happened to be directly under the spot where we would impact.

I continued upward pressure on the collective, hoping like hell that the throttle compensator was keeping the engine and torque within limits. As I pulled on the collective, I pushed on the right pedal, remembering the relationship between increased lift in the hover and the requirement for more pedal to stabilize the aircraft. A quick smile passed over my lips. Nearly every other helicopter in the world, like the Schweitzer I had trained in, had rotor blades that rotated clockwise, requiring left pedal to counter the rotation. It figured that the one time my skills would be required in an emergency situation, I'd be in one of the few helicopters in existence that had counter-clockwise rotating blades and required opposite inputs.

Maybe I wasn't so lucky after all.

Our descent to the roof began to slow, as did the rotation of the aircraft. The roof was a few meters below the skids, and because it was a series of pitched rooflines, landing on it wasn't an option. Besides, I knew I needed to get Bill and Fred to a hospital as soon as possible. I watched the tan and gray brick of the Balmoral hotel go by slowly, off the nose of the helo, like the gradual pan of a movie camera. Then the shops and buildings of Princes Street passed in front of us, even more unhurriedly. The descent stopped, and my view of the buildings around us remained level. I applied a little more right pedal, and the rotation ceased as well. The Eurocopter settled into a stable hover, just a few feet above the apex of one of the pitched rooflines of the train station. I looked through the windscreen to see the faces of hundreds of people, staring at me from the road in front of the Scottish National Gallery, just across the railyard.

I looked downward. We were so close to the rooftop, I could see the lines in the pattern of the metal.

"You saved us," Fred said weakly over the intercom.

"Barely," I said.

I flexed my fingers on the cyclic and collective and kept my eyes on the road in front of the gallery. Smooth inputs and eyes on the horizon were the keys to a stable hover. It was the one area of my training I had spent the most time practicing and the one in which I had the most confidence. The fact that the Eurocopter was a much heavier ship than the Schweitzer and inherently more stable in the hover than the smaller aircraft didn't hurt.

"Fred, how bad are you hit?" I asked.

"Bullet went through my chest," he said, now wheezing a bit as he spoke.

I glanced over at Bill. The inertial reel in his harness had held him upright. If it weren't for the huge red hole in the center of his chest, he could have been napping.

"Not sure about Bill," I said. "Fred, we need to get to a hospital. Where do we go?"

"Royal Infirmary of Edinburgh," he said, his voice barely audible. "Get higher; I'll show you where it is."

"Might be easier said than done," I muttered. "But here goes."

I pushed forward on the cyclic, flying us directly towards the Scottish National Gallery. As the helo gained speed and passed through the magic window of transitional lift, 16 – 24 knots, I had to apply left pedal to keep the nose aligned. We accelerated through 40 knots, I pulled up on the collective gradually, and the helo rose into the dull Scottish sky. I glanced down to see the faces of the onlookers in front of the gallery looking up at us as we climbed above the roof of the Gallery. Some had their hands over their mouths; others were pointing up at us.

"Uh-oh," I said to myself, "I wonder if we're trailing smoke or something."

We accelerated through 90 knots and climbed through 800 feet. I could see the Edinburgh airport in the distance and gave some thought about going back to where we had come from, but it seemed that minutes could matter for Fred and maybe even for Bill if he was still alive. I leveled the helo at 1,000 feet and began a slow turn to the south, just to the west of Edinburgh Castle.

I felt around on the cyclic for a microphone switch and pushed each of the two red buttons I found, listening for a click in my headset. There was nothing. Then I remembered my Schweitzer days and felt for a trigger underneath the cyclic with my right index finger. It was there. I squeezed the trigger twice and heard two clicks in my headset. Then I held it down.

"Mayday, Mayday, Mayday. This is Police Helicopter 10 over downtown Edinburgh. We've taken sniper fire and are proceeding to the Royal Infirmary of Edinburgh."

"Police 10, Edinburgh Approach, roger the emergency. The infirmary's helicopter pad is under repair, recommend you proceed to the Edinburgh airport."

"Negative, approach," I replied. "I've got two men aboard who were hit by sniper fire. One is probably dead, but the other is severely wounded. Need to get him to hospital as soon as possible. Please call them and tell them we're coming."

"Roger, Police 10. We'll call."

"Find the University," Fred said over the intercom. His voice sounded like he was fighting unconsciousness.

I looked to my left and saw the white dome we had discussed earlier.

"I see the dome," I said.

"Fly toward it for now…" His voice trailed off.

"Stay with me, Fred," I said, as I turned the helo toward the dome. "Stay with me. We'll have you in a doc's hands in just a few minutes."

I rolled the Eurocopter out of the turn and observed the nose wasn't pointed exactly in the direction of flight. I applied a little right pedal to align it. Nothing happened.

Oh shit! I thought. *Did the fucking bullet go through to the tail rotor?*

The tail rotor on a helicopter was what kept it from turning in the opposite direction of the rotor. If the tail rotor failed, forward flight might not be affected much because the helo had stabilizer fins to keep it aligned, but slow speed flight and hovering would be impossible without the ship rotating, as it had done a few moments earlier. Only this time, I wouldn't have the controls to counter it.

I pushed the right pedal a little harder and the nose of the ship slowly, almost begrudgingly, moved to the right.

This is going to fucking interesting.

"When we get to the University, what then Fred?" I asked.

"Three roads," he said. "Three roads going south on the far side. Follow the road furthest east."

We flew over the dome of the auditorium, and I picked up the three roads he had mentioned. There was a two-lane road, nearest the University, a four-lane road a few blocks over and then another two-lane road a few blocks after that.

"Road in sight, Fred," I said.

"Infirmary only a few miles south," he wheezed. "On east side of road. Look for golf course and small castle."

"Got it."

I turned us to fly down the road and saw the gardens of George Square and a huge tennis court complex go down the right side of the helo. I looked across the cockpit at the PDU display on Bill's instrument panel. 1,100 feet and 120 knots. We needed to get down and slow down if I was going to land this thing. I moved the collective down slightly to begin a descent and pulled the cyclic back to slow us, paying very close attention to the amount of pedal I needed to keep the aircraft aligned as we decelerated.

It's funny the skills that can come back to you after a long time of disuse. In my younger days, during the Cold War, I had flown the A-10 all over the UK and western Europe at 250 to 500 feet and had perfected the fine art of finding targets at low altitude. Without my willing it, my brain and eyes went into target acquisition mode, analyzing terrain features and man-made ones, looking for lead-in clues to the place we were going. I looked down the and saw a building that looked like a drum kit on the east side of the road and another building with a large, white, square roof. Beyond the rectangular roof was a golf course but I didn't see anything that looked like a small castle or a hospital.

"Golf course but no hospital," I said to myself.

"That's Prestonfield," Fred said weakly. "Look for the next course further down. Liberton. On the other side of the road."

"A lot of golf courses," I said, my eyes already looking beyond the course in the foreground.

"You're in Scotland," Fred said with a barely audible chuckle. "We invented the damn game."

I laughed. "Good point, Fred."

I scanned the road further down and found the next golf course. Then I looked across the road and saw the hospital complex, a large group of modern buildings with silver roofs, looking oddly out of place in the midst of the farm fields and golf course surrounding it.

"I see the hospital, Fred. We're almost there."

"That's great," he said, wearily. "The superintendent is going to be miffed. I've made it grotty back here."

I continued the descent down to 300 feet on the altimeter and slowed us to 50 knots. As the helo decelerated, the nose started to rotate slowly to the left. I pressed the right pedal further, and the rotation stopped. I had less than an inch of pedal left before I hit the stop. There was no question that the tail rotor was damaged. I wasn't going to be able to hover and land the helo.

Well shit.

I pulled the mic trigger. "Edinburgh approach, Police 10. I'm not going to be able to do a hover landing at the hospital. I'm going to need to do a run-on landing, probably on one of the roads around it. Tell the hospital, please. Also tell them the crewmember in the aft part of the ship has a bullet wound to the chest, probably through one of his lungs."

"Police 10, Edinburgh approach, roger. Suggest you return to the airport."

"Fuck that," I said to myself as I released the mic trigger. "He'd never make it."

The infirmary complex came up on the left side of the helo as I leveled us off at 250 feet on the altimeter, just over 100 feet AGL. The complex was massive. The center of the main building was rectangular and attached to several smaller quadrangle complexes, arranged in an arc on the southwest side. I orbited the complex and looked for a place to set the helo down. There were roads on all sides of the complex, but some had trees that were too close to the paved surface, and other roads had too much traffic on them for me to land. As I came around the west side of the complex, I saw the helicopter pad the controller had mentioned. The surface was torn off it, and there were several construction vehicles parked around. A few members of the construction crew pointed up at me as we flew by.

"Probably think I'd be stupid enough to try to land there," I said to myself.

As I came around the north side of the complex, I could see an ambulance with its emergency lights flashing parked in front of the main entrance of the hospital. There were two police cars parked next to it with their lights on as well. I nodded. That was our welcoming party. Now all I needed to find was a place to land.

"Police 10, Edinburgh approach. Police on the ground there advise you land on western part of Little France Drive, where it's under construction."

"Which road is Little France Drive?" I asked myself as I turned down the east side of the complex.

I was about to key the mic and ask when I looked at the road along the south side of the complex and saw the brown section of it to the east.

"Understand that's the road that goes approximately east-west along the south side of the hospital, and the part under construction is the westernmost part of the road?"

There was a delay while the controller communicated with whoever had given him the instructions.

"That's affirmative, Police 10."

"Roger that. I'll put down there. Please tell them I'll need to make one more circuit to get set up."

"Understood Police 10."

I turned the helo in a lazy arc to the left to get spacing from the road and line up on it. I flew directly over the infirmary complex and saw the ambulance and the two police cars exiting the parking lot and heading for the intersection of the infirmary's southeastern access road and Little France Drive. I nodded to myself. They were going to wait for me to fly by and then follow me down the road. I rolled out parallel to Little France Drive and tried to gauge my spacing for the base turn. Several things ran through my mind, none of which were good. I realized that in my whopping 12 hours of helo time, I had done a run-on landing exactly once. Now, I not only had to do one, but I also had to do it at relatively high speed, with a lot of precision and no idea when

I'd run out of right pedal. And, to top it all off, as I gazed downward, I gauged the wind by the deflection of the trees below me and noticed they were bending westward. That meant the winds here were approximately opposite what they were at the airport. I'd landing downwind – which would increase my ground speed.

This just keeps getting better.

I crossed the north-south road and flew out over the Liberton Golf Club. As the green sea of the golf course appeared around me, I began a gradual base turn to parallel the north-south road, and I released pressure on the collective to allow the helo to descend further. When I rolled out of the turn, I noticed four tall apartment buildings, in a line, directly in front of me. Like a barrier.

"Jesus," I said. "If it's not one thing it's another."

So much for a square landing pattern. I banked to the left slightly to round out the turn to final and stopped the descent about 100 feet above the ground. In my peripheral vision, I could see golfers on the course, braving the November weather. I smiled as I looked down at them.

"Bet you guys didn't think you'd see a flyby."

I flew over some houses on the edge of the golf course and began my turn to final, watching the nearest apartment building go by on the right side of the ship. Little France Road stretched in front of me as I rolled out, with a row of tall fir trees lining the southern edge of it. Up ahead, I could see where the road turned from gray to brown, and the construction began. There was a police car parked in the construction area, well away from the road with its light bar flashing. There were no personnel or vehicles in my path.

I breathed a sigh of relief. *At least that's something*, I thought.

I crossed the north-south road and flew along the left side of Little France Drive so that the trees wouldn't be a factor as I descended. I didn't have much of a plan. I was going to get as close to the ground as I could and slow the helo until I ran out of right pedal. Once that happened, I was going to put the skids on the ground, drop the collective and hope for the best.

The intersection of Little France Drive and the infirmary access road went by and I saw the ambulance and a police car moving to pull out behind me as I passed. I let off a little more collective and allowed the helo to drop lower. Even as there were trees on the south side of the road, there were bushes on the north side. I stopped the descent just above the bushes, about 10 feet or so above the road and offset to the left of it. The greenery flashed underneath the helo, and I saw a walking path paralleling the road on the left of the aircraft. A large parking lot went by on the left, filled with cars for patients and staff and whomever. It was the middle of the day, so people were coming and going, probably for lunch. Up ahead, there was a big square building south of the road, and beyond that, the road turned brown. I passed the parking lot and saw the trees on the right side of the road getting smaller. I moved the ship a little to the right with bank instead of pedal, trying to save the pedal for when I'd need it most.

The glass front of the square building went by on the right, and I had the impression of faces pressed against glass, probably getting their day's entertainment watching some fool trying to land a helicopter on the road.

Then another road to the north went by on the left, and the building faded past on the right and Little France Drive went brown underneath.

I let up on the collective a little more and let the helo sink, even as I banked slightly to center us on the road. The brown dirt flashed by, now mere inches below the skids, and I looked up to see the end of the road and a forest beyond that, far too close for comfort. I eased the cyclic back to continue to slow the helo through 40 knots and applied a slight pressure on the collective to maintain altitude. For the moment, it seemed that I had enough right pedal to keep us straight.

Decelerating through 30 knots, I took my last glance at the airspeed indicator. The helo would go through transitional lift at any moment, and that would be the test. A little more aft cyclic, a little more collective. A little more pedal. So far, so good.

The brown dirt below the skids was going by slower now. I could see tire tracks clearly and even see detail of the tread marks in the tracks. I aligned the helo with the most visible set of tracks as it continued to slow. Then, the Eurocopter's nose started to rotate to the left a bit more, and I pushed harder on the right pedal to line the ship back up. But even as I applied pressure to the pedal, I felt it hit the stop.

I was out of pedal.

Here we go.

I had no idea how fast we were going. I was estimating 20-25 knots, which sounds slow, but in a helicopter with shit turning all around you, it seemed pretty damn fast. I let the collective down slowly, and we sank to the dirt. A cloud of brown dust surrounded the helo, and I lost all depth perception as well as my view of where the road ended.

Should have thought about that. Idiot.

I let the collective down a little more, and there was thud and vibration as the skids contacted the dirt. I was moved forward in my straps, and I pushed the collective to the floor, effectively killing all the lift in the rotor disc. The skids dug into the dirt then, and I was thrown violently forward into my shoulder harness. I felt the helo skidding sideways, and I had a mental image of us rolling on a side and rotor blades breaking and going everywhere, but fortunately, that didn't happen and we stayed upright. I searched the panels for engine controls frantically and found them on the forward console, just above the center pedestal. I flipped both engine switches to the off position and heard the twin turbines whine downward as the fuel supply to the engines was closed.

The helo slid to a stop a few moments later.

I wanted to take a moment and breathe, but there wasn't time.

As the engines continued to spool down, I released my safety belt and harness and reached over to put my hand on Bill's throat to feel for a pulse. His head rolled back into my arm, and I saw that his eyes were open and unseeing. He had a slight smile on his lips.

"At least you died happy, my friend," I said.

I closed his eyes and exited the helicopter quickly, disconnecting my com cord as I stepped out. I dashed around to the side. The door of the ship was open as was the normal practice, so I jumped inside. The helmeted figure in blue coveralls was covered in blood, and there were oozing red bubbles coming from a gaping wound in the chest.

But Fred was still breathing.

As I reached to unstrap him, the medical personnel and police reached the helicopter.

"We've got him, sir," said a man in a white coat with a stethoscope around his neck, reaching in from the other side of the ship. He wore a lanyard with an ID badge, sporting the name of D. LIVINGSTONE.

Another member of the team, a female, had entered the helo from my side. She wore dark blue scrubs, had a bag at her side and an intent look on her face.

"Could you clear out sir? We'll take him now."

I nodded and backed out of the helo.

A British Police constable was waiting for me as I stepped to the ground, an attractive woman in her mid-thirties with chestnut brown hair. She reminded me of Gail. I smiled at her. "Thanks for coming. Sorry to put you to the trouble."

"No bother at t'all," she said in the British idiom. "Probably the most eventful day I've had in a while." She extended her hand.

"Constable Rachel MacDonald," she said.

"Colin Pearce," I replied, shaking her hand. Her grip was firm and businesslike.

"I probably should turn this thing off," I said, gesturing to the cockpit. "I'm just not sure how and I don't want to disturb the pilot's body in case your forensic team wants to do some analysis."

She smiled and stepped past me to the open cockpit door. I saw her reach up to the overhead panel and heard the click of several switches being turned off. The helo's external lights extinguished and the avionics cooling fan wound down. She stepped out of the cockpit and inclined her head toward it.

"I've flown as observer on these things and watched them shut it down. Anything else you need from in there?" she asked.

"Nope," I said. I unstrapped my helmet and removed it. "I should probably leave this behind."

I stepped up and placed the helmet on my seat. Then I closed the cockpit door. As I turned back to her, I could see her looking me over, taking in the wrinkled French flight suit, the disheveled hair and tired look on my face.

"You seem to have had quite a day," she said.

I nodded. "You could say that."

"He's stabilized enough for us to move him," Dr. Livingstone said from the aft compartment. "Let's get him to the operating theater."

I stuck my head into the compartment. "What do you think, doctor? Will he make it?"

He looked up at me from Fred's side. "Hard to say with certainty at this point but we've kept him breathing, and we've stopped the bleeding. He's got a really good chance."

"Glad to hear that."

"It's a good thing you brought him here," he said. "Another five or ten minutes and he wouldn't have made it. What sort of weapon made this injury? So, we know what we're up against."

".50 caliber BMG round," I said. "Although I think they're specially loaded and have ballistics that are somewhat unique. One round killed the pilot, went through Fred and did some damage to the tail rotor boom of the aircraft."

He nodded. "I used to be in the Army, and I spent some time in Afghanistan. I'm familiar with the damage that sort of round can do."

"Then he couldn't be in better hands."

He smiled wearily. "We'll see," he said.

I nodded and turned back to the constable.

"I'll need you to come with me and give a statement," she said.

"I'll give you one," I said. "But I'm not sure you'll believe it."

CHAPTER TWENTY-SIX

Friday, November 5
1000 Hours Local Time
Flight Level 430 in a Falcon 900LX
Over the West Coast of Scotland

The leather seat was comfortable, but I always had trouble sleeping in the ass-end of airplanes I wasn't flying. So instead, I looked out the window and watched the cloud-covered coast of Scotland go by underneath us. I glanced at the Airshow display in the small monitor that was by my window. We were flying over the island of Islay, the origin of nearly all the peaty single-malts I loved.

"Get enough sleep last night?" Dave Smith asked.

I turned toward him. He was seated across the aisle from me and was nursing a bloody mary made by our very attentive flight attendant, Marsha. I had a similar drink in the cup holder next to my window. The drink was excellent, but I had only finished about half of it.

"I guess," I said, answering his question. The truth was that I didn't sleep very much at all. Once again, thoughts of Alina and St. Moritz swam through my consciousness, refusing to allow me the bliss of undisturbed rest. And after seeing her handiwork yesterday, at close range, and almost dying as a result of it, I couldn't unscramble the thoughts of her from my growing concern about the darkness inside of myself. I didn't take her shot at the helicopter personally. She didn't plan to shoot at us. We got in the way. We stood between her and the mission, so she took us down. Exactly as I would have done. We would have been collateral damage. And I had caused my fair share of that as well.

Jesus, I thought for what seemed like the millionth time, *we are the same.*

"We need to get you to Tahoe," Smith said, interrupting my introspection. "We'll give you a quick stop in Wilmington to swap your clothes out and for John and I to get reequipped. But then we fly to Tahoe so we can be in place for the Shadow's next event."

"So, assuming Alina makes it out of the U.K. without getting nabbed by the Brits. She'll be after someone at the WANO thing?"

"Yes. And our intelligence folks have done a little digging. It's a two-day event with a reception tomorrow afternoon, a boat cruise on the lake tomorrow night and meetings the next day."

"Who's the target?"

Smith sighed. "With all the high-ranking WANO directors and members coming in, it could be anyone, but our money is on Mark Lane, the CEO of Enteron, the largest nuclear operator and largest utility in the U.S."

"Why?"

"Because he's the keynote speaker," Smith said. "And he's vehemently against WANO's supporting the Russians' breeder reactors for worldwide distribution."

I nodded. "When's his speech?"

"During the meetings in the morning day after tomorrow," Smith said. "But he'll have tomorrow evening to mingle and drum up support on the boat cruise. And according to our background folks, this guy is an artist. He's a high school graduate who came up through the nuclear ranks and is incredibly smart and perceptive. He knows how to work people. If anyone can get WANO to vote against the Russians, he can."

"When does he arrive at Tahoe?" I asked.

"Tomorrow about mid-day," Amrine said. "And by that time, we need to know what airport servicing Tahoe presents the least risk and how we can better protect him."

I looked over to Amrine, who was across the aisle from me as well but seated a row behind Smith. "That's easy. I've flown into both airports that service Tahoe. The airport you want for Lane is Truckee, north of the Lake. You don't want the South Lake Tahoe which is obviously south of the lake. Especially with Alina to deal with."

"Rationale?" Amrine asked.

"If you're online, you can call up a terrain map." I shut my eyes and looked away from both of them. "South Lake Tahoe Airport is in a valley, and a sniper could sit up on one of the hillsides and shoot down into it. Truckee's airport is out in the

237

open, but the nearest terrain or concealment is quite a distance away. A shot there would be considerably more difficult."

Amrine nodded. "Makes sense," he said. "I'll reach out to Enteron's Chief of Security. He used to be the Agency. We've worked an op or two together in the past."

"I guess the big question is how could Alina know, in advance, what airport he'd be landing at?" I asked. "If she can get intel like that then it would seem that nothing is off limits for her."

Amrine shook his head. "Can't ever underestimate the Russians," he said. "The day you do that, they kick your ass. We don't know if she'll know where he's landing. We just have to assume she knows. Every one of the hits she's made has shown incredible attention to detail and planning. She's getting the intel from somewhere."

I nodded. "I think the boat's your biggest problem," I said. "Out in the middle of the lake and exposed. The terrain around Tahoe could make lining up a shot difficult. But out in the middle of the lake, the target will be a sitting duck."

Amrine nodded. "You're right. I'll work with my contact at Enteron and try to talk the CEO out of it. But I'm not optimistic. This guy is passionate about wanting to tube the breeder reactor deal. He'll want to grip and grin with everyone on the boat."

"And let me guess," I said. "That's where we'll be."

Amrine smiled. "What you mean we, paleface? You'll be on the boat. We'll be in a helo looking for her from above."

"It'd be nice if you had a date or something, T.C.," Smith said. "All the CEOs attending will be bringing their wives, and Lane will bring his. You should have someone with you. You'll blend in better. Think General Peterson would be game for it?"

"Who knows? It's short notice for her, and she's not spontaneous. Besides, if it interferes with her job or her schedule, she won't go for it. God, forbid she prioritize something else over her job."

Or someone else, I thought.

"As you have frequently reminded us, she knows about the Shadow," Amrine said. "It would make the arrangements much simpler from a clearance perspective."

"Text her, T.C.," Smith said. "See if she can join you tomorrow night."

I dug my phone out of my jacket pocket and turned it on.

"Don't get your hopes up," I said as I waited for the phone to boot. Once the screen illuminated, I connected the phone to the jet's wifi system and began to type.

ON A PLANE HEADED TO U.S. MAKING A QUICK STOP ON EAST COAST THEN HEADED TO CA FOR POSSIBLE EVENT. ANY CHANCE YOU COULD BE IN LAKE TAHOE TOMORROW NIGHT?

The bubble appeared on the iPhone screen while Gail composed her reply.

NEED A REASON TO JUSTIFY TRAVEL, she wrote.

"Of course, you do," I said, looking down at the phone.

"Tell her we'll send a plane for her," Smith said. "This is pretty important. We've uncovered some additional material that makes us think the Russians may be up to more than cornering the market on nuclear energy."

CIA WILL SEND PLANE FOR YOU, I wrote. Then I thought for a moment. S & A WANT YOU WITH ME FOR COVER. MATTER OF NATL SECURITY.

The reply bubble appeared and remained for a long time. She was obviously thinking carefully about her reply. After a long moment, her words came through.

K. SEND DETAILS PLZ.

"Well, don't sound so enthusiastic about it," I said, staring at the screen. I looked over at Smith. "Apparently, she's on board. I'll need the details of the flight for her when you have them."

He nodded. "I'll get with our flight ops folks and have them schedule something for her ASAP."

I nodded back and turned to gaze out the window. I took a sip of my bloody mary as I watched the clouds go by. Thoughts of Alina occurred to me again, but this time interspersed with thoughts of Gail. I wondered how I could feel such a strong connection to a woman I barely knew and hardly any connection at all to a woman I had known for several months.

I sighed to myself. For someone who saw himself as a loner, it seemed that I hadn't been alone much over the last year or so. Since I couldn't be with Sarah, I had moved from one recreational relationship to another and sometimes, got people killed along the way.

I knew I needed to end things with Gail. Our relationship, if it could even be called that, was a waste of time and energy and it was going nowhere. Besides, after the close call in Crystal City, she could end up caught in the crossfire again and I didn't want that on my conscience. I decided to have that conversation with her in Tahoe and let her go back to her Air Force life without me. I doubted it would even bother her.

Alina and I would end as well. It was inevitable. Sooner or later we were going to have to confront one another without the guarded civilities we had shown in Switzerland and our true natures would come out. And one of us was going to die.

Hell, I thought as I took another sip of my drink, *maybe we both will.*

CHAPTER TWENTY-SEVEN

Saturday, November 6
1300 Hours Local Time
Truckee-Tahoe Airport (KTRK)
Truckee, California, USA

It was one thing flying into this airport at the controls of a business jet. It was quite another waiting on the ground for a jet to arrive, knowing one of the passengers could be the target of a professional assassin, and having very little ability to make a difference. I felt completely useless.

I was sitting in the passenger seat of a pickup truck parked in front of the Truckee-Tahoe Airport FBO with its manager, a pleasant fellow named Joe Keating. We were waiting for Mark Lane's jet to arrive and were going to lead them to a more enclosed area where the passengers could disembark. When the CIA and I had arrived earlier, we had met with Keating in his office and described the threat. He nodded like he knew exactly what we were talking about and then admitted he had been a former FBI agent and a specialist in undercover work and intelligence. That made the rest of the discussion easy.

The ideal scenario would have been for Enteron's Falcon 2000LX to land and taxi into a hangar and have Lane and his wife disembark inside the hangar. But the FBO didn't have access to a hangar large enough to contain the aircraft. Keating had suggested having the jet taxi to a ramp area well behind the FBO to facilitate concealment for Lane and his wife to exit the aircraft and get to their ground transportation without being engaged. The buildings around the parking area would obscure the line-of-sight from almost all of the terrain around the airport.

Smith, Amrine and I had all nodded in satisfaction as Keating had shown us the area where the jet would be unloaded. It wasn't perfect, but it was better than unloading on the open ramp in front of the FBO.

"We'll leave the jet here after the crew shuts it down and puts it to bed," he said. "I assume you're going to have a security crew stay with the aircraft."

"You bet," Smith had said. "Three teams working 8-hour shifts."

"I'd like to meet all of them if you don't mind," Keating had said. "So, I can tell if there are any imposters later."

"You'll be able to remember all the faces?" Smith had asked. Then he had held his hand up in apology. "Sorry," he said. "I forgot you were an undercover guy. John and I used to go under as well. You have to have a photographic memory for faces."

"And names as well," Keating added.

"And you've briefed the pilots?" Amrine asked me.

I nodded. "You bet. Right after you put me in touch with them. It turns out Enteron's Aviation Director is a classmate of mine from the Air Force Academy. His name is Mark Hill. He'll be flying the aircraft when it lands."

"Is this Hill guy reliable?"

"Absolutely. I'll vouch for him anytime. And he thinks very highly of his CEO and his wife. He had more questions than I had answers. I told him we'd have everything under control."

That ended the consultation a few hours ago, and now Joe Keating and I sat in the truck, waiting for the jet to arrive.

"So, tell me how you ended up here?" I asked. "After spending a good portion of your life with the FBI?"

Keating shook his bald head slightly as he looked through the windshield at the runway in front of us. "Everything happens for a reason, I guess. I was getting fed up with the bureaucracy of the Bureau, especially with the current DOJ staff. My folks own the FBO here, and my dad's health was failing. My dad would never make the call but my mom did, and I came back to run the family business. It wasn't a hard choice. I've always loved it here, and I hate the city."

"Can't fault you there," I had said.

"Besides," he said. "The pay's about the same here as it was while I was in the Bureau and no one is trying to kill me." He winked at me. "Although my wife may have considered it a time or two."

I laughed.

The radio in the truck crackled. It was tuned to the common traffic advisory frequency for the airport. Truckee-Tahoe

242

airport didn't have a control tower so pilots made advisory calls about the position of their aircraft so other pilots would be aware of them.

"Truckee-Tahoe Airport Traffic, November 497 Delta Charlie is rolling out on a five-mile final to runway one-one, Truckee-Tahoe Airport."

I keyed my hand-held radio, which was on a different, scrambled frequency. "They're about five minutes out."

"We're ready," Smith replied. "Vehicles in place."

"Roger," I acknowledged.

The sun was out, and it was a beautiful afternoon in the Sierra Nevadas. As I squinted my eyes and looked to the west, I could see the twin landing lights of the approaching business jet as it descended to the runway, its white shape just visible above the rolling, tree-covered hills west of the airport and the mountains beyond.

"You don't think your sniper will try to take them in the air or while they're taxiing?" Keating asked.

I thought about it for a moment then shook my head. "I don't think so," I said. "She's not a sniper. She's never been tactically trained or under fire. She's a former target shooter, and she needs the conditions to be controlled when she shoots."

He looked over at me and nodded. "That's good intelligence," he said. "You guys seem to know your adversary."

You have no idea, I thought.

The Falcon 2000LX touched down gracefully a few moments later and passed in front of us as the thrust reversers deployed and it slowed to taxiing speed. I had a quick glimpse of it before Keating put the truck in gear and saw a white jet with three stripes of orange, blue and green. It was a catchy paint scheme.

"Here we go," Keating said.

I keyed my mic. "We're moving," I said. "We'll be in the parking area in about three to five minutes."

"Roger," Smith replied.

Keating drove the truck out to the parallel taxiway and turned right, following the taxiway to meet the airplane when it turned off the runway and to lead it to the designated area.

"Tahoe-Truckee traffic, November 497 Delta Charlie is clear of the active, Runway 11, Truckee-Tahoe."

The sleek jet turned onto an adjoining taxiway, just before the cross runway, then made another turn onto the parallel taxiway, facing us. I watched the landing lights extinguish, and the flaps and slats on the wings retract as the first officer ran the AFTER LANDING checklist. Then, as Keating blinked his headlights at the jet and made a 180 degree turn on the taxiway to lead the jet to parking, I saw the jet's taxi light go out as well.

Keating turned off the parallel taxiway at the first adjoining taxiway to the ramp and led Enteron's Falcon between two buildings and down another taxiway that was bordered by a row of hangars for small aircraft on the east side and the airport's fire station on the west side, just in the corner.

"This is good," I said as we led the jet to the spot. "This is very good. No high terrain with a line of sight. Just like we thought."

"It's funny," Keating said. "I've been out of the Bureau for a few years now, and I was never on a protection detail, but I can't help thinking about scenarios when I drive around the airport. You know? How would a vehicle or a jet be taken here or there? How many men would be required? How would they gain access? That sort of shit. It just never leaves you."

"I know what you mean," I said.

"But this area isn't perfect, like we discussed," Keating said. "She could still shoot from that tree line on the other side of runway 11-29 if she found a good position."

I shook my head. "Not her style," I said. "I can't tell you how I know that. I just do. There's not enough advantage for her. It's not high ground. It's not particularly far, and there's no quick avenue of escape. Like I said, she's not a sniper in a ghillie suit and lying in the mud. She's a target shooter looking for a nice mat to lie on or a nice even surface for the bipod of her rifle. Everything would need to be perfect for her. Everything would need to be certain."

Keating nodded. "She sounds pretty fucked up," he said as he made a slow 180 degree turn with the truck, showing the pilot of the jet behind us the path he needed to follow. "But that's true of all killers."

Yes, it is, I thought.

Keating parked the truck, retrieved a pair of orange marshaling wands from the side pocket of the vehicle and exited it. I opened my door and joined him on the taxiway. The 2000LX taxied by us, and I saw Hill looking out the left cockpit windscreen at Keating. Joe had his arms in the air and provided the signals for Hill to make the left turn to parallel the far edge of the taxiway and then another left turn to complete the 180-degree turn and face us. Keating had one of his line crew members next to the row of hangars with his hand up in the air with a "thumbs up" displayed so that Hill knew his right wing would be clear of the hangars as he turned. Hill straightened the jet out and taxied it very slowly toward Keating as Joe motioned it forward. A few moments later, Joe made an X with the two wands above his head, and Hill stopped the jet. Keating's line crew personnel quickly installed chocks in front of the main gear, and Joe took the wands to waist level, pointed them inward and moved them toward each other, indicating the jet was chocked. Hill nodded, and the jet's engines wound down a few moments later.

Almost immediately, three black Chevrolet SUV's, Tahoes as luck would have it, drove planeside. The rear hatch on the center one opened, and the driver exited to take charge of his passengers. The other two SUVs dispensed men in black tactical gear with M-4 carbines strapped to their chests. The men formed a cordon around the jet, and several of them gathered below main entry door. A few seconds later, the door slowly lowered to the boarding position.

I made my way through the cordon of men and shouted up the ladder. "Permission to come aboard?"

"Granted!" said a tall figure at the top of the stairs.

I walked up the airstair and shook hands with Mark Hill.

"Good to see you, Hill-man!" I said.

"Same to you, T.C.," he said.

Hill was about the same height as I was but slightly stockier and with less hair. Time had taken its toll on him as it had on all of us, but the "don't' fuck with me" look was still embedded on his features. Even so, he smiled easily like he always had.

"You've kept yourself in pretty good shape," I said.

"Not as good as you!" he answered. "You must work out like a fiend."

I shook my head at him. "No," I said. "I just don't have a real job like you do."

I looked into the passenger compartment and nodded my head when I saw it was empty.

"So, you took my advice, huh?" I asked.

Hill nodded. "I stuck to the plan you and I discussed. We dropped into Reno, offloaded them into an SUV with your security folks at the FBO there and popped over the mountains to the airport here. Lane and his wife are probably already at the Ritz-Carlton north of the Lake. We changed their hotel at the last minute, so they're away from the Hyatt where everyone else is staying. They took the southern route through the mountains instead of coming via the interstate. Hopefully, they weren't observed."

"That's perfect," I said. "If the Shadow is here at the airport, and she probably is, she's about to discover her intel isn't as good as she thinks it is. That should shake her up a bit."

Even as I said the words, I had the same sensation I had in Trafalgar square several days ago. I nodded my head unconsciously as it came over me.

"What are you thinking, T.C.?" Hill asked.

"She's here," I said. "I just don't know if she's watching us with her eyeballs, binoculars or through a telescopic sight on top of a .50 caliber rifle."

"Well, I hope it's not the last one!" Hill said, laughing. "My director of maintenance is an Irish guy named Costello, and he gets pissed if I bring his jet back with a bird strike. He'd probably kill me if I brought it back with a bullet hole!"

I slapped his arm and stepped outside of the jet onto the top level of the airstair and looked north, across the runway and into the tree line that Keating had mentioned earlier.

I looked down at the security folks at the base of the stairs. "Any of you guys have a set of binos?" I asked.

One of the men went over to the nearest Tahoe and retrieved a binocular case and brought it up the stair to me. I took the binos out of the case and trained them on the tree line. As I zoomed them in, I was rewarded with a view of a blonde woman in a black down jacket and black pants looking back at me. I focused on her face and saw a smile there.

Fight's on, honey. I thought. *We know you're here and we know who you're after.*

As I watched, Alina removed the binoculars from her eyes. She winked at me and blew me a kiss.

Then she disappeared. I felt the same, intense pull for her inside of me. And I sighed. *Goddamn it!*

He was alive!

The Shadow raised her binoculars to survey the flight line at the Truckee-Tahoe Airport, and she saw him. Sitting in a pick-up truck parked in front of the main terminal building, next to a younger, balding fellow who seemed to smile a lot.

She felt mixed emotions of anger and happiness.

Anger at Anton for lying to her and telling her that Pearce had died of a heroin overdose and that Jean and Abby had to remain in Switzerland for questioning. She had texted Jean and Abby and had not received a response from either in days. The three of them had formed a very tight bond over the last year. She knew they were dead. Anton had probably had them killed, cleaning up loose ends.

But then she wondered. Maybe Colin had killed them.

They were supposed to drug him. Maybe Anton instructed them to administer a fatal dose of heroin? Maybe Colin had foiled their plot and killed them instead!

Yes! That must be what happened! She was certain of it. And it made her want him even more.

She had mourned his supposed death on the long drive across Scotland and the ferry ride over to Belfast. She had relived their time together over and over as she rode the train from Belfast to Dublin and then on the chartered flight from Dublin to South Lake Tahoe airport, all the while wondering if she could ever find another person who could be her other half. Her equal.

And here he was! On the other side, once again, but that would be over soon. She had only come to the airport to see what the target looked like and what the security arrangements would be. She already had the nest prepared for the event tonight and had built a full range card for all the possible engagement zones. Her target had no chance of escape.

Then the airplane landed, and she watched it taxi in behind the pickup truck and park on the back of the ramp area. Alina had to walk eastward in the tree line to keep the aircraft in sight as it was parked. Once she regained an observation position, she saw her Colin standing on the ramp and marveled again at what strong, handsome figure he was.

Three black SUVs pulled up, and several men in black got out of them. She nodded. She was expecting the target to have security. This was impressive.

The door on the aircraft opened, and Colin went up into the jet. But the target and his wife didn't come out.

The Shadow smiled. They had been dropped somewhere else. Clever my angel! she thought. Very, very, clever. This makes the game even more fun. Our last game on opposite sides. We will be together soon!

Colin stepped outside of the jet and said something to one of the men in black. The man brought Colin a set of binoculars.

The Shadow stepped out from behind the tree she was using for cover and stood in an open area between three different trees, just inside the edge of the wooded area. She wanted him to see her. She watched him raise the binoculars to his eyes, quickly sweep the area and then settle on her.

She smiled, winked at him and blew him a kiss.

She left the area, found the motorcycle where she had parked it and rode south. She smiled for the entire ride back to her hotel. The sun seemed brighter today, and the cool November air felt good through the vented leather of her riding clothes.

The shot tonight would be challenging, so she needed to get a nap before the event and as well as perform the ritual cleaning of her weapon. She would also take a long bath and lay in the tub, thinking of Colin.

That made her smile even more.

CHAPTER TWENTY-EIGHT

Saturday, November 6
1700 Hours Local Time
Highlands Bar, Ritz-Carlton, Lake Tahoe
Truckee, California, USA

"What can I get you sir?" the bartender asked. She was 30-something, brunette, cute and shapely, with a bubbly personality. The tag on the uniform said her name was Gail and I found that ironic since I was waiting for her namesake to join me before the limo came to take us to the evening's event.

"Sapphire and tonic would be great," I replied.

"With a lime?"

"Yes, please."

Gail scurried away to make the drink, and I looked out of the bar's back window at the patio area behind the hotel and at the hillside beyond. There was a light dusting of snow on the higher terrain behind the hotel, barely visible through the thicket of pine trees on the incline. It seemed like a promise of the winter to come for the ski-resort that surrounded the hotel.

I glanced around me. While perhaps not quite as opulent as the hotel in Switzerland, the Ritz was a perfect combination of ski-lodge and five-star hotel. There were wooden beams and fireplaces everywhere, but the furniture, carpet and wall coverings were all very high end. The service was especially noteworthy. I was greeted by name at the front desk and offered a full suite of hotel services that were related to my Marriott profile. I was amazed by the attention to detail.

"Here you go, sir." Gail, the bartender, placed a bar napkin with the hotel's logo in front of me and placed a tall tumbler of sapphire and tonic in front of me.

"Wow," I said. "Is that a double?"

She smiled at me. "At the single price. You looked like you could use it."

"Thank you, Gail," I said. "You're very perceptive. I appreciate it. It's been a long day."

I took a long pull at the drink, and it was nice and strong, just the way I liked it. I nodded at her. "Well made, ma'am. Thank you very much."

She seemed to be taken aback. "Ma'am?" she asked. "I don't think I've ever been called that before."

I smiled at her. "No offense meant, Gail. It's a habit. Twenty plus years in uniform and then a decade in the customer service business."

"I think it's darling," she said. "Very polite and endearing."

"Well, well," a familiar voice said. "Getting to know the *staff* are we."

I had never been married in my life, but I suddenly identified with every henpecked husband I had talked to or heard of. I turned to see Major General Gail Petersen standing next to me, clad in a gold sequined top with a neckline that walked the line between risqué and discreet and a floor-length black skirt. Her dark hair fell to her shoulders, and her brown eyes flashed in the light of the bar.

"Hi honey," I said. "Gail, the general, meet Gail, the bartender." I inclined my head toward the bartender. "And she makes a hell of a gin and tonic."

Gail, the bartender, instantly turned on her professional voice.

"What can I get you *ma'am?*" she asked, without even looking sideways at me. I felt a smile form on my lips.

Women, I thought.

"What's your house cabernet?" Gail, the general, asked.

"We have three," Gail, the bartender, answered. "Mondavi Reserve, Beringer Reserve and the Stag's Leap," she answered.

"Which do you like best?"

Gail, the bartender, brightened a bit, pleased to have been asked.

"The Stag's Leap is my favorite," she said. "It's fruity and bold all at the same time."

Gail, the general, looked at me and didn't spare a moment. "I'll take one of the other two. Doesn't matter which one."

"Very good...ma'am."

Gail, the general, shot a cold glance at Gail, the bartender, and I couldn't help but smile again.

"Everything ok?" I asked as she sat down.

"I'm giving up my weekend for this?" she said, with a peevish expression on her face. "I had a round of golf lined up with General Ashley, the Deputy Chief of Staff for Manpower, Personnel, and Services."

I sipped my drink and sighed. "Sorry to interrupt your career with this national security stuff," I said. *Or a relationship*, I thought. I looked over at her. "There's a mad chick out there with a big-ass rifle, and she's going to try to kill someone tonight and possibly influence energy policy for a good part of the world," I said. "Your being here may help us stop it." I turned back to my drink. "Sorry to keep you from golf with your boss," I added.

I felt Gail stiffen next to me and I didn't care. She had arrived at the hotel a few hours earlier and had insisted on separate rooms for 'appearances' since her superiors knew she'd be here. We'd hardly exchanged ten words since I had returned from the airport and found she'd arrived. I had arranged for adjoining rooms with the hotel staff, and after a quick, awkward greeting that consisted of quick kiss and hug, Gail had made her way to her room and begun her preparations for the evening's event, and I had done the same.

"Room okay?" I asked her.

I saw her nod in my peripheral vision. "It's nice actually," she said, showing an unexpected touch of humanity. "I've only stayed in a Ritz once before. The service is amazing."

I nodded in return. "It is that," I said, staring out the window and sipping my drink.

"Colin?" Gail asked. "What's the matter with you? You seem different than you normally are."

I sighed and took another sip of my drink. The interludes with Alina ran through my head like teasers for a movie.

"Nothing," I said, after a long moment. "I just have a lot on my mind."

Gail edged closer to me and put her hand on my arm. "I moved a lot of stuff around to be here," she said. "You know how I am. That says something."

I looked at her. "It does, and I'm grateful."

"Here's your wine…ma'am," Gail, the bartender, said as she delivered the glass of cabernet, once again not looking at me as she used the personal pronoun she had never heard of before she met me.

I couldn't help smiling again.

"What?" Gail asked.

"Nothing," I said, shaking my head. "Just a random thought."

"So, what's the deal tonight?" Gail asked.

I shrugged. "Hopefully nothing more than a dinner cruise. An SUV is going to show up outside the main door in a few minutes and drive us to the Tahoe City Marina along with the CEO of a company called Enteron, Mark Lane, and his wife, Amy. When we arrive at the marina, we'll board a dinner party boat with the CEO and his wife and go on the cruise. You and I will work the crowd and stay close to Lane and his wife."

"Do we have a cover story?" Gail asked.

I nodded. "You'll love it," I said, not looking at her. "You're being recruited to be Enteron's new head of HR, and this is your look at the energy industry. I'm just your male sidekick."

"Why was it so imperative that I be here?" she asked. "From what you said earlier, it's going to be a group of executives. You could have worked that crowd…"

"Executives and their wives," I corrected her. "And a single male in a crowd like that stands out like a turd in punch bowl. We need to blend in. We're going to stay close to Lane and Amy," I said. "I might see something before it happens."

"So, you might see something?" Gail asked, aghast. "I gave up a chance to move my career to the next level for a maybe?"

I didn't look at her. Instead, I stared straight ahead and breathed in and out very deliberately. Another sapphire and tonic appeared by my right hand without my asking for it. I saw Gail the bartender subtly move away after delivering it. I looked down into the glass I had been sipping. It was empty.

Damn, I thought. *The service here is good.*

I looked over at Gail, the general. "You know, some day, before too long, probably sooner than you think possible, you're going to retire from the Air Force. And the day you walk out the door of whatever office you're in at the time, people will shake your hand and hug you and tell you how much you meant to them, but you know what?"

She looked at me with a defiant, disbelieving look on her face.

"After about a month or so, it won't make a difference that you were even there. Someone else will take your position, and the Air Force will go on. And Gail Petersen will have been just a cog in the bureaucratic wheel."

She snorted. "I don't care," she said. "It's who I am. I enjoy it."

I shook my head and took the first sip of my new drink. "No," I said. "It's who you choose to be. And in the big scheme of things, it will mean nothing. Yes, you will have served your country, and that's about all that will have mattered."

We both sipped our drinks in silence for a few moments. I could feel the tension building between us.

"Listen," I said. "I'm glad you came. You've got a free evening in Lake Tahoe at government expense. Tomorrow morning, the CIA will fly you back to San Antonio, and you can go on with your life with your ex or whomever. But tonight, we have a role to play, and I need to try and stop the Shadow from taking another life."

Gail nodded slowly and solemnly, seemingly accepting my statement and terms. She turned toward me and touched my arm. I looked at her and found her beautiful brown eyes looking up at me.

"I care about you," she said. "I don't want anything to happen to you."

I took a sip of my drink and looked away. "Neither do I," I said. "But this woman and the people she works for have tried to kill me three, maybe four times. Twice in the last few days. And I'm still here. Hopefully being lucky instead of good will continue to work out for me."

My phone buzzed. I looked down and saw a text from Smith and Amrine. CAR IS OUT FRONT, it said. I nodded and looked at Gail. Her eyes were wide with concern and fear.

"We're on honey," I said. "It's show time."

CHAPTER TWENTY-NINE

Saturday, November 6
2000 Hours Local Time
Touring the West Shore, Aboard the Anna Marie
Lake Tahoe, California USA

The dinner cruise boat was well-appointed and comfortable. It featured two decks. The main-deck was enclosed and housed the band, the bar and the dining tables. The upper deck was open to the elements and featured an obstruction-free view of the lake and shore around us. The upper deck didn't attract many of the boat's guests tonight, due to temperatures of the November air and the breeze across the cool waters of the lake. But a few couples made their way up there, and I wondered how much of that was about the view and how much was about a good cigar or just getting away from the crowd below.

Throughout the pre-dinner cocktails and the meal itself, Lane did what CEOs do, working the group and engaging the WANO directors and their spouses in conversations that ranged in topic from the climate to intricacies of nuclear energy. Lane was a few inches shorter than I was and looked trim and fit. He sported a full head of gray hair and deep green eyes in a face that was lined with the worries and cares of the job he held. But he smiled easily and laughed a lot. His wife Amy was an attractive brunette with a body that bespoke of a religious attention to her diet and exercise. She too was good-humored and gracious.

I admired the way they moved through the crowd, making the mingling and conversation look so easy.

"God, they're good at that," I said.

"Yes, they are," Gail replied.

We stood about three feet away from them, never too close nor too far away. I made sure we stood so we were looking toward the shore, and between glances around the room, I watched every niche of the shore go by, even though it was three miles away.

"I bet you're good at this sort of thing as well," I said. "I've never gotten to see you work an official function but you've got the personality for it."

"I love it," she said. "But you know how the military is. It's like a reunion every time I go to one of those functions. It's like catching up with old friends."

"How did the ex deal with it?" I asked. "Or is he attending functions with you now, at Randolph?"

She stiffened alongside me. It didn't particularly bother me. She and I were going to be through after tonight anyway. I just wondered how addicted she was to the guy.

"I only ever took him to a few functions, while we were in DC before the divorce. He had a habit of getting drunk and embarrassing me, so I stopped bringing him."

I kept my eyes on Lane and his wife. They were talking to a couple that seemed to be from the Middle East judging by the apparel and complexion. Lane had the four of them laughing in seconds.

"So you see that?" I said. "He's got a partner he can be proud of in public. A partner that's worthy of him."

Gail nodded slowly. "I understand," she said. Then she lowered her voice. "Does he understand how much danger he's in?"

"He does," I said. "I had a brief conversation with him while you and Amy went to the restroom before we got into the limo."

##

"What do you need me to do?" Lane had asked.

"Just stay in the crowd," I said. "The Shadow is very good, but she's also loath to cause collateral damage. She's very surgical. If we can keep her from getting a clean shot, we might be able to prevent her from shooting at all."

"Will my wife be safe?" he asked.

I had nodded. "Absolutely. She's not the target. You are."

"I can't believe the fucking Russians are doing this!" he said. "It's outrageous."

"But it's working, isn't it?" I asked. "How certain are you about the breeder reactor endorsement vote tomorrow?"

He shook his head in disgust. "Not certain at all. The damned Russians have bought, intimidated or convinced nearly every member of the organization. There are a few of us who are holding fast, but we're dwindling. That's the only reason I'm here with this sniper threat you guys have told me about. If this meeting was about anything less important, I would have canceled. But this is too damned important. If I didn't speak out about it, I couldn't live with myself."

A man with principles, I thought. *No wonder Hill likes this guy.*

"Well it may be even more at stake here than bad reactor technology," I said. "There was a Swiss journalist that was killed by the Shadow a few days ago. It turns out that he was going to publish an article about how the Russians are intentionally building valves into the design that can be remotely controlled and can vent radioactive steam into the air around the plants."

Lane's eyes widened, and he nodded. "That's the part we couldn't figure out when we saw the plans for the plants! You can't believe how attentive we are about cyber security and communication security in nuclear plants. Having someone on the outside control the reactor is our worst nightmare."

"I can imagine," I said. "But according to the article this guy was going to publish, the Russians have taken that even further. Do you remember anything unique about the specifications for the concrete around the reactor units?"

Lane looked at me for a moment and I could almost see the gears turning inside his head. "I do," he said at last. "Some special steel rebar to reinforce the concrete. Comes from some place in the Ukraine. Some economic incentive for the workers and the economy there."

"It's not just steel. It has a specially developed explosive compound woven into the fibers of the steel itself. Impossible to detect without special equipment and several times more powerful than C-4 or Semtex."

"Jesus," he said. "They're turning the reactors into dirty bombs."

I nodded. "Exactly. And were you to go back through those plans, you'd see electrical wire running into the concrete and linking up with the steel. The wire was there to detonate the steel.

"I remember!" he said. "We couldn't figure out why the wires were there, but there were so many other issues with the plans we didn't dwell on them."

"So the bottom line is that your speech tomorrow is important. And we're going to do our damnedest to keep you alive to make it. We'll have a helicopter over the lake at all times with night vision gear and a sniper of our own. The tour operator has been instructed to keep the boat at least three miles off shore for the entire evening. And I presume you're wearing that special garment you were given."

He nodded and smiled thinly. "I had to get in on quickly and then put my t-shirt and dress shirt on top of it, so my wife didn't see it."

"That will help," I said. "If she gets a shot off at you and if she does hit you, it will be at extremely long range, and the bullet won't have much energy. It shouldn't penetrate the armor."

He chuckled. "Shouldn't being the operative word in that sentence."

I laughed with him. "You have an awfully calm attitude for a man that's risking his life to make a speech."

"Hell," Lane said. "I risked my life in nuclear control rooms twelve hours at a time for twenty years. This is nothing."

The conversation groups seemed to be breaking up, and Lane and his wife went over to the band. After a few quick words with the band leader, the band began playing an upbeat version of a recent pop song that a had a bit soul mixed in, and I could sense Gail moving her hips next to me. Her love of music was one the things that attracted me to her. When there was a good beat, she couldn't keep herself from moving.

The boat's crew cleared an area of the floor of tables and chairs and Lane and Amy took to it, moving together smoothly to the beat of the music.

I nodded to myself as I watched them together and I understood his strategy. He wasn't trying to change the minds of the people present as he worked the crowd. He was building relationships. He was getting the members of the group to like him and trying to get their spouses to like his wife. If people liked him, they were more likely to listen to him, and if they listened to him, he might just sway their opinions.

"Classic politics," I said to myself. "I could never do that job."

The band transitioned into another song that had a much more intense beat. I sensed it was a rap song that was civilized for the present crowd. Gail grabbed my hand and led me out to the floor where we joined Lane and his wife. As one who has never been comfortable dancing, I marveled at how easily Gail moved to the music and how happy she looked as she danced.

We danced several songs together along with Lane and his wife and a few other couples. The boat's crew had managed to bring the lights down a bit, so the atmosphere around us seemed more intimate. There were a few slow songs where I was able to hold Gail against me and feel her hard body against mine.

During one of the quiet moments, she raised her face to mine and kissed me lightly on the lips.

"I will miss you," she said.

"I'll miss you too."

She raised herself to kiss me again. Our lips parted and I smiled down at her as she put her head against my chest. Then I raised my gaze to look outside.

The lake shore looked closer than it had previously. Much closer. I looked around to the other side of the boat and saw shoreline close on that side as well.

"Jesus!" I said. "We're in Emerald Bay! How the fuck did we get in here?"

The phone in my pocket began buzzing like crazy and I was sure it was exploding with text messages or calls from Smith and Amrine about the boat's position.

I suddenly became aware that the four of us, Lane, his wife, Gail and I, were the only four people on the dance floor and the other people in the room had seated themselves or dispersed such that the view of the outside shore was unobstructed, which meant someone could see in as well as we could see out.

Lane seemed to become aware of the conditions about the same time that I did. He looked over at me with a questioning look on his face. I looked back at him and beyond him to the shore in the near distance. There was a full moon tonight and the reflection on the water and on the hillside of the shore made it easy to see nearly every detail.

For just a second I was torn about whether run upstairs to the bridge and tell the boat's captain to get us out of here or to throw Lane to the ground.

But Alina made that decision for me.

For in the distance, on the inclined shore off the far side of the boat, about twenty feet above the waterline and a few feet back in the trees, I saw what I had been looking for all night and hoping like hell I wouldn't see.

The muzzle flash of a heavy rifle.

The Shadow had settled into her nest. She was ensconced in an isolated alcove of rock about twenty feet above the water in an area of Emerald Bay where there was no beach below and no trails above. There were thousands of huge boulders, stones and rocks lining the hills around Emerald Bay and her nest was formed by four large boulders on the hillside. Two of the huge stones formed the sides of the alcove, another formed a sort of roof, and a fourth one formed a half wall across the front of the alcove and gave her a flat surface upon which to rest the bipod of her rifle. The rear part of the alcove had a narrow area between the rocks and the hillside that the Shadow had managed to squeeze through, both when she found the position yesterday and built the range cards and an hour ago when she made her way back and prepared for the evening's event.

She had brought a camper's stool with her, in the backpack, and upon which she was sitting, while she regarded the glassy surface of the bay and beautiful green reflection of the water on the moonlight. She was happy that this was the last event for her uncle. She loved him but she wasn't sure she trusted him anymore, especially since had lied to her about Abby, Jean, and her Colin. She smiled when she thought of Colin and a future with him. He would try to foil her attempt on the target tonight, but he would fail, and she would comfort him later when they found each other. Then, they would get away and spend a restful long time together, lying in the sun and making love.

The Shadow looked over at the entrance of the bay and saw the lights of the dinner boat as it turned into the bay. The things you could buy with money, she thought. All it had taken was $2,000 to get the captain to ignore the instructions he was given and bring the boat into Emerald Bay during the evening. She knew she wouldn't be able to get a shot at the target while the boat was out on the lake. Lake Tahoe was 12 miles wide and 22 miles long and a boat out in the middle of it would take the target out of range. But Emerald Bay, at the southwest part of the lake, solved that problem. It had a narrow entry, less than 300 meters wide, and *was only about 1,000 meters at its widest point from the north side to the south side.*

It was like a shooting gallery.

The only real issue was visibility through the side windows of the boat. The Shadow normally liked to shoot down on a target whenever possible. The boat had forced her to choose a nest that was lower, so she could shoot directly into it without the roof to contend with. She knew that this orientation might make collateral damage more likely, but she also knew the time of flight of the bullet would be short and she'd be able to time the shot much more closely.

As the boat entered the bay, the Shadow settled into her weapon. She turned on the low-light feature on the telescopic sight, although as bright as the moonlight was, the low-light feature wasn't necessary. She verified the ranges and settings for the sight as well as the engagement zone for the shot and checked the wind and humidity readings once again.

She was ready.

Her position was on the north side of the bay, about 400 meters west of the mouth of it. She had two chances to make the shot, once when the boat entered the bay and once when it left the bay. She was patient. If the first pass wasn't optimum, she'd wait until the second.

As she focused her eyes into the scope, the Shadow heard a helicopter nearby but instantly dismissed it. A helicopter would be foolish to fly into a bay with 600 – 1,000-foot walls around it.

The lights of the boat were coming closer. The Shadow looked into the scope and trained it on the main deck. She heard the strains of music as the sound reached her across the water and it made her happy. She loved music. She wondered what kind of music her Colin liked. The shapes of people on the main deck became visible, and the Shadow increased the zoom on the scope. As the boat came closer, she could start to discern individual people on the main deck. She could see two couples dancing! That made her smile. She thought about dancing with Colin. Just the two of them, dancing to their own band, all by themselves, under the moonlight.

She trained the scope on the two couples and increased the zoom. She could see and a gray-haired man and a younger woman, swaying to the music together. The man's face looked like that of the target, Mark Lane. The Shadow pivoted her sight to the other couple and what she saw crushed her heart.

It was her Colin, in the arms of another woman, kissing her and holding her.

The ire and rage that filled her was instantaneous.

He was a cheater! He was cheating on her! He knew the two of them were meant to be together! Why would he even be looking at another woman?

For the first time in her short but precise career, the Shadow didn't turn the video on to record the shot, nor did she take the time to align the shot with the exactitude she had displayed in the past.

She pivoted and noticed that the couples on the dance floor had stopped moving and had separated a bit. She centered the crosshairs of her scope on the gray-haired man's chest and squeezed the trigger. The heavy rifle recoiled against her, but she recovered it quickly. She turned the weapon back to the right and saw a dark-haired woman in a gold-sequined top looking directly at her with fear in her eyes.

"He was mine," the Shadow said.

And she squeezed the trigger again.

CHAPTER THIRTY

Saturday, November 6
2030 Hours Local Time
Aboard the Anna Marie in Emerald Bay
Lake Tahoe, California, USA

I leaped toward Lane as he stood there, already aware that I was too late to prevent the bullet from hitting him. I knew the approximate dimensions of Emerald Bay and my recent education in sniper ballistics told me that I wasn't close enough. My hands impacted his shoulder, and the bullet went through him milliseconds later, the vest being far too light to stop a .50 caliber projectile at a distance of a few hundred meters. I saw the hole materialize on the upper left part of his chest and he fell to the floor of the main deck, a look of disbelief in his eyes that made me sorry for the reassurances I had given him earlier in the evening.

The suppressed report of the shot reached my ears as he hit the deck and I snatched a tablecloth from the nearest table on the sidelines and put it on the wound immediately. Amy, his wife, was at his side next to me in a moment. Her eyes were glassy with tears, but her expression was one of purpose, not fright or panic.

"Keep pressure on this wound," I said. "He's going to make it. The bullet didn't hit anything vital."

"How do you know?" she asked, a look of fear and skepticism in her eyes.

"First-hand experience," I said. "I've been shot enough to know what will kill and what won't. This will be painful for him, but he'll recover."

And then I heard the report of a second shot.

I swept my head through the crowd to see who had been hit, but there was no reaction to the shot that I could see. And then, as I looked further to my left, I saw Gail, standing on the dance floor, just a few feet away from me, with a perplexed look on her face – like there was something she couldn't understand. She turned toward me, took a step or two and then fell to her knees.

And I saw the red hole, near the center of her chest, just slightly visible among the gold sequins.

I slid across the wooden surface and caught her as she sank to the deck from her knees.

"Doctor!" I screamed. "Is there a doctor here?"

The silence and lack of feet scrambling to assist me was deafening.

"Can someone find a fucking first-aid kit? We've got two gunshot victims here!"

There was the report of another shot, and I felt air displaced near my head and sensed the force of a projectile passing by. I wanted to turn my head toward the direction of the shot and curse Alina in the name of all that was holy, but my attention was on matters of more importance. I ripped the jacket from my body and placed it under Gail's head and then I tore the dress shirt from me to use as a bandage to apply pressure to her wound.

But even as I lay her down, the light was ebbing from her eyes. I could see her lips moving, and it was apparent that she was trying to speak. I lowered my ears to her mouth so I could hear her.

"You…were…right," she whispered. "Job…was bullshit."

"Don't' think about that," I said. "We're going to get you out of here. We're going to get you to a hospital."

Even as I said the words, I heard a helicopter roar over the top of the boat at low altitude, and moments later, I heard the unmistakable sound of a Browning .50 caliber machine gun in full auto mode. It had been nearly 20 years since my tour in the first Gulf War, and I still remembered what it sounded like.

"That's a .50 cal, honey," I said. "The boys brought the heavy artillery tonight. They're going to kick her ass."

I turned my attention back to Gail to find her looking up at me and smiling. It was a content smile, but it was also a sad one.

"You…were… the best …thing that ever …happened to me," she said. "Only one…who …ever got me….so sorry…didn't see it…too much bullshit."

She coughed then, and blood came out her mouth. Bright red blood. I shook my head in sadness as I saw it. I knew what it meant. She smiled again and then her eyes went sightless.

The problem with death is that it is so damn permanent. I had experienced it many times and was intimate with the intransigence it bestowed. I felt grief, anger, helplessness, and anguish all at the same time. I pulled Gail to me and held her against me, even as I heard the helo return to the boat and felt the shift in the vessel's weight as it touched down on the upper deck. I heard the clumping of boots on stairs, and the distress of the crowd on the main deck as multiple men in black descended on the crowd. I had my eyes closed with Gail against my chest when I felt the presence at my side.

"Help Lane," I said. "He'll make it." I stroked Gail's hair while I held her in my arms. "This one won't."

The presence went away.

Later…much later…I felt the boat stop, like it was docking. I could hear men boarding the boat, and I sensed flashes of red and blue light, like the lights from emergency vehicles. I disregarded all the stimuli and still held Gail against me. I didn't know where she was on her journey to whatever world lay beyond, but she wasn't going to make it alone. I was going to help her.

Then I heard the familiar voice at my side.

"You've got to let her go, T.C.," Smith's voice said. "They've got to take her."

I opened my eyes and looked at him. I could barely see him through the moisture on my eyes.

"Why, Dave?" I asked. "She didn't have anything to do with any of this."

He put his hand on my shoulder and comforted me as the coroner's team gently extracted Gail's body from my arms and carried it away. I remained, kneeling on the deck of the boat, trying to process what had happened.

"Lane's going to make it," Smith said to me. "You pushed the shot off center of mass. He's not going to be playing tennis anytime soon, but he's going to live. The helo took him to Reno general."

I nodded my head in slow motion, acknowledging Smith's words. But I remained kneeling on the deck, my crumpled jacket in front of me, where Gail's head used to be and my dress shirt, now red with Gail's blood, to the side of me, cast away like a piece of random litter. I reached in front of me and gathered both garments into my arms and held them to me, burying my face in the jacket that still had traces of her scent.

"We need to get you out of here, Colin," Smith's voice said. "We need to keep you away from the press."

I hardly heard him.

I felt myself being stood up and walked to a waiting vehicle. While I sensed activity around me, I was barely aware of the sights or sounds of my surroundings. As I took my seat, another door opened.

"Did you get her?" Smith asked.

"Not sure," Amrine said. "After that third muzzle flash, we pummeled that area with .50 cal, but I'm not sure if we hit anything."

I felt something stir in myself as the vehicle began to move.

"We'll have the locals search the area as soon as possible," Amrine said.

I laughed then. It was a bitter, humorless laugh. "You missed her," I said. "She got away."

"We engaged her seconds after she fired the third shot, one that was aimed at you, T.C. How do you know she got away?"

"Because she's who she is!" I said. "She's gotten away with over 50 of these killings. She knows how to plan the egress and look normal, and in any of the towns around here, she'd fit right in. She's already in a vehicle and on her way to an airport. She'll be back in Russia in hours."

"So, we've lost her?" Smith asked.

"Maybe not," I corrected him. "She's normally very deliberate, and she's never had to egress under fire. You guys changed that tonight. I'm betting she left something behind that will tie her to the shooting, maybe another shell casing or even the weapon itself." I looked between the two of them. "You have a forensic crew en route to the scene, right?"

Amrine nodded.

"Then they'll find something. If you get evidence linking her to the shooting tonight, can you link it to any of the other events?"

Amrine shrugged. "In a court of public opinion, maybe. In a court of laws, who knows," he said.

There were a few moments of silence as the driver of our vehicle made his way through the winding roads around the edge of

Lake Tahoe and back to the Ritz hotel. I stared out of the window of the SUV and watched the lights and the rocks go by. I thought about the women I had seen die, at my side or close by. Until now, they had died because of something they were involved in that was independent of me. But tonight was different.

"T.C.," Smith said. "I have to ask you something, and you're not going to like it, but I have to ask you anyway."

I exhaled and shook my head. "Don't bother," I said. "I know what you're thinking." I looked across the expanse of the Tahoe's back seat to him. "You're wondering why she shot Gail. Right?"

Smith's face looked like he had been caught in a guilty moment. He nodded slowly.

"She died because of me," I said. "She died because she kissed me and Alina saw her kiss me. In some fucking world that only she understands, Alina owns me and Gail was intruding on her turf, so Gail had to die."

"That shot against Lane was almost careless," Amrine said. "She nearly missed him."

I looked at him. "She didn't miss by much," I said. "If I hadn't gotten to him, that bullet would have punctured a lung or maybe his heart."

Amrine shook his head. "Until recently, she's been a machine. We only have her on record as missing twice, in 57 shots. She missed Essex because he sneezed at exactly the right moment. That was a coincidence and could happen to any shooter. But she missed the Swiss journalist with the first shot after she met you and now, tonight, she rushes the shot on Lane and then concentrates on the shot on Gail. Do you know what means, T.C.?"

I shook my head slowly and looked over at him.

"You're the key to bringing her down," Amrine said. "You push buttons in her that she can't control."

I shook my head and leaned back against my leather seat. I glanced out of the windows of the SUV and watched the lights and the rock continue by us.

"Lucky me," I said. "Lucky fucking me."

CHAPTER THIRTY-ONE

Sunday, November 7
1030 Hours Local Time
Ritz-Carlton Lake Tahoe
Truckee, California, USA

The warmth of the sun through the window of the hotel finally woke me. I wasn't sure how long I had slept because I wasn't entirely sure when I went to bed. I lay there and tried to recount the previous evening's events, which were somewhat fuzzy as it turned out. I forced myself out of bed and made myself a cup of the superb in-room coffee. As the hot beverage made its way through me, I slowly recounted the events of the evening.

After the SUV deposited me at the entrance to the hotel last night, I dismissed Smith and Amrine's offers of company and proceeded, alone, to that place where I was always at home – the nearest bar.

I stopped in the restroom on my way down to the bar level, and took a few difficult moments to wash Gail's blood off my hands. Watching the red fluid swirl down the drain seemed to cheapen Gail's death somehow, like it was easily cleaned up. Like it didn't matter.

Gail, the bartender, was still on duty when I walked into the bar, wearing my now soiled dress slacks, a t-shirt, and a crumpled jacket. I still carried my bloody dress shirt under one arm. As I walked through the door, the hostess tried to intercept me but Gail, the bartender, waved her off with a quick but intense gesture.

I seated myself on the barstool nearest the entrance. The bar had a few couples sitting at it, away from me around the curve of the bar, enjoying drinks and cordial conversation. The conversation paused somewhat as I took my place at the bar. I could see a few of the faces recoiling at my presence. I was sure my t-shirt was also bloody from holding Gail against me, and I was also sure that my attire probably didn't match the dress code at the Ritz.

But I didn't give a shit.

Gail, the bartender, was in front of me in seconds, her eyes looking me up and down and the expression on her face one of sympathy and understanding. She knew something terrible had happened but had the good judgment not to ask what.

"What do you need?" she asked.

I smiled thinly. "Scotch," I said. "Something peaty. From Islay, if you've got it."

"Ardbeg 10 okay?" she asked.

I nodded. "Neat. Club soda on the side please."

Gail, the bartender, went off to pour and I sat there, at the bar, staring at my hands, which still had spots of Gail, the general's, blood on them. I wondered if they would ever come off.

In short order, a generous pour of the Ardbeg arrived at my place.

"Thank you, Gail," I said. "You're a gem."

"You're welcome," she said. She paused for just a moment and then when she realized I was through speaking, she moved away to deal with the other customers at the bar.

I took a long pull at the Ardbeg, relishing the peat and smoke and let it rest on my tongue for several moments before I allowed it to ease down my throat, warming my insides as it made its descent.

"Hey buddy, don't you think you should have changed clothes before coming into the bar? All the blood on you, it's making my wife sick."

I blinked my eyes and returned to the real world. I looked to my left and saw a younger man standing there, clad in designer slacks and a shirt, and sporting a chic tattoo on his left forearm. He was about my height and judging by the veins in the arms and the flat stomach, had spent some time the gym.

The tone in his voice was amusing. He was trying to scare me. I couldn't help myself from chuckling.

"What's so funny, old-timer?" he asked. "You got a problem?"

I turned my head and looked at him. "What's it to you?"

In another world, I would have been courteous. I would have apologized. I would have been civil. But that world wasn't here. And it wasn't now.

I slowly rose to my feet. As I did, he saw that he and I were about the same size and that my gaze never wavered from his.

"Go sit down youngster," I said. I inclined my head toward the area where he had been sitting. "And enjoy the evening with your wife. And just be fucking grateful she's sitting next to you and not lying in a fucking morgue somewhere."

A smarter young man would have realized he was dealing with an unbalanced adversary and would have retreated gracefully, understanding that the emotion coming from his potential opponent wasn't an expression of masculinity but instead, a function of shock and grief. But this young man was more about his balls than his brains and apparently, he had a point to prove.

The left jab was quick, but not that quick, and I easily tapped it aside with my right palm.

"Don't do this," I warned him.

The right cross came next. It was clumsy and predictable. I stepped inside of it and blocked it with my left elbow. I had several options then, but I chose the one that was the least ostentatious as well as the least damaging. I swept his legs out from under him with my right leg and let him fall to the floor while I retained his right arm. As he hit the bar's wooden floor, I put my right foot at the juncture of right shoulder and arm and twisted his right arm with both of my hands. The expression on his face when from surprise to anger to agony in a fraction of a second.

I pointed down at him with my right index finger.

"If you get off that ground, I'm going to put you in it," I whispered to him, with venom in my voice. "Just crawl back to your bar stool and thank the universe you still have a place to crawl back to."

I released him and regained my seat at the bar. I reached for my glass and took another long drink of the Ardbeg. In my peripheral vision, I saw the young man on the floor struggle to his feet and return to wherever it was that he came from.

"I'll pay for their next round," I said to Gail, the bartender. "Sorry to disturb the peace," I said. "That was not my intention."

She leaned toward me. "He's been in here a few times this week. He's an arrogant ass," she said. "Maybe tonight, he met his match."

I sighed. "Maybe."

Then I finished the Ardbeg. It was the first of several that night.

My head pounded as I slowly rose from the luxurious bed, the pain as excruciating as the awareness that once again, I was alone. I wandered across my room and through the doors into the connecting room. Gail's things were still there. Her traveling clothes were strewn across the bed, her suitcase was open, and toiletries were still scattered about on the bathroom counter. It was like she had just stepped out of the room. It seemed impossible that she was gone. Forever.

I wandered about the room aimlessly for several moments, like I was trying to gain a sense of her, or maybe even a spiritual glance of her. Eventually, I sat on the edge of the perfectly made bed and scooped up the discarded clothes into my arms.

Then, I held them to me, and I sat there and cried.

Eventually, I heard my phone buzzing in the other room. I ignored it as I sat there, but it continued to buzz. Slowly, unwillingly, I rose from Gail's bed. I folded the clothes I had been holding very precisely, and placed them in the suitcase on the stand at the foot of the bed. Then, even as the phone in the next room continued to buzz, I went to the bathroom and carefully, even tenderly, packed the toiletries and sundries that I found. Finally, I checked the closet and all the drawers in the room, folding what I found and stowing it in the suitcase, taking care not to wrinkle anything. Gail hated to iron, and she would have loathed dealing with wrinkles.

The phone continued to buzz. I slowly wandered back into my room and raised the thing to my ear, pushing the answer button in the process.

"The vote passed," Smith said, without hesitation. "WANO endorsed the reactors."

I sank to my bed. "You've got to be kidding me," I said. "Even after last night?"

"Maybe because of last night," Smith said. "They watched the keynote speaker get gunned down before he spoke out against the Russians. Maybe they're scared."

"Jesus," I said. "What a bunch of wimps."

"Anton holds all the cards now," Smith said. "He has control of the breeder reactor project, and he's brought all the organizations opposing him to his feet through bribes or threat of assassination. There's nothing we can do to stop him...legally."

The implication was clear, and I was ready for it. Anton was Alina's uncle, but more importantly, he was Alina's boss and mentor.

"Where is his office?" I asked.

"One of them is in Saint Petersburg," Smith said.

"Any idea when he'll be there?"

"He's there now, and his schedule is somewhat unpredictable, but there's a ceremony he's bound to attend in two days. It's a meeting between the government's energy leaders and their supporters." Smith laughed humorlessly. "And rumor has it that he's going to be giving Alina the Hero of the Russian Federation medal there."

"How could you possibly know that?"

"We have someone on the ground there. I think you might know her. She's our Plan B."

"No fucking way," I said, without a moment's hesitation. "Anton is mine. Besides, don't you guys need that plausible deniability thing?" I asked. "Unbalanced freelance contractor kills Russian Energy Minister? Something like that?"

Smith sighed. The silence that ensued was poignant.

"You already thought of this," I said.

"Yes," Smith said. "Of course, we did. This day and age, we have to protect ourselves. Especially with our wimpy president who is willing to throw anyone of us under the bus for political gain."

"Then you need to get me to Saint Petersburg. Quickly."

Smith thought for a moment. "We couldn't take you in through conventional means. We'd have to develop a disguise and a legend and construct all the documents to support it. That takes a lot of time."

"I could ingress by air. If you have something available to help me do that. Without getting detected."

There was a long silence as Smith pondered this suggestion. "What exactly are you planning to do if we get you there?" he said at last.

"You know the answer to that. Take Anton down of course. With a big-ass rifle from as far a distance as I can manage it. It should tube their entire plan. I can take Alina down as well. Make it a two-fer."

"No. We need you to take her here. She left her rifle behind when she left the nest. If we plant it with her body, we can expose the Russians. Alina's just psycho enough that if you kill her uncle, she'll come after you."

"Amrine said I was the key to bringing her down."

Smith ignored me. "You're good at learning new airplanes, right?" he asked.

"Yes, I am. I pick them up quickly; it's like a gift. If it's built and has jet engines on it, I can fly it."

"There isn't going to be time for much instruction. Just what you can absorb in a simulator in a few hours."

"Understood," I said. "If I have checklists and good first officer, I can make it work."

Smith chuckled. "There's no first officer. The jet is single-seat. It's one of the test birds we've been working on at Eglin Air Force Base."

"A Viper? I need something fast."

"No. They'd see you coming miles away in a Viper, and you couldn't land it vertically. We've got something we might be able to arrange that's better for you."

My mind went into several different places but soon returned to the moment. "Dave, there aren't a lot of different platforms that can do that. I'm mediocre at the controls of a helicopter, and I have no idea how to fly a Harrier or an Osprey."

"No problem at all," he said. "We've got fast stealthy jet that has incredible technology, and even you can land it vertically."

In a second, I knew the jet he was talking about.

"No way," I said.

"Yep. We've got a few F-35Bs we took from the production line to test for covert force close air support. I'll get you into the one of those. Get to the Truckee airport as soon as you can. We're going to fly you to Eglin."

I felt a something pull my glance to the open door of the adjoining room. I could see Gail's now packed suitcase on the stand at the end of the bed. In a few hours there would be no trace of her in the room. In a few days, there would be no trace of her on the earth. The excitement about avenging her was instantly doused in a profound sense of loss.

"What about Gail?" I said. "What about Gail and her things?"

"We've been talking to the Air Force. They have a mortuary affairs team en route. Our people will be working with them."

"I packed her things," I said, still looking at the suitcase. I could see her the Delta Airlines Diamond Medallion luggage tag hanging from the handle. Gail had loved to travel. Now she only had one journey left for her. Her body would make one final trip, and that would be it. It just seemed so damn unfair.

"That's helpful," Smith said. "Now snap out of it and get your ass to the airport. We'll have a car standing by to take you there. We need you downstairs ASAP."

"Okay, Dave," I said, tearing my eyes away from the adjoining door. "Fifteen minutes or so. I'll grab a shower and throw my shit in a suitcase."

"Sounds good, T.C."

I was going to hit the END key, but Dave wasn't hanging up. There was obviously something else he wanted or needed to say.

"What is it, Dave?"

"This is awful fucking risky, T.C.," he said. "We have minimal presence on the ground and minimal intel. You're going to have to kill one of the most visible figures in Russian politics and then make it out of the country without being caught. And you'll be doing it all in a jet you've never flown before with all this emotional shit in the background between you and Gail and you and Alina. Are you sure you're up to this?"

I closed my eyes and silently commanded all the compartmentalization power I possessed. In my mind, I could envision three metal doors closing, slamming shut from ceiling to floor. Behind the first one went Alina, still clad in the amazing black dress I had seen on her in Switzerland. Behind the second door, was Gail, lying on the floor of the dinner boat, her eyes shut in final slumber. And finally, behind the last one, I ripped the heart out of my chest and locked it away. I opened my eyes with new sense of clarity and a renewed purpose.

"I am, Dave. I'm ready."

"Cool," he said with a satisfied tone in his voice. "One more thing, the jet we're going to put you in is fucking expensive. Like hundreds of millions of dollars expensive. For the love of God, try to bring it back in one piece."

I smiled grimly into the phone. "No promises, Dave."

CHAPTER THIRTY-TWO

Monday, November 8
2330 Hours Local Time
250 Feet AGL, At 600 knots
Somewhere over the Baltic Sea

So now here I was, in the cockpit of a borrowed F-35B, racing over the dark water of the thin strip of sea between Finland and Estonia. The small cockpit, with its single 8 x 20-inch LCD screen or panoramic cockpit display, side stick controller and single throttle, felt foreign and familiar all at once. If I had more than six hours of simulator time and eight hours of flight time, I might have felt a little more at ease. But at the end of the day, it was a cockpit, and cockpits, like bars, always felt like home to me.

My thoughts on the inadequacies of the F-35 had come a long way in the last 24 hours. After shooting three of them down with a Viper last summer to keep them from being sold to the Chinese, I wasn't terribly impressed with the platform at the time.

I felt differently now.

The time I had spent in the simulator yesterday afternoon and the flight time on the way here had given me the opportunity to explore the technology in the jet and the more I investigated, the more I found myself amazed. The panoramic cockpit display or PCD was a touchscreen computer on steroids and its four main display areas offered a full menu of options, including basic flight instruments, a sophisticated tactical situation display using data fusion technology, infrared and synthertic aperture radar imagery and the stores management system. Any option could be selected using the cursor control on the throttle or a gloved finger on the screen itself. Below each main display area were two smaller sections where the larger picture could be dragged to and dropped, to allow an additional option to be displayed. In all, it was possible to have 12 different displays available, providing more information than a pilot could probably assimilate, especially one with my scotch-impaired brain.

Yet while the capabilities of the PCD were impressive, it was the helmet mounted display, or HMD, that set the F-35 apart.

Unlike previous fighters I had flown, the F-35 had no HUD. Instead, all the applicable flight data like airspeed, altitude, heading, and attitude, was projected onto the HMD. Weapons employment information, like gunsights, bombsights and missile launch data was projected on the visor as well. Had the display stopped here, the HMD would have been about the same as the helmet mounted cueing system that I had flown with at Luke Air Force Base in the Viper during the summer. But the HMD took the concept of data fusion to the next level. In addition to flight data and weapons employment symbology, the HMD combined information from all the aircraft's sensors and projected it on the visor. Radar information, electro-optical imagery, and infrared imagery were present, and when I turned my head, the HMD took feeds from six cameras built into the skin of the aircraft and provided 360-degree vision to the helmet display. I could see all around and even through the aircraft. The HMD's night capability put standard NVG's to shame and as I flew on a moonless night, the amount of awareness I had about the terrain and threats around me made me as comfortable as if I was flying during the brightest sunlight. Of course, the fact that I had a terrain-following-radar or TFR mode didn't hurt.

"Terrain following radar? Seriously?" I had asked the CIA's Tactical Aviation Manager yesterday when I was in the simulator at Eglin.

"This is an electronically-scanned radar," the TAM had said. "All it takes to add a mode is more software. We wanted the TFR mode in case we needed to ingress at low altitude and provide air-support for covert ops well inside national borders."

"I thought the military had sworn off low-altitude flight," I said. "I thought it was all about stealth now."

"We're not the military," the TAM had said, smiling. "And stealth doesn't make you invisible, just hard to detect. If you're stealthy and at low altitude, at night, you're almost impossible to detect and engage."

That's good logic, I had thought.

I nodded to myself as I looked out over the cold water below me and monitored the rock-steady altitude control the TFR was demonstrating as it was coupled to the F-35's autopilot. The jet was flying at exactly 250 feet over the waves. While planning the mission, we had decided on 250 feet as a compromise altitude for the ingress. 500 feet would have been too high for both radar and optical/infrared system detection, assuming the Russians even had those systems in an alert mode in peacetime. 100 feet would have forced the F-35's radar into a much higher scan/update rate. Higher update rates required more pulses of energy and more pulses of energy increased the probability of alerting radar warning systems. So, 250 feet it was, and it felt damn comfortable. I had lived at this altitude when I flew the A-10 all across the U.K. and West Germany during my Cold War days, and it felt good to be here again. Even if it was late at night in a strange jet.

Like the ingress altitude, the choice of ingress route had been driven by the need to avoid detection. If I had approached Russia from the sea, there would have been nothing to hide behind and the odds of being acquired, either optically or by radar, would have been greatly increased. After a last aerial fueling off the northern coast of Norway, I followed the procedure I practiced in the simulator to make the jet stealthy, including retracting my radio antennas and extinguishing all of my external lights. Then I began a gradual descent over northern Norway and Sweden. The jet's onboard acquisition systems easily found the few aircraft that were between me and where I needed to be and the locations of those aircraft, relative to me, were projected on the HMD, like everything else. Avoiding them was easy. Soon I was leveling off over the Gulf of Bothnia at 1,000 feet above the waves and headed for northwestern Estonia. Just moments ago, I had passed the group of small islands between Finland and Sweden and then descended to the final ingress altitude of 250 feet.

The plan was to coast in on the northwestern tip of mainland Estonia, in a sparsely-populated area between the cities of Haapsalu and Vihterpalu, turn east and fly approximately 100 nautical miles before crossing into Russia just north of Lake Peipus. Once inside of Russia, I'd continue east until I passed south of the city of Slantsy and then turn northeast toward St. Petersburg. The final set of coordinates in my route was a large clearing in a forest about 30 miles southwest of the city.

Finding a deserted place near the city that provided concealment for a jet-sized object and could be easily controlled had been quite a challenge, or so I had been informed. The ground ops team got in place about the same time I landed at Eglin and using local guides and imagery, were able to locate a landing site only moments before I left Eglin. While I was en route, they were to secure the area and set up an infrared beacon they would use to signal me as I approached. If there wasn't a place for me to set down, the only choice I had was to turn around and depart without landing.

If the ingress and landing scenarios weren't challenging enough, the fuel situation didn't make things any easier. The F-35B carried over 13,000 pounds of gas, more than an air-to-ground configured Viper did, but stealthy aircraft weren't necessarily aerodynamic, and the vertical takeoff and landing phases of flight burned a lot of gas. After running the calculations repeatedly, the team at Eglin and I found that I barely had enough fuel to fly the route, land, takeoff, and egress to the landing site.

But it was possible, so here I was.

The dark coast of Estonia loomed ahead. This time of the evening there were few ships in this area of the sea cruising between the Port of St. Petersburg and the Atlantic Ocean, so those weren't a factor. As I approached the coast, I marveled at how good the vision in the helmet was. Even with very little ambient light, the jet blended optical and infrared energy and overlaid it with a synthetic vision display so that that I could see the precise outline of the coast and the small hills beyond it.

In seconds, I was "feet dry" and flying between two small rocky hills just a few hundred meters in from the coast. In another moment of technological magic, I watched the F-35's radar detect and paint the hills and then automatically adjust the aircraft's course to even the distance at which we split the gap between them.

"Jesus," I said to myself. "What an airplane."

A datalink message popped up on the screen in front of me. SEE YOU ARE FEET DRY.

The jet was automatically transmitting position information to Smith and Amrine, wherever they were, and they had acknowledged I had crossed from the sea to the land.

The jet banked to the left slightly, to avoid a small ridgeline to my right and then rolled out as another incoming message appeared on the screen.

SEE 10000 POUNDS OF GAS. TAM SAYS TO TAKE IT EASY ON THE HORSE.

"Whatever," I mumbled into the intercom.

I noticed that in message reply window, just under the message I had received, the word "WHATEVER" had appeared. I had forgotten that some of the systems in the jet, including message reply, could be voice-controlled.

Using the cursor slew switch on the throttle, I slewed the cursor to the CANCEL softkey, displayed on the screen next to the message, and pushed the cursor slew switch down to enter the command. Then I slewed the cursor over the ACCEPT key and pushed on the cursor switch down again. ROGER was displayed as my response to the boys.

The jet crossed over another set of small hills and then began a slow turn to the east for the approach to the Russian border. In the F-16, we would have never made a slow turn on an ingress route. We'd drive to the turn point, roll into 70-80 degrees of bank and pull the nose to the next heading to minimize the time in the turn. But we were using a different philosophy tonight. Abrupt changes in the heading or attitude of the airplane might make it easier to detect if someone was watching. And hard turns required G and G required more throttle to maintain airspeed. Smooth turns were going to be the norm tonight.

Even with the superb night-vision optics of the HMD, the countryside below appeared dark and featureless, just a continuous mosaic of tree lines, small hills and farmland as far as the optics rendered it into the distance. While the terrain may have been unremarkable, at least it was going by rapidly. At 600 knots groundspeed, I was covering ten nautical miles or 11.5 statute miles every minute. The jet's power was set to auto-throttle mode, so it regulated itself to maintain speed. Another thing that had amazed me about the F-35 was the incredible thrust the engine produced. Even with heavy vertical fan system mounted in the jet, the throttle position wasn't anywhere near the 100% or MILITARY power setting as the auto-throttle held the airspeed at 600 knots.

The jet banked up slightly as it made another 5-degree turn. I looked underneath the visor of the HMD and down at the navigation route in the tactical situation display on the LCD screen, in time to see another turn point symbol pass under the airplane symbol that represented my jet. The route to the east wasn't quite a straight line. We had inserted a few turn points before the major turn to the northeast toward St. Petersburg in order not to fly directly over some of the small towns in Estonia.

I looked back up at the destination ETA display in the HMD and nodded to myself. 2355 hours arrival time at the clearing. Perhaps another 3-5 minutes to land and shut down. On the road into St. Petersburg by 0015 hours. Plenty of time to get into position for the 1000 ceremony tomorrow. It seemed like the plan was all coming together.

The jet banked up again. As it rolled out of the turn, I could see the hills just north of Lake Peipus appear in the synthetic vision of my HMD. Soon, they'd transition from being synthetically displayed to infrared/optical imaged and that would mean I was about to cross into Russia. It would also mean that I'd be in range of any low altitude radar detection systems the Russians had in place any moment. I touched the LCD in front of me until I found the appropriate menu screen and ensured the electronic countermeasures suite on the jet was set appropriately. I also ensured that the radar warning system subscreen was displayed and I smiled when I called it up. The small screen looked almost exactly the same as the radar homing and warning display in the F-16.

While the F-35 relied on stealth to elude detection, it had electronic countermeasures, or ECM, in the event a radar became too interested in the aircraft. When I had been flying the Viper, ECM didn't activate until an enemy target-tracking radar had locked onto my aircraft. The F-35's ECM could perform that function, but it could also fool acquisition radars, assuming the Russians had any sites that were active and searching at low altitude.

As if on cue, I heard an alert tone in my headset and a red radar shape appeared on the PCD tactical situation display as well as in my HMD. It was about 30 degrees left of my nose and about thirty miles away, just inside the Russian border.

"Acq radar," I said to myself, looking at the symbol. "Maybe even an ATC radar." Based on its position, I was betting it was monitoring the approaches from the Gulf of Finland. The F-35's sensors were letting me know it was there, but wasn't a threat yet. "Keep looking the other way, baby," I said into the intercom.

The dark expanse of Lake Peipus appeared on the right side of the jet, barely visible at my altitude and the hills to the left of the jet transitioned from synthetic display to infrared in my HMD. As quickly as the hills transitioned, they went by on the left side of the jet as the lake went by on the right and I was in Russian airspace.

"Holy shit," I said to myself. "That was fast."

About thirty seconds later, the F-35 banked up and made the 30-degree turn to St. Petersburg. I was in the home stretch.

Another alert tone sounded, and a datalink message appeared on the LCD.

SIX MINUTES FROM LANDING. SITE IS READY. BEACON WILL ACTIVATE AT 1 MINUTE FROM LANDING. DO NOT DESCEND OR BEGIN CONVERSION UNTIL YOU HAVE BEACON IN SIGHT.

I slewed to the ACCEPT softkey with my cursor and clicked on it.

The terrain remained somewhat featureless as I flew toward St. Petersburg, but the number of small towns increased significantly. There was no way I could avoid every one of them. When we planned the route, we had theorized that the average Russian family wouldn't be terribly surprised or alarmed at the sound of a jet roaring over their house in the middle of the night. That hope seemed a little feeble now, as I saw the small clusters of lights go by me or directly under me. Everyone in every house down there had a telephone, and any one of them could make a call. I could feel my gut tightening up as I flew.

Looking out in front of me, I could see the lights of St. Petersburg illuminating the sky in the distance and growing brighter as I neared the city at 10 miles per minute. I crossed another small town, and the jet made a course correction to the landing site. Twenty miles to go now. I toggled off the auto-throttle and slowly retarded the power to idle. The F-35 decelerated slowly, almost begrudgingly, seemingly reluctant to give up the comfort of high-speed flight. The lights below me were going by more slowly now, but the jet was making much less noise, so the possibility of disturbing someone enough to make a phone call was probably less. Or so I hoped.

The clearing had been carefully chosen so I could ingress without crossing any major highways. It was outside of the main St. Petersburg ring road and south of a major east-west highway that led into the city. It was also 3-5 miles away from the nearest towns or settlements so that the high power required for the vertical takeoff and landing wouldn't attract attention from the local populace. But the requirement to keep it away from civilization also meant it was isolated. And even with the F-35's enhanced vision systems and precise navigation, I wasn't sure I'd find it without the infrared beacon from the ground crew.

As the jet decelerated through 300 knots, the distance to the landing site decreased to ten miles – about two minutes to go now. I peered into the HMD and searched the forests and fields in front of me to look for the beacon. When the jet decelerated through 250 knots, the HOOK/STOVL button to left of LCD would begin to flash, indicating that the F-35 was ready for conversion to the vertical mode. If I didn't see the beacon soon after that, I was going to be forced to make 180-degree turn and egress. We would have come all this way and expended all this effort for nothing.

And Alina wouldn't have to pay the price she deserved. Thoughts of Gail in my arms as she died passed through my mind, and I locked that down immediately.

"Goddamn it," I whispered into the intercom. "Fucking be there."

The green light blinking behind the plastic front of the HOOK/STOVL button drew me out of my reverie. I scanned the terrain in front of me. The landing site was 4.5 miles away now. About 90 seconds or so at my current speed. The airspeed was decreasing through 220 knots. I eased the throttle forward to keep the airspeed from deteriorating further. The massive Pratt and Whitney F135 spooled up quickly and held the airspeed at 190 knots. I smiled to myself. 190 knots was a familiar number. It was the slowest airspeed the Falcon 7X was supposed to be flown in the clean configuration.

Three miles to the landing site and the terrain in front of the jet remained still and dark. No beacon.

"Fuck," I said to myself. "C'mon guys!"

As I closed the few remaining miles to the landing zone and eyed the trees in front of me in my HMD, I could see the waypoint symbol for the landing zone in the middle of a dense expanse of forest just ahead of me, across a large open field. I had a mental flashback to my time as a ground forward air controller, driving through the farm fields of Bavaria in West Germany in an M105 jeep with a pallet of communications gear in the back. I remembered trying to find an advantageous position to control the ground attack aircraft that were assigned to support us and trying to gain sight of them as they popped up from low altitude to roll-in on their simulated targets.

And then I realized why I didn't see the beacon.

When we were doing all our last-minute planning, we didn't count on the trees blocking line-of-sight from the beacon to the jet as it flew at low altitude.

The clearing was less than two miles away, and I wasn't going to be able to see it, or the beacon, until I was right on top of it. At that point, it would be too late to make a landing.

"We're fucking idiots," I said to myself.

I lifted my left hand from the throttle and pushed the HOOK/STOVL button.

The miracle of technology took over then.

The throttle moved itself to the center position, and the autopilot disengaged as the control stick transitioned into the vertical control mode. The engine spooled up to a higher power setting as the doors for the vertical thrust turbine opened, and the engine nozzle rotated downward. I could feel a tingling behind my back as the vertical turbine wound up to speed. The entire conversion process took about 8 seconds. Mimicking what I had practiced in the simulator, I eased the throttle back to slow my airspeed, while I loosened my grip on the sidestick so that I didn't command any vertical movement of the aircraft. The F-35 slowed to 150 knots, then to 100 as I continued across the field.

The navigation readout showed one mile to go.

"Too fast, too high," I said to myself.

I pulled the throttle back to slow the jet further and pushed forward on the side stick slightly. The jet slowed to 50 knots and descended, in a level attitude, to 100 feet.

"Perfect," I said to myself.

.5 miles to go.

I was using the virtual speed brake switch on the throttle to control airspeed now. I could make fine adjustments as required. I crossed a small farm road in the middle the field. I could see some small shacks around the edges of the field. Hopefully, there were no people in them.

.3 miles to go. I was at 50 knots and 100 feet and the trees on the northeast edge of the field went under the nose. I had no idea how much noise the jet was making but I was betting the noise would carry across the still night. I needed to get this thing on the ground and shut it down quickly.

.2 miles to go, about 1200 feet or so.

I moved the speed brake switch aft and slowed the jet to thirty knots. I was probably only about 50-70 feet above the trees now, and I knew I wouldn't see the beacon until I was on top of it, but at least I'd be able to land if I saw it. I gave some quick thought to our fuel planning and wondered if I was burning more fuel in this maneuver than we had estimated.

No time for that now. We're committed.

.1 mile to go and no beacon.

I didn't doubt the accuracy of the jet's navigation systems as much as I doubted whether human beings on the ground with a GPS could get to the right place.

Jesus, I thought. *Are they lost? Do they just think they're in the right place?*

The jet crept over the edge of a clearing, and I squinted down looked down to see a few shacks and some farm equipment in the glow of the electro-optical display. It amazed me again that I didn't need to worry about visibility over the nose of the jet. With the HMD, I could see through the nose and to the ground beyond.

But there was nothing to see. No personnel, no vehicles.

"Where the fuck are you guys?"

I slowed the jet to 20 knots and moved the last few feet to the coordinates I was given. The landing gear handle turned red, and a stern female voice said LANDING GEAR, LANDING GEAR in my headset.

"Shut the fuck up," I said to myself.

I canceled the verbal warning with my cursor, but the light in the gear handle stayed illuminated. I flew over a small group of trees and found a much larger clearing beneath me. It was the perfect size to land the F-35 in. The distance to go indicator read 0. And there was still no beacon.

I slowed the jet to a hover and flew out over the center of the clearing. Then I gingerly applied some left rudder and made the equivalent of a slow pedal turn to examine the edges of the clearing in detail. Nothing there. No people. No vehicles.

Then I saw the bodies.

Three of them. Just inside the north tree line of the clearing. The infrared energy emitting from the bodies made the shape of them unmistakable.

Holy shit! I thought.

Then I received an alert tone in my headset, and the message screen came up in my display.

LOOK SOUTH, the message said.

I pivoted the jet to a southern heading and saw the infrared strobe of the beacon, a few miles away. I positioned my head to put the marking cue in my HMD on it and pressed the MARK button on the right side of the sidestick. Instantly, a steering cue appeared in front of me, and I pushed forward on the speed brake switch to accelerate. I held the switch forward until the airspeed was up to 100 knots and flew across a few more groups of trees and fields. When I was a mile from the strobe point, I slowed the jet to 50 knots and looked through the HMD to try and make out the ground party. At first, the IR energy from the beacon was so bright it masked anything around it, but as I closed to a half a mile and slowed to 20 knots, I could see one vehicle and one, lithe person holding the beacon.

I felt a smile form on my lips.

She was standing in front of a long rectangular building with a high, angular roof. The building was at the edge of a field and had a road that came to the front of it but then went around the west side of the building and behind it. I followed the road with my eyes in the other direction and saw that it went diagonally across the field to the northwest and vanished into another tree line.

My headset dinged again.

LAND ON SOUTH SIDE, the message said. OTHER SIDE.

I nodded to myself and slowed the jet to 10 knots.

I decreased my altitude slightly and slowly moved the jet around the building to the southern side. The asphalt pad on this side of the building was exactly the length of the building and about 100 feet wide. It was lined by trees on the east and south sides and the building to the north.

Perfect, I thought.

I brought the jet into a hover over the asphalt pad and tapped the right pedal to align it with the orientation of the landing area. Then I lowered the landing gear handle and waited for the down and locked indications. Once I was satisfied with the gear, it was time to put the jet on the ground.

"Don't try to overthink it," the TAM had said to me. "This isn't a helicopter. The jet knows where it is. Just hold the stick forward and let it land. Don't try to flare it or grease it on. You'll mess up the landing logic."

I did as I had been instructed and pushed forward on the control stick.

The F-35 descended smoothly to the ground and settled on its gear with a minimal bounce on the struts. As soon as it went weight on wheels, the engine spooled down to idle. I pushed the HOOK/STOVL button to deactivate the vertical mode and to stow the vertical turbine doors as well as return the engine nozzle to its normal position. I gave the jet about 10 seconds to make the conversion. Then, I lifted the guard on the engine control switch on the left console and raised the engine switch to the OFF position. The engine wound down and I raised the canopy switch and began to unstrap. As the canopy raised, a van pulled around to the west side of the building and parked next to the jet. As soon as the car stopped, the familiar figure of Sharona/Isabelle/Janine leaped out of it. She was dressed in tight black pants and a sweater. Even in the darkness of the asphalt pad, the cappuccino tone of her flawless skin was easily visible.

"C'mon hero," she yelled at me. "We don't have all night."

"Trying my best," I said. "Do you know how to deploy the boarding ladder?" I asked her.

"No," she said. "But Bart sent me instructions."

I set the HMD on the left console of the jet and unsnapped my PIC, or pilot interface connection from my harness. Lockheed Martin's engineers had combined the F-35's g-suit, oxygen and communications connections into one, easy to use fitting. I silently commended them on the simplicity of their design. Outside, I could hear the quick release catches on the skin of the aircraft being opened and soon after I heard the three metallic clinks as the boarding ladder deployed.

"Keep all your flight shit on," she said. "You can change in the van."

I nodded, turned the jet's battery switch off, and began to rise off the seat. Then I noticed the ejection seat was still armed.

"Damn it!" I whispered. I retrieved the seat and canopy safety pins from my g-suit pocket and inserted the seat one in the hole underneath the lanyard between my knees. I stood up and tried to remember exactly where to place my left foot so that it found the top step of the ladder and lowered it slowly. Sharona grabbed my left ankle and guided it to the step.

"Thanks for that," I said over my shoulder. "Do you have a day job that I don't know about?"

"It's possible I may have infiltrated a fighter squadron in a past life," she said.

I inserted the canopy jettison safety pin and completed my descent unassisted, damn proud of myself for doing so.

"Welcome to Russia, comrade!" she said as I made landfall.

"Good to be here, I guess."

I turned to the side panel and lowered the canopy with the switch inside. Once it was locked into place, I raised the ladder and closed the panel.

"What happened at the other site?" I said. "I saw three bodies there."

"That was never intended to be the real site," she said. "We were a little suspicious of our Russian contractors, so we provided the coordinates to them without telling them what was going to happen there. The coordinates were leaked almost immediately. The Ops team and I arrived at the site after they did and discovered that there were not only the two I briefed but also a third guy who was hiding and waiting to ambush us. I took him out first and the team took care of the other two."

"What do you think that means?" I asked.

She shrugged. "No idea. Besides Hansen, the only people who know what's going down here are you, the boys and the team and me. Hansen hasn't even briefed it up-channel yet."

I nodded. "Compartmentalization and all that."

"Words to live by," she said.

"Do you have it?"

She nodded. "Barrett .50 with a monster scope. Pre-sighted and ready."

"It's time to go kick some ass," I said.

She smiled. "You bet it is. Let's do this, baby."

CHAPTER THIRTY-THREE

Tuesday, November 9
0945 Hours Local Time
St. Peter's Church
St. Petersburg, Russian Republic

It was a dingy morning in St. Petersburg and a blanket of low clouds, heavy with pending precipitation, hung over the city. I could feel the cold moisture in the air as I gazed out of the church bell tower and across the drab rooftops to the Palace Square, a little less than a half a mile away. So named because of the massive building that stretched across its north-western border, the Palace Square stood before what was once the Winter Palace of the Emperors of Russia and now housed the State Hermitage Museum. I was no student of architecture, but I found the palace's white and green baroque facade impressive with its two levels of columns. The top part, or capital, of each column, seemed to be coated or painted in gold, as was the area above each of the windows. The Emperors of old had plenty of money to spend on themselves.

The square itself was one of the larger public spaces in the world, but it wasn't shaped like a square at all. The shape was somewhere between a semi-circle and a triangle. It was bordered on the northwest side by the Winter Palace and the southeastern side by the curved yellow and white building that housed the Imperial Army Chief of Staff back in the days of the Emperor. The open area of the square was vast, and I estimated it at about 50,000 square meters. In the center of the square stood the Column of Alexander, a monument to the Russian Military victory over Napoleon and built to honor Alexander I, the Russian Emperor who had ruled during the Napoleonic Wars. The red granite column was nearly 156 feet tall and featured an angel with the face of Alexander standing at the base of a cross and looking down on the square below.

It was there, at the base of the column, the award ceremony for Alina was supposed to take place, sometime in the next hour. As I gazed out over the rooftops and into the square, I wondered if Alina would see the irony of her uncle dying at my hands, in the same manner, and in the same sort of area, as the British prime minister had died at hers.

Sharona and I were in the northern bell tower of St. Peter's Church, or more properly, the Lutheran Church of St. Peter and St. Paul, in the Nevsky Prospect of the city. It was the only structure high enough to allow an unobstructed view of the Square and yet provide enough distance from it that we would have a decent chance to escape once the shot was taken. Since the Winter Palace and the Square were near the geographic center of the city, there would be quite a distance to travel after I took Anton down. In fact, finding our through the confusing array of streets, canals and bridges to the church had been quite a challenge last night, even with little traffic and the help of a military-grade GPS.

Sneaking into the church, however, had been surprisingly easy. Sharona had picked the lock on one of the side doors, and we had made our way through the dark sanctuary and into the northern bell tower without seeing a single soul. The walk up the stairs of the tower, lugging the 30 plus-pound Barrett rifle and other gear, had been a bit of chore, but soon we were in a room below the floor of the bell area, which turned out to be somewhat cozy, in spite of its lack of insulation and its vertical distance from the warm sanctuary floor below.

We went up to the bell area and surveyed the area and its view of the target area. Then, after choosing the most advantageous place to set up the rifle, we had returned to the room below to get some rest before the events of the morning. Sharona had brought an air mattress and a sleeping bag with her gear, and she inflated the mattress, rolled the sleeping bag out and without preamble, she stripped off her coat, kicked off her shoes and crawled into it. I stood there watching her.

"Well what are you waiting for?" she had asked. "Get comfortable and get in here. We need to get some sleep, or we won't function, and you won't shoot straight."

I shrugged and doffed my coat and shoes. Then, I crawled into the sleeping bag next to her. She reached around me and zipped the bag up. Then she curled up against me and put her head on my chest and her arm around my waist.

"Better to keep warm this way," she said.

Ordinarily, my over-active libido would have taken notice of the presence of an attractive woman in such proximity, but I was confused by the events of the last several days and exhausted by the flight here. There was so much to work through, and I didn't have the energy or the time.

I felt Sharona's left hand reach up and stroke the side of my neck. "I'm sorry about Gail," she said in a soft tone that I was unfamiliar with. "Bart and Bruiser are sorry too. No one had any idea that the Shadow would engage a non-combatant. She's been so businesslike up until now. It just seemed out of character."

"Gail and I were dancing together," I said. "I kissed her a few times. Alina must have been jealous. That's the only thing that makes sense."

Sharona nodded her head against me.

"We agree. That's one of the reasons we were able to get approval from Hansen for you to take Anton down. If the Agency did it, it wouldn't be personal, and she probably wouldn't come looking for anyone. But she's fucked up enough that if we make it personal between you and her, she'll come out of hiding to get you. And we need her to do that."

I felt a series of emotions go through me as Sharona spoke. First, there was the connection between Alina and I and the powerful desire for her that still lurked inside of me. Then there was the pain of holding Gail as she died and the sense of anger at the needless death of another person because of me. Finally, there was the anger at Alina for taking Gail's life. Gail had an incredible career and life in front of her and Alina had taken it all. A line from Clint Eastwood's character in the movie *Unforgiven* came to mind.

"It's a hell of a thing, killin' a man," he had said. "You take away all he's got, and everything he's ever gonna have."

I thought about Gail in her uniform and about how ravishing she had looked the night she had died. I thought about how she felt in my arms and how playful she could be, in bed and out of it. I thought about the hours we had spent talking with her head in my lap, or watching T.V. and just being together.

I felt a tear roll down the left side of my face. It landed on the top of Sharona's head, and I was sure she felt it, but she didn't move. Instead, she squeezed me and let me mourn in the darkness.

Eventually, we slept.

Later, much later, I felt Sharona unzip the sleeping bag and reach across me to her backpack of gear. Her body felt warm on top of mine. I felt a smile creep onto my face.

"I...didn't... hear... an alarm," I said, groggily.

"I don't need one," she whispered. "I just tell myself what time I want to wake up and I do."

"That must be handy," I said, trying to blink the sleep out of my eyes. "What time is it?"

"7:13 local," she said. She retrieved two sets of earplugs from a pocket on the side of her bag and handed me a set.

"That's an odd time to wake up," I said as I watched her put her earplugs in. Then she looked up at the ceiling and back at me. I remembered the grandfather clock my mom had in our house growing up.

"Oh yeah," I said as I stuffed the earplugs into my ears.

The time 7:15 registered on my watch and the bells above us sounded the typical four-note refrain of the first quarter hour of the day, shaking the tower slightly and vibrating the floor beneath us.

"Just in time," I said.

Sharona sank back into the sleeping bag and snuggled up against me, pulling the side of it over us.

"We don't have to get up just yet," she said. "But I doubt we'll get any sleep with that thing ringing every 15 minutes."

"Of all the places we might have slept together, I never thought we'd do it in a church," I said.

She patted my chest and laughed. "You must be feeling better." She lifted her head and kissed me on the left cheek. "But I think if I'm going to take advantage of you, I'd prefer more slightly more luxurious accommodations."

"Yeah, you're right, besides a wood surface like this would be hard on my knees."

"Your knees? Whoever said you were going to get to be on top?"

"It's where I seem to do my best work," I said, laughing.

Several hours later, after rising, eating some protein bars, and relieving ourselves into plastic bags with gel inside that Sharona had bought for just that purpose, I was peering out of the bell tower to the Square below. Watching for Alina and Anton, I wondered if I'd be able to pull the trigger when the time came. I smiled grimly to myself as I looked over at the Barrett M107 rifle resting on its bipod on the ledge next to me. I probably wasn't the first person to set up a sniper's nest in the spire of a church but if there was an almighty and he was keeping a ledger, the act of assassinating someone from holy ground would add to my considerable tally in the negative column.

"This place has an odd history," Sharona said, looking at the square through binoculars one window over. "The stones for the original foundation were laid in 1728. Eventually, it grew too large for its congregation, and it was razed, only to be rebuilt from 1833 to 1838. It functioned as a church until even after the Bolshevik Revolution in 1917 when the Soviets nationalized it. But Stalin, that eternal party pooper, closed it in 1937. All of the interior was confiscated or stolen. It was used as a warehouse in the 40s and 50s, then Nikita Khrushchev turned it into a swimming pool in 1962. It remained as a swimming pool for 30 years until it given back to the church in 1992 and re-ordained in 1997. Some of the locals still call it the 'swimming pool church.'"

I looked over at her. "You've done your research," I said.

"I always do," she replied without looking at me. "Knowledge is power. And sometimes it can save your life."

I nodded.

"It's getting close to ten. Let's verify the range and the sight setting and get you settled into the weapon."

Using a laser rangefinder and the Barrett Optical Ranging System (BORS) mounted next to the rifle's telescopic sight, we verified the range to the column as just under 522 meters, well inside the tactical effective range of the powerful rifle. There was no wind to account for, so that made the windage adjustment a no brainer. The rifle had been zeroed for 1,000 meters, so the elevation had to be lowered, but with the heavy humidity, we didn't lower it as much as we would have if the air had been less dense.

I settled into the weapon's stock and placed the side of my face against the cheek guard. The view through the Leupold 14 power telescopic sight was clear, and I settled the crosshairs on the chest of the angel at the top of Alexander's Column. I could see the figure of the angel easily, and the folds of the angel's gown were discernible, but my field of view was wide enough that I could see the entire length of the column. I smiled to myself as I heard Gunnery Sergeant George Phillips' words ringing in my ears.

"It's a tradeoff," he had said. "When you choose a mag level. You want precision sight placement for the shot, but you also need a wide enough field of view to see the target's surroundings and to shift your point of aim to other targets when required. You have to select a magnification level that allows you to do both and it's always a compromise."

The 14 power scope seemed to be doing the trick, at least at this range. After having shot targets at ranges up to 1200 meters in Arizona, I felt confident I could hit my target at 522 meters, especially with the powerful Barrett. The M107 was probably the best sniper rifle in the world, although some might characterize it as an anti-material rifle more than a sniper rifle. The brainchild of Ronnie Barrett, whose goal was to design a shoulder-fired .50 caliber rifle, the weapon I held had its roots in the 1980s with the M82 series and was adopted by the US Army at the M107 in 2002. It could engage targets at ranges over 2000 meters and with its recoil-operated, semi-automatic action, it made rapid follow up shots not only possible but easy. I had heard about this incredible weapon multiple times and had even been on the wrong end of it in my last adventure with the CIA, but I never dreamed I'd end up firing one.

"Life plays tricks on you sometimes," I murmured to myself.

"What'd you say?" Sharona asked.

I shook my head slightly. "Nothing important," I said. "Definitely nothing important."

"Head's up," Sharona said. "There's a group of black sedans approaching the square."

I nodded. *Showtime.*

At that moment, the rationale behind having snipers operate as part of a two-person team became clear. While the sniper was the weapon, the spotter was the acquisition and situational awareness system for the sniper. Looking through his sight, the sniper saw the world through a soda straw. The spotter saw the big picture.

I tilted my sight downward and saw three official-looking sedans approach the square from the west. The traffic in this area of the city wasn't heavy, but the sedans weren't moving very quickly.

"Probably just came from the Admiralty building next door," Sharona said. "Anton is a former Soviet-Russian Navy guy, a submariner in fact. He still maintains an office in the Admiralty building."

The three sedans stopped along the side of the square closest to us and began to disperse personnel as soon as they halted. The drivers opened the passenger doors, and a stream of men and women in black winter garb exited the vehicles, formed up into small groups, and made their way to the base of the column. As I watched the center vehicle, I saw a woman with long blonde hair exit it, followed by a tall, thin man with gray hair, just visible under the edge of his *ushanka*, the stereotypical Russian fur hat with ear flaps.

"Anton," I said to myself.

"Possibly," Sharona said. "But we have to wait to have positive ID before you take the shot."

"Copy that," I said.

I centered Alina's face in the cross hairs of my scope and marveled at the beauty I saw there yet again. She was talking to the thin man and smiling. She looked happy, and her blue-gray eyes were sparkling in the dull light. I felt the involuntary and compulsive desire for her once more, and I fought it down inside of myself.

"She's hot," Sharona said. "What was she like up close and personal."

"Fucked up," I said, after a moment too long.

"But there's more. Isn't there? There always is."

"Yes there was," I said. "She was human. Disturbingly human." *And I wanted her. Goddamn it.*

"That's one of the oddest things about this line of work," Sharona said. "You run into people who seem absolutely nice and normal and you find out they're capable of doing some of the most fucked up things."

The procession of people made their way across the expanse of open stone to base of the column. Then a shorter, dark-haired man began to give directions to form the group into an orderly gathering for the ceremony. Soon there was a semi-circle of people to the left and four people to the right, the short man, the tall, thin man, Alina, and another woman who stood next to the thin man with a box in her hand.

"Our line to the target is almost perpendicular to the group," I said. "I hope I can get a clean shot."

"The alignment should work in our favor," Sharona said. "At some point he'll have to turn and then you can nail him, assuming this gadget works and I can ID him."

"What gadget?" I asked, still looking through the Barrett's sight.

"These binoculars can capture an image and then run a facial recognition routine on it. I just need the thin guy to turn just a bit…more."

The small man stepped forward and then began reading something from a folder in his hands. A photographer, with a commercial 35-millimeter camera, separated himself from the larger group and began snapping photos as the small man spoke. A few moments later, Alina and the thin man stepped forward and then turned to face each other. Anton's face was clearly in view. While I had studied photos of the man, it was different looking at him through a telescopic sight and knowing that he was going to die at my hand. The lined face was smiling broadly, and the gray eyes were beaming with pride. Today was a happy day for him. The breeder reactor project was a go, and his country would not only make billions of rubles, but it would also have the power to blackmail a good portion of the western world because each reactor site was a potential dirty bomb. It would take years before all the reactors were in place. But that would suit the Russians just fine. They were planners. They were in it for the long haul.

And here was the man who was responsible for it all. As well as the deaths of 55 people who were killed at his command.

"Gotcha," Sharona said. "Hey Bart, I just sent you a vacation photo."

I smiled. She was talking to Amrine through a headset that I had never seen her put on.

"Well thanks, Bart," she said after a moment. "I'm sure we'll have a great time." She lowered her voice. "Definitely Anton. Cleared to engage."

"Roger."

I had observed and participated in many medal ceremonies in my life, and they all followed essentially the same format. The person receiving the medal and the person giving it stood while a citation was read. Then, once the reading was over, the person giving the medal pinned it on the receiver. Normally there would be handshakes, but today, since we were in Russia, there would be hugs and kisses.

Almost on cue, the speaker finished his reading and turned to Alina and Anton. The other woman in their group opened a box with a hinged lid and offered it to Anton. He reached inside it and retrieved a medal with large gold star suspended below a tri-color ribbon of red, blue and white. Then he leaned forward and pinned it on Alina. When he finished, he kissed her formally, on her right cheek, her left cheek and her right cheek again. Alina, not content with the formal greeting, threw her arms around his neck and hugged him as the small crowd broke into applause.

"Damn," Sharona said. "If they don't stop with the lovey-dovey stuff we're going to lose the shot opportunity."

"No, we won't," I said as I watched the proceedings through the scope.

"What makes you so sure?"

"Because. They'll want pictures."

Once Anton and Alina stopped hugging each other, the photographer marshaled the two of them over in front of the base of the column, turning their bodies slightly toward one another for the formal photo.

It was perfect.

I clicked the Barrett's safety to the FIRE position with my right thumb and positioned the crosshairs on the center of Anton's chest. With many weapons, a single shot to the center of mass wouldn't be a certain kill. With the powerful .50 cal, it was a death sentence. I began to control my breathing as I put pressure on the trigger, but even as I concentrated the sight placement on Anton's chest, I could see his smiling face alongside Alina's. It didn't seem fair that a man responsible for so much death should die with no pain and no angst in the last few moments of his life.

No.

Without really being aware I that I did it, I shifted the crosshairs to a point in space just to the left of Anton's right ear. Then I squeezed the trigger slowly and deliberately.

The huge rifle fired and shoved itself into my shoulder while 750 grains of steel-cased death closed the distance to the target at 2,650 feet per second. I kept my face to the sight and returned my point of aim to the center of Anton's chest.

"Clean miss!" Sharona said. "What the fuck T.C.! I thought you practiced."

"Wait for it," I said.

The .50 caliber slug had closed the distance to target in just over half a second and struck the column just behind Anton, digging out a huge chunk of marble and splintering into thousands of pieces as it impacted. I wasn't worried about the people on the ground finding our location. By now, the sound of the shot would have reached them, but the rifle's suppressor was military grade and dispersed the sound effectively. I watched Anton's face as I held the crosshairs on target. It was like watching a slow-motion sequence in a movie. First, his head had turned as the bullet went past his ear. Then, he turned forward again with a look of surprise in his eyes, like he didn't understand what had happened. But then, I saw a look of comprehension find its way onto his features, and his eyes slowly widened. And in those eyes, comprehension turned into fear, and a millisecond later, fear became terror.

I squeezed the Barrett's trigger once, and huge red hole appeared in Anton's chest. I realigned my sights and squeezed the trigger again. Another huge hole appeared less than a centimeter away from the first.

Anton staggered as the bullets impacted him and the crowd of people dissolved into a mass of running, screaming individuals, eager to leave the open square for some kind of cover. All of the crowd except for one. Alina caught her uncle as he fell to his knees and then eased his descent to the hard stone. Her eyes were full of disbelief and tears. She cradled his head to her chest, just as I had done with Gail's, and looked down at him with her mouth open in what I was sure was a silent scream.

Then, she slowly looked in our direction and raised her eyes. She found our position immediately because it was the same place she would have chosen. I positioned the crosshairs on a point in space just to the right of her left ear and squeezed the Barrett's trigger a final time. The bullet went by her head so closely that her hair was moved by the air disturbance of its passage.

She didn't flinch.

Instead, she stared at me, across 522 meters of open, Russian, air. And the look of sadness on her face turned into one of bitter, raving hatred.

"That's it, sweetheart," I said as I watched her. "Now you know it's me. Come, and fucking get me."

CHAPTER THIRTY-FOUR

Tuesday, November 9
1113 Hours Local Time
Somewhere in the Ligovsky Prospekt
St. Petersburg, Russian Republic

I turned the Lada van around the corner of the busy street, barely missing two pedestrians in the process. They were old women, clad in the typical black winter garb and I glimpsed just enough of their faces to detect looks of disbelief and anger there.

"Easy, Jeff Gordon," Sharona said from the van's right seat. "We're not going to get anywhere if you hit somebody."

"I'm doing my best," I said. "Goddamn it!" I swerved to avoid a car that pulled out of a parking garage without looking. "Explain again why we're not only staying off the freeways but also going the wrong way?"

"St. Petersburg and Moscow lead Europe in traffic jams," she said. "So, getting onto the freeway is unpredictable. There was a 120-mile long traffic jam here once." She looked down at her GPS. "And going the wrong way, at least for now, ensures that if we pick up a tail at some point, we won't be leading them to the jet."

"Tail?" How would that happen?"

"I always assume there's a tail. Until I'm sure there isn't." She glanced over her shoulder. "But, I think we're okay." She pointed to the ear bud in her left ear. "And from what I hear from our mission support folks, there hasn't been much of an organized response from the local police. They're reacting, but they're not responding."

"That's good," I said.

"Turn right on Boravaya," she said. "Two blocks ahead. That will get us started in the right direction."

"The street signs are all in Cyrillic. How will I know it?"

"Second right. It will be a major road."

I kept my eyes on the road as the traffic moved around me, seemingly in random order. I was reminded of some contract trips I had done to Cairo, Egypt and the passenger van rides from the airport to hotel and back. Those rides had been some of the most harrowing experiences of my life. Today's traffic didn't feel that much different. Eventually, I felt Sharona's eyes on me. I glanced over at her and found here looking at me appraisingly.

"What?" I asked.

"I guess sending you to sniper school *was* a good investment," she said. "You were pretty good with that Barrett today. A shot past Anton's ear and two center of mass in just a few seconds. That was tight work. Remind me not to piss you off. At long range, anyway."

I shrugged. "Not sure how much of it was me and how of it was the gun. That Barrett is a damn nice weapon."

"That's true. But it takes a skilled operator to get the most out of it. And the warning shot you put past that bitch's ear. So close it moved her hair! That was epic!"

"Just wanted to make sure she got the message."

"Well if that didn't do it, the love note you left on the Barrett will."

"Hopefully they'll find it," I said.

We had left the Barrett in place on the tower window ledge. Sharona had poured a vial of acid compound down the barrel of the gun and into the weapon's action to ensure it couldn't be used again. On top of the gun's receiver, I had left a note.

I bet you're sorry you kept me alive, I had written. *You took someone I cared about, so I took someone you cared about. You know where I live. Let's finish this. Love, CP.*

Sharona tilted her head.

"And speaking of the rifle, they just found it." She listened for a few moments. "Shit. They have a rough description of us."

"How?"

"Security camera in the church, most likely. They're everywhere these days."

"We wore these worker coveralls on the way down. Between the smudges on our faces and the high collars, how much do you think they can tell?"

"All they need is enough to trigger the facial rec software. Then they can pull good photos of us out of their files and disseminate them."

I turned the van onto Borovaya lane or road or boulevard or whatever it was and immediately found myself behind a Russian Politsiya car with its roof lights flashing.

"Well shit," I said.

Sharona looked up. "Don't sweat it. They can't have the pictures yet, and they definitely don't have the vehicle."

A uniformed Russian policeman got out of the car and waved us by. He had a bored expression on his face and a cigarette hanging out of his mouth. His blue shirt and gray pants were wrinkled, and the large gray and red service cap sat on his head at an odd angle. He eyed us as we drove by and then turned back to the car in front of his.

"Writing a ticket," I said. "With traffic so heavy you can't go any faster than 30 miles per hour. That makes sense."

"Don't forget, you're in Russia," Sharona said. "Things don't have to make sense." She looked out the Lada's dingy windscreen. "We're going to follow this road for about a mile. Eventually, we'll get to Ligovsky Avenue. There we'll turn southwest and start heading for the jet."

"Roger that," I said. I was following a large Russian tractor-trailer rig as we drove down Borovaya at 50 kilometers per hour, about 30 miles per hour.

"Shit," Sharona said a few moments later. "They've made the car. We'll need to ditch it." She looked up and down the street. "And of course, there's no parking garage to be seen."

"Parking garage?"

She nodded. "Best place to ditch one car and pick up a new one." She looked to her right. "Hey, make the, next right. This looks like a shopping center. We might be able to do a swap here."

As I came to the turn a few minutes later, I saw a formal building on the left-hand side of the road.

"Medical center," Sharona said. "Or meditsinskiy tsentr." She looked down the street intently as I completed the turn. "There's a parking garage under the health store there. That should be perfect."

"Unless someone sees us," I said.

We cruised up the street behind the inevitable stream of slow-moving cars. I was starting to wonder how people in St. Petersburg got anywhere on time. After waiting for an excruciatingly long time, I finally was able to make the left turn and into the garage underneath the health store building. I blinked to adjust my eyes to the darkness as I drove down the ramp.

"Just keep going down until I tell you to stop," Sharona said. "We'll need to find a car that blends in and is easy to steal."

"I'll have to trust your judgment on that," I said. "Don't have much experience there."

"I've boosted cars all over the world," she said. "The Agency has a course in it. I'd like to tell you there's an art to it, but most of the time it's just about finding a hidden key."

Ten minutes later we were driving out of the garage in a black Mercedes E320 station wagon that was about ten years old. It was dingy and dusty and perfectly anonymous. It had been parked in a corner on the second level down, and as Sharona predicted, the owner had left a spare key in a magnetic box under the bumper. We discarded our coveralls and left them in the van. We donned heavy Russian winter coats and *ushanka* hats and transferred the few bags we had remaining into the wagon.

"Back out to Borovaya," Sharona said. "We'll stick with the same route. At least for now."

We drove on into the late afternoon and early evening, doing our best to stay off of the freeways and avoid other major roads. It took us several hours to get out of urban St. Petersburg and the suburbs around it, such as they were. During that time, we learned that our photos and descriptions had been dispersed to law enforcement agencies and that road blocks were being set up to keep us from leaving the city. We also learned that Pulkovo airport was being watched, as were the train stations throughout the city.

"They don't know about the jet," I had said. "At least not yet."

"Let's hope we stay that lucky," Sharona said. "The only problem is that the general route we need to follow is about the same as someone trying to drive out of the country to Estonia. And they will anticipate that."

"So, what are we going to do?"

Sharona shook her head. "Once we get past the ring road and the airport, there aren't any neighborhood streets we can hide on. We'll have to get on a major road and take our chances." She clicked a mic button near her collar. "Any word on the E95?" she asked.

We were actually on the E95 at the moment, a major artery into and out of the St. Petersburg metroplex. It was a four-lane, limited access road that passed just southeast of the St. Petersburg/Pulkovo airport and went to the city of Gatchina to the southwest, and beyond. We were moving slowly, at 30-40 kilometers per hour, about 20 – 25 miles per hour due to the volume of traffic on the road. But at least we were moving. The problem was the volume of the traffic was steadily increasing because we were getting into rush hour and due the fading light of the early autumn evening, drivers were slowing down.

"Okay, copy that," Sharona said. "Let us know ASAP if you hear anything." She released the mic button. "So far so good. The checkpoints haven't gotten out this far yet, and there's nothing at all on the E95. They must not have thought we'd try to drive out of the city immediately."

"So where would they think we'd go?"

Sharona shrugged. "They'd have to know that we wouldn't be stupid enough to try to get out on a commercial flight. Trains would be a better option, but unless we took a train that went deeper into Russia, the border police could stop us." She thought for a moment and then snapped her fingers. "They probably thought we'd try to get out on one of the ferries to Helsinki or Stockholm. It would be very easy to hide aboard one of those ships because they're fairly large vessels. There are also a lot of them, and they depart regularly from the harbor."

"Makes sense," I said, nodding. "Let's hope they stay with that thought."

As we passed the airport, we transitioned from urban sprawl to farmland, as far as I could see into the distance. Like many big cities, the transition was nearly instantaneous – one moment we were driving through suburbs, the next moment we were in the countryside. I looked ahead of us and saw the trail of taillights ahead of us on the road.

"Where the hell do all these people live?" I asked. "There's nothing out here."

"Gatchina is a pretty big town," Sharona said. "Maybe they all live there."

We drove along in silence for next several minutes, and then the roar of afterburning jet engines caught my ears. I looked out of the left side of the Mercedes just in time to see two Russian fighters, one in trail of the other, taking off from an airport just a few miles to the east. The blue-yellow glow of their afterburners highlighted them against the darkening sky.

"Probably MiG-29s," Sharona said. "There's a depot repair station for them there at Pushkin Airdrome."

The pilot of the lead aircraft commanded his jet into a graceful climbing turn to the south while the pilot of the trail aircraft banked up and pulled his nose inside his leader's turn radius to make the rejoin. I sighed involuntarily.

"Aren't you quite the storehouse of knowledge," I said as I watched the jets. "It would seem you're not a stranger to these parts."

She looked over at me, raised her eyebrows and smiled. "I can neither confirm nor deny…"

"Yeah, yeah," I said. "You spooks and your need to know and all that."

The traffic had lightened a bit, and our speed had increased to 50-60 kph. The countryside was going by more rapidly and ahead of us, the stream of taillights was spreading out. The sun had disappeared below the horizon, and red glow of the sunset was giving way to another dull Russian evening.

"This is awesome," Sharona said. "Once we get to Gatchina, the site is only about another 30-40 minutes away."

"What are the odds someone will be there waiting for us?"

She shook her head. "Zero. We own the land through a shell company, and the Ops team secured it shortly after we left last night." She looked over at me. "We couldn't leave an F-35 unguarded in the Russian countryside. I'm sure the team has it wired for demo in case something bad happened. We'll have to make sure they remove that shit before you fly out of here."

"If you guys had all of this planned, why the ruse on the initial landing site?"

She looked over at me. "We didn't have it planned. It was a last-minute operation, but it also allowed us to deal with a few moles in the local support team. Sometimes things just come together."

"Jesus," I said after a few minutes. "You guys have put a lot of money and effort into this deal."

Sharona nodded. "We have. But if we get Alina to come after you it will all have been worth it. If we take her and can pin all the killings on her, it will bring down all of Anton's work and quite possibly save the energy world from the Russians."

"Hell of a gamble," I said.

"We've bet more on worse odds." She pointed to a sign coming up on the right side of the road. "The E95 will go to the east in a few miles to go around Gatchina, but we'll stay right and take the main road through the center of town. We've tempted the checkpoint gods on the freeway here long enough."

We exited the E95 a few minutes later and took a street that had the word "Lenningradskoye" in it, or at least that was the translation Sharona rendered. Ahead of us, the lights of Gatchina glowed in the mist of the early evening. On the street lights that lined the road, rainbow-like rings were forming around the lamp bulbs, adding notes of color to the gloomy darkness.

"Shit," Sharona said. "They've mobilized the FSB. Goddamn it."

"That doesn't sound good," I said. "I only know what I've seen on T.V. or in the movies, but those guys don't fool around."

"Think KGB mentality focused on internal counterintelligence. They're brutal and ruthless."

"Experience talking?"

Sharona didn't reply.

"Change of plan?" I asked.

She shook her head. "I don't think so. We're close enough to the jet that we should be ok. It's just that the FSB adds a variable to the equation that I wasn't counting on."

The tail lights of the cars on the road in front of us started illuminating as the cars braked with the inevitable speed limit reduction of an urban area. The street we were on merged with another road from the left, and the traffic volume increased significantly. Soon, were in stop and go traffic again. I sighed. We had spent most of our day negotiating this kind of traffic, and my patience was wearing thin.

We drove for another few blocks to an intersection with one major city street, between two warehouse looking buildings, and around a small plaza. Then, as we approached another T-intersection, a car darted out into the traffic from the street to our left and the car in front of me, a small four-door sedan, slammed on its brakes. I saw the situation developing and already had my right foot on the brake pedal, but the car in front of me came to a sudden halt, and even though I pushed the Mercedes' brake to the floor, there simply wasn't enough distance between our vehicles. We hit the rear end of the car at about ten kph, about 6 miles per hour. There was a mild thump and a barely audible crunch.

"Shit," I said.

"No big deal," Sharona said. "You barely tapped him. Maybe he won't even notice." She peered through the Mercedes' windshield. "That car's a total POS anyway. It looks about twenty years old."

I saw the driver's side door of the car fly open, and a large, bearded man with a ferocious expression on his face seemed to grow onto the street from the driver's seat. He was so big and the car so small, that his exit from the vehicle appeared to be an optical illusion and it fascinated me for a moment or two. I lost my fascination as he gained his footing and marched toward us. I could feel the strength of his glare through the grimy windshield.

"Sharona?"

She was already opening her door, and the look on her face was one of pure, icy, calm. I swallowed hard. It was a look I had seen a few times in our association, and it never worked out well for whomever she dealt with.

She began speaking in rapid-fire Russian as soon as she exited, gesticulating wildly as she spoke. The large man seemed surprised, and he stopped in front of the Mercedes and turned his attention from me to her.

"You probably thought you were having a bad day, pal," I said to myself. "Well, it's about to get a whole lot worse."

Sharona seemed to pirouette around the right front corner of the Mercedes and reached the man in seconds, using movements that would have made a ballet dancer jealous. She stepped close to him, waving her right hand and as his eyes followed it, her left hand swung in an arc that started low and ended underneath his chin. The man's eyes registered shock and surprise for just a moment, and then they were empty.

"Colin?" Sharona said. "Do you think you could help me put this nice man back into his car? I think he fainted."

I was out of the car in seconds and at her side. Together, we moved the dead weight of a large, inert, human being and placed him back in his car. It took quite an effort. We got him into the driver's seat, and Sharona put his hands back on the wheel. I never saw the stiletto that I knew she had used on him. It vanished like it never existed.

"We need to get on the first side street we come to and get the hell out here," Sharona said. "If you don't mind, I'll drive."

"No problem with that at all," I said.

We got back in the car, and without even buckling her seatbelt, Sharona put the Mercedes in reverse and backed up hard, intentionally slamming into the car behind us. Then she put the car in drive and managed to squeeze around the sedan in front of us and turn right onto the first side street that we came to.

"We need to ditch this car," she said. "I'm just not sure we'll have time."

We were on a small street that weaved between apartment towers on the left and right of us. There were cars parked along the road and a few in odd parking lots on both sides of the street.

"Not a huge selection anyway," I said.

Sharona nodded. "Too early. Everyone is still getting home from work."

After meandering around a few other buildings, we came to a cross street, and Sharona turned left. We now seemed to be traveling in approximately the same direction as we had been when we had the accident.

"Get the GPS off the seat and tell me where to make the next turn," she said. "The mission support folks should be feeding it with the best route."

I picked up the iPhone-sized device and looked down at the color screen. It was a high definition map with a route highlighted in green and several alternate routes illuminated in light green, yellow or red.

"Okay, you're going to need to explain the color scheme," I said.

"The coding is a function of traffic and police activity. Green is obviously the best route. Light green is alternate routes that are clear. Yellow routes are risky but passable. Red routes are no go."

I nodded. "You'll turn left onto a major street. I'm not even going to try to pronounce it. In about half a mile. I think this road dead ends into it."

"Great," she said.

Sharona stepped on the gas pedal, and the Mercedes accelerated. The side street we were on was free of traffic so we could move very quickly. Several more tall apartment complexes went by on the left and right. In a few moments, we reached the major street, and Sharona floored the gas and pulled right out into traffic, disregarding the cars on either side of the intersection. There were a few honking horns, but we were back on a main road and headed toward the road we had been on originally, just a few blocks down from the collision.

"This is where it's telling us to go?" Sharona asked.

I nodded. "Yes, it is. Back to that road we were on."

"Then it isn't compromised. At least not yet."

We reached the main road, now labeled "Dr. 25" and turned right as soon as a break in traffic would allow. As we rolled out onto the road, we passed a police car parked against the curb on the right side. The inside of the car was dark, but the dashboard was illuminated, as were the car's parking lights, indicating the engine was running and the driver of the car was waiting for something. A few other cars passed the police car before its headlights suddenly came on and it pulled out into traffic, 2-3 vehicles behind us.

"Now we have a tail," Sharona said.

"What are you talking about?" I asked. "He could be after anyone."

She shook her head. "If you believe in coincidences in this line of work, you end up dead."

We drove into an area with buildings on the left and a wooded area on the right and one by one, the vehicles between us and the police car made turns that took them off the road into neighborhoods or apartment complexes. The police car pulled up behind us as we crossed a bridge with lakes on either side of the road. As we moved along, I could see Sharona looking into the rear-view mirror as much as she was looking at the road ahead.

"He's radioing something in," she said. "Maybe the license number of the vehicle or something else."

"Would they have the license of the car this soon?"

She shrugged. "If the car was reported stolen and the information had been updated in their system, maybe," she said. "But no doubt he's also calling up the vehicle registration."

"So, what do we do?"

"Find out," Sharona said.

The road briefly transitioned into limited access freeway, and Sharona accelerated and took the first exit that came up on the left. The police car accelerated and stayed with us, still keeping its light bar off. Sharona made a sharp right turn onto an access road and stomped on the gas. The Mercedes seemed to remember its German roots and sped up rapidly, the accompanying engine noise providing a reassuring sound of power as the car gained speed. The police car materialized onto the road behind and began to fall back as the Mercedes continued to accelerate. Then, the light bar on top of the car illuminated, and flashing blue lights came on, the reflections bouncing off the buildings around us.

"And that's what they do," Sharona said. "When they can't catch you, they play the intimidation card." She looked over at me and cocked her head. "Too bad they don't know that we're not easily intimidated."

I looked down at the GPS. "If you make the next left, we can follow the road until it tees into another road and turns right, that will keep us going in the same direction."

She nodded. "How far?"

"A few hundred meters," I said. "After we pass this complex of buildings on the left, it will be the next left you can take."

"Ok. But we may have to do something about this cop."

The buildings I mentioned went by on the left. I had a brief glimpse of a long brick building with a metal roof. Then some other buildings along with a huge parking lot came up on our right.

"Next left," I said.

Sharona nodded a few times, rapidly.

As soon as the car approached the intersection, she turned the wheel to the left, and we entered a full, skidding turn that had us on the westbound road in seconds, with no appreciable decrease in speed. I blinked in surprise.

"Damn," I said. "That was impressive."

"CIA driving school," Sharona said. "Best training on the planet."

We sped down the road between rows of trees on either side. I couldn't tell whether it was treed farmland or private property of some kind. The intersection where the road ended was coming up rapidly, and I could see the arrow signs directing turns left or right reflecting in our headlights.

"Right at the end of the road?" Sharona asked.

"Yes," I said. "I'll give you vectors from there."

"Let's lead this guy astray just a bit."

We reached the end of the road just as the police car made the turn onto the road behind us and Sharona turned to the left and ducked into a small parking lot that appeared on the left-hand side of the road. She spun the car so that the rear end of it was facing the parking spaces furthest from the road. Then she backed into the spot and killed the lights. As soon as the car was dark and the transmission was in park, she reached under her jacket and removed a Glock of some sort that I never knew she had. From another pocket under her jacket, she removed a suppressor and screwed it onto the threads of the Glock's extended barrel.

"This cop has a choice now," she said as she worked. "He can go on by and live or turn in here and die."

"Hopefully he'll do the smart thing," I said.

Sharona looked at me with her eyebrows raised. Her facial expression was barely visible in the dark light of the car. "Since when have the Russians been smart?"

"Good call," I said.

She pulled on her door handle. "I'm slipping out," she said. "You've got the gun I gave you in Switzerland. Don't be taken alive."

I nodded as I reached under my jacket and retrieved the Kimber .45. As I was checking the magazine and chamber, Sharona went out of the driver's side and shut the door behind her. The inside of the Mercedes went dark, and suddenly it was me, all alone, in the front seat of a stolen car, in the parking area of a city in Russia I had no right to be in. I screwed the suppressor onto the Kimber's threaded barrel. Then I rolled the hammer back to the fully-cocked position and clicked the thumb safety on, all while feeling a remarkable sense of calm.

Flashing blue lights appeared to my right as the cop car reached the end of the road and paused at the intersection as the driver pondered which way to turn. He made up his mind quickly and turned left and then pulled into our parking lot.

"Bad move, pal," I said in the darkness.

The police car moved slowly through the lot, the driver obviously looking for our car among the few that were parked there. I eased down in my seat to blend into the shadows of the Mercedes' interior. The police car stopped a few cars down from me and paused. I could see the driver's face illuminated by the dashboard lights as he consulted something in front of him and compared it to the cars he saw the parking lot. The police officer was a young man with dark hair and a mustache. The look in his eyes was one of excitement and intrigue. He obviously thought he was on the verge of something important.

He pulled forward another few feet and looked at the car next to the Mercedes. His eyes ran up and down the car and then turned to ours. Almost immediately, his eyes lit up, and he lifted the microphone to his mouth.

It was the last move he ever made.

The passenger window of his car shattered and his head shuttered with the impact of multiple bullets. Then he leaned against the driver's side window and collapsed.

Sharona rejoined me in the car a few moments later.

"They'll come here and find him, and that should buy us some time," she said. There was no breathlessness or excitement in her voice at all. She could have been reading a daily weather report. "So out and to the right, yes?"

I nodded.

She started the Mercedes and nosed out of the parking space, around the police car and onto the road. She turned right and headed northwest, accelerating into the dark, Russian night.

"Look at the upper right portion of the GPS display. What's the ETE to the site?"

I looked down at the map and picked up the time she wanted from the GPS unit.

"Thirty minutes even."

She nodded and clicked the mic button on her collar. "Tell the team we're thirty minutes out," she said. "We don't have company right now but we might when we show up." She looked over at me. "Next turn?"

I looked at the GPS.

"A left," I said. "It will be a bridge across the railroad tracks that are paralleling us to the left. First left you can make. Just a few hundred meters."

Sharona nodded and then frowned as she listened to something in her headset.

"Great," she said. "Roger." She released the mic button. "Fuck!" she muttered under her breath. Then she looked at me. "The FSB is on to us for sure. The cop was following us on their orders after he phoned the license number in. They know we're down here, but they don't know exactly where we are. Yet."

I looked down at the GPS. The screen was flashing.

"What does it mean when the screen flashes?" I asked.

Sharona took her foot off the gas. "Usually a reroute. The data feed from mission support uses real-time intel about police movements, roadblocks and that sort of thing."

The screen stopped flashing, and a new route was revealed.

"Okay, change in plans," I said. "We're still turning in a few hundred meters, but now right instead of left. They're going to take us back out onto the main road we initially turned off of to lose the cop."

We reached the turn, and Sharona pulled the Mercedes around it to the right and applied the gas.

"Left at the next intersection," I said.

"What's the designation of the road we're turning left on?"

I looked at the map and pinched the screen to increase the magnification. "Something like 41K-011. Does that make sense?"

She nodded. "They're keeping us on the faster roads to get us through more quickly. If we stick to the neighborhoods and go slower, it will give the FSB the opportunity to create more roadblocks."

We reached the next intersection, and Sharona pulled out into traffic, cutting off a car that had been accelerating into the intersection. I had brief glimpse of a middle-aged woman with impossibly blonde hair and a cigarette hanging from a mouth lined with blood red lipstick.

"Guess they never got the word about the whole cigarettes-causing-cancer thing over here," I said.

Sharona floored the gas, and we accelerated up the road. The traffic was lighter than it had been before and she wasted no time getting around the vehicles in front of us, either using the opposing traffic lane to the left or the shoulder to the right. She looked over at me. She was smiling with the high of pure adrenaline, and her eyes were radiant. "I know you're probably thinking that I'm driving like an idiot and it makes us more visible," she said.

"The thought had occurred to me."

"Earlier, it was about stealth. Now it's all about speed. The FSB knows we're here and if they stop us all bets are off. We need to get west of the city as quickly as we possibly can before they can set up checkpoints or roadblocks. If we give them even a few moments more time, it could cost us."

"I'll take your word for it. You're the one who has done this before. I'm just the baggage at this point."

"Okay Samsonite," she said, grinning at me. "When is the next turn?"

For the next several minutes, Sharona drove us through the western suburbs of Gatchina with the guidance of our intel-fed GPS. We alternated between the main streets and side streets and managed to avoid traffic jams and altercations with local authorities and the FSB. Sharona pushed the old Mercedes mercilessly, keeping the accelerator on the floor whenever possible and taking the corners at speeds that just kept the vehicle upright and on the road. Finally, we turned onto the main westbound highway, the 41K-102, and left the lights of Gatchina behind us. The tension level in the car decreased noticeably.

"Time to go?" Sharona asked.

I glanced at the GPS. "About 20 minutes from this point at posted speeds. Which means we'll probably get there in 10 – 15 minutes. Who's playing Jeff Gordon now?"

"Hell with Jeff Gordon," Sharona said. "I'm a darker version of Danica Patrick."

"Well, hopefully, you'll win more races than she has."

The road made gradual s-curve that took us north, through a small area with houses and barns for about half a kilometer and then back to the west. As we finished the turn back to the west, we saw groups of several official-looking vehicles on both sides of the road about a half mile ahead. The vehicles were barely visible, just silhouettes with parking lights in the darkness. There were no obstacles or personnel on the road yet, and as we neared, we could see the shapes of people working in groups near the vehicles, off-loading road barricades and placing them on the ground near the edges of the road's asphalt surface.

"Couldn't time this more closely," Sharona said. "Damn, I'd give anything for a pair of NVGs right now." She clicked the mic button on her collar. "Checkpoint being deployed just ahead," she said. She tilted her head as she listened to the response in her earpiece. "Roger," she said after a few seconds. She turned to me. "They obviously didn't expect us to get here so fast." She looked back at the road. "What's the time to go now?"

"Ten minutes," I said. "According to the GPS."

"Let's make it less," she said and pushed the accelerator to the floor.

The Mercedes' headlights illuminated the two groups of people and the vehicles, and we could see a large military-style truck and two cars on the left side of the road and an SUV and motorcycle on the right side. The people were clad in classic Russian Stormtrooper gear, with the long coats and *ushanka* hats with rifles hanging on their shoulders and pistols holstered. As they worked, their faces were lit with the dull glow of their cigarettes.

We raced between the two groups of vehicles a few moments later, and I saw faces turn towards us and watch us go by. One of the figures seemed to raise a radio or something to his ear.

Next, to me, Sharona was looking in the rear-view mirror. She clicked the mic button on her collar. "They just called us in," she said.

I looked around behind us and saw headlights illuminate on two of the cars and the motorcycle. Then the vehicles pulled out onto the road, and the motorcycle passed both and moved into the lead, accelerating rapidly towards us.

"The bad guys are coming," I said.

Sharona nodded and spoke into her mic. "Tell the team we're coming in hot. Tell them to get the demo off the jet and clear the camouflage." She released the mic. "You need to get your flight shit on. You're only going to have a few minutes to get airborne once we get you there."

I unbuckled my seat belt and grabbed the bag from the back seat with my flight gear. Then I shrugged out of my jacket, not an easy task in the front seat of normal-sized sedan. I glanced behind us.

"You're holding your distance with the cars," I said. "But that motorcycle is gaining. Do you have anything I can reach out and touch him with, besides my .45 or your Glock?"

She nodded. "There's an AR-15 pistol in one of the other bags."

"AR-15 pistol?" I asked.

I tore off the turtle neck shirt I was wearing as I pushed my shoes off with my feet.

"Yep," she answered. "Handy little thing. 10-inch barrel and collapsible stock. Fits in a backpack but has a tac effective range of 300 yards or so. You'll need to attach the upper receiver to the lower receiver."

"Nice," I said, shimmying out of my pants. "What kind of optics do you have on it?"

"Just a two-power red-dot. Should be child's play for you after what I saw this morning."

"The conditions are slightly different."

"No excuses."

I glanced behind us again. The motorcycle was definitely closer. The headlight was distinct, and the sound of the engine was barely audible.

"I feel like we're in an Indiana Jones movie," I said.

Sharona glanced down at my legs. I was sitting on the front seat of the car clad only in boxer briefs, a t-shirt and a pair of wool socks. She took one hand off the steering wheel and ran it down my left thigh.

"Ooh la la!" she said. "You *have* been working out. You're getting me all hot. Too bad we're in the middle of a chase right now."

I looked over at her and shook my head. "Promises, promises." I looked down at the GPS. "The turn-off is going to be in about a kilometer. You'll make a left turn and that will take us on that narrow road through the woods. If you can make the turn and stop, I'll deal with our friend."

"Sounds good," she said.

I retrieved one of the other bags, opened it and reached inside. I felt the hard iron of the AR-15's upper receiver. I pulled the bag into the front seat and opened it. The upper receiver, lower receiver, suppressor and a thirty-round magazine were all fastened into individual compartments. I assembled the components in about thirty seconds, inserted the magazine and charged the weapon.

"Turn coming up," Sharona said. "Stand by."

I braced myself with a hand on the dashboard as we approached the turn to the narrow road into the forest. Sharona took the turn at speed, and we skidded slightly as we departed the main road for the forest road. While there had been some ambient light on the main road, here on a one-lane road between two rows of pine trees, it was almost completely dark. Sharona drove another 100 meters, stopped the car and turned off the vehicle's lights. I jumped out of the side door, weapon at the ready and looking quite fearsome in my underwear and t-shirt. For just a few moments, there was utter silence on the small forest road and the sounds of the nighttime woods were audible. I could hear the wings of birds flapping and movement of small creatures in the underbrush.

Then the silence was shattered by the roar of a motorcycle engine at high RPM, and the cycle's headlight appeared on the road behind us. The light was almost blinding in the insulated darkness of the forest road, and it made the trees that lined the road appear willowy and ethereal. I quickly centered the red-dot of the aiming reticle on the space just above the headlight, but even as I started to squeeze the weapon's trigger, I saw a series of bright flashes appear in the reticle and heard the staccato sound of an assault rifle firing in full auto mode. Bullets began to impact the car and the ground around us. I heard the unmistakable buzzing sound of a slug passing just to right of my right ear.

The AR-15 spat a three-round burst of 5.56 slugs into cold Russian air. I squeezed the trigger again, and another three rounds went down range. The motorcycle's head light suddenly veered to the left and into the forest. There was a crunch of metal as the cycle impacted a tree and a sickening thud that sounded like a sack of potatoes hitting the ground at high speed. The cycle's headlight stayed on, and the motor stayed in idle, but the rider and the bike were out of commission.

I jumped back into the car.

"He's down," I said. "Let's go."

Sharona nodded stiffly and hit the accelerator. She turned the vehicle's lights on, and the rows of trees were illuminated again. I put the AR-15 aside, dragged my flightsuit out of the other bag and began pulling it on. My legs went in easily, but as I tried to twist my torso and squeeze my arms into the sleeves, I notice a few, small, bullet-sized holes in the fabric.

"I guess some bullets came through the car. This the first time I've ever worn anything resembling holy cloth," I said.

Sharona remained silent, and the car sped down the forest road toward the clearing where the buildings and jet were. I looked behind us and saw twin sets of car headlights far behind, just turning onto the narrow road.

"Well this is going to be close," I said.

I slid my feet into the boots and pulled the quick closure zippers up.

We were suddenly in the clearing, and I could see the buildings on the other side, about a kilometer in front of us.

"Almost there," I said.

Sharona reached down to the car's headlight switch and flashed the lights off and on several times, varying the time between each actuation of the switch. Then she returned her left hand to the wheel, and her head nodded, just slightly. I looked over at her, and it was then that I saw that the plastic covering the instrument cluster was shattered. She was holding her right hand to her chest, and there was a slow but steady stream of blood seeping onto the smooth, cappuccino-colored flesh of her delicate but deadly hand.

"Jesus!" I said. "You're hit!"

She shook her head. "Doesn't matter," she said, her voice gravelly with moisture from her lungs. "You're the mission, and you're almost there." She looked over at me and attempted her usual playful smile. "Got to keep you alive for the ladies."

Time seemed to slow down at that point. We drove on, across the clearing and into the small complex of barns where I had landed, less than 24 hours ago. Sharona stopped the Mercedes on the side of the long barn and shut off the vehicle's engine. Ever the conscientious operative, she quickly extinguished the vehicle's lights as well.

I saw the shape of a man in black tactical gear materialize next to my window, but I paid no attention. I unbuckled Sharona's seatbelt and turned her toward me. Even in the dim light and with the dark fabric of the Russian winter coat she wore, two bloody holes were visible. One of them was emitting foamy blood, an indication that her lung had been punctured.

"Sharona!" I pulled her to me. "Not you too!"

My door was opened, and I could feel the presence behind me.

"You've got to get that jet out of here, sir," said a low, authoritative voice. "We'll take it from here."

"But she's been shot," I said. "Twice."

"We've got a trained medic on the team," the team member said. "She'll be fine. We've fixed folks a lot worse off."

"Go, Colin," Sharona said, her voice barely a whisper. "You've got to get back, or this whole business will mean nothing."

She lifted her right hand slowly, with an effort and placed it on the back of my neck. Then she pulled my lips down to hers. Out in the distance, somewhere, I could hear automatic weapons firing. The FSB reinforcements had arrived. And every moment I lingered meant that someone else could die.

She pushed me away from her. "Go. We can't leave until you do."

I nodded at her. "Okay."

I lowered her gently, with her hand still around my neck. As I disengaged her fingers, she squeezed my hand and looked up at me, through eyes that were barely half open.

"C'mon, sir," the operator said. "You've got to get that jet out of here."

I laid Sharona's head down gently and then exited the Mercedes. I walked around the side of the barn and didn't look back. Instead, I focused on the F-35, its squat form appearing as a shadowy, menacing creature in the darkness. Two more team members stood guard on the machine, one of whom stood near the nose. I approached him holding my gear bag and opened the door on the side of the aircraft where the boarding ladder deployed. Then I hit the switch to open the canopy and donned my anti-g suit as it raised. I gave him a quick tutorial on how to secure the boarding ladder and the door.

"Once you hear the engine start to wind up, get you and your guys away from this thing," I told him. "Because I'm going to get it out of here as quick and as low as I can."

He nodded at me with a calm expression on his face. Like he had seen this sort of thing many times before.

I scurried up the ladder and sat down in the cockpit. As soon as my butt hit the seat, I activated the battery switch and lowered the canopy. I could feel the boarding ladder being pushed back into position and the outer door being shut by the man on the ground. As soon as the electronics in the jet came to life, I hit the integrated power package (IPP) switch and set the engine switch to the RUN position. Beneath me, the huge Pratt and Whitney F135 engine spooled up to idle, while I clicked into the PIC, strapped into the Martin Baker ejection seat and armed the seat for flight. Then, I donned the HMD and once again entered the world of composed situational awareness, with optical, infrared and synthetic systems displayed.

I recalled the egress route from the navigation computer and selected the first point of the egress route as the next waypoint.

NAV RDY, the jet told me.

"Perfect," I said. I looked at the panel to left of the display and pushed the HOOK/STOVL button. As soon as the button illuminated, I pulled back on the side stick controller. Below me, I felt the jet shudder as the huge engine wound up to full power. Behind me, I could sense the door above the vertical lift turbine open and then I heard the high-pitched whine of the turbine itself as it engaged. In mere moments, the F-35 lifted off Russian soil and into the dark Russian sky, leaving a small cloud of dust in its wake. As I rose, I saw the muzzle flashes from the weapons of the ops team and the oncoming FSB forces. I wished I had some air-to-ground ordnance on the jet to help the ops team but there was nothing loaded, and even if there had been, I didn't know how to use it. I looked down, through the floor of the aircraft and saw the long, gray shape of the barn and saw the dark outline of the Mercedes wagon. I wondered if Sharona was still inside it and if she was still alive.

But there was no more time to wonder.

I stopped the jet's ascent at 100 feet, and pedal turned it to line up the navigation cues in the HMD. Then I pushed the throttle forward as far as it would go. The jet shot into the darkness, accelerating rapidly. I raised the gear handle, and as the wheels retracted, the HOOK/STOVL button blinked at me. I hit the switch and continued to let the jet accelerate as I engaged the autopilot and auto-throttle. The jet slowly climbed to its TFR programmed altitude of 250 feet and planned speed of 600 knots.

I sighed and sat back against the F-35's seat, once again at home in a cockpit, with a throttle under one hand and a control stick in the other. I gazed out through the F-35's canopy at the Russian countryside, now rushing by in the darkness, just a few hundred feet below. As I settled in my place, in my office, in my womb, I wondered how many good people I was leaving to their deaths behind me.

The cost is getting too high, I thought. Way too high. Too many good people are dying because of me.

It has to stop.

CHAPTER THIRTY-FIVE

Tuesday, November 9
2012 Hours Local Time
250 feet, 600 knots over Northeastern Russia
30 miles from the Estonian Border

As it turned out, I had no time for self-reflection. The F-35 had barely settled into the first leg of the navigation route when the jet's onboard warning system started talking to me. Literally.

"AIRCRAFT THREAT," said a stern female voice in my ear. On the tactical situation display on the PCD, two square symbols with radar dishes in front of them appeared at the three o'clock position to my aircraft, off my right wing. In the radar warning display below the tac display, two airplane symbols appeared at the same relative position. The F-35's threat system took a moment or two to resolve the information it was receiving and then the pneumonic MI31 appeared next to the symbols in the tac display.

I stopped myself from marveling at the technology of the F-35's threat detection system and focused on the information displayed. MI31 probably meant one kind of aircraft – one I was familiar with.

"MiG-31s," I said to myself. "Damn. Where the hell did you guys come from?"

As I watched the display, the two shapes moved closer to me. They were now about 50 miles away. I did a quick mental review. I knew that the F-35's onboard warning and jamming system had been programed to require no action on my part. I also know that some warning information could be data linked to the jet. So just because the onboard sensors detected the MiG's unique radar signature or because an airborne radar platform saw them didn't mean they were necessarily targeting me.

"I sure hope this stealth shit works," I said into the intercom.

I pushed the talk to text softkey on the PCD's text message window. "Two MiG-31s at my right 3 o'clock for 50 miles. Are they being vectored to me?"

The message appeared just as I had spoken it on the datalink window and I pushed down on the throttle cursor control switch to send it.

STANDBY, came the response a few moments later.

"Great," I muttered.

"AIRCRAFT THREAT," the female voice said again. I looked at the tactical situation and radar warning displays. A second set of jets appeared, at my dead six o'clock. A second or two later, MI29 appeared next to them. There were two MiG-29's on my tail. But these guys were a lot closer, more like 30 miles behind me. About the same distance away as the airbase Sharona and I had passed earlier.

"That's not good," I said.

As I watched, the two MiG-31s to my right stayed fixed at my three o'clock position and they closed to 35 miles range.

"Jesus," I said to myself. "You guys are hauling ass."

But then the obvious occurred to me. By not falling aft on the threat display, like down to my four or five o'clock position, the MiG-31s had altered course to intercept my jet.

"I'm supposed to be fucking invisible! How are you seeing me?"

It had been a long while since I had reviewed any threat briefings about Russian aircraft, so my knowledge was rusty at best. I knew the MiG-31 Foxhound was the follow-on to the MiG-25 Foxbat and was built to intercept the SR-71 Blackbird, the USAF's premier high-altitude reconnaissance jet. It wasn't a turning machine, but it had an electronically-scanned radar, just like the F-35 did, just with more dated features and abilities. The MiG-31 was capable of speeds above Mach 3, and in spite of the fact that it was roughly 40 years old, it still performed intercept duties in Russian airspace. The MiG-29, on the other hand, was a turning and burning machine and in the right hands, could outfight an F-16 or F/A-18. But it was limited in range due to its relatively small internal fuel capacity. It wasn't going to be able to follow me at 600 knots indefinitely without running out of gas, assuming it continued the pursuit into Estonian airspace.

I glanced at the tactical situation display as the F-35 banked to make a small turn of about five degrees. About 20 miles to go before I crossed the Estonian border. On the tac display, the MiG-31s had closed to 18 miles. The MiG-29's were slowly closing the distance as well. They were now 25 miles astern.

And the tactic became clear.

The MiG-31's were supposed to get me to turn and then MiG-29's would engage me.

How in the hell did you guys put together an air effort like this with so little time to react? I wondered. But the answer was obvious. *Because you had eight hours to prepare.*

I was 15 miles from the Estonian border now. The MiG-31's were 10 miles off my right wing. I turned my head to look there, and sure enough, the F-35's infrared and optical sensors found the two aircraft for me. They appeared in my HMD as two squares, one superimposed on the other with the label MI31 next to them. The warning system had interfaced with the optical and infrared sensors and combined the data. The two targets were well above me and maintaining altitude.

I turned my head to look at my six o'clock. The HMD showed the MiG-29's as well. They were much lower on the display, just 1,000 feet or so above my altitude. I turned around to the front and regarded the tactical situation display again. The MiG-29's were inside of 20 miles range – mere minutes away. In spite of how close they were, as long as they were in a tail chase, there wasn't a missile they had that could reach me, purely due to the energy limitations the missile would suffer against a receding target. So I was safe from them, at least for now.

The MiG-31's were a different story. They would catch me, and they could look down and shoot down.

A square corner was building, and I had no idea how to escape it. Worse, I still had no idea how the MiG's were tracking me, so I had no idea how to defeat them or how to disappear.

I looked high and to my right and saw the targets inside the two squares on my HMD growing larger. The optics in the helmet were so good that I could see the infrared outline of the two MiGs' afterburner plumes in the display.

Infrared, I thought. *Jesus, of course! They're tracking me with IR!*

The F-35's designers had gone to great lengths to build an airplane that was nearly impossible to detect with radar and difficult to detect with infrared sensors. Difficult, but not impossible. As long as there was a jet engine back there emitting heat, an IR tracker would be able to see it. There were certain laws of physics that were inviolate.

I was about to weigh my options, but the decision was made for me. As I looked toward the MiG-31's, I saw a bright flame suddenly appear in the HMD. Almost instantly, the F-35's warning system blared in my ear.

"INFRARED MISSLE LAUNCH – RIGHT 3 O'CLOCK."

My response was automatic.

I toggled off the autopilot and auto-throttle as I rolled the F-35 to place my lift vector on the MiG-31s. Then I applied back pressure to pull the jet's nose up to them. I also smoothly retarded the throttle to idle. My right thumb found the countermeasures switch on the sidestick and I pushed it in all four directions, not sure which one dispensed flares or any IR decoys that were loaded on the aircraft.

Whatever IR signature the F-35 was providing for guidance, both to the MiGs and to the missile, suddenly vanished. The missile was visible in the HMD, and as I watched it, it slowly biased upward as the heat source it was tracking disappeared. The trick now was to be nowhere near it so the proximity fuse it carried didn't command detonation of the missile's warhead close to me. I pulled the F-35's nose to the right of the missile and continued my ascent towards the MiG-31s, still not sure what my final game plan would be.

Reflexes from the Viper took over then. Without my willing it, my left thumb moved from the cursor slew button on the throttle to the weapons management switch or WMS, located nearby, and pushed the WMS forward twice. Immediately, the stores management system or SMS screen appeared in the rightmost section of the PCD and a diagram of F-35's internal weapons bays appeared. Inside the two weapons bays were the white symbols for a total of four air-to-air missiles. The pneumonic next to them read AIM120. I felt a smile creep onto my face.

"Slammers," I said into the intercom. "That was nice of you, guys."

The Slammer was the AIM-120 Advanced Medium Range Air-to-air Missile, more properly known as the AMRAAM and probably the most deadly radar-guided air-to-air missile in the world. When I flew the Viper, we jokingly called it the "wish you were dead missile" because when we used it, the target died nearly every time.

As I glanced down at the MiG-31s in the tac display, I saw dashed red circles around each aircraft, indicating the AESA radar was tracking them. I slewed the cursor to the MiG on the right, the one closest to me, and designated it with the TMS switch on the sidestick. The circle around the aircraft went from dashed to solid. I looked up into the HMD and saw the familiar rectangle of the designated launch zone or DLZ. The triangular carat on the left side of the rectangle indicated the lead aircraft was within range. I smiled underneath my oxygen mask and pressed the red "pickle" button on the sidestick.

Nothing happened.

It took me half a second to understand why and it dawned on me that even in an aircraft as advanced at the F-35, there still had to be a MASTER ARM switch, somewhere.

It took me a second or two to find it, because it wasn't where I expected it to be. In the Viper, it was on the left quarter panel. In the F-35, it was between my legs on the lower portion of the center console, just to the left of the standby attitude indicator. I flipped the switch into the ARM position.

STAS AIM-120 RDY appeared under the missiles in the weapons bay diagram and the missiles themselves changed color from white to green.

I looked back into the HMD to find the MiG-31s and located them immediately, but now they were directly ahead of me and only about 9,000 feet away. They were flying in a wedge formation, with the leader in front and the wingman 45 degrees aft and about 1-2 miles behind and to the leader's side. I looked at the DLZ and saw that I was inside minimum range for the missile targeted on the leader. Instinctively, my right thumb moved the TMS button on the sidestick to the left. The active missile switched to the wingman, and the DLZ showed min range was adequate. I smiled as my thumb reached for the pickle button.

"You're about 10 seconds from being dead pal," I said.

But I didn't push the button. The MiGs weren't showing further awareness, and they weren't shooting. If they weren't shooting, the odds were high they didn't see me. No need to highlight myself if I didn't need to. I pushed down on the sidestick slightly and flew directly underneath the lead MiG-31 with about 500 feet of altitude separation a few seconds later. I knew enough about the MiG-31 to know that the visibility from inside its cockpit was severely limited and I was betting they were going to have a damn difficult time finding a dark jet against a dark background with no IR emissions to highlight it. As we passed, I waited for them to begin a turn to engage me, but instead they continued down in their previous trajectory. I looked at my threat display to confirm the two MiG-31s were staying on course and it quickly became evident they were. I found the MiG-29's on the display, and the system showed them well below me and beyond the point where I had turned. They were now making a slow, lazy turn back to the west. As far as they were concerned, I had vanished into the Russian night.

I looked down into the screen and saw the STAS AIM-120 RDY still illuminated. I nodded to myself and moved the MASTER ARM switch back to the SAFE position.

I heard the text message warning tone in my headset and looked over at the text display.

HOSTILE TARGETS ARE UNDER POSITIVE CONTROL BY RUSSIAN AIR DEFENSE.

"Well no shit," I said, and acknowledged the message.

The F-35 was climbing through 15,000 feet now, and I decided to let it climb. Fuel was going to an issue for the return leg, and I was going to need to conserve every drop of it I could. I gradually increased the power as I went through some clouds and began a turn back to the west. I left the clouds behind a few moments later and beheld the clear heavens above, lit with the myriad of stars surrounding the earth. I felt a tremendous sense of freedom as I viewed the stars for the first time in about 24 hours, like I had been in captivity and released. Even though I had spent less than a day in Russia, the time had seemed much longer somehow, and I was grateful to be headed westbound.

I leveled off at 20,000 feet and designated my landing site as a final destination. Even though I was traveling at typical airliner altitudes, I had no concerns. The jet's stealth would keep me invisible to ATC radars, and the HMD would show me any aircraft in front of me in time for me to get out of the way. I set the auto-throttle to maintain .85 Mach and engaged the autopilot. Then I settled into cruise.

A few hundred miles ahead of me, the undercast of clouds dissipated and I could see the outlines of Denmark and Norway, traced with the lights of their cities. In the distance, I could see the glow of Aberdeen Scotland, beckoning to me. I was almost back in the land of the civilized.

"AIRCRAFT THREAT," said the F-35's warning system, startling me from my contemplation of the horizon before me.

"What the fuck?" I asked myself as I looked down at the threat warning display.

There were four of them again. Two Mig-31s and two SU-27s. I didn't know if the MiGs were the same ones I had encountered earlier or not, but the SU-27s were newcomers. And the SUs were even better in a dogfight than the MiG-29s, with the additional advantage of having more gas to fight with.

"Jesus," I said into the intercom, "you guys must want me bad."

A text message alert buzzed in my headset.

WE SEE FOUR HOSTILES CHASING YOU, it said. DO WHAT YOU HAVE TO DO.

"Well thanks, guys," I said, shaking my head as I looked at the words. "I'm glad I'm allowed to try to stay alive."

The tactical situation and radar warning displays depicted them clearly. The two MiG-31s were about 10 miles behind me, closing rapidly. With the rate their range was changing, it was apparent they were close to their maximum speed of Mach 3, and they would be in firing range in seconds. Behind them, the SU-27s were closing as well, albeit at about half the speed of the MiGs. It was déjà vu all over again. If I didn't turn, the MiG's would shoot, and if I did, the SUs would finish the job. The Russians weren't imaginative, but they weren't stupid either.

There wasn't a lot of time to think or formulate a game plan. The first encounter could have been dismissed as a token effort but this second attempt showed a degree of coordination and determination. The Russians wanted to stop me, and I couldn't let them. I also knew that if their pilots saw me or got footage of my jet, U.S. relations with Russia could regress to the Cold War era.

I pulled the throttle to idle and applied aft pressure to the sidestick. There was no doubt the Russian jets were tracking the infrared signature of my exhaust. I needed to take that away from them and try to show them something they hadn't seen before. I hoped that would give me enough time to decide what to do.

The stocky jet climbed into the vertical eagerly, and as I continued to apply pressure to the sidestick, the nose tracked smoothly upward and over, until I was inverted over the Baltic Sea, looking down at the clouds far below. After a 180 degree turn in the vertical, the flight data display in the HMD showed me at 28,000 feet and 220 knots.

"Jesus," I said. "Even after an Immelmann at idle power. Holy shit, this thing has thrust."

"INFRARED MISSILE LAUNCH. TWELVE O'CLOCK." the system alerted me.

"C'mon, guys," I said. "It didn't work before. It's not going to work now."

The MiG-31s had fired on me, but I wasn't worried. My infrared signature was nearly non-existent, and while the missile might bias toward my last known position, it wouldn't be able to guide on me.

I pushed forward on the sidestick to unload the jet and pushed left to roll the jet upright. As I rolled, I saw the wispy vapor trail of an air-to-air missile above me. I glanced back, over my shoulder, and saw the missile warhead detonate, well behind my jet, with an orange flash that reflected on the clouds below. I turned my head forward and looked up. The two MiG-31s were visible in the enhanced imagery provided by the HMD. They were 15,000 feet above me and headed east at over 1,800 knots. They flew in the standard Russian intercept formation, with one aircraft in front and the other in an offset trail position, about two miles astern of the first. I found myself wondering how many sonic boom complaints the Russian Air Force would receive as a result of tonight's activities.

As they passed overhead, I did some quick mental math and realized the MiGs were out of the fight for 2-4 minutes, the time it would take them to realize they had overshot their target and make the 180-degree turn back to the last position of their prey. In the meantime, I wasn't taking any chances. The two SUs were 20 miles off my nose now, closing at well over 1,000 knots and they were looking to engage anything in my vicinity. The F-35's AESA radar was tracking both of them, and as the bottom arm of the tried and true vertical pincer tactic, they were 10,000 feet below me. I looked down at them in the tactical situation display and touched the square symbol for the lead aircraft with my finger. A red circle appeared around the aircraft and a DLZ appeared in the tac display and the HMD. The AIM-120 was in range. I toggle the MASTER ARM switch to ARM.

The SMS display in front of me changed to STAS AIM-120 RDY. I nodded and pressed the weapons release button on the sidestick once, used the TMS to step the target designator to the other SU and pressed the button again. I didn't know what to expect regarding how quickly an internally-carried missile would be fired compared to the externally carried ones I had shot in the Viper, but there didn't seem to be much difference at all. I felt the airframe vibrate as the weapons bay doors opened. The first missile left the jet while I was stepping the TMS switch, and the second one left mere milliseconds after I pushed the pickle button a second time. As usual, the AIM-120 took a second or two to ignite after departing the aircraft, but when the motors lit, the missiles roared away like dragsters on steroids and accelerated to their maximum speed of Mach 4 at an impossible rate. Both missiles biased high into the atmosphere to maximize their range and left a trail of condensed vapor in the form of ice crystals in their wake. I knew the two SU-27s, who were under the clouds below me, had no way to know missiles had been fired at them – the F-35's radar was too agile for their warning systems to detect. Both jets would get hit with no notice, and the pilots would have no chance to escape. Such was life.

"Dos vendanya, boys," I said into the intercom.

The F-35 had slowed to 170 knots, and with two MiG-31s turning to reacquire me, I wasn't going to give them a heat source to make their task easier. I checked my throttle in idle, banked the jet up to about 135 degrees and applied gentle aft pressure to the sidestick. The jet's nose tracked slowly but smoothly downward in a gentle arc, oriented about halfway between the vertical and horizontal planes – a sliceback we called it, years ago. As I came through about 90 degrees of turn, the two SU-27s vanished from my threat display, and I nodded to myself.

"Two down, two to go," I said into the intercom.

As I continued the 180-degree vertical turn back to the west, the two MiGs reappeared in the HMD, about 20,000 feet above me and twenty miles off my nose. They had rolled out of their turns and were headed east.

I nodded to myself. "Smart move guys. Get plenty of lateral separation before you re-engage."

Now that I was nose on to them, I designated the lead aircraft. The F-35's radar was tracking both jets and was able to assess their speed and the closure rate between them and me. It was immediately apparent they had pulled their power way back and bled a lot of airspeed with g in the turn.

I leveled off after trading altitude for airspeed, and was in idle power at 250 knots. The MiGs had slowed to 450 knots, trying to build more pre-merge time for target acquisition into this pass. Where I had no worries of being acquired by the Su-27's radar due to its conventional nature, the MiG-31's radar was something else. Even though it was an older aircraft, the MiG had an electronically scanned radar that was much more agile than the mechanically scanned radar in the SU. In the amount of time required for the F-35's fire control computer to open the weapons bay doors and fire two AIM-120s, radar acquisition by the MiGs might be possible, since the opening of the weapons bay doors would break the stealth profile of my aircraft. If the MIGs could acquire and lock, they could shoot. With the size of the warhead on a radar-guided missile, even a proximity blast could do serious damage to my jet.

And at my low airspeed, I couldn't perform much of an out-of-plane maneuver to defeat it.

The Russians had put me into a tight corner. If I shot at them, they might see me on radar and launch. If I pushed up the power, they'd see my infrared signature and launch. All they had to do was hold me here until another pair of fighters with better turning capability showed up. But I had something they weren't counting on.

The F-35 continued to slow, and I maintained aft pressure on the sidestick. The HOOK/STOVL light blinked enticingly at me.

"Not yet," I said.

The MiGs were at 15 miles, and the F-35 was slowing through 150 knots. The nose of the aircraft was staying level, but the sidestick was at the aft stop. At some point, the jet's digital flight control system would intervene with my input and force the nose down to keep the jet from departing controlled flight, but that moment hadn't come yet.

My airspeed bled down to 100 knots. The MiGs were at ten miles. I pictured the crews looking into their radar and infrared displays and searching frantically for traces of my aircraft. By now they knew the SU-27s had been destroyed, so they knew I was still here, but they couldn't see me. The MiG-31 had a two-person crew, and the rear-seater was dedicated to the operation of the MiG's sophisticated radar. I was sure the two weapons systems officers in the back seats were burning up the intraflight com frequency with intense chatter about targeting and radar modes. And I was betting none of the four crew members could understand why I wasn't showing up.

At about 70 knots the F-35's nose began to move downward. The digital flight control system was taking over. The MiG's were now descending, still trying to find and engage me. It was time.

I pushed the HOOK/STOVL button, and the F-35 began the conversion to its vertical mode. I had no idea how well the vertical mode would work at this altitude, but I knew it would change the flight control laws of the aircraft and let me get even slower. Even though the MiG-31 had an electronically-scanned radar, I was betting it still had a Doppler notch, a speed below which the radar's logic unit would filter out any targets detected as ground clutter and not display them to the crew. Even with the increased radar signature of the vertical turbine door, my lack of speed would make me invisible on radar, and since they were above and in front of me, my infrared signature would be hidden as well.

The F-35 completed its conversion to STOVL mode, and my airspeed had slowed to 30 knots. The jet was maintaining a level attitude, but I was sinking slowly, at about 200-300 feet per minute. The thinner air at high altitude wasn't giving the jet enough thrust to maintain a level hover at the default power setting. I applied some aft pressure to the sidestick to increase the vertical thrust.

The MiGs were at five miles now and coming right at me in the descent. The F-35's radar was tracking both of them, and the Slammers were ready to go, but the lead jet was inside of minimum range, and his partner was approaching minimum range. I wasn't going to take any chances. I needed to wait for a better shot.

The MiGs were inside of two miles now, and I could see the aircraft clearly in the HMD, thanks to its infrared/low-light capability. I was briefly concerned that they would see me, but the clouds were well below me, and there was no moon to highlight my presence. To get eyeballs on me, the crew members would need to know where to look, and with nothing to cue them, they'd be searching the heavens with a soda straw.

Then the lead MiG went by me, about 1,000 feet above me and a mile to my right. I watched him pass to see if he demonstrated any awareness of me, but he didn't commit to any turn or maneuver. I looked back to the front, in time to see his wingman directly at my twelve o'clock and getting larger in my display very rapidly. I pushed down on the sidestick and put the F-35 into a vertical descent. At the last moment, the MiG made an evasive maneuver to my right and then flew just past me and above me. As it went by, the aircraft banked up in my direction, and I saw two helmeted heads looking down at me.

I was made.

"Fuck," I said.

The MiG-31's lack of maneuverability saved me. I pushed on the right rudder pedal and pivoted the F-35 around to the right, even as I stopped its descent. The radar was tracking both aircraft again, and the AIM-120s were ready. Since the Russians were going away from me, instead of closing, minimum range wouldn't be a problem for the missiles. I knew the number 2 man was talking to his leader over the radio even as he flew away from me and I needed to stop that communication ASAP.

The leader was 3 miles away now and wasn't turning yet. I stepped the target designator to his jet with the TMS switch, and when the DLZ stabilized, I pushed the pickle button. The F-35 vibrated slightly as the weapons bay doors opened and then the AIM-120 ignited and took off after its target like a greyhound after a rabbit, the flame of its rocket motor lighting up the darkness. The Mach 4 missile was still accelerating when it slammed into the lead MiG-31 several seconds later. The resulting explosion generated a huge fireball that illuminated the dark heavens even more and left a gray and black cloud that blanked out the stars as it expanded into the night sky.

Number 2 was smarter than his boss. After he passed me, he started an easy turn back to the right to keep me in sight. As soon as I fired on the leader, Number 2 transitioned to a hard turn into me. Having seen what happened to the lead jet, he correctly assumed he couldn't outrun the missile and decided to stay in the phone booth with me to complicate matters. It was a good decision. As long as he stayed beam aspect to me, keeping his right wing on me and flying around me, the F-35's radar would track him, but I might not be able to shoot him. The DLZ display had him right on the verge of minimum range, and with no opening velocity and the fact that he was beam aspect, there was no guarantee the Slammer would hit him.

"Shit," I said to myself.

I was screwed. He could hold me here indefinitely by flying an orbit around me, and I would be forced to expend fuel to stay in the vertical mode and continually pivot to keep my nose on him. I probably wouldn't be able to do that for long because the longer I stayed anchored in the same place, the more vulnerable I was. The Russians seemed to be committed to stopping me. I had little doubt there was another formation of fighters being scrambled even now to bring me down. I needed to do something quickly.

I pushed forward on the throttle and commanded the F-35 to fly toward the MiG. At the same time, I continued to pivot my nose to point at him with the right rudder pedal. The MiG pilot did what I would have done in the same circumstances. He tightened his turn to take maneuvering room away from me and force me to overshoot his turn.

I smiled to myself. "You still don't know exactly what you're dealing with, do you, pal?"

I continued flying toward him. If I had been in the conventional flight mode, and not the vertical mode, his tactics might have worked. But he couldn't take turning room away from me because, while I remained in the vertical mode, I didn't need any. I was one mile away from the MiG now, and his energy was bleeding down. He had to assume I was armed with infrared seeking missiles, so he had to maintain idle power to keep his heat signature as small as possible. He had entered his hard turn at 450 knots, and as he continued the turn, his airspeed had constantly decreased with the g he was applying to his jet. Now, according to the data my radar was providing as it tracked him, he was slowing through 225 knots. As I looked at the large jet and took in its large angular features, it was easy to see that it was going to be on the edge of the controlled flight envelope soon.

I was 3,000 feet from him now, and the MiG was slowing through 175 knots. I could see the jet vibrating with pre-stall airframe buffet in the HMD. His turn rate was down to 5-6 degrees per second, but he was still holding the turn. The MiG pilot wasn't concerned about the infrared air-to-air missile threat any longer. Now he was worried about an air-to-air gunshot. He couldn't know that the B model was the only one of the three F-35 models that didn't have an internal cannon, so he had to honor my nose. I watched the MiG pilot continue to hold his turn and had no idea how his jet was still preserving level flight with the high angle-of-attack he had to be maintaining. I closed to about 2,000 feet from him, drifting toward his 5 o'clock position, inside of his turn. I began to pivot my nose forward. As the MiG pilot watched it move, he'd perceive that a gunshot was coming as soon as my nose was pointed in lead or ahead of his aircraft. And based on his training, he'd believe he'd have to do something in the next few seconds to survive.

As my nose swept through the nose of the MiG, the aircraft suddenly rolled out to about 20 degrees of bank and the nose began to track slowly upward.

"Not much of a jink," I said into the intercom, "but it will do."

I countermaneuvered. I pushed the sidestick down and pivoted the nose of the F-35 to put it front of where I knew the MiG's nose was going to be.

The MiG rolled hard to the right, past 90 degrees of bank, and the pilot tried to pull his nose downward in another jink. The-jet's nose tracked for a few seconds, but then it suddenly moved rapidly to the right. Immediately, the MiG snap-rolled to the right until it was inverted. Then, the tail end of the jet fell downward, and the MiG began to rotate to the left. As I watched it, I thought I was a hallucinating at first, but it only took another few seconds to understand what had happened - by commanding high angle-of-attack and inducing a rudder input, the pilot had put his jet out of control.

The MiG went into an inverted spin, which increased in speed of rotation as the aircraft continued to fall. I didn't know what the out-of-control recovery procedures were for the aircraft, but given the shape of the wing and the design of the jet, I was willing to bet that they wouldn't be very effective. As if to echo that thought, as the MiG fell to earth, I saw the glow of the crew's ejection seat rockets reflected on the clouds below and saw two parachutes inflate. Moments later, the jet and the crew members disappeared into the white strata beneath me.

I nodded to myself, pivoted the F-35 to the west, and pushed the throttle forward. When the HOOK/STOVL light blinked a few moments later, I turned the F-35 back into a normal airplane for the last time and headed for the recovery base.

An hour later, I landed the F-35 on a carefully chosen concrete pad just south of intersection of the runways at RAF Lossiemouth, the last operational Royal Air Force base in Scotland.

The pad was away from the hubs of activity on the base and allowed me to touchdown without attracting a lot of attention. It was black and cold and clear on this north coast of Scotland, and I was a little remorseful that I wouldn't be able to see more of this beautiful part of the country by daylight.

As soon as I touched down, I hit the HOOK/STOVL button, gave the jet 10 seconds to make the conversion, then I killed the engine and opened the canopy. Once again, there was an odd silence. I looked around and felt an eerie sense of familiarity. I was surrounded by the hardened aircraft shelters so common on NATO bases in Western Europe during the Cold War. The structures looked like large half-cylinders and were built with enough steel and concrete to withstand a direct hit by a 2,000-pound bomb. RAF Bentwaters, the A-10 base of my former life, had many of them. I felt like I had taken a step back in time.

"Well done, T.C.," Dave Smith said as he opened the side panel and deployed the jet's boarding ladder. "You brought it back in one piece after all."

"It wasn't easy," I said. "The Russians wanted me pretty badly."

Smith nodded. "We watched the whole thing on satellite. The Russians aren't saying anything yet. Probably too embarrassed by the fact that one guy in one jet evaded four aircraft and knocked down another four."

"Hopefully it will stay that way. By the way, tell the Lockheed Martin folks that an IR search and track set can still see this thing."

I ensured the seat and canopy were safe, and collected my gear. As I was about to exit, the CIA TAM I had met at Elgin walked up in full flying gear, helmet bag at his side.

"You're taking it home, I guess?" I asked him.

He nodded. "I have a tanker waiting over the Atlantic," he said. "Thanks for not breaking my baby. You can leave the battery on. While they're refueling, I'm going to prep the cockpit for the next flight."

"Roger that."

I performed my usual awkward exit and slow descent down the ladder and reached the pavement a few moments later. I noticed a fuel truck had arrived and was deploying its hose for the refueling operation.

"Any squawks?" The TAM asked, using the USAF vernacular for maintenance discrepancies.

"Not a one that I could see," I replied. "But I didn't know what the hell it was doing most of the time."

He smiled and smacked my arm. "You did pretty well for a guy who didn't know what he was doing. We'll be analyzing the footage of your engagement for a while. And thanks for validating my push to have the air-to-air weapons available while flying in the vertical mode. I insisted on that capability for our jets. The standard F-35B won't do it."

"Wow," I said. "I'm glad it worked! I never thought about that."

"I've heard you tend to be lucky," the TAM said.

"At some things," I said, as I turned away. "Only at some things."

I walked over to the car with Smith. Amrine was waiting for us. I could only assume a long debrief would follow. It wasn't going to happen without some form of alcohol, that was for sure. Before I reached them, I turned back to the F-35, sitting on the pavement as it was serviced, its squat form looking like a creature hiding in the darkness, ready to spring.

"It's still uglier than shit," I said so that the TAM could hear me. "But it is a hell of an airplane."

He smiled at me and gave me a thumbs up with a gloved hand.

I turned back to Smith and Amrine. "Where to boys?"

"Other side of the field. One our jets is waiting to take all of us back to the states. We'll do the debrief on the flight back."

I nodded. "Any news about your team on the ground there or Sharona?"

Smith's face was a grim mask. "No. It's like they've vanished. We've heard nothing."

"Damn it," I said, staring at the ground. "Damn it to hell."

"We don't like it either," Amrine said. "We're using every resource to find them and get them out of there."

"As bad as the news about Sharona may be," Smith said. "She's not the woman you should be thinking about right now."

"Alina?" I asked.

He nodded. "She's chartered a jet from St. Petersburg to the states, destination TBD."

"She's coming for you, T.C.," Amine added, unnecessarily. "Just like we hoped she would."

"Of course she is," I said. "So, let's get to Delaware and get this over with."

CHAPTER THIRTY-SIX

Thursday, November 11
2330 Hours Local Time
Pearce Townhouse
Wilmington, Delaware, USA

It was a still night, and I was enjoying the stillness. The fireplace was crackling with a log fire, and since it was the only light in my study/living room, the fire was producing a fascinating array of shadows on the bookcases and furniture in the room. I sat in my recliner, watching the shadows and nursing a healthy shot of the Balvenie Portwood 21. Enya was singing in the background, and between the music and the fire, the ambiance in the room could have been very relaxing.

If a team of Russians led by a mad chick with a gun wasn't coming to kill me.

I lay my head back against the recliner and contemplated the room around me. There had been a time when this room and even this house, had been a retreat, a place in which I could escape the world. Now, for the second time in just over a year, it would be a death trap. Early last fall, a man and two women had died in my dining room, mere feet away. The man had been taken out by a CIA sniper, one of the women, someone I had cared about, had been killed by the other woman. And then I had killed the killer, with a knife, across her throat, and I had watched her life run out before my eyes.

Tonight, there would be more death. Here. In my home.

It seemed that my house was the best place in which to trap/engage Alina, or at least that's what the CIA thought. Amrine had listed the advantages, ticking them off one-by-one on his fingers.

"Limited entrances and exits," he had said. "Easily monitored, free from public scrutiny, fewer chances of collateral damage, easier cleanup and disposal, plus the most important advantage of all..."

"What would that be?" I had asked.

"You know your way around in the dark," Amrine replied. "If she brings a team with her, they'll undoubtedly cut the power before they breech. It's standard procedure for forced entry."

"Along with a flash-bang grenade or two," Smith added.

"By the way," Amrine said, looking me directly in the eyes, "just so we're clear, she goes down tonight. We can't have any of this go public. In addition to the damage it would do to the credibility of the law enforcement and counterintelligence agencies of the world, it could cause a civil panic. She's no use to us alive. You can put her down, or one of our guys can put her down, but she does go down. Do we understand each other?"

I nodded slowly.

"And she needs to be dealt with in a manner that leaves her identifiable and could be attributed to other causes…like government authorities."

"That means no knives, T.C.," Smith said.

I shook my head. "I couldn't cut her anyway."

The boys seemed taken aback by that statement.

"You mean T.C., the throat cutter, couldn't use a knife on her?" Smith asked.

"No," I replied. "I couldn't." I looked away from them. "I can't tell you exactly why. It just wouldn't be right."

"Well don't let your trigger finger suffer the same limitation," Amrine said. "We don't have any idea how good this woman is with a handgun and if you hesitate, she could kill you."

There could be worse things, I thought.

"We'll be watching and listening," Smith had said. "Keep your earpiece in and keep the mic in your collar. We'll let you know what they're up to before they breech and we'll have a team ready to back you up."

I nodded absently. "I'll be fine."

I took another sip of the Balvenie and marveled at the crispness and complexity of it. The nose featured the aroma of peaches and a very subtle, ever so delicate, whisp of smoke. On the tongue, it was dainty and elegant with notes of fruit, raisins, white grapes and honey. The finish was slow and lingering with a note of pleasant bitterness combined with a bit of cocoa. It was light and thoroughly satisfying.

I looked down at the table next to me as the scotch warmed its way down my throat. The faithful .45 ACP combat commander was there, as was a Mossberg 12-gauge pump shotgun. Both weapons were loaded and ready. As I contemplated the flames and amber depths of the scotch, I wondered if I was.

So much death. So much death related to me. Sharona was still unaccounted for, and she was just the latest in a toll that extended back to this very house and this very room over a year ago.

I looked at the fire, the whiskey and the guns and took another sip of the Balvenie. It probably wasn't the best idea to drink scotch in anticipation of a possible gun fight, but I needed the resolve the alcohol would provide.

The truth was that I didn't know if I could kill Alina. While I was certain I could point a weapon at her, I just wasn't sure I could pull the trigger. Despite all the events of the past week or so, a part of me still craved her and desperately wanted to lose myself in the sickness we both had. I had resigned myself to the fact that we were, in fact, alike, and in mutual misery, often mutual solace could be found. Several times this evening, my thoughts had wandered back to the time we shared in Switzerland. While the time was limited, the moments of excitement, of tenderness and of understanding, still tugged at me and I was having trouble letting them go.

I took another sip of the scotch and enjoyed the flavor of it on my tongue and the warmth of it in my throat. I contemplated the amber nectar in the light of the flames. Scotch was one of the few constants in my life. It was always there, always reliable, and it never let me down.

If only people were like that, I thought.

Then Enya's voice went silent. A few moments later, I heard the crack of the downstairs door being forced open.

The CIA would have probably warned me about this if I had worn the earpiece I was given. I probably would have known how many of them there were, and I might have even known what their armament was.

But I wanted to face them alone. Without assistance. I needed to face them alone. Perhaps to regain some self-respect. Maybe to give Alina a sporting chance.

I took a last sip of the scotch and rose from my chair.

I placed the pistol in the rear waistband of my trousers and checked that the shotgun had a round chambered before putting my head through the bandoleer/sling attached to it. Then I walked the few steps to my kitchen in the darkness and knelt just to the side of my kitchen counter. In front of me was the dining room, with my fine collection of single malts on the credenza on the opposite wall. To my left, was the door from the garage and to my right, around the counter, was the sliding glass door that led to my backyard. They would come through one or both portals, I was certain of it. The front door was too public, too visible and too risky. The front window, in my study, was visible as well and it was too high off the ground. The kitchen window would not offer quick ingress to a normally-sized human being, even it if was thoroughly demolished.

I strained to hear the sounds of them coming up the stairs from the lower level, where my garage was. The steps were wooden and several years old, and they routinely creaked when I ascended them.

But there was no sound.

As I waited, kneeling on the ceramic tile of the kitchen floor, I felt an usual lack of emotion. Normally, in a situation like this, the rage would have been singing in my veins, raising my adrenaline level with anger and craving satisfaction with the blood that would invariably follow.

But not tonight. Instead, I felt an icy calm. I was ready, and I knew what had to be done. While the emotions about Alina were yet to be dealt with, whatever else came through these doors would be going down hard.

The silence was interrupted by the tell-tale "clink" sound of something breaking the kitchen window. I nodded to myself.

There's the grenade, I thought.

I scooted around the kitchen counter and quickly shoved the earplugs deeper in my ears.

WHUMP!

The flash-bang grenade detonated in the kitchen with the usual blast and overpressure. At nearly the same moment, the glass on the sliding door shattered, raining down on my table and scotch bottles. I was on the floor, with a pair of protective glasses on and the moment I saw a figure outside the door, I fired two rounds of 00 buckshot at it, before pivoting toward the door. The knob was turning as I rotated and I put another two rounds through the door. Two patterns of ragged holes appeared in the thin wooden door, one about head height and the other slightly lower. I yanked the door open, shotgun at the ready.

The crumpled figure of Vassily, the former Spetnaz soldier, lay on the staircase, his face a meaty mess of gore and blood, but the dual colored eyes were still visible. I pulled the fighting knife out of the sheath on his leg and cut his throat open, before shoving the knife into the underside of his chin, all the way to hilt. His eyes remained fixed and sightless. I nodded and proceeded carefully down the steps.

A few moments later, I silently stepped out the back door of the lower level, into my backyard and up the cement stairs to my patio. There, I found Sergei, the other Spetnaz guard from Switzerland. He was still breathing. He lay on his back with a good portion of his right shoulder gone and the upper part of his left thigh looking like it had been run through a meat grinder. I looked down at him for a moment so that he could see my face. As his eyes showed the glint of recognition, I removed his knife from its sheath and slashed his throat with it. The dark eyes showed a moment of surprise and rage, but then transitioned to a look of helplessness and fear. I nodded, tossed the knife aside, and stepped back into my house, leaving Sergei to die alone under the stars.

The smell of cordite hung heavily in the air as I entered the dining room and my shoes crunched on the shattered glass on the carpet. I let the adrenaline settle in my veins as I contemplated the room and found myself oddly relieved that the carpet in the room wouldn't have to be replaced after tonight's incident. Vacuumed a lot, yes. Replaced, no. I looked behind me at the inert body on my patio and through the garage door at his companion, lying on my stairs.

So, where's Alina? I wondered.

I realized it was probably time for me to call the boys, even though I was sure their surveillance people had captured much of what had happened. I sighed, removed my earplugs, and walked the few steps into my study/living room to retrieve the headset they gave me.

"I love this room," said a feminine voice. "It looks like you."

Alina was sitting in my recliner, just where I had sat moments earlier, sniffing my scotch glass and pointing a suppressed semi-automatic pistol at me. She wore a black cocktail dress with a modest neckline and high heels. She had an expensive looking purse at her side. A coat of some sort was thrown over the sofa down from the chair.

"I'm sure I don't need to tell you what happens next," she said.

I nodded and reached down for the shotgun.

"Slowly, Colin," she said, raising the pistol just a bit. "Use your left hand."

I reached across my body with my left hand and removed the shotgun and its sling from my right shoulder. Then, I slowly placed it on my desk a few feet to my left.

"Very good," she said.

She raised the scotch glass to her lips and drank the remaining drops of liquid. She seemed to relish it.

"Maybe my last chance to taste you," she said, smiling. "The scotch is awesome. What was it?"

"Balvenie Portwood 21," I said. "One of my favorites." I looked around the room. "So how did you get in here? With the …commotion."

She smiled back at me. It was an odd smile. A distant smile but an affectionate one. I remembered the smile she had given me the first time at the bar at the Dukes Hotel, and the smile after our dinner in St. Moritz, and I had the context. It was a smile that meant she didn't expect to see me again.

"I came in through the front door of course. While you were dealing with Vassily and Sergei. No one suspects a woman in a dress coming to a door in the evening."

"You're right," I said. "They don't." I thought about her words for a moment. "So, you expected me to take care of those two?" I motioned with my right hand toward the room behind me.

"I would have been disappointed if you hadn't," she said. "They were the last spying eyes. I needed to be rid of them. Before…" Her voice trailed off.

"Before what?" I asked. I placed my right hand on my right hip, trying to make it look as nonchalant as possible. I drew my left hand up on my left hip to balance it.

Alina's expression changed. Like one door in her mind had shut and another had opened.

"Who was the woman in Lake Tahoe?" she demanded.

"Huh," I said, hoping the CIA's sound equipment was collecting the conversation. "So, you *were* there. The shooting was so poor I wondered."

Her eyes were fiery. "The shooting was good enough. I accomplished my mission."

"You didn't really," I said. "Mark Lane is still alive, and you missed me. But the one person you did manage to kill had no relevance at all to your mission. She was an innocent bystander. A non-combatant."

Alina slowly rose from the recliner, holding the pistol on me. "You were kissing her!" she screamed. "Who was she?"

Damn, I thought. *The Boys were right. I do get to you.*

I sighed and looked down at the floor for a moment. "Her name was Gail Petersen, and she was probably the finest Air Force Officer I've ever met. We had a …a…relationship…if that's what you can all it…for several months."

"Did you love her?" Alina's voice was lower and her tone less accusatory and more interrogative. Her eyes seemed calmer but distant.

I glanced at the gun in her hand. It was wavering a bit. I thought about how to answer the question as I performed a quick emotional inventory to assess my feelings. There was a profound sense of loss for Gail, but was it love? Had it ever been love?

"No," I said, after a few moments. "I didn't. I cared for her, but I didn't love her. So you fucked up. You killed someone who didn't need to die."

Alina swallowed hard. "But you slept with her," she said, softly. "You made love to her."

I nodded. "Not after I met you, but many times prior to that."

"You never made love to me." Alina's voice was almost a whisper. I couldn't decide if she was talking to me or to herself.

"After the amazing time we had together, I thought about it. Especially on that afternoon after the massage. But then you drugged me and your uncle tried to have me killed. That sort of put a damper on things."

Alina let her gun drop slightly.

"I didn't intend that," she said. "I was trying to save you and keep you out of all of this. I never thought Anton would have you killed. Especially when he knew how I felt about you."

"You mean killed, again," I said. "There were two earlier attempts on my life. A man and woman team. They tried to kill me while I was running. Then there was a team in a car in downtown Crystal City, Virginia. One of them was Vassily. He had the weird eyes."

Her eyes went out of focus for a minute, like she was somewhere else. The gun drooped a little lower.

"I didn't want that either," she said, softly. "I liked you from the first moment I saw you. That's why I wanted to watch you land the airplane. But after I told Anton you were at Duke's bar that one night, he didn't want to take any chances on you." She raised her gaze to mine. "I was happy when I learned you hadn't been killed. That's when I knew we'd be good together. That's when I knew we were the same."

Yes, we are. A switch was thrown in my subconscious and the longing for her rose inside of me, suddenly and powerfully, like the water inside a geyser, seeking an immediate, explosive outlet.

"We're free now, Colin," she said, her eyes glistening in the firelight. "That's why I tried to keep you out of this. So we could be together. Now with Anton gone and those two dead," she waved her hand dismissively toward the dining room, "there's nothing holding us back."

She lowered the gun and smiled radiantly. "I have almost 60 million U.S. dollars in my bank account," she said. "We could run away and live together forever!"

"That's a lot of money," I said. "What is that, about one million for every hit you made?"

"Isn't that crazy?" she said in a giddy voice. "I got two million for the British PM. And set a record too!"

"How did Anton afford to pay you so much?" I asked.

"Through Vladimir's company," she said. Then she lowered her voice and whispered conspiratorially. "But some of that money might have come from the government. There was a huge push to get that reactor project in place. Everyone was calling it an investment in the future of the Motherland. I even got to meet Putin once!"

That should give you everything you need boys, I thought.

"But none of that matters," she said. "We can go to an island somewhere! We can get one of those rooms on stilts over the water and lie in the sun and swim all day and make love all night. For as long as we want to!"

The longing felt even stronger now. I looked at the beautiful face and the luxurious blonde hair and the amazing body that was perfectly accentuated in the flowing black dress. My quick glimpse of her nude body in Switzerland rushed into my mind. I tried to force it away but it remained. I remembered every curve of it and the memory tantalized me.

Alina tossed her gun onto the sofa and took a step towards me. "A lot of people will never know what is truly in the heart of the person they're with. Especially if there is some darkness in the heart. But you and I know the darkness well," she said. "Because it lives in us. It's part of you. Just like it's part of me."

She reached up and slid one of the straps of her dress off her right shoulder.

The longing inside of me increased in intensity.

"Make love to me, Colin. Be one with me and we can live in the darkness together."

She slid the strap off her left shoulder and stepped out of her shoes.

My eyes fixated on her. More memories of our time in St. Moritz coursed through me. I could feel my eyes sting with the sudden onslaught of unbidden emotion and I could feel my heart being pulled in a way that was both intense and terrifying.

A kaleidoscope of mental images cascaded through my mind's eye. She and I swimming together, walking the beach together, laughing together, making love together, and sleeping together. But in the background there would always be darkness, the darkness inside of us that drew us to each other. We would never be free of it.

She reached down to her sides and began to lift her dress up. The flowing black fabric collected in her hands in a sensual, enticing way. It took me a moment to understand what she was doing, but then her hands reached under the hemline of her dress and moved downward. A few seconds later, a pair of lacy black panties slid down to her ankles, and she kicked them aside.

I was utterly paralyzed. Frozen where I stood and unable to breathe, let alone, think. I was helpless and hers to command. I wanted her. I wanted the darkness. I wanted it all.

Until I saw the gun.

It was a small, black automatic that had somehow materialized in her right hand. She was raising it even as she continued to smile at me, lovingly, enticingly.

Reflexes kicked in then.

My right hand reached back to my waistband and found the Colt's rubber grip. As I brought the weapon forward, I dropped to my right knee and threw myself to the right. I heard a sound like loud pop and heard a thud in one of the walls behind me. I heard another pop, and there was a sound of glass cracking.

By then, the Colt was up and centered on her chest.

I fired. Two times in quick succession. Two red spots, about half an inch wide appeared between her breasts. The beautiful gray-blue eyes expressed pained surprise for a moment and then her eyelids closed and she sank to the floor as if she fainted. There was no sound as she collapsed to the carpet. I walked over and looked down at her. The blonde hair lay strewn about her head, contrasting with the tan carpet below. She had let go of the gun. Her arms were outflung and her legs were slightly bent. The black dress clung to her splendid body perfectly and but for the two ragged red holes in her chest, she would have looked like she had merely fallen asleep. Tears came to my eyes and streamed down my face as I looked at her. I sank to my knees at her side and gazed at her, not able to decide whether I felt horror or relief at what I had done.

Eventually, I heard quick footsteps on the walk outside my home and on the patio in my backyard. The ops team was on the way in. I reached out with my left hand and touched the smooth skin on the side of Alina's face. There was a slight smile on her beautiful features. A knowing smile. A beckoning smile.

The team came through the doors behind and around me. I put my weapon on the floor to show them there was no threat. But putting the gun down was a much greater struggle than I anticipated. Alina was still calling me, still enticing me, still compelling me. And there was a large part of me that wanted to put the gun in my mouth, pull the trigger and join her.

EPILOGUE

Saturday, November 13
1015 Hours Local Time
United States Air Force Academy Cemetery
United States Air Force Academy, Colorado

The four F-16's flew over slowly, at about 250 knots, the shapes of the gray-blue jets contrasting starkly with the bright blue Colorado sky. At precisely the right moment, the number three jet, the one between the leader and the number four wingman, pulled up out of the formation, climbing above the other aircraft and disappearing into the sky overhead. Then, the three aircraft, now in the "missing man" formation, flew directly over Gail's gravesite, and continued north, along the front range of the Colorado Rocky Mountains. A few moments later, three UH-60 helicopters flew over the gravesite as well, also aligned in the missing man formation, with a gap in the formation where the number three helicopter should have been. This flyby was in tribute to Gail's years flying rescue helicopters. I had never seen a helicopter formation flyby before, and between the amount of time the aircraft took to fly over us and the amount of noise they generated, it was perhaps even more impressive than the jets. Seeing a missing man formation had always created a lump in my throat, regardless of who it was commemorating. But today, knowing the two were for Gail, gave them special meaning.

I lowered my gaze back to the gravesite after the aircraft passed. The blanket of grass on the cemetery had gone dormant, so it was a mixture of brown and light green, contrasting with the tall, dark green pine trees that surrounded the cemetery. It was a typically beautiful Colorado day. The sun was almost overhead, and it was illuminating the cemetery and the area around it. Just over a mile west of the cemetery, the USAF Academy Cadet Area gleamed in the sunlight, with the white marble expanse of Fairchild Hall, the academic building, in the foreground, alongside the blue and silver edifice of Vandenberg Hall, one of the dormitories. In the background, closer to the mountains, stood the seventeen spires of the Cadet Chapel, perhaps the most iconic building on the vast campus. We had been at the Chapel earlier, for the memorial service, before we came down to the cemetery for the interment.

The many rows of graves in front of me were perfectly aligned in military fashion, and they bore many of the Air Force's most illustrious names. General Curtis LeMay, the father of Strategic Air Command, was buried here, as was General Carl "Tooey" Spaatz, first Chief of Staff of the Air Force and Brigadier General Robin Olds, one of the greatest fighter pilots and tactical leaders the Air Force has ever produced. It seemed only fitting that Gail should rest among such company.

I stood many yards away from the other mourners and regarded the gravesite. It didn't seem appropriate to me that the man who had gotten her killed should share the bereavement of her friends and family. There were many people in attendance. Gail had been a well-respected leader and friend. There were at least fifty people in Air Force Blue, most with stars or eagles on their epaulets. One of them was my friend and classmate Bob Barnett, who stood in the front row of mourners, with his wife, Kristin. They had motioned for me to join them graveside, but I waved them off, content to gaze from afar. Thirty to forty more people were present in civilian clothes, some were spouses of the officers, mixed in with the small sea of blue uniforms, others stood in a separate group, and I guessed that they were members of Gail's family.

And of course, Gail's ex-husband was there, seemingly distraught over the passing of his ex-wife. He was unimpressive in stature, short, squat and overweight, with black hair and dark eyes. For the millionth time since Gail had mentioned him, I wondered what the hell she had ever seen in him. I had watched him closely throughout the memorial service in the Cadet Chapel and at the graveside service. While he seemed tearful, every once in a while, a grin would slip onto his face, when he thought no one was looking.

Gail told me that she never changed the beneficiary on her life insurance policies after the divorce, something about not having anyone else to give the money to. Now that he had followed her to San Antonio, there seemed to be no doubt that he'd be receiving the funds. He would also be the recipient of the survivor's portion of

Gail's military pension, and would be receiving a substantial monthly stipend for the rest of his miserable life.

I shook my head as I watched him trying to keep the smirk from off his features and pay his respects to the woman he had been married to for over fifteen years. He kept sneaking glances at his watch as the graveside eulogy was spoken. Apparently, he had somewhere more important to be.

"You always said he saw you as nothing more than a meal ticket, Gail," I said to myself. "Looks like you were right."

After the graveside ceremony had concluded, I waved to Bob and Kristin as they departed, and waited for the other mourners to make their way to their vehicles and drive away. Gail's ex-husband had a stretch limo waiting for him. Evidently, he was too important to ride with anyone else. He waited for a driver to open the door and as it opened, I saw a flash of lingerie and blonde hair inside. I shook my head. It seemed he needed some entertainment on the way to the wake.

I walked to the grave alone and spent some time looking down at the gleaming brown casket therein. The service in the chapel had been closed casket, and I was grateful. There had been a viewing earlier, in a funeral home nearby, but I didn't attend it. It would have been hard to explain my presence and I wasn't sure I could handle looking at Gail's beautiful face artificially made up and lying there in a semblance of sleep. I had watched her sleep so many times when we had been together, and I didn't want to see her that way in death.

"Gail, I am so sorry," I said, as I looked down at the casket. "It wasn't my idea for you to come to California, but I'm the reason you did." I bowed my head. "And I'm the reason you died."

I squatted down and pulled a handful of Colorado soil from the ground and gently tossed it onto the lid of the coffin.

"You had such a life in front of you," I said, as the dirt hit the wooden lid and rolled off the sides. "And I'm the reason it's all gone."

I brushed a tear aside with the sleeve of my suit jacket.

"So, let me tell you something that might make a difference, wherever you are. Your death mattered. It counted. When the Shadow shot you it started a series of events that put me in place to kill her and avenge you. The CIA took her body and planted it in a car outside of London with the rifle she used at Lake Tahoe, and it's all over the news that a Russian assassin was killing people who opposed the Russian breeder reactor thing. The whole scheme has fallen apart, and now a good portion of the free world won't be subject to nuclear blackmail. It was your sacrifice that made it possible."

I stood up and looked back down into the grave.

"So you served your country until the very end," I said. "And I know that mattered to you. I know we had differing views about the career thing, but you were about service. It's who you were and that will be remembered." I rose to my feet, came to the position of attention and saluted her. "Rest in peace, General," I said. "The world is a poorer place without you."

I turned from the gravesite and walked to where my rental car was parked, in the cemetery parking lot, about 100 yards away. When I reached my car, I stood there for a moment and surveyed the scenery in front of me. Behind the cadet area were the brown rock and treed inclines of the front range of the Rocky Mountains, stretching far to the south into New Mexico and north to Wyoming and Montana. And south of the cadet area, west of Colorado Springs, lay the brooding mass of Pike's Peak, looking down upon the city and dominating the view to the southwest. The mountain had already seen its first snowfall of the season and sported a white peak that seemed to be a scenic omen of the winter season to come.

"God this place is beautiful," I said to myself. "It's just too damn bad you can't appreciate that while you're here."

I opened the door to my car and slid inside. I had just strapped in and started the engine when my phone rang.

"Pearce," I said.

"Sharona's alive, T.C.," Smith said without preamble. "And so is the rest of team. They got out through Estonia. She's been flown to the U.S. Army hospital at Landstuhl, and she's going to make it."

I leaned back against the seat of my car and pressed my head against the headrest. I felt a surge of grateful emotion well up within me.

"That's the best thing I've heard all day," I said.

"You and me both," Smith said. He paused for a few moments. "How was the service for Gail?"

"As good as a funeral could be," I said. "Seems like I've been attending too many of them recently."

"Comes with the turf sometimes," Smith said. "Sad but true."

It was my turn to pause. "So Dave, about that," I said.

"Yes, Colin?" The tone of his voice went from friendly to businesslike. It was a subtle change but a noticeable one. I had played the resignation conversation over in my mind several times, but now that it was time for it, I wasn't sure I could say the words. The sad fact was that Dave Smith and John Amrine were probably the closest things to friends or family that I had. Or at least, the only two people I had access to. And that was fucked up.

"How are Sarah and Colleen?" I asked, surprising myself with the question.

"They're great," Smith said. "We just checked on them. Sarah appears to like being a stay at home mom, and she takes Colleen with her everywhere, walking, hiking, running, you name it. Both are adapting to their new lives well."

"I'm glad for that," I said. "And I'm really glad the Sharona is going to be ok." I thought for a moment. "So what the hell is her real name anyway? If it's Isabelle, why do we all call her Sharona?"

Smith laughed. "I'm not sure anyone even knows," he said. "She's gone deep cover so many times; she may have forgotten it herself. When she told you her name was Isabelle in July, it was the first time any of us had heard that. Sharona has been her most used legend, so that's the one that seems to stick. It suits her too."

I nodded. "Sure seems to." I let several moments go by before I spoke. I thought that Smith might eventually hang up, but he didn't. "Dave?" I asked.

"I know what you're going to ask," he said. "And it's okay."

"What's ok?"

"Taking some time off. You should probably do that."

"How did you know?"

"Because you're human," he said. "And it happens to every operator after they've been in action repeatedly. We all have needed time to decompress at some point and come to terms with what we've done in the name of our country. It's the only way you can deal with it and not go crazy. John and I have expected this from you for some time. Frankly, we're shocked it took this long."

As I listened to him speak, I looked out over the cemetery and to the Cadet Area and the mountains beyond. Clouds were starting to form just beyond the hills of the front range and with temperatures predicted to go below freezing tonight, I wondered if Colorado Springs and the Academy would get the first snowfall of the year this evening.

"Colin," Smith said. "You know how you wondered whether you had some sickness that makes you good at the violence?"

I nodded even though I knew he couldn't see me. "Yes."

"This proves you're not sick. If you were, you wouldn't want a break. You'd just want to get to the next opportunity to kill. The fact that you need to take the time to recover from the killing means that it doesn't own you. Remember that."

The intellectual part of me processed Smith's words, but they failed to provide much consolation to the other half of my brain. Or to my heart.

"So where do you think you'll go?" he asked.

I thought for a moment. "I don't know," I said.

"Doesn't matter. Take as much time as you need. Come back when you want."

Hearing him say the words, 'come back,' pushed the button that I needed.

"Dave, I'm not sure I can keep doing this. I've gotten too many people hurt or killed. I'm not sorry for the ones I've taken out, even though I might have enjoyed it a little too much. But there have been too many others, like Gail, caught in the crossfire and others still, like Sarah and Colleen, who could be caught in a potential crossfire."

"So what are you saying?" Smith asked after a long moment.

"I don't think I'm coming back."

There were a few moments of silence, and then Smith laughed. I could picture his jade green eyes twinkling.

"What's so damn funny?"

"You're by far not the first person to feel that way. You should have seen me after my first few ops, I was a mess. But that's not the biggest thing."

"And what would that be?"

"You'll be back because this is who you are, T.C. You can't run away from that. Not now. Not ever."

Smith's words rang in my ears as I drove the rental car down Parade Loop and made a left turn onto Stadium Boulevard, and then a right turn onto North Gate Boulevard. I had given some thought to driving around the Academy for a few minutes to indulge in some nostalgia, but given the reason I was here, it didn't seem appropriate.

A few moments later, I was southbound on Interstate 25. My plan was to head south to US Highway 24, turn right and head west. Beyond that, I had no idea where I would go or what I would do.

Even as I drove, my townhouse in Wilmington, Delaware was being packed and the boxes and furniture put into storage. The townhouse would be placed on the market in the next few days and would sell quickly, according to the real estate agent I had hired. My car would be sold as well and within days, all my worldly possessions, such as they were, would be liquidated or stored away.

And I would be free. I had nearly ten figures in various bank accounts and wouldn't need to work for a long, long time. I didn't ever want to come back. I wanted to prove to Smith that he was wrong about me. Hell, maybe I wanted to prove it to myself.

I turned on the car's radio and heard the strains of a Metallica song I knew from years ago, but the lyrics had renewed meaning for me.

What I've felt
What I've known
Never shined through in what I've shown
Never free
Never me.
So I dub thee unforgiven.

That was me: unforgiven. For all the death I had caused. Certainly, those I had killed needed to die and perhaps it was all for a greater good. But the toll of collateral damage was rising and my conscience, even such as it was, couldn't deal with it any longer. The deaths needed to stop. As I turned westbound and saw the huge mass of Pike's Peak filling the windshield, I felt my resolve solidify inside of me. I needed to escape from the drama and the killing and the relationships. Hell, maybe I even needed to stay away from airplanes as well.

But even as the last thought entered my mind, I looked skyward and saw the contrails of a jet, flying high above and leaving a white, wispy trail in the terrific blue of the Colorado sky. I smiled as I saw it. I knew I'd never be able to stay out of the cockpit for long. The sky would always beckon to me. And I would always answer.

COLIN PEARCE WILL RETURN
IN
THE BRONCO CONTRACT

About the Author

Chris Broyhill is a retired U.S. Air Force fighter pilot who flew the OV-10, A-10, and F-16 while on active duty. He holds a bachelor's degree in computer science from the U.S. Air Force Academy, a master's degree in national security studies from California State University at San Bernardino and a Ph.D. in aviation from Embry-Riddle Aeronautical University. Chris is an outstanding graduate of the U.S. Air Force Fighter Weapons School and is a National Business Aviation Association Certified Aviation Manager. Chris has flown in and led aviation organizations for over 30 years and currently works for an aviation consulting firm in the Dallas-Fort Worth area of Texas.

www.ingramcontent.com/pod-product-compliance
Lightning Source LLC
Chambersburg PA
CBHW072013110726
47910CB00005B/1741

* 9 7 8 0 9 9 8 8 2 5 0 0 7 *